"Maniacal Laughter"

Angelo was pinned down by an unknown, unseen, and merciless entity. Panic seized her. She was unable to move or fight. She didn't like the feeling. Not one bit.

The stranger's harsh laughter grabbed her attention and she looked to her left. It seemed the only thing she could move was her head. In the pitch darkness, she saw what appeared to be a steel table. A morgue table, commonly used to dissect dead bodies.

Like a macabre theater play, a spotlight illuminated the table and she found herself staring in horror at a corpse. He had a dagger protruding from his chest and the look of death in his cloudy eyes. Eyes, that were wide open and staring back at her.

The room was filled with hateful, maniacal laughter again. Angelo was starting to hate this unseen force that held her captive.

"Stop! Stop! Why are you doing this to me?"
"Because I can," it told her.
"I won't let you! Damn it! I won't!

Just My Best , Inc.
1746 Dailey Road
Wilmington, Ohio 45177
937-987-9948

http://www.jmbpub.com

This is a work of fiction. All names, characters, locations, and incidents are products of the author's imagination or used fictitiously. Any resemblance to actual events or locales or persons, either living or dead is purely coincidental.

ANGEL OF JUSTICE

By Rosanna Filippello-Sztuba
Copyright © 2004
All rights reserved.

No part of this book may be reproduced, stored in a retrieval system, or, transmitted by any means, electronic, mechanical, photocopying, recording, or otherwise, without written permission from the author.

Just My Best Publishing, is a subsidiary of
Just My Best Incorporated.

Manufactured in the United States of America

Library of Congress Control Number: 2004114961

ISBN 1-932586-09-1

Books in the Angelo Mystery Series

Angel of Death (Book One) - ISBN 1-932586-08-3

Angel of Justice (Book Two) - ISBN 1-932586-11-3

Other Books by *Rosanna Filippello-Sztuba*

Caught in the Crossfire (Sci-Fi)
The Best Medicine (Romance)

www.detective-angelo-mysteries.com

eMail - rosanna.filippello@justmybest,com

Special Thanks goes to the Inspectors from Northwest Division and the Forensic Science Unit for the fascinating and informative tours.

Also to all the guys and gals in the Special Victims Unit and in the Crime Scene Unit.

You Rock!

Affectionately R.F.S.

Angel of Justice

A, B. Angelo Mystery

By

Rosanna Filippello

Prologue

The snow was falling fast and furious, covering the tops of the short bushes in front of the stone twin home in the Holmesburg section of Northeast Philadelphia. Christmas tree lights on an Evergreen blinked blue, red, and green, off and on, throwing colorful hues onto the snow covered ground. The street was eerily quiet, yet serene. People slept peacefully in their beds, feeling nothing amiss. Nevertheless, there was something very amiss lurking on the tranquil street.

Somewhere in the distance, there was an annoying tinkling of *Jingle Bells*. He really hated Christmas. All that damn, *good will toward man*. Sure, it was easy to say that, but he knew the darkness in people's hearts. A cold, black, evil. The holiday was bull in his opinion. It was just a way for the rich to get richer and spoiled brats to get that car they've been hounding their parents for all year.

He could hear them now. *Mommy, I want that red Mustang. And boom! They'd have that car.* His mother never gave him anything but grief. If she gave him anything at all. He hated her. She made him what he was now. A predator. He would always hate her and himself for that *gift*.

These decorations were modest compared to some of the other houses on the block that went completely overboard with the holiday spirit. It was a wonder anyone got any sleep around there with all the bright lights blazing. He could imagine their expensive electric bills.

The redheaded woman in the dark green business suit lived alone in that modestly decorated house on Ashburner Street, not too far from Pennypack Park. Very convenient for what he had in mind. Watching the house, he licked his dry lips, waiting for her to return. No one was home in the house next door. He checked. They were away for the weekend. He decided that tonight would be the perfect time to make his move and play his hand.

He didn't anticipate any trouble from her. She was short, petite, and fragile looking, but he'd bet a week's pay that she was a tiger in the bedroom. He was tall and strong. She would be no match for him. He liked them that way. He hated it when they fought. It only made him angry and he couldn't control himself when he was angry. Having to hurt them ruined the experience for him. He wanted his *date* to enjoy it. He *wanted* to enjoy it.

He had been watching her for two weeks now, knowing her schedule better than she did. He knew when she got up in the morning, when she went to work, who she hung out with, even who she slept with. He made it his business to know his prey. That was the best part of the thrill of the hunt. He was her personal Santa Claus. He started to hum, *Santa Claus is Coming to Town* under his breath, watching the steam from the cold escape his lips.

Her name was Jennifer Tully. *A corporate lawyer and a fine looking woman to boot*, he reflected, thinking back to the first time he spotted her in the coffee house across the street from her office building.

The perfect date.

She must have been on a lunch break. Blending into the background, she didn't notice him observing her. No one ever noticed him. He was a fly on the wall.

Tonight, after work, she did a little shopping at the mall, picking up some last minute Christmas gifts for her friends. Meeting a few of her co-workers for drinks, they stopped by the local pub around the corner. He watched in amazement as she downed three Kamikazes in the span of an hour. She was feeling no pain.

Luckily, she was only a few blocks from her house and she didn't need to drive. He wouldn't have wanted anything to happen to her on the way home. That would be tragic. The streets at ten in the evening were very dangerous for a woman, drunk, or sober, to be walking around unprotected.

Feeling a little tipsy, she stumbled up the front steps and fumbled with her keys, dropping them a few times. She giddily laughed at her own clumsiness. Finally, after a minute she was able to slip the right key into the lock and open her front door. That was when he struck, coming up behind her and pushing his way into her home. She cried out, dropping her shopping bags as he clamped a hand over her mouth to silence her.

"Shhh!" he hissed, "scream and you'll regret it!" Using his free arm, he grabbed her around the throat in a headlock. He could easily snap her neck with his muscular forearm if she fought too hard.

She could not move, paralyzed with fear and unable to concentrate. She was dizzy and nauseous; the alcohol she had consumed earlier that evening was now revisiting her. Who was this stranger in her home? Her sanctuary!

"You understand that, don't you, my little lamb?" he breathed in her ear and inhaled deeply through his nose. He enjoyed the scent of the opposite sex. So clean. So fresh. So...feminine.

She shook her head in an affirmative. He removed his hand from her mouth. "Who...Who are you?" she asked, tears streaming down her face. Almost gently, he wiped them away with his thumbs. He stuck his thumb in his mouth, tasting her tears. The gesture made her shudder even more than she already was. It made her sick to her stomach. It would be a miracle if she didn't throw up. She had to keep some sort of control.

"Don't you know? I'm the big bad wolf," he laughed, sensing her terror.

She started to cry louder.

"Shhhh!" he said, almost kindly. "It'll be all right, Jennifer. Don't cry." The house was dark. She couldn't see her assailant's face. He was wearing a surgical mask over his nose and mouth. She could only tell that he was big and smelled like sweet pipe tobacco. He could easily overpower her if she tried to fight. But damn it, she was going to fight. She could feel her adrenaline kick in.

Why the hell did I have those drinks? I can't think straight, she thought frantically.

"Your bed room. Where is it?"

Pointing with a shaking finger, she gestured toward the stairs.

"Upstairs? Which room?"

"Front bedroom to the left. Please don't hurt me," she whimpered.

"Cooperate and you won't be harmed. Do exactly as I say and you will enjoy this."

"Take what you want. I've got money. You can have it all. Take my credit cards, just don't hurt me."

"Oh, I don't want your money. I'm not a thief. That would be wrong." In some twisted way, he truly believed that.

"What do you want?"

"I want you, of course. I've wanted you for weeks. This is our first date. The first of what I hope will be many. Now here we finally are. I don't want to hurt you, really I don't. I want to make this as pleasant as possible for you."

Pleasant! Who the hell does he think he is? Casanova?

"No!" she screamed, pushing back from him and turning to run. She had to take the chance to escape. She was not going upstairs with him. She kept thinking of the advice she was given in a self-defense class—a lot of good it did. *Never let them take you to a second location.* However, there was nowhere for her to run. She knew she was going to be sexually assaulted—that was plain as day—but only God knew what else he intended. She'd be damned if she was going to make it easy for him.

He spun her around and backhanded her across the face. She fell into an end table, knocking the lamp over. It crashed to the floor with a thundering noise. *Surely, someone heard the commotion,* she thought frantically. She started screaming, but he hit her again, causing her nose to bleed.

"I told you that I wouldn't hurt you if you cooperated! Your neighbors aren't home to hear you, so shut up! You didn't keep your word so now I might not keep mine!" he stormed furiously.

"Please. Please. I'm sorry," she whimpered, holding her hand to her face and trying to stem the flow of blood. Blood dripped on the carpet, staining it, but that was the least of her problems.

"Get up!" he ordered, yanking her to her feet by the arm. He propelled her toward the stairs. She stumbled over her feet and fell to the floor. He knew she was stalling and nudged her in the ribs with his foot, making her move again. "Move or we'll do it here on the rug! I don't care where we do this. I like adventure. But wouldn't you be more comfortable upstairs?"

No, no, no! she screamed in her head. He yanked her to her feet again and pushed her toward the stairs.

As they started to climb, her eyes darted around the house, looking for an escape route or a weapon, but there was no escape. She knew she was walking up the stairs to an unknown fate. All she could hope for was that she would survive. She would submit and let him do what ever it was he wanted to her. Silently she prayed that he'd just leave the house without killing her.

She continued to pray as she slowly descended into hell where only the angels would hear her plea.

Angel of Justice

A, B. Angelo Mystery

By

Rosanna Filippello

Chapter One

Angelo was exhausted. She didn't know why, she hadn't been in work for over four weeks. On IOD, injured on duty, status ever since the last incident that nearly cost her life, her left hand was in a cast, the broken pinky finger healing nicely. Bored out of her mind at home she decided it was time to go back to work even if that meant in a limited duty capacity. Not that she didn't love being home with her husband, Sam, but she had to do something or go mad.

Sam's therapy was going well. The fall down the stairs miraculously freed the damaged nerves pressing on his spine. It could have gone the other way and he could have died or become a quadriplegic, but God was on his side that night. He was on both of their sides.

He was regaining mobility every day, but the doctors told him he would need years of intensive therapy before he would be walking without assistance. He was told to continue to use the wheelchair and crutches. Sam intended to prove them wrong, determined to walk down the isle when they renewed their wedding vows for their twentieth anniversary in two years.

Sam was ordered to take it easy. No strenuous activities and that included making love to his wife. *The hell with that*! However, there was nothing said about her making love to him. She was only too happy to oblige him and do all the work.

Their bedroom was all decked out in the holiday spirit. Sam always loved Christmas. Last year was the only time in eighteen years Sam didn't' decorate the house for the holidays and Angelo didn't have the energy or the desire to do it herself. She was in a bleak place and no amount of Christmas spirit was going to bring her out of that darkness. Sam's recovery was the only thing on her mind at the time.

There was a gigantic Fir tree in the corner of the room next to the fireplace, its blinking lights flashed off and on, twinkling. Angelo had no idea how

Sam managed to set it up without her knowing. It was hard to get anything past her in her own home, especially something that big. She hadn't even detected a fallen pine needle on the floor. She was taken by surprise when she walked into their bedroom. The look on her face was all Sam needed to feel pleased.

A small nativity scene was set up on the windowsill. Mary and St. Joseph sat huddled together watching over their precious baby Jesus with love and joy. Stable animals, shepherds, and angels bowed down before the Lord, paying homage to Him. A few inches away, three kings marched toward the manger, following the bright star above. The set had been in Sam's family for generations.

His parents had always been big on the Christmas decorations too. Angelo always remembered the festivities at his house with delight when they were children. Angelo could see where he got the knack for it.

Although Catholic herself, she never felt the same as Sam did about the holiday. Sure, she went to church and honored the Lord, but as she grew older, she felt as if Christmas was taken way out of context. It was more about Santa and presents than about the Lord Jesus' birth.

Still, as long as it made Sam happy, she'd let him have his fun. He was a big kid at heart anyway. He said it made him feel younger. Secretly it made her happy too, but she'd never admit it. She was an adult, so she told herself.

Angelo cuddled next to Sam in bed, snuggling close to his chest. The lights from the tree bathed his face in a white hue. He looked peaceful and sedate. He looked *alive*. She watched him breathe, steady and sure, as she played with the hair on his chest. She thanked God for His mercy. Sam opened his eyes and looked at her.

"What's wrong, Bee?" he asked, seeing slight worry on her beautiful face.

She replied, "Nothing. I'm just thinking."

"About what?" He stroked her head, brushing her hair out of her eyes to gaze at her face.

"You. And how much I love you."

He kissed the top of her head. "You're sweet."

"No, just hopelessly in love with you." She snuggled closer to him and he wrapped his arms around her.

He knew what was on her mind. He could always tell. "When are you going back to work?"

"In the next few days."

"Bored of my company already?" he teased. "It can't be *that* terrible, Bee."

"Of course not, but you know me. I can't sit around and do nothing all day. At least you have your writing, your cooking, and now your decorating to keep you busy."

"You make me sound like a housewife."

"I don't even take vacation or sick days."

"Yes, I know. But you really needed the break." The last time she took time off was when he was in the hospital after the accident. She was up to the max on accrued vacation and sick time.

She held up the cast. "I didn't need this one," she joked.

"Seems to be the only way to get you to take some time off. Force it on you."

"Come on, Sam, you know work is the second most important thing in my life."

"Oh, yeah? What comes in first?"

"You do, of course."

"What about your hand?"

"The cast can come off after the New Year, but I'd like to go back to work even if that means I'll have to be on limited duty status."

"No street work?"

"No. However, I'm sure I have a ton of work to catch up on. You know O'Malley isn't going to do it all by himself."

"God forbid," he laughed. "Wouldn't want him to work for his tax payer's salary."

"No, of course not."

"So are you going back on last out? I kind of liked having you home at night."

"Yes, so did I, but you know three squad is the only place for me."

"Oh. I'm going to miss cuddling you in bed."

She smiled. "Well, we better make up for lost time," she said, climbing on top of him and straddling his midsection.

"Whoa! Down girl!" he said surprised by her amour.

She laughed out loud, her hair falling back in her face. He brushed it away again, wanting to see her. "Hmmm, I should say the same for you," she giggled, leaning over and kissing him full on the mouth. She made sweet, gentle love to him for over an hour. They fell asleep in each other's arms exhausted, but relaxed, as the clock struck midnight.

* * *

The shrill ringing of a telephone woke Angelo from a restful sleep. Opening one eye and blinking twice, she looked at the digital clock radio on Sam's side of the bed. Two a.m. *Who the hell would be calling at two o'clock in the morning?*

Reaching over Sam's sleeping body, she picked up the receiver. "Hello?" she said groggily.

"Bee, you've got to help me," a female voice cried.

"Who is this?" Angelo asked, sitting up and trying to wake her sleepy mind.

"Help me, Bee, please," she begged. The phone was suddenly disconnected.

Angelo looked at the telephone, confused.

"Who was that?" Sam mumbled, half asleep himself.

"I'm not sure." She climbed over Sam and out of bed, turning on a light. Looking at the caller ID, she said, "The call came from Jennifer Tully's house."

"Is she in some sort of trouble?" he asked concerned.

"Beats the hell out of me. Let me call her back." Angelo dialed the number and waited a full two minutes for someone to pick up the line. "That's weird. No answer."

"What did she say?"

"She needed help. That's all. Sam, I'm going over to her house and see what's going on."

"I'll come with you," he said, reaching for his shirt.

"No. Stay here," she told him, getting dressed. "I'll call you when I get there."

"At least call for some back up. I don't want you going there alone."

"I will if I think I'll need it. I wouldn't want to jump the gun with this. Jenny's a private person. I don't think she'd appreciate a house full of cops there if it's nothing." After checking to see if her off duty weapon was loaded, she holstered it.

"Be careful."

"Aren't I always?"

Sam was still upset about the time she almost got herself killed serving a warrant. He would never take her leaving the house for granted. One never knew if their loved ones would be coming back. "I mean it."

"I will. I'll call you as soon as I get there, okay?"

"You better. Or I'll be calling you. Take your cell phone with you."

Holding up her cell phone to prove to Sam that she'd call, she said, "Love you."

After kissing him goodbye, she ran out the door and into the snow covered driveway. Angelo hopped into Sam's four-wheel-drive Lexus and headed north on the Roosevelt Boulevard. Traffic was nearly nonexistent except for a few salt and plow trucks trying to keep one step ahead of the storm. It seemed to be a losing battle against the elements. Mother Nature would always be the victor in these matters. There was no point fighting God.

Angelo made it up to the Northeast section of the city in less than a half an hour. A personal best.

She pulled up to the house and noted that all the lights were out, even the

Christmas decorations. Walking up to the front door, she noticed that there were no footprints on the ground. A fresh layer of thick snow covered the tracks of the last person who entered or exited the house hours ago.

Angelo knocked on the door and rang the doorbell. *The Carol of the Bells* chimed softly inside the home, but there was no answer. She pressed on the door handle and the door opened with a creak. Pulling back her coat and reaching for her gun, she entered the house. She tripped over something lying on the floor. She prayed it wasn't a body.

Reaching around in the darkness for a lamp, she found it overturned. After righting it, she switched it on and illuminated the room.

The living room was a mess, looking as if there was some sort of struggle. Glancing down at the floor, she saw what she tripped over—wrapped Christmas gifts. At least it wasn't a body. She did notice what appeared to be dried blood on the carpet. It stuck out like a sore thumb on the white rug. Not a good sign. Not good at all.

"What the hell is going on?" she quietly asked herself. She was about to call for backup when she heard someone moaning. "Jen! Jen! It's Bee! Where are you?" The sounds were coming from the second floor.

The moaning turned into sobbing as Angelo took the stairs three at a time, rushing up to the front bedroom. Standing to the side, she pushed the door open and peered into the darkened room. She reached around the door and turned on the light switch. When her eyes adjusted to the light, she found her friend curled up in a fetal position, naked and bleeding.

"Oh, Jesus, Jen," she said, swiftly moving over to her side. She placed a hand on Jennifer's shoulder. Jennifer freaked out, jerked away screaming and swinging wildly at Angelo.

"Get away from me! Don't touch me!" Jennifer shouted.

Angelo grabbed her arm to restrain her as gently as possible. "Jen, calm down. It's me, Bee. Calm down! Look at me."

The hysterical woman stopped swinging and looked up at her friend. "Bee?" she said in a small voice.

"Yes, Jen, I'm here. You're safe." Angelo turned and reached for a folded blanket at the foot of the bed. Pulling it off, she covered Jennifer and hugged her to her chest.

"Bee," she said, crying on her shoulder. She kept saying her name repeatedly. She was in shock.

"Jen, what happened here? Who did this to you?"

Pulling away from Angelo, Jennifer clutched her knees to her chest and rocked silently. She shook her head. "No, no, no," she said to no one in particular.

"Jen, look at me." Angelo came around and kneeled in front of her. "Look at me. Look me in the eye and tell me what happened. Focus on my face."

Jennifer refused to look Angelo in the eye.

"Okay, I'm calling the police." She reached for the overturned telephone lying by the bed.

"No! No police!" Jennifer screamed, grabbing Angelo's arm. She gripped her so tightly that Angelo knew she was going to have bruises in the morning.

"Jen, why not? You're hurt. You need Rescue."

"No! I'm fine!" she yelled, knocking the telephone out of Angelo's hand.

"Okay, okay. Relax. Then tell me what happened here tonight. You called me for my help and I'm here to help you. You trust me, don't you? Jen? I'm your friend, right? Look at me."

Shaking her head and looking into Angelo's eyes, she replied, "Yes."

"Okay, then, talk to me. Whatever it is, I'll understand." She took Jennifer's hands and waited for a reply. She'd wait all night if she had to do so.

Finally, Jennifer said, "I was coming in the house and he grabbed me from behind. I thought he was going to kill me."

Thinking like a cop, Angelo asked, "What did he look like?" She needed details.

"I don't know. I didn't see his face. He was wearing a mask. It was dark in the house."

"What kind of mask?"

"The kind a doctor uses. Cloth or paper. The flat kind."

"Okay, how about his size? His build?"

"He was big. Tall. Thin, but muscular. He smelled like tobacco." She started crying again. Angelo had to get her to focus.

Pointing at her never wavering eyes, she said, "Jen, look at me."

She did.

"Cigarettes?"

"No, sweet pipe tobacco."

"How about his voice? Could you tell if he was a white male, black male?"

"White. He was definitely white."

"Accent?"

"I...I don't remember."

"What was he wearing? Color?"

"Black. Sweats, I think. Had one of those black air force jackets."

"Bomber?"

"Shorter. Cloth, not leather."

"Flight jacket? M-1?"

"Yes. Black on the outside, orange on the inside."

"Then what happened?"

"I tried to fight, but he overpowered me. I...I had a few drinks earlier. I couldn't think. It's all my fault! I was asking for trouble drinking like that."

It was common for victims to feel that they were responsible for what happened to them. "No, Jennifer, listen to me. It was *not* your fault. None of this is your fault. No one *asks* for it."

"I should have fought harder."

"You're alive, right?"

"Yes," she sniffled.

"Then you fought hard enough. You survived. You're not a victim, but a survivor. Okay?"

"Yes."

"Say it."

"I'm not a victim. It was not my fault."

Angelo pulled Jennifer into a tight embrace, hugging her to her chest. "Tell me what happened next."

"He forced me up here. And...and...he raped me. I thought it would never end."

"It's over, Jen. He's gone."

"He said he'd be back for our second date." Jennifer's voice trembled in terror, her eyes darting around the room. She truly believed he'd return.

"Date?"

"Yes. He told me that this was our first date and he looked forward to seeing me again. Oh, Bee, I was so scared. I was powerless to do anything to stop him. Oh, God, oh, God!" Jennifer tried to stand up, but her knees buckled out from under her. She collapsed to the floor.

Angelo steadied her and said, "It's okay. He's not coming back."

"How can you be so sure?"

"I'll make sure of it. We have to call the police."

"No. I don't want anyone to know about this," Jennifer murmured.

"Jennifer, if you don't report this he'll rape some one else," Angelo told her to make the point stick in Jennifer's conscience.

"No! You always said it was the victim's choice whether to go to the police. I choose not to call them. I don't want anyone to know my business. I don't want anyone to know this happened to me."

"Okay, but we need to, at the very least, get you to a hospital."

"Bee, no!"

"Please. Look, you are hurt. You're covered in bruises." Angelo could see the dark bruises around her throat and shoulders. Jennifer was probably very close to dying that night. "You could have internal injuries. Think of yourself."

Shaking her head, Jennifer said, "It doesn't hurt that bad."

"Jennifer, you can get pregnant."

She looked up at Angelo with scared eyes. "But he...he used protection."

"A condom? Did he leave it here?" she asked, hoping he left his DNA behind. Something that would identify him.

"No, I think he took it with him. Yes. Yes. I remember him putting it into his jacket pocket after...after he was finished."

"Okay, but those things aren't 100% effective. You need to get to a hospital. They'll keep it confidential. They won't call the police unless you want them too. I'll make sure they don't. Trust me. If nothing else I just want you to get medical attention."

Biting her lower lip, she thought about it for a moment. "You'll stay with me?"

"I'm not going anywhere, Jen. If you want me there I'll be there through the whole thing."

"Can we wait a few minutes? Just so I can get myself together?"

"Take all the time you need. I'm not going to leave your side."

"Thanks, Bee. I'm sorry to have called you like this, but I didn't know who else to turn to."

"I'm glad you did and I'm here for you. Okay? I'll not let anyone else hurt you."

Angelo reached for the telephone, but Jennifer grabbed her hand. "Who are you calling? You promised no police."

"I have to call Sam and let him know I'll be a while. Okay? I don't want him to worry and send the cops here. You know how he is. Very overprotective."

She knew exactly how overprotective Sam could be. Angelo was just as bad as her husband in that respect and she was proving it now. "Oh, okay," Jennifer agreed.

Angelo dialed the number and it was answered on the third ring. "Sam, it's Bee. Listen, Jen's okay. She had a little—accident. I'm going to take her to *Episcopal* Hospital."

"Episcopal?" he repeated, making sure he heard her correctly.

"Yes." Her voice was cold and without emotion, but he could tell she was enraged.

Sam knew instantly why his wife was taking her friend to Episcopal and not the closest hospital only a few blocks away. Episcopal, located in North Philadelphia, was one of two hospitals in the city, which dealt with rape victims. They were known as Rape Crisis Centers.

"Okay, honey, give Jennifer my love."

"I will. Thanks. I'll talk to you later."

"Right. Goodbye."

Angelo replaced the receiver. Turning to Jennifer, she said, "Let's get you dressed. Then I'll drive you to the hospital. I'm going to warn you, the exam is not pleasant, but no worse than what you've already been through tonight. However, this time, we're on your side. Okay?"

Jennifer nodded her head. Angelo made her dress in the same clothes she was wearing when she was attacked. She hoped to find some evidence left behind on them.

"You're going to be fine. I promise I will not let anyone else hurt you."

Jennifer placed a hand on Angelo's arm. "Thanks for being here for me, Bee."

"Anytime, Jen, anytime," she answered, hugging her friend tight.

***

Episcopal Hospital located at Front and Lehigh in the heart of East Division was usually a very busy place, but tonight, because of the snowstorm, there were hardly any cars in the parking lot.

Angelo parked close to the entrance in the Emergency Room lot and cut off the engine. Jennifer was silent the whole trip, looking vacantly out the window. Not once looking at Angelo, she just sat there chewing her bottom lip. Angelo was sure Jennifer was reliving the incident over and over again in her head.

"Are you okay?" Angelo asked, engaging the parking brake.

"Fine. Yes. I'm okay," she said softly. Angelo didn't believe it for a minute. "Ready?"

Shaking her head, she said, "Bee, I'm not so sure about this. I'm afraid."

"I know, honey. It's okay to be scared, Jen. But remember, I'm here for you." She patted Jennifer on the arm. "Look, they are going to want to call the police."

"No cops, Bee. I mean it. I won't go in there if they call the police."

"I'll talk to them, okay?"

"Okay."

Angelo got out of the car and walked over to the passenger side, opening her door. She helped Jennifer out and holding her by the arm, escorted her inside. There were only a few people in the waiting room. The only injuries seemed to be from a few motor vehicle accidents.

Angelo walked over to the guard at the window and tapped her badge on the glass. The guard looked up from his newspaper. "Can I help you, ma'am?" he asked, slightly annoyed that his reading was interrupted.

In a quiet voice, Angelo said, "I've got a rape victim." She held up her badge for his inspection.

His tone changed, becoming softer. "Okay, Officer, bring her through," he said.

Angelo waved Jennifer over and the guard pressed the door release to let them into the Emergency Room. They entered the ER and Angelo directed her to the triage area.

Jennifer looked around her. She imagined everyone in the emergency room would be staring at her—knowing what had happened. However, she soon realized that the few people in the ER had their own problems and weren't concerned with her.

An alarm sounded somewhere in the ER. A nurse and an orderly rushed past Jennifer, pushing a crash cart. They disappeared behind a curtain. She could hear orders and shouts of, 'clear!' Someone had coded. Listening to the commotion behind her made Jennifer realize that she was lucky to be alive. She was a lot more fortunate than the poor individual behind the curtain was.

Angelo could see that Jennifer paled, looking rather ill. She took her by the hand and steered her away from the commotion.

"Sit here a minute while I talk to the nurse." She walked over to the triage nurse, a Hispanic woman in her mid thirties. Pulling out her badge and showing it to the nurse, she said, "Excuse me."

"Yes, Detective? Can I help you?"

"Detective Angelo. Look, I have a rape victim, but there is a little problem."

"And that is?"

"I'm not here in an official capacity. The woman I brought in is a friend of mine. I know it's your policy to contact the police, but the only way I could get her to come to the hospital was to promise not to contact them. She really needs medical attention."

"You want me to disregard policy?"

"No, but I'd like to contact Special Victims myself and explain the situation."

The nurse looked over at Jennifer who was quietly looking down at her feet and wringing her hands. "Look, if you want to handle it that way, I guess it would be all right as long as someone is contacted."

"I appreciate it."

"What's her name?"

"Jennifer Tully."

"Okay, let me talk to her." The nurse got up and went over to Jennifer. "Ms. Tully, would you come back with me, please?"

Jennifer looked at Angelo pleadingly. "It's okay, Jen. I'll be right out here. I'm not going anywhere."

The nurse pointed to the telephone on her desk, indicating to Angelo that she could use her phone to call Special Victims. Then she took Jennifer gently by the arm and helped her back to a private exam room. When she was out of sight, Angelo picked up the telephone and dialed the number for Special Victims.

"Special Victims, Officer Parks speaking. May I help you?"

"This is Detective Angelo; could I please speak with Corporal Grosse?"

"Sure, hold on a second."

After a minute or so, another voice came over the line. "Corporal Grosse."

"A.J. it's Angelo."

"Hey, Bee, what's up?"

"I need a favor."

"Anything."

Angelo explained the situation to her in vivid detail. "And I don't want him to get away with this," she finished.

"Look, tell you what. I'll send Officer Thompson over to collect the kit. We'll write up a '48' and say that the victim does not want police involvement at this time. This way if she changes her mind we'll have the evidence."

"I really appreciate it."

"No problem."

"I'll call you later for a follow up."

"All right. How are you feeling?" Corporal Grosse asked as an afterthought.

"Better."

"Sorry to hear about your partner."

"Thanks." Angelo still didn't like to talk about it. "I've got to go see how Jen is doing. I'll call you."

"I'll send Thompson over right away to talk to you."

"Okay. Goodbye, A.J."

She hung up the phone just as the nurse returned to her station. "You talk to SVU?"

"Yes. They are sending over an Officer Thompson."

"Good. You're doing the right thing. Your friend is seriously injured. She needs to report this."

"I know, but she is a strong willed and proud woman. Maybe she will change her mind once she has time to think about it."

"The doctor is in there with her right now doing the kit. Did you bring an extra set of clothes for her?"

"In the car."

"Good. SVU is going to want the old ones."

"I know. I used to work Sex Crimes a few years ago."

"Then you know the drill."

"Yes."

"They are going to be in there a while, so you might as well give me all the information. I need to start the paperwork."

Angelo sat down and gave the nurse all the information she could. About an hour later, the officer from Special Victims entered the ER. Walking over to Angelo, she held out her hand. "I'm Officer Thompson."

Angelo looked at the petite woman in the blue blazer. She guessed she was in her early twenties, five feet six, thin, with blonde hair and green eyes. The officer was a pretty, young woman who could have probably been a model if she wasn't a cop. Angelo wondered why she was a police officer, making no money whatsoever, when she could be making a small fortune doing something else. Like her, the young officer probably had *the calling*. She looked sharp as a tack.

"Detective Angelo," she informed the officer, holding out her hand. Officer Thompson took it and shook it enthusiastically.

"I'm sorry for taking so long to get here, but the drive from the unit to here is a bit of a distance. The weather did not help either. I'll be happy when the unit makes the move to this location in a few months. It'll save valuable travel time."

"Don't worry about it. I understand. It gave me time to sort all this out."

"The Corporal told me about the situation. Sorry to hear what happened to your friend. You're doing the right thing."

"I know, but I feel like I'm going behind her back and breaking a promise. But I also know the policies."

"Yeah, the Corp said you used to be at the unit. Homicide now, right?"

"Yes, but I'm on IOD."

She looked at her hand. "Yes, I heard about the incident. Good work, that."

Angelo didn't reply. She didn't want to talk about it. Thompson was smart enough to see that and dropped the subject.

"Okay, so tell me what happened?"

She told the officer everything Jennifer told her. How she called her and how she found the house a wreck. She mentioned that the offender used a condom and took it and any evidence with him. There wasn't much of a scene. Thompson wrote the information down on a 75-48 incident report.

Another hour past before the doctor came out of the exam room, holding a rape kit. He handed it to Officer Thompson. "Your friend is asking for you," he said to Angelo.

"Let me go and get her clothes out of the car. Officer, will you walk with me?"

"Sure."

They walked outside and over to the Lexus. The snow was still falling at a pretty good clip. Brushing the snow from her face, Angelo said, "I appreciate the help, Officer Thompson."

"You can call me Susan."

"Bee."

"Nice car. You guys in Homicide must make a lot of overtime."

"It's my husband's car. My car is an '89 Toyota. Would never make it in this snow."

"Oh."

Angelo smiled. "But the OT is great."

"I'd like to get into Homicide one day."

"Maybe you will. It's hard work and long hours, but it's very satisfying. Anyway, I'll call you about this when I return to work in a few days."

"All right. Well, it was nice meeting you although I wish it were under better circumstances. Again, sorry about your friend."

"Thanks. Goodbye, Susan."

"Goodnight, Detective. Merry Christmas."

Another holiday ruined for me, Angelo thought drearily. "Yeah. Right."

She watched as Officer Thompson got into her city issued car and drove away. Angelo scooped up the clothes out of the back seat and returned to the ER. Going back to the private exam room, she knocked on the door before entering.

"It's just me, Jen. I got some fresh clothes for you."

"Thanks," she replied quietly.

"Are you all right?"

"No worse than when I came in here," Jennifer answered, wiping a tear from her eye. She was still in a state of shock. Angelo knew she'd be numb for some time to come.

Angelo wrapped an arm around her shoulder. "I know it's pretty bad in here, but at least it's all over now."

"It'll never be over, Bee. Never," she said.

She was right. He would be with her forever. Angelo handed her the clothes and watched as she got dressed. When she saw her friend's battered body, bruises covering her back and chest, she winced. She had seen her fair share of brutal rapes in her time at the Special Victims Unit, but this was her friend who was the victim and it bothered her. Bothered her to no end. She'd make sure the SOB paid for his crime. Pay tenfold!

"Do you want to go back to your place?"

Jennifer hadn't thought about it. "Uh, I don't know. What if he comes back?"

"Look, if you want you're welcome to stay at my place for a while."

"What about your husband?"

"Oh, he won't mind. The house is huge. All those bedrooms going to waste."

"You sure?" she asked.

"Positive."

"Well, maybe just for a few days. I wouldn't want to wear out my welcome. You've already done so much for me."

"Hey, we're pals. You could never do that."

"Yes, but you know what they say about fish and houseguests after three days."

Angelo laughed. At least Jennifer still had her sense of humor. "Not a problem. Probably won't even notice you there. Besides, you can keep Sam company while I'm at work. But remember—hands off!" she joked.

It was difficult, but Jennifer cracked a slight smile. "I've met your husband. Quite yummy, but I promise to behave."

"You better." She smiled back.

"Besides, I wouldn't want to piss you off. I've seen you mad."

"Glad you remember. Come on, I'll take you back to your place so you can get a few things. Don't worry; I'll be with you the whole time. Nothing will hurt you."

"Thanks, Bee. I don't know how to repay you."

"No need. I'm sure you would have done the same for me."

On the way out, the nurse gave Jennifer a prescription for an antibiotic just in case of the possibility of a sexually transmitted disease and two tablets that Angelo assumed was a *Morning After* pill.

Angelo drove Jennifer home. She was worried for her friend and she wasn't sure how to deal with it. As many rape cases as Angelo handled in her career, this one hit a little too close to home. Her jobs were never personal; they were always strangers. Just another case number in a long list of victims. Never was it a close friend. She prayed she'd be able to focus and handle everything in a professional, detached manner. It wasn't going to be easy.

Chapter Two

By the time Angelo brought Jennifer back to her house on Cliveden Street it was eight in the morning. She knew Jennifer was both mentally and physically exhausted. She'd also bet that Sam didn't sleep a wink either, worrying. She pulled up the driveway and parked in front of the house. Grabbing one of Jennifer's suitcases, she helped her to the front door. Jennifer stopped at the door, hugging her arms to her chest.

Sensing Jennifer's apprehension, Angelo asked, "What's wrong?"

"Are you sure Sam won't mind my staying with you guys? I don't want to be a burden."

"Are you kidding? He'll love to see you again. He doesn't get many visitors," Angelo responded, unlocking the heavy Oak door. Placing the bag on the floor, she closed the door behind her. She punched in the security code for the alarm, deactivating it. "The house is alarmed at all times. Very secure. You have nothing to fear here."

"I'm sure. You have a beautiful home," she said, glancing around the foyer. Sam had done more decorating in the hallway. He was trying to make the house feel as happy and comfortable as possible. Angelo couldn't imagine where he got so much stuff. Where'd he keep it all?

"Thanks. Sam and I are rather proud of it. Ah, speaking of Sam, here he comes now."

Sam wheeled himself around the corner. Angelo looked at his handsome face and smiled. She was right though, he didn't look like he slept much at all.

"Good morning, Jennifer," he said. "Nice to see you again. It's been way too long." He would have greeted her with a kiss, but he wasn't sure how she would react.

"Hello, Sam. You're looking well," she replied.

"Getting better every day." He patted his thigh gently.

"I'm happy for you. Really I am. I love what you've done with the place."

"I try, but Bee is such a humbug."

"Hey!"

Sam ignored his wife's protest. "Would you like some breakfast?" Sam was a man who believed everything could be fixed with a good, home cooked meal.

Good thing he did the cooking, Angelo thought, or they'd starve to death if it were up to her.

"As I recall you are an excellent cook, but I must decline. I'm not feeling very well. The doctors gave me medication that is making me sick to my stomach. I hope you didn't go through any trouble."

"Nonsense."

"Sam," Angelo said, "I'm sure Jen is just tired. I'm going to show her to the guest bedroom. She needs to get some sleep. I'll join you for breakfast after I settle her in."

"Well, if I can't have two beautiful women to dine with me, I guess I'll have to settle for one." He winked at her.

Angelo smiled. He was such a charmer.

"All right, Jenny, I hope you feel comfortable here. If you need anything at all don't hesitate to ask," Sam told her.

"Thanks, Sam. Thanks for your generous hospitality."

"Anytime."

"Come on, Jen, let's get you upstairs and settled," Angelo said, gently taking her by the elbow and showing her the way to the stairs. They walked upstairs and over to the guest quarters. "Your room is going to be down the hall from ours, okay? If you need anything there is an intercom."

"You've been so kind, Bee. I don't know how I'll ever repay you."

"We've been friends, how long? Ten years?"

"Yes. About that."

Jennifer was an assistant district attorney before she went into corporate law. She prosecuted some of Angelo's cases in court. She always won. She had tenacity and was a good lawyer. No, she was an excellent lawyer. Angelo missed her in the courtroom. The city needed more lawyers like her as prosecutors. Of course, it didn't hurt that Angelo dotted every 'I' and crossed every 'T' in her investigation reports.

"Jen, you know me. I don't have a lot of close friends, but I consider you one of the few. I don't just invite anyone to my humble home. My partner hasn't even been here."

"Humble? You have a gift for understatement. This is a wonderful home. Not just the way it looks, but there is love here. So full of love. I hope to have a fine husband some day." Her voice trailed off. "But I guess that will never happen now."

"That's the biggest pile of bull I've ever heard, Jen. This is just a setback.

Just like Sam's accident. You won't always feel afraid. In time, you'll heal. I'm here for you until you do."

"You're the best, Bee." Jennifer hugged Angelo so hard she thought she'd break a rib. Opening the bedroom door, Angelo ushered Jennifer inside.

The guest room was tastefully decorated. The queen size bed was covered with a pastel colored down comforter. There was a writing desk and an entertainment system in the room. Everything she would need could be found in the guest room, including a private bathroom and a small kitchenette.

"Boy, you sure know how to treat guests."

"Only the best for my friends," Angelo told her and meant it too.

Jennifer sat down on the bed and looked at her hands. Angelo sighed and squatted in front of her, taking her hands. She stroked them gently as if comforting a small child.

"Jen, I know how you are feeling."

Jennifer started to cry. "How could you, Bee? Have you ever been raped?"

"Well, no," she answered honestly.

"Then you can't understand," she said, shaking her head. She wiped away a fallen tear from her cheek with the back of her hand.

"But I do know how it feels to be defenseless."

"You? Defenseless? Never."

"Look," she said, getting up and sitting next to her on the bed, "you know how this happened?" She held up the white plaster cast on her left hand.

"I heard something about it on the news. You got hurt arresting a serial killer."

"Yes, but they didn't report everything. There was a lot more to it."

Jennifer's eyes widened. "What happened?"

Angelo took a deep breath. "My partner and I were on a stakeout and when we tried to apprehend him, my partner was killed."

"I'm sorry. I did hear about that."

"I was powerless to stop it. He died in my arms."

Jennifer could say nothing in reply.

"That wasn't all. He came here and planned to kill me next. He was insane. Not just with physical and mental problems, but with hate and jealousy for me. I was sleeping and he attacked Sam who was outside my bedroom door. Sam was trying to defend me and he almost took my husband from me. He shot me with a Taser gun and I went down. All I could do was watch as this man hit Sam on the head and pushed him down the stairs."

"I didn't know. They never mentioned that on the news."

"No they didn't. They didn't mention that I was powerless to stop him. I was a victim, not the hero. He tied me to a chair and I wasn't sure what he had planned for me. It could have been anything. I couldn't fight. I couldn't do anything to stop him. He broke my finger, just to cause me pain. I was at his

17

mercy. He told me he would have me—dead or alive. He did this to me."

Angelo unbuttoned the top of her shirt and showed Jennifer the X mark on her chest above her left breast. The jagged scar was a permanent reminder of what she could have lost. Even if she had plastic surgery to remove the scar, it would always be there in her mind.

"I'm…I didn't know."

"So, I might not know what it's like to be raped, and I hope I never do, but I do know what it's like to be afraid and powerless."

"I'm sorry. I'm being selfish."

"No you're not. You're just scared and you have every right to feel scared, but you are with friends now. You have plenty of other friends too. They'll understand. They'll help you also."

"Not like you."

"Give it time. You might want to call your job."

"Jeez, I hadn't thought about that."

"Just tell them that you're ill. Take a few days off. Feel free to use the phone. Call whoever you feel the need to talk to."

"I'll do that."

"Take a nap. When you are feeling a little better and rested, come downstairs and eat something. Mi casa es su casa."

Jennifer produced a weak smile. Angelo got off the bed and left the room. She went downstairs and into the kitchen. Sam was cleaning up the dishes.

"How is she?" he asked.

"Surviving."

"I'm sure she'll be fine after she rests. She just needs time to heal."

"Yes, time."

"You want something to eat?"

"Uh, no thanks. I have some things to do."

"What you need is some sleep."

"I'm fine. I really have to get some things done. Today if at all possible. It's really important."

"Work stuff, right?"

"Yeah, work stuff. Sorry."

"Fine. I guess I'll keep an eye on Jenny."

"You're a dear."

"You owe me."

"I'll make it up to you. I promise."

He grinned.

"See if you can occupy her mind."

"I'll try. She likes to read, right?"

"I believe so. Yes."

"Maybe I'll let her read my new book."

"You haven't even let me read it yet. I guess I'll have to wait like all your other fans."

He stood up and kissed her on the forehead, before falling back into his chair. "Sorry I really needed to do that."

"You're not following doctor's orders."

"Neither are you, so there."

"I'm taking the Lexus," she said, grabbing the keys.

"Hey, don't get used to it. It's mine," he teased.

"Next time get a Hummer."

"If this weather keeps up, maybe I will."

"Bye, Sam. Love you."

She headed out the door. The snow had finally stopped and the streets were at least passable on the main roads. Angelo drove to her doctor's office, needing a note to get her back on duty. The doctor agreed only to limited duty. She knew she wasn't going to get any more than that. It would have to do.

Her next stop was the city's medical unit in Fairmount to get cleared to return to duty. They were hesitant, but agreed to let her return to limited duty. The Safety Officer then cleared her to go back to her unit.

Being that she was an important component of the Homicide Unit, she was allowed to go back there instead of *Police Limbo*, AKA, the Abandoned Auto Unit. Officers who were injured, on limited duty, or pregnant on the job were sent there. She would have rather stayed home or have her fingernails ripped out than end up shuffling someone else's paperwork. She had enough of her own to shuffle at the Homicide Unit.

The last thing on her list was to contact her captain and inform him that she would be returning to work for her next tour of duty in two days. He was happy to get her back, even if it was for just desk work. Apparently, O'Malley was driving everyone crazy. They needed her to put him in his place. *Good old Patty O'Malley*, she mused.

She finally returned home just in time for an early dinner. She walked in the door and hung up her coat in the closet. Sam was setting the table.

"How is my little house Frau?" she teased.

"Humph!" he grumbled.

"Has Jenny come downstairs?"

"No. I checked to see if everything was all right, but she locked the bedroom door. She said she was fine, but tired. She spent about an hour in the shower. I think the only reason why she got out was because we ran out of hot water. And that is not an easy task."

"I'll go check on her. She needs to eat something."

"That's what I told her. I left a tray by her door, but she didn't touch it."

Angelo sighed. "If I have to force feed her, I will!"

"Bee, take it easy on her."

"No more babying. I'm putting my foot down," she stormed.

"Bee, temper! Keep a lid on it."

"I will." Angelo put on her tough face and marched upstairs to the guest quarters. She tried the door and found it locked from the inside. Knocking on the door, she announced herself. "Jen, It's Bee, open this door." She didn't yell, but she made her point. She could hear Jennifer shuffling behind the door. She opened the door and looked at Angelo.

"Sorry, Bee."

She was still wearing the same clothes that she put on in the hospital. She didn't look like she got any sleep either.

"It's time for dinner."

"I'm not hungry."

"Look, I have to put my foot down about dinner. Poor Sam slaved in the kitchen all day."

"I'm sorry. He didn't have to go through the trouble."

"Well, he did. We have one rule in this house and that is that everyone eats dinner. I expect you to abide by that rule."

Jennifer looked down at her feet again, her lower lip quivering. She was about to cry. Angelo started to feel bad that she raised her voice. Sam was right. She needed to control her temper.

"Look at me, Jen," she said softly. Jennifer looked up. "You have to eat something or you'll make yourself sick. You're taking antibiotics. You can't take them on an empty stomach. I wouldn't ride you so hard if I didn't care."

"Okay. I know you mean well."

"What have you been doing all day?" Angelo asked, looking around the room. The bed was still made and not slept in. Only the chair by the window was out of place. The setting sun was beaming through the window. It would be dark again soon.

"Just thinking."

"Get any sleep?"

"A little." Unless she slept in the chair, Angelo doubted she slept at all.

"Jen, you're going to need to talk to someone. I know a few counselors."

"The doctor at the hospital mentioned this to me already. I don't need a therapist."

"You don't have to go through this alone."

"I'm just not ready, Bee, don't push me!" she snapped.

Angelo didn't even blink at the outburst. *Ah, getting into the anger phase*, she mused.

"I'm sorry."

"Stop apologizing to me."

"I called work," Jennifer said, changing the subject. "I told them I was not feeling well and needed a few days off. I have vacation time saved. I might as well use it. Thankfully I don't have any pressing clients to attend to."

"That's a good thing, but maybe work will help you."

"I can't concentrate. It wouldn't be fair to my clients."

"Okay."

"I'm sorry I'm being such a big baby, Bee. I'm sure you've got better things to do than baby sit me."

"I wouldn't call it babysitting. However, I just got clearance to go back to work. Will you be all right here with Sam?"

"I'm sure I'll be fine."

"Think about talking to someone. Even if it's to Sam. He'll understand."

"Does he know?"

"Yes. I don't keep things from my husband."

Her face turned red with embarrassment. She was mortified. If she felt that way around close friends, how would she feel around others?

"Come one, it's time for dinner. Sam made something special just for you. He doesn't do that for just anyone."

Jennifer attempted a smile, but it fell flat.

* * *

Jennifer went to bed right after dinner. She picked at her food, but at least it was an attempt to eat something. Angelo worried about her. She needed more than Angelo could give. She had to get professional help. She needed crisis counselors and support groups.

Angelo and Sam retired for the night after the eleven o'clock news. Angelo still had a strong dislike for the media; they hounded them for a week after the serial killer incident. She didn't know how Sam could watch it. Same stuff, different day. She saw enough death and destruction at work; she didn't need to bring it home too.

"I'm going back to work tomorrow night," she told him as he turned off the television with the remote control.

"I kind of figured that was what you were doing all afternoon. How much did you threaten the doctor?"

"I didn't," she said innocently.

He looked at her, smiling.

"Okay, maybe I did. Just a tiny bit." She laughed. "However, until the cast comes off, I'm on limited duty."

"I know it's been hard for you, Bernadette. Being cooped up here isn't fun at all."

"How do you do it?"

"You go to work to have something to do, right?"

"I don't just go to have something to do. I beg your pardon!"

"I didn't mean it that way. I mean, you enjoy working."

"I get something out of it, yes."

"Well, when I'm home writing, I'm enjoying it. These books don't just crank themselves out of the computer, y'know."

"I know. That's where we are different. You like the quiet job at home and I have to be on the streets fighting injustice."

"I love you so much. I love that brain of yours, your integrity and sense of justice."

"And I thought it was just for my body."

"Oh, yeah, that too," he said, grinning.

She snuggled close to him. "Sam, I'm so lucky to have you."

"So am I. What was it you told me? We're soul-mates."

"Forever bonded."

"Yeah." He kissed the top of her head.

"I'm really worried about Jen."

"Give her time. All those years you did in Sex Crimes should make you realize that the victims need time."

"I know, damn it, but this is personal. She's my friend."

"You really are her friend, so give her the time she needs to heal."

"I'm going to find out who did this to her."

Sam sighed out loud. "I figured you would. Don't let it cloud your judgment."

"My judgment has never been clearer."

"It's a Sex Crimes job, not Homicide."

"Not yet, but I have a bad feeling it will be one day. Did you see the bruises on Jenny's neck?"

"No. She's covered up."

"He almost strangled her. One day some poor girl is going to be dead because of this bastard. He needs to be stopped before it becomes my job."

"What can you do? You're on limited duty. And besides, you told me Jenny didn't report it."

"Well, that's not strictly true."

"What?"

"I reported it. I called on a favor. Special Victims took a report from me and gathered the evidence from the kit. I'm hoping to convince Jenny to prosecute."

"Does she know?"

"No. But I couldn't let him get away with it. Besides, it's policy. I couldn't ignore policy."

"Yes, policy."

"The officer assigned seems to be a straight arrow. She's a little young and I'm sure hasn't been at the unit long."

"Sort of like you back then?"

"Yeah, she kind of reminds me, of well, me."
"Are you going to work with her?"
"I'm going to try. I said I'd call when I got back to work."
"Taking a young one under your wing. That's sweet."
"I'm nobody's rabbi."
"God, I bet half the department wishes to have you as their rabbi."

Angelo blushed. That was one of the nicest things he ever said about her and the job. "Goodnight Sam," she said, kissing him.

He cuddled closer to her. "Goodnight, Bernadette."

***

Jennifer woke up screaming. In fact, she woke up the entire household. Angelo jumped out of bed and ran down the hall to the guest quarters. The door was locked. Battering on the door, she shouted, "Jenny, open the door!"

"Get away from me! Don't touch me! Ahhh!" Jennifer screamed.

"Jen!"

The door was thick and solid. Angelo couldn't budge it even after a few attempts at putting her shoulder into it.

"Bee, here!" Sam shouted, tossing an extra set of keys at her. Angelo caught them in one hand. Unlocking and opening the door, she rushed inside the guest quarters. She found Jennifer cowering in the corner of the room. She was holding an iron fireplace poker in front of her.

Slowly, Angelo approached her. "Jen, it's just me. Give me the poker before you hurt yourself."

"No! Stay away!" she screeched, swinging the iron poker. Angelo used the cast to block the blow.

Pain smarted up her arm. It would have been worse if not for the thick plaster cast. "Jen," she said softly. "Jen, calm down. There is no one in here but me, okay?"

"No, no, no," she whimpered.

"Jen, listen to me. You're safe."

Jennifer stopped swinging the iron poker and seemed to return to reality. She blinked a few times; focusing on Angelo's concerned face. "Bee? What?" she said, confused.

"Yes, Jen, it's just me," she replied, holding out her hand and taking hold of the makeshift weapon. Jennifer refused to let it go. "Jen, let me have the poker."

She looked up at Angelo's face and let go, crying. Placing the poker on the bed and out of arm's reach, she gathered Jennifer up into her arms.

"It's okay; it was just a bad dream. Just a dream."

"No, he was here." She was shaking so bad that the muscles in her body were starting to spasm and lock up.

"There is no one here but me and you." Angelo looked at the door and saw Sam's worried face. Without even saying anything to him, he got the message to leave them alone. "Jen, he's not here. Look around. Everything is secure. The alarm is set. You're perfectly safe."

"Bee, I don't understand. It was so real."

"I know, sweetheart."

"Oh, God, I don't think I can take this," she whined.

"It'll get better in time. I swear. He will never hurt you again."

She looked Angelo in the eye. "You promise?"

"On my life, I will."

Jen continued to cry on Angelo's shoulder. Angelo gathered her closer to her chest and rocked her like a child. *Damn him! I'll find you and make you pay for this*, she swore under her breath.

Chapter Three

He was home preening himself for his next date. He was always preening himself, a compulsion he'd had since childhood. Time to find another lovely woman to pursue in his endless quest to make all girls his. He'd be at the coffee house again—one of his many haunts. There were plenty of redheaded Irish lasses in there for him to choose. He loved redheads. They were so fiery.

He wondered how Jennifer was doing. He knew she enjoyed their date. Then again, was it too much for her to handle? She did seem a little bit upset that he left her. Did she report him to the authorities? The others did, those whores. They weren't worth a second date. He found out just what they were made of. Dirt. Too bad, all of them were quite attractive.

He hoped not. He would like to pay her a second visit. She was hot! He may have been a bit rough with her, but not any more or less than the others. They all liked it rough. He could tell. It was just a game to them. They wanted to be dominated and that was what he gave them. It was all part of the role-playing game.

Looking in the bathroom mirror, he brushed his unruly hair, smoothing it down with his hand. *I need a haircut,* he thought absently. He smiled, his bleached white teeth grinned back at him. *Damn, I'm a fine specimen of a man*! He didn't care that he was so vain. Nothing wrong with a little pride in oneself. The women loved him for it. He smelled so clean and fresh. Not flowery, but manly.

He removed his shirt and admired his smooth, hairless torso and chest. His skin had a golden glow all over. Not that fake, artificial, painted on look, but the real thing. Everything about him was real. He took time out of his busy schedule to go to a tanning salon once a week during the winter. He thought himself a bronze god.

If he didn't, because he never went out in the sun, he'd be pale and white as snow. The sun was not good for his delicate skin. He didn't want to risk skin cancer. That would not do at all. He preferred going out after the sun had set. He was a night creature, a creature of the dark. The dark was his friend.

Modeling for himself in the mirror, he flexed his muscles and posed. He worked out five times a week after working in that dreary building day in and day out. He hated his job. He hated his co-workers who thought they were above him. He hated that bitch of a boss. *She'll get hers someday,* he thought bitterly.

Still looking at himself, he said, "Yes, sir. Fine body, fantastic lover. Mr. Universe, look out!" He giggled at himself. There were no shortages of compliments. He was sure and confident in himself. What was wrong with that? Any girl who couldn't see that wasn't worth his time. He had plenty of girls, but the thrill of the hunt, picking his prey from the herd and pursuing until he pounced. That's what it was all about.

He didn't like it when girls were too forward. He preferred them submissive, giving into his masculinity. His dominance. His power! He knew they all enjoyed it, even encouraged it. Every last one of them. They only reported it to the cops because of the feelings of guilt and shame from enjoying it.

Yes, they enjoyed it a little too much and now they wanted to cover up for their sins. They needed an excuse for why they cheated on their husbands and boyfriends. Yes, of course, that was it. No other reason. He did nothing wrong but satisfy them in ways they couldn't even admit to themselves. A fantasy.

"I am the greatest lover of all time," he said to himself. "*Of all time!*"

Strolling out of the apartment door, he smiled again as he stole one last glance at himself in the mirror.

Chapter Four

Angelo was glad to be back at work. She missed the ugly green paint on the walls, her co-workers, and yes, even her pain in the ass partner, Patrick O'Malley. Slipping into the unit, she hoped no one would notice her and ask too many questions. She still wasn't up to talking about the incident. Her co-workers showed concern after it happened and she was thankful for that, but she also knew that cops were nosey and liked to talk. They all knew what happened, having to do their jobs by interviewing Sam after he had to kill her attacker. He was cleared soon enough. Self-defense and the defense of a police officer. He was hailed a hero, and of course, he was.

Sitting at her desk, it wasn't long before Lieutenant Kenney walked over to her. He smiled and was delighted to have her back in the squad. "Angelo," he said.

She glanced up from her paperwork. "Yes, sir?"

"The captain said you'd be coming back. I still think you should take more time to recover."

"I'm recovered, Lou."

"How is your husband?"

"Fine. Healing more every day."

"How about you?"

"My hand is fine. Should be back to full duty shortly. Can't wait. This thing itches like crazy."

"I can't let you out on the street until you're cleared."

"I know. I have a ton of paperwork to deal with anyway. It'll give me a chance to play catch up." She held up several folders.

"You could have done that at home."

"You sound like you don't want me here," she replied disappointed.

"That's not true."

"Lou, I understand that you think I should take more time, but my hand is fine. You know me; I get stir crazy at home."

"Yes, but I'm not so much concerned about your physical injury. It's your mental state I'm worried about."

"There is nothing wrong with my mental state. I'm as crazy as ever," she joked.

The lieutenant gave her a serious look. He was not amused by her joke.

"I took those EAP counseling sessions like I was ordered to. I'm fine. No stress. Ready to return to duty. The doctors said so."

"Bee, you lost your partner. It can't be easy for you." His tone was serious. She knew he meant well, but harping on the subject wasn't going to help how she felt. It wasn't going to bring Ronalds back from the dead.

"It's not." She looked down at her desk. "I'm working on that, Lou. But I have to do it my way and in my own time. This is the way I deal with things. It's the way I am."

"I know exactly how you are and burying yourself in paperwork isn't going to help."

"It'll help me fine, Lou. I know what is best for me. I *am* an adult, y'know."

"All right, but if you feel the need to take more time, you let me know."

"I will. Thanks for your concern. I appreciate it."

"I want you in top form, not distracted."

"When have you ever known me to be distracted?"

"Never and I don't want to see it."

"You won't. You can bet on that."

He smiled, patting her on the back. "Yes. Well, then, good to have you back. It wasn't the same without you."

She returned the smile as he walked away. There was just no arguing with her when her mind was made up.

"Angelo!" O'Malley shouted across the room.

"Jeez! Why don't you take out an ad, Pat?" Walking over to her, he thumped her on her back so hard that she pitched forward. "Ow!" she whined, straightening up as he planted his butt on her desk. Nothing ever changed. She rolled her eyes at him.

"You're back. Great. I was getting tired of having to do all the work myself," he said playing with the pens and pencils on her desk. Angelo noticed that he couldn't keep his hands still when he was nervous. She wondered why he was uneasy.

"Do you mind!" She snatched the pens out of his hand and put them back in the *Far Side* cartoon novelty mug on her desk. "Well, now you know how I feel."

"Ouch! You wound me," he replied, picking up another pen.

"Pat, would you leave my pens alone and quit stealing them. I could have sworn I had more than this. Don't you have any of your own?"

He handed her the chewed up pen and put his hands in his pockets. "Yes and they aren't all damaged like yours."

"That's how I know they *are* mine. Dental impressions. So if you don't want me to put those impressions on your ass, you'll leave them alone."

"Ah, I see you're back and meaner than ever."

She grinned at him. "Did you think I wouldn't be?"

"One could only hope."

"Sorry to dash your hopes, Pat."

"Seriously. What are you doing back so soon? You could have been on IOD status until the New Year. Free vacation."

"I don't like to get paid for doing nothing. Staying at home, watching the soaps, and eating bon bons is not my style. Unlike some people."

He ignored her. He knew she didn't mean it. "So, how's the hubby?"

"Fine."

"I guess you were telling the truth about him. And I always thought he was a fantasy to keep your mind off of me."

"You keep on believing that, Pat."

He sighed heavily. "I guess that blows any chance I have with you."

"Sorry. You're eighteen years too late."

"Besides, he'd kill for you. I ain't messing with him." As she recalled, so would her partner. O'Malley saved her life too. He saw sadness in her eyes. "Sorry, I shouldn't have said that."

"Never mind."

"Quite a hunk though. I see why you hold on to him."

She raised an eyebrow. "O'Malley, are you hitting on my husband?" she teased.

He jumped up off the desk, coughing. "No, no, of course not!"

She laughed out loud. "So, what do we have to catch up on?"

"Glad you asked." He reached over to his desk and picked up a stack of files. Plopping them on her desk, he said, "Have fun."

"Hey!" she said, fingering through the paperwork. "These are the same cases we had before."

"I didn't want to mess with your system. So I thought it would be best if I didn't touch them."

"You're so kind," she said sarcastically.

"Aren't I, though?"

"Get away from me, Pat. Now!"

He winked at her. "Nice to have you back and in not-so-rare form as usual."

She laughed. He was right. She wouldn't have been happy if anyone, including him, messed with her paperwork. She continued to work through the night. No one bothered her or asked any questions. They were happy that she was back and unharmed. The unit wouldn't be the same without her.

***

About half way through her tour of duty, Angelo was paid an unexpected visit. She was looking down at her work when someone cleared her throat, announcing her presence. Angelo glanced up and saw a young woman wearing a pressed business suit standing in front of her.

Angelo smiled. "Officer Thompson. How are you?" she asked, indicating with her hand for Thompson to have a seat. Thompson sat down. "So what's going on?"

"We need to talk, Detective Angelo," she said softly.

"You can call me, Bee."

Just because Angelo outranked her, didn't mean she was superior. They were all cops. Most officers knew the rules. After all, the police department was a paramilitary organization. When talking to a superior officer in the presence of other officers they were to be called by their rank. However, off duty or alone, it was permissible to call them by their first name if allowed to. Angelo didn't mind being called by her nickname. As long as no one called her Bernadette.

"Okay, as long as you call me, Sue."

"Deal. What's up? You seemed concerned."

Thompson lowered her voice to a whisper. "It's about your friend."

"Jenny? What did you learn?" she asked, leaning forward.

"Nothing about her case since she's refusing to cooperate, but I took the initiative and went over some cold SVU cases. I came across some similar assaults. I ran it by the supervisor, but he shot me down. He doesn't think I'm experienced enough to know any better."

She sounded bitter and Angelo guessed that poor Officer Susan Thompson of the Special Victims Unit was left out of the loop quite a bit. Sometimes squads had their own cliques and those who weren't part of the group were shunned or ignored. It was worse than high school. She would just have to prove her worth to the unit. It would take time, but unless she was a total screw up, they'd eventually accept her input. Angelo didn't believe that Thompson was a screw up. She had a lot on the ball.

"How long have you been at the unit?" Angelo asked.

"Five and a half months."

"Did he at least listen to your concerns?"

"Oh, he listened to them all right. Said he'd look into it and bring it to the lieutenant's attention. I found out that meant the lieutenant gave the jobs to her *Golden Boy*, Officer Trevor Seymour."

"It happens." Angelo wasn't surprised at that either. There was always a teacher's pet.

"But it's not fair," she whined.

"Never is, Sue. You have to get used to it on this job or you won't have a job for long."

"I guess so."

"You didn't mention Jenny's case, did you?"

"No. I didn't want Seymour to take that from me. I know it sounds petty. Besides I thought you wanted it kept quiet."

"I do and I appreciate it. That's fine."

"What am I to do?"

Thinking about it, she replied, "Did you make copies of the other cases?"

She smiled. They were on the same wavelength. "Yes." She held up the files in her hand.

"I don't see anything wrong with following up on *your* case. As it happens, it just coincides with the others," she said slyly. "Just don't get in Golden Boy's way."

"I was worried. I'm still on probation at the unit. I don't want to rock the boat."

"You're not. You were given Jenny's case, right?"

"Yeah, because it was a dead end. Sorry, I didn't mean it that way."

"I know."

"Without her cooperation, there isn't much I can do about it."

"There is plenty. And if anyone has anything to say about you checking out the cold cases, use it as an excuse to follow up."

"That's kind of backhanded."

"If you're worried about it, then don't take the case. But sometimes it's the only way."

"Will you help me?"

"Me? Sue, I can't officially help you. I'm on limited duty and I don't work sex crimes anymore."

"Oh," she said disappointed.

Seeing that she let Thompson down, she said, "But I'll help you with advice—on my own time."

Thompson beamed. "Really! Oh, thank you so much!" She clasped Angelo's hand.

"Hey, no touching the superior officer," she joked.

"Sorry," she said, pulling back her hand.

"Let me see the files." Thompson handed Angelo the copies. "Tell me what you have so far. Explain to me, how you think these cases are similar. The trick is to talk out loud."

"Okay. This is what I've got. There are five—six if you count Ms. Tully's assault—in the cold cases files. Same physical description—well, what there is of one. No one has seen his face. He always strikes in the dark. He wears some sort of mask to hide the lower part of his face. It's usually different each time. A surgical mask, bandanna, scarf, or full face mask. That sort of thing. They all occurred at night or in the wee hours of the morning. All were white females with red hair."

"So our guy likes redheads."

"That's what I thought."

"That's good, go on. How far apart are the assaults?"

"I believe they started about seven months ago."

"The last one being Jenny?"

"Yes."

"The one before Jenny was when?"

"Two weeks ago."

"Six women in seven months," Angelo said thoughtfully. "Does the time between each attack get shorter and more violent?"

"I think so. I've done a time line. Victim number one was Barbara Cotton, a twenty-seven year old storekeeper. She was attacked in her home in May. Next one was Francine Tabor, a thirty-year-old bartender. She was attacked six weeks after Barbara. The next one occurred five weeks after that and her name was Paula Clydesdale. She's a twenty-year-old college student. Within the next month, he struck his forth victim, Sydney Bayberry, a forty-year-old businesswoman. Now the fifth one was attacked just two weeks ago. Heather Donnelley. She's only sixteen. Not even out of High School yet. He messed her up pretty bad. Mentally, not physically. And of course you know about Jennifer Tully, a thirty-three year old lawyer."

"He doesn't seem to have an age range or working class."

"No. Sixteen to forty so far. He swings from students to professionals to blue collar."

"The only factor is the red hair?" Angelo was chewing on a pen thoughtfully.

"Seems that way."

"Hmmm," she said, thinking out loud. "He's tightening his pattern."

"All the victims stated that he called them *his date*. He'd force his way into their home as they were entering or sleeping in their homes. There he would overpower and rape them. All the complainants state that there was something taken. A small trinket. Wait, I should rephrase that."

"Why?"

"He asked them for something."

"He asked? That's weird."

"Yes. I guess they gave it to him to pacify him. Why does he do that? Take something, I mean."

"It's a trophy."

"Excuse me? I don't understand."

"He's taking something to remind himself of the experience."

"Oh, I see. Interesting."

"It's very common in serial rapists. Or any criminal for that matter. Let me ask you this question. Do any of these women have husbands?"

"No. Boyfriends, but none of them live with the victims."

"Independent women who live alone."

"Yes. Except for the teen. She lives with her parents."

"Ten to one odds, he's stalking them first."

"I'd take that bet."

"Any description at all?"

"White male in his twenties or early thirties. Tall. Very muscular and cocky. Oh, and he had no body hair."

"Not any?"

"Except for his head. Not even any *short and curlies*," she told her.

"Doesn't want to leave DNA. No hair or semen left at the scenes?"

"Always used a condom and took it with him. Crime Scene narrowed the brand, but that's it."

"And you say not one victim saw his face?"

"Nope. Like I said before, he always wears a mask of some sort."

"Has his violence escalated?"

"No, not really. The sixteen year old was the most traumatized, but she was not beaten. Her injuries were more mental than physical. Poor kid. Only Ms. Tully sustained serious bodily injury. You saw Ms. Tully's neck, right?"

"Yes." She remembered the bruises in vivid purple detail. "That's what I'm worried about. Eventually he's going to kill someone."

"No doubt about it. I'm told that you were good at getting into their psyches. What do you think?"

"I think that he is arrogant and as you said, cocky. He doesn't think of himself as a rapist, but a lover. A Don Juan, if you'd like. He feels that being forceful is flattering to these women. It's all a fantasy."

"A rape fantasy? What woman wants that?"

"There are some, I'm sure, but not these women. I think he stalks them. Maybe he sees them in a bar or at work. Find out where these women work. See if they are connected in any way. Are they friends? Do they run in the same circles? Do they go to the same movie theater or club? A social gathering place? Church?"

"I did pick up on the fact that they all lived up in the Northeast section of the city. All local."

"All six of them?"

"Yes. Holmesburg, Torresdale, and Pennypack. Lower northeast. Nothing above Grant Avenue."

is of one. No one has seen his face. He always strikes in the dark. He wears some sort of mask to hide the lower part of his face. It's usually different each time. A surgical mask, bandanna, scarf, or full face mask. That sort of thing. They all occurred at night or in the wee hours of the morning. All were white females with red hair."

"So our guy likes redheads."

"That's what I thought."

"That's good, go on. How far apart are the assaults?"

"I believe they started about seven months ago."

"The last one being Jenny?"

"Yes."

"The one before Jenny was when?"

"Two weeks ago."

"Six women in seven months," Angelo said thoughtfully. "Does the time between each attack get shorter and more violent?"

"I think so. I've done a time line. Victim number one was Barbara Cotton, a twenty-seven year old storekeeper. She was attacked in her home in May. Next one was Francine Tabor, a thirty-year-old bartender. She was attacked six weeks after Barbara. The next one occurred five weeks after that and her name was Paula Clydesdale. She's a twenty-year-old college student. Within the next month, he struck his forth victim, Sydney Bayberry, a forty-year-old businesswoman. Now the fifth one was attacked just two weeks ago. Heather Donnelley. She's only sixteen. Not even out of High School yet. He messed her up pretty bad. Mentally, not physically. And of course you know about Jennifer Tully, a thirty-three year old lawyer."

"He doesn't seem to have an age range or working class."

"No. Sixteen to forty so far. He swings from students to professionals to blue collar."

"The only factor is the red hair?" Angelo was chewing on a pen thoughtfully.

"Seems that way."

"Hmmm," she said, thinking out loud. "He's tightening his pattern."

"All the victims stated that he called them *his date*. He'd force his way into their home as they were entering or sleeping in their homes. There he would overpower and rape them. All the complainants state that there was something taken. A small trinket. Wait, I should rephrase that."

"Why?"

"He asked them for something."

"He asked? That's weird."

"Yes. I guess they gave it to him to pacify him. Why does he do that? Take something, I mean."

"It's a trophy."

"Excuse me? I don't understand."
"He's taking something to remind himself of the experience."
"Oh, I see. Interesting."
"It's very common in serial rapists. Or any criminal for that matter. Let me ask you this question. Do any of these women have husbands?"
"No. Boyfriends, but none of them live with the victims."
"Independent women who live alone."
"Yes. Except for the teen. She lives with her parents."
"Ten to one odds, he's stalking them first."
"I'd take that bet."
"Any description at all?"
"White male in his twenties or early thirties. Tall. Very muscular and cocky. Oh, and he had no body hair."
"Not any?"
"Except for his head. Not even any *short and curlies*," she told her.
"Doesn't want to leave DNA. No hair or semen left at the scenes?"
"Always used a condom and took it with him. Crime Scene narrowed the brand, but that's it."
"And you say not one victim saw his face?"
"Nope. Like I said before, he always wears a mask of some sort."
"Has his violence escalated?"
"No, not really. The sixteen year old was the most traumatized, but she was not beaten. Her injuries were more mental than physical. Poor kid. Only Ms. Tully sustained serious bodily injury. You saw Ms. Tully's neck, right?"
"Yes." She remembered the bruises in vivid purple detail. "That's what I'm worried about. Eventually he's going to kill someone."
"No doubt about it. I'm told that you were good at getting into their psyches. What do you think?"
"I think that he is arrogant and as you said, cocky. He doesn't think of himself as a rapist, but a lover. A Don Juan, if you'd like. He feels that being forceful is flattering to these women. It's all a fantasy."
"A rape fantasy? What woman wants that?"
"There are some, I'm sure, but not these women. I think he stalks them. Maybe he sees them in a bar or at work. Find out where these women work. See if they are connected in any way. Are they friends? Do they run in the same circles? Do they go to the same movie theater or club? A social gathering place? Church?"
"I did pick up on the fact that they all lived up in the Northeast section of the city. All local."
"All six of them?"
"Yes. Holmesburg, Torresdale, and Pennypack. Lower northeast. Nothing above Grant Avenue."

"He must live or work up there. They don't usually stray far from home. Run a check using what you have in your description through the computer and see if anything pops. See if anyone was arrested or accused of sexual assault. Even look into wife beaters, stalkers and harassers."

"Right," Thompson said, writing down everything Angelo was telling her. "I just remembered something about one of the victims."

"What's that?"

Opening the file again, Thompson pointed out an interesting fact. "Victim number two, Francine, has a restraining order on a guy named Ben Moody. He's her ex-boyfriend. I believe he's an auto mechanic or something."

"See if he violated that order. Also check if he has any priors."

"Will do," she said, happy that her suggestion wasn't shot down like it was by her supervisor. "I'll let you know what I dig up."

"You know, this is going to take a lot of legwork on your part."

"It's not like I have anything else to do."

"Give it time. You'll earn your keep."

"How long did it take for them to accept you?"

"Oh, well, I was already a detective by the time I got to SVU. I didn't have anything to prove to my supervisors. You're only an officer—no offense."

"None taken."

"How long have you been on the job?"

"Five years."

She smiled. "Eventually you'll earn that respect you want. Look at it this way, if you didn't have anything to offer Special Victims, they wouldn't have transferred you."

Thompson smiled at the compliment. "I'm going to prove it to you and the others that I have what it takes."

"You don't have to prove anything to me, Sue. I can see that you want to help these women, not just get a pinch."

"How is your friend anyway?"

"Not well."

"I'm sorry to hear that. I'm sure it's hard on her. And you too, for that matter."

"Yes," Angelo admitted. "She needs time, but she also needs counseling. She's stubborn. I think if I hound her enough she'll get the help she needs."

"You're a good friend. I know how she feels. I wish I had a friend like you."

"Sue, you have my friendship."

"I appreciate that. I asked to be transferred to SVU because I want to help these women." Angelo got the feeling there was an underlying reason, but it wasn't her place to ask about it. If Thompson wanted to tell her something, she would.

O'Malley sauntered over to her desk, interrupting them. "Why, *hello* there," he said to Thompson.

Angelo grumbled. "Officer Thompson, this is my partner. Detective O'Malley," she announced, pointing her destroyed pen at him.

"You can call me Pat. In fact, you can just call me." He looked her up and down, winking.

Angelo rolled her eyes and Thompson smiled. "Hello, Detective. I've heard many good things about you."

"You have? Oh, of course you have." His chest swelled and he sucked in his gut.

Angelo laughed out loud. "Sue, don't encourage him. What do you want, Pat?"

"Nothing. I just wanted to meet your lovely friend."

"Officer Thompson is here just visiting."

"Oh, taking on a protégé?"

"No."

"Well, sweetheart, if you're looking for a rabbi, I'm your man." He patted his puffed out chest.

"Go away, Pat!" Angelo ordered.

He smiled at Thompson and walked off.

"Sue, one thing you have to learn is never to encourage the men on this job. Especially Patrick O'Malley."

"He seems nice."

"He's harmless, but a pain in my ass."

"Most men are. Anyway, thanks for all your help, Bee. I appreciate it."

"Look, here is my card and home number. Call me if you find out anything or need help."

"Thanks. You've done so much already. Here is mine." They traded business cards.

"It was nothing."

"If I get anything solid I'll let you know right away."

"Listen to me. If you get anything, don't go in alone. Don't do anything by yourself. Call for backup. Call me. I've got your back."

"Really?"

"Of course. I mean it. Don't do anything on your own."

"I should be getting back to the unit. Thanks again, Bee." She stood up and waved at O'Malley on the way out the door.

"You can let your gut out now, Pat!" Angelo yelled across the room.

O'Malley wandered back over to her desk. "So what is going on?"

"It's personal."

"She's cute."

"And almost half your age. You leave my *cousin* alone. You hear me?"

"Your—your cousin?" he coughed. "Another Angelo on the job? Great.

She looks nothing like you."

"Mother's side. Mess with her and you mess with my crazy family." It wasn't true, but he didn't have to know that.

"It figures."

"I mean it, Pat."

"Oh, okay. You are such a party pooper, Angelo," he said disappointed.

"You remember that, my friend."

***

Angelo got off work on time, something she hadn't done in a long time. She was happy about it though, finally able to get some rest and maybe run a few errands later. Walking in the front door, she called out for Sam, but there was no reply. *Was he in the kitchen?* she wondered.

He must have cooked early. She could smell fried bacon and eggs, but when she entered the kitchen, she didn't find anyone. Puzzled, she looked in the dishwasher. There were two sets of dishes in it. Well, at least Jenny had eaten that morning. That was a good sign.

Wondering where they could be, she made her way toward Sam's office. She could hear voices inside. Someone was laughing. Something stirred in Angelo's gut. It wasn't jealousy. Sam wasn't the type of man whom she had anything to worry about. Their marriage was solid. Her heart stirred because Jenny was laughing.

She knocked on the door before entering. "Ah ha! Caught you!"

Sam looked up from his computer and smiled. "Oh, no, she suspects," he laughed. Jenny looked horrified, not knowing what to say.

"Relax, Jen, he's only kidding," Angelo told her. "What's going on?"

"Jenny is proofreading for me. Apparently she thinks my writing is funny."

"You're a funny guy," she said, planting a wet kiss on his lips. They were always so soft and welcoming.

"Hey! It's supposed to be serious romantic stuff," he huffed.

"It's really good," Jenny told him. "I don't think I've ever read any of your books though."

"Now, I'm insulted." He gave her the hurt puppy expression.

"I'm sorry," she said seriously.

"Relax, Jen, Sam is only yanking your chain."

"It's just that law books are my thing."

"Maybe you should try a few. Get your mind off of the law for a while," Angelo suggested. "He's really a good writer. I'm rather proud of him." She patted his head like she would a puppy.

"Thanks, honey. You're my inspiration."

"Perhaps I will," Jenny said.

"I'm sure Sam has a few of his books lying around here somewhere."
"Heck, I'll even autograph it for you."
"Really? Thanks."
Sam looked at his watch. "It's only nine o'clock. You're home early."
"That's why I trust you so much. You never know when I'll pop home. There wasn't much for me to do on limited duty. I played catch up with all my paperwork. There certainly isn't a shortage of it."
He grinned. "You want breakfast?"
"If you wouldn't mind, Sam. You're a love. I'll be there in a few minutes. I'd like to talk to Jenny alone for a moment."
"Sure. It'll be ready for you," he said, taking his leave of the women.
Angelo sat down on the edge of the desk. Jenny got the feeling she was about to get a lecture. She wasn't wrong. "Jenny..."
"I know what you're going to say," Jenny said.
"How could you? I haven't even started in on you yet."
"But you were."
"Of course I was. I'm really worried about you. About what happened last night."
"It was only a nightmare."
"I know, but I still think you should talk to someone about it."
"You should talk. I don't see you going to a head doctor about your problems."
"I've worked out my problems. With professional help, thank you very much."
"I'm sorry. I'm just not ready, okay?"
"No, it's not okay, Jen."
"I'm doing much better. Sam is a pleasant distraction. I'll think about it."
"Okay, fine. But what I'd really like to talk about is much more serious."
"What?"
"I think you need to make a formal complaint to the police."
"No, Bee, no! Do you bully all your victims?"
"My victims are usually dead. Look," she said, holding her hands, "I had someone look into it."
"You promised me, no cops! Bee, you lied to me! How could you!"
"What did you expect? I can't let him get away with this."
Jennifer stood up angrily, pulling her hands from Angelo. "It's over. I want it to be over!"
"It will never be over, Jen. Not until he is caught and punished!" Angelo yelled.
"Let someone else file a complaint."
"That's just it. You aren't his only victim. He's attacked before. You're not the first and probably not the last."

"What are you talking about?"

"You're victim number six. Six that we know of, Jen!"

"What?"

"He's attacked five other women besides you. There are probably even more than that. The one before you was only sixteen freaking years old. Just a baby. She'll be scarred for life. Look what he's done to you. Those marks on your neck didn't just appear out of nowhere. He put them there. He tried to strangle you. You could have been killed."

Jennifer's hands went up to her neck, covering the bruises. She turned her back to Angelo, looking out the window. "No. That was my fault. I made him angry," she said softly.

Angelo couldn't believe what she was hearing from Jennifer. Jennifer, the tough as nails prosecutor. "You made him angry!" she shouted, grabbing Jenny by the arm and forcing her to look at her. "You make it sound like you think it was all your doing!"

"Bee, it was my fault. I shouldn't have fought. I should have just submitted and gotten it over with. Instead I tried to be tough and fight."

"Bull shit!"

"Bee, not everyone is like you. Tough and unafraid. Able to hold your own in a fight."

"This isn't about me. It's about you."

"I don't want it to be about me, goddamnit! I want nothing to do with it! I want to be left out of it!"

"Can't you help me out just a little bit here? Give me a description."

"I didn't see his face. I didn't *want* to see it."

"You felt him. You know his physical description. Tell me about his body."

"No! I will not! You're not being fair. You're not my friend. You're just an unsympathetic cop!"

"I am your friend even though you don't think that right now. I want to help."

"Well, I no longer want or need your help! Tomorrow I'm going back to my house."

"Jen, you don't have to go back just yet."

"Yes, I do. I need my life back."

There was just no arguing with her. She needed more time. "You know I'm here for you."

Jennifer refused to speak further. Angelo could hear Sam calling for her. Shaking her head in dismay, Angelo left her alone in the office. *Give her time*, Angelo told herself repeatedly, hoping she'd believe it.

Chapter Five

Angelo's body clock was out of whack. She was hoping to get a little extra sleep, but it wasn't in the cards for her that day. A little after noon the telephone rang, waking her from a restless nap. "Hello?" she said sleepily.

"Bee, this is Sue. Sorry to wake you," Thompson said apologetically.

At first the voice didn't register in her muddled mind, but it didn't take long for her brain to snap into action. "What's up?" She sat up in bed, rubbing her eyes.

"Did you see the news?"

"I don't watch the news, Sue," she told her. Any mention of the news media put Angelo in a foul mood.

"He struck again. Last night. This time they don't think she's going to make it."

"Jesus!"

"She's on life support. Her brain is dead and it's only a matter of time before they pull the plug."

"Damn it! I knew it!"

"Be sure to watch the six o'clock news. Golden Boy is going to have a press conference. They are calling him the *Don Juan Rapist.*"

"Jeez, that's all we need. As if this guy's head isn't big enough. Can't you stop it?"

"*Me?* Who am I? I've got no pull with the brass."

"Okay. How long has she got?" She tried not to sound so unsympathetic, but it was hard for Angelo not to automatically go into cop mode.

"They'll probably unhook her tonight. They are planning to harvest her organs first. Then she'll be on your turf."

"Yes, okay. Listen to me, Sue, I'll call you tonight."

"Why?"

"Just be at work."

"Whatever you say, Bee."

"Thanks for informing me about this."

"No problem."

Angelo hung up the telephone and got dressed in a hurry. She ran down the stairs and headed out the door. Sam stopped her before she could leave without being spotted. Sam had some kind of radar when it came to his wife. He always caught her before she left the house.

"Where are you going in such a rush?"

"I have something to do," she told him, slowing down just enough to put on her coat.

"Who was that on the phone?" he asked as if he didn't know.

"Work."

"Ah, of course. Work. You're on limited duty, remember? You shouldn't be going anywhere work related."

"Thanks for the reminder, Captain," she said sarcastically. She immediately regretted snapping at him. "Sorry. It's important."

Shaking his head. "It always is."

"I have to go. I can't argue about it now."

"Who's arguing? Don't get into anything. Remember you have a cast on your arm."

"Not for long," she mumbled.

"Excuse me?"

"Nothing. I'll be home before dinner. Keep an eye on Jen."

"Bee!" he shouted as she exited the house.

"Trust me," she replied.

He hated it when she told him to trust her. That usually meant she was going to do something rash. "Fine. Whatever," he said as she bolted out the door without another word.

***

Angelo drove to her family physician and made a beeline into the doctor's office. She ran past the nurse at her desk. "I have to see the doctor!" she announced to the surprised nurse.

"You just can't..." the nurse protested, chasing after her. The nurse knew better than to try and physically restrain this particular patient. Dr. Framer was even more surprised than the nurse to see her. "I tried to tell her that she'd have to wait."

"It's okay, Nicole," the doctor said to his harried nurse. With a dirty look in Angelo's direction, the nurse turned and left the room.

"What's going on Bernadette? This is very unlike you to come running in here like a mad woman."

"Sorry. I have a lot on my mind, Doctor."

"You're not scheduled for a visit until the New Year."

"You've got to take this thing off me now," she ordered, holding up her cast.

"Excuse me? I can't do that."

"You will do that, or I'll get another doctor who will!"

"Bee, what's gotten into you? If it's not healed right, your hand could become permanently damaged. Then that will be the end of your career."

"Take it off now!" she insisted.

"Just tell me why?"

"I have to go back to work tonight."

"You're already back to work. Limited duty. Why? What's going on?"

"I can't explain to you right now."

"It's against my better judgment as your doctor."

"Doc, I have to return to full duty," she explained.

It wasn't a good enough excuse for him, but he'd listen to her side of the story. "Let me look at it first, tell me what's going on and then I'll decide."

"That's all I asking."

She did eventually tell him why she needed the cast removed. He could appreciate her devotion to duty, but her health should come first. He x-rayed her arm, and was relieved to see that the bone was healing nicely. However, he was concerned that she could re-injure it. "I'm not so sure about this, Bee."

"Doc, I am. It's my goddamn hand. I'll do what I want with it. If you're worried I'll sue…"

"Of course not."

"Then take this damn thing off me now. I promise to be careful. If I have to punch anyone, I'll be sure to use the other hand."

"Not funny."

"Please. I'm begging you to do me this favor. I'll owe you."

He huffed. "You can be a real pain in the tailbone. Okay, have it your way. But I'm not responsible."

He cut off the cast. She flexed her hand. It felt good to be free of the burden. Wiggling her fingers, she stated, "Feels good."

"You're not just saying that, are you?"

"Would I lie to you, Doc?"

"I mean it. You have to be careful with it."

"I will. I promise. Now, about that full duty note."

He sighed heavily.

"Playing hardball, Doc? Don't make me get ugly. Remember how I helped you out with that little—uh incident?"

"I knew that was going to come back and bite me on the ass."

"So?"

"You've really got me by the *cojones*, don't you?"

"Cough, Doc."

"That's the last time you're going to use that particular piece of blackmail on me."

"Will never speak of it again."

"You're used to getting your way, aren't you?"

"You bet."

He signed a note stating that her hand was healed and she was fit for duty. "If you re-injure that hand, I swear to God, Bee, you'll have the cast all the way up your arm that won't come off until spring."

"You're the best, Doc."

"I hope we both don't regret this."

She smiled. "Trust me."

* * *

Sam was even more dismayed than the doctor was about her having the cast removed so early. She was going back to full duty if it killed her. There was no talking her out of it. And did he ever try. She just told him to watch the six o'clock news and to make sure Jenny was there also. That surprised him even more than her going against doctor's orders. She despised the news.

The three of them gathered in front of the living room television and watched the press conference being held at the Special Victims Unit Headquarters in Tacony. Angelo finally got to see what *Golden Boy* looked like.

He was tall, young, handsome, and built like a brick house. He stood a head taller than his lieutenant, looking the perfect spokesperson. Sadly, he reminded her of Dwayne Ronalds. She decided not to go there. She wouldn't judge this book by its cover as quickly as she did with Ronalds.

"It has come to our attention that apparently six known sexual assaults have occurred in Northeast Philadelphia," Seymour said. "While going through the cold cases files, the unit found a distinct pattern and got a general description of the offender."

Angelo could picture Thompson throwing a fit as she had done when Ronalds talked to the media about her case. At least Thompson was prepared. It wouldn't come to her as such a shock.

"What's the description?" a reporter asked, holding up her microphone.

Flashbulbs popping, Seymour replied, "White male in his twenties or early thirties. He's between six feet and six six. Muscular build."

"Any description of his face or a composite?"

"No. He wore a mask during the attacks."

"Anything else you can give us and the viewing public?"

"No. Not at this time."

At least he didn't mention the lack of body hair, Angelo mused.

"How many victims?"

"He's attacked six women that we know of. If anyone else was assaulted by this male, we would like you to come forward."

"What were the ages of his victims?"

"Sixteen to forty."

"Officer! Officer! We are told that the last victim is in bad shape. That she is in a coma!"

Seymour turned to his lieutenant. After getting a go-ahead nod from his superior, he replied, "Yes, she is."

"Will she make it?"

"We aren't sure. We certainly hope so for her and her family's sake. Our prayers go out to her."

"If she dies, will the case go to the Homicide Unit?"

"We hope that will not happen, but if it does, we will work hand in hand with homicide and pool our resources."

In other words, no, Angelo thought grimly. *They won't cooperate. They want this guy and won't want to share the pinch with Homicide.* However, SVU would have no choice in the matter. A murderer trumped a rapist—even a serial rapist—every time.

"That is all for now. We will have more information for the public as it becomes available."

The lieutenant took the podium. "We would like to stress to the women of the Northeast section—and everywhere else in the city—to be vigilant and travel in pairs. Take precautions. Report anything suspicious, especially prowlers. Don't worry about feeling silly because you called 911 and it turned out to be just a cat in your back yard. Better to err on the side of caution."

"Lieutenant!"

"That is all for now. Thank you all for coming."

Angelo turned off the television and looked at Jennifer who was staring at her hands. Sam suddenly got the urge to leave the room. "I'm going to make some coffee."

When he was gone, Angelo said to Jennifer, "See. I told you."

"What do you want from me, Bee?"

"Give me more information."

"I told you everything."

"You didn't tell me all of it. I know you're holding something back from me."

"I can't! I can't! Don't you understand that?" She put her face in her hands.

Not letting up, Angelo said, "His body. Tell me about his body?"

Looking up, she said, "You get a sick thrill about hearing that sort of thing, don't you?"

"Of course not, don't be silly. I only want to stop him before he hurts someone else."

"I wasn't actively participating in the act. It wasn't like I was feeling him up."

"His body. Did he have any deformities? Something different?"

Seeing that Angelo was not going to stop hounding her, she thought about it. "The only thing I remember was that his body was very smooth. He had no body hair. Waxed."

"Now we're getting somewhere. How about on his head? Was his hair, short, long, curly?"

"Kind of medium length. Curly. And a bit unruly."

"Anything else you remember?"

"He had a nipple ring."

"Did he now?" That was something she hadn't disclosed before. Now they were getting somewhere.

"Yes. I remember because it hurt me."

"Jen, you have to go to the police with this information."

"No!" she said, shaking her head. Tears fell from her eyes as she looked away.

"At least let me talk to one of the officers assigned to the case."

"Not him!" she shouted, pointing at the television.

Surprised, Angelo asked, "Why not?"

"I don't know why."

"How about if you spoke with a female officer? One who can understand?"

"Not now, Bee. Maybe in a few days."

"We might not have a few days."

"What do you mean?"

"Every assault is getting closer in time. The time between your assault and the one before was only two weeks. The last one was only three days ago. Who knows when he'll strike again. Maybe tonight. Another woman will go through the whole ordeal just like you. She might even die."

"I can't do it, Bee. Can't you get that through your thick skull!"

Angelo growled through her teeth. "Fine. Let it be on your head."

"Bee, that's uncalled for! Don't make this my fault. It's not fair!"

"Life isn't fair, Jenny. It isn't fair that the last woman is going to die."

"They just said she's in a coma."

"She's brain dead, Jen. They plan to pull the plug tonight. When I get to work, she'll be in my hands. And God help the bastard!"

"That's why you got the cast removed early. So you can take over the case."

"Damn right. If you won't help. I will!"

"I'll think about it. That's all I can promise."

Calmer, she said, "Are you still going back to your place tomorrow?"

"I have to. I've obviously worn out my welcome here."

"Don't be silly."

"I have to get my life back. I need to get on with it."

"Okay, but if you need anything, even just to talk, don't hesitate to call me immediately."

"Thanks, Bee. I'm sorry I yelled at you."

"Me too. I lose my temper when I think about that bastard getting away with it. Getting away with what he did to you and the others. I've probably been way too hard on you. But it's for your own good."

"I know you mean well."

"I do, Jenny. Really, I do."

***

Angelo arrived at work a little earlier than usual. She needed to catch the lieutenant the moment he came into the unit before anyone else got the chance. Waiting patiently behind her desk, she jumped up the second he walked in the door. He saw her coming and braced himself. He knew that look in her eye—determination. She was on a mission.

"I want the Victoria Sterling case," she stated.

Taking a step back, he replied, "Excuse me, Detective?"

She handed him her full duty authorization. "I want the case."

"Wait a minute, Angelo. What's with you tonight?"

"I'm back on full duty." She showed him her hand and wiggled her fingers at him. "I want the case."

"She's not even dead yet. Aren't you jumping the gun just a little bit?"

"She died twenty minutes ago. You should be getting a call in minutes."

"Don't you have enough of a case load to catch up on?"

"Yes, but this is important to me."

"I'd like to know why this case is so critical to you."

"Personal reasons."

"Did you know her?"

"No. I told you, Lou, it's personal."

"Then you can't have it," he said matter-of-factly.

"Lou!"

"Unless you tell me why I should give it to you, Magee is going to handle it. He's up on the wheel."

"No!"

"Excuse me, Detective, but who is the supervisor here in this unit?" He raised his voice just loud enough to attract the attention of the others in the room.

"You are, boss," she mumbled.

"Damn right."

"I'm sorry, sir." She resisted the urge to look down at her feet like a chastised child and continued to look him straight in the eye.

He paused a beat, watching her expression. "I'm listening to your pitch."

"Can we talk in your office, sir?"

"This better be good." They walked into the office and he closed the door. He sat down behind his desk, folding his hands in front of him. Not offering her a chair, he made her stand. "Well?"

She stuck her hands in her pockets and paced around the room a few seconds before speaking. "Okay, this is the deal, Lou."

"I'm listening."

"This Don Juan character attacked a close friend of mine four nights ago."

"What? Why wasn't this reported?"

"It was, sort of. She didn't want to file a complaint and report it, but I called SVU anyway. They sent out a rookie officer to take care of it for me."

"And?"

"The officer did a little investigating on her own and came across the similar cold cases. She called me for advice."

"I thought…"

"Yes, well, she went to her supervisor and the lieutenant gave it to Officer Seymour."

"Well, Seymour is an up and coming."

"An upstart more like it." They both knew how the game was played.

"So, then what?"

"I knew something like this was going to happen. I felt it in my gut. I knew he would kill someone sooner or later. Too bad it was sooner. It's a pity that woman had to die, but now it's homicide's turn."

"So what do you want?"

"I told you. I want the case."

Thinking about it, he replied, "You'll have to work with SVU."

"I don't have a problem with that. Remember, I came from there."

"I'm not sure you'll get any help from them. The whole place has been revamped since you left. They're going to want to handle all of the jobs."

"Let them handle the other five jobs. Homicide is my gig. They let this guy continue for seven months before a rookie caught on. Seven freaking months, Lou!"

"You'll need a liaison with SVU."

"I was thinking about that. I want Officer Thompson to help me. She's bright and is the one who put it all together in the first place."

"All right, but don't let this get personal. If you let it get to you, I'll pull you off the case so fast it'll make your head spin."

She had never been pulled off a case in her career. He knew that would be devastating to her ego. He didn't want to hurt her, but if he had to do something that drastic, he would in a heartbeat. He would do it to protect her even though she wouldn't see it that way.

"I won't."

The telephone rang and Kenney picked up the receiver. Angelo listened to the lieutenant's one-sided conversation. "Homicide, Lieutenant Kenney. Yes? Right. I'm aware of the situation and I'm assigning Detective Angelo to the case....No, she is no longer on IOD....Yes, full duty. She's going to need a liaison and requests Officer Thompson....I know she's a rookie. Just tell her to come over to Homicide right away....Yes, now! Right. Goodbye." He replaced the phone on its cradle, turning back toward Angelo. "I hope you know what you're doing."

"Don't I always?"

He shook his head. "If you weren't such a fine detective, I'd bust you for insubordination."

She smiled. "Thanks, Lou."

"Just remember, Thompson is a rookie."

"Weren't we all rookies at one time?"

"Hmm, yes."

"I'll keep a sharp eye on her. Don't worry." *I won't let her down like I did Dwayne. I swear*, she thought to herself. "You won't regret it."

"I better not. Let's shake on it." He held out his left hand. Confused, Angelo looked in his eyes, trying to read his motives.

"But that's your left hand," she said dimly.

"I know."

Oh! she thought. He wanted to test her hand. She gave him her hand and winced as he squeezed it. Not very hard, but it smarted, making her grimace. She didn't make a sound, but it hurt like hell.

"I better not," he repeated.

***

Officer Thompson walked into the Homicide Unit and looked around for Angelo. She was standing by the coffee machine, filling up on departmental sludge. Waving Thompson over to her, Angelo offered her a cup. Thompson smartly declined the offer. Going back over to her desk, Thompson followed like a faithful puppy.

"Are you going to tell me what's going on? I was totally prepared to spend the night at my desk doing nothing while Seymour played super detective."

"Didn't SVU tell you?"

"No, but Seymour gave me a dirty look. I'm telling you, if looks could kill

I'd be one dead cop."

Angelo laughed. "You've been detailed to Homicide on my request."

"Excuse me?"

"Victoria Sterling died not too long ago. I've been assigned the case."

"You? But I thought…"

Angelo held up her cast free arm. "Not anymore."

"Okay, so why am I here? Not that I'm complaining. I thought Seymour would be working with you."

"I requested you."

"Really?"

"Yes. Why does that surprise you so much?"

"I don't know. It just does. I'm nobody at SVU. Or the job for that matter."

"Who says? You're smart and resourceful. I've checked out your jacket. You are destined to go places, but you need to get your feet wet first."

"And a bloody nose, if Seymour has anything to say about it."

"Here's your chance. Never mind him. He's got his hands full with the other cases. We have the homicide."

"A competition to see who can catch the creep first, huh?"

"It's not a game, Sue!" she said crossly. "This is life and death."

"Sorry, Detective," she responded, looking down at her feet.

"You are the liaison between this unit and SVU. We aren't here to make enemies, but work together."

"Yes, ma'am."

"I sure hope you are up to some long, hard working hours. We here at Homicide don't work just the eight hours. It's twelve and sixteen hours. Some times it's twenty-four."

"I don't mind. It's not as if I have a life. My boyfriend, Matt, is pulling doubles himself."

"Is he on the job?"

"He's a paramedic with the Fire Department."

"That's nice."

"He's a sweetheart, but our work schedules conflict. I'm not sure how much longer we'll last."

"If you want relationships to work out you have to make it happen."

"You're married, right?"

"Yes."

"How long?"

"Eighteen years."

"Really? Wow! You don't look that old."

"I'm not that old. We married young."

"How do you do it? How do you keep it fresh?"

"We are madly in love with each other."

"I hope I have that some day."

"Maybe you already have it. Just give it a chance. Gosh, I'm sounding like Dear Abby."

"I'd like to meet your husband one day."

"We'll see. Sam's not really a public person."

O'Malley walked up behind Angelo. "Please, I've known Angelo for years and I just met him a few weeks ago. I think she keeps him in a closet."

"Shut up, Pat. Keep it up and it'll be another ten years."

"What's your cousin doing here tonight?" he asked.

"Cousin?" Thompson queried, raising an eyebrow.

"Tell you later," she mumbled. "O'Malley, Thompson is going to be working with us on the Victoria Sterling case."

"We have the Sterling case? When did that happen? I thought Magee was up on the wheel?"

"Don't you listen to the lieutenant when he talks to you?"

"Not really."

She huffed. "Yes, we got the job. Thompson is our SVU liaison."

"Cool. Be fun to work with a younger woman."

"You're not going to be working with her, I am."

"Hey, no fair. I have seniority."

"No, you're just old. Besides, I have important interviews for you to conduct. Guy stuff. You're a man, right?"

"Yes, of course I'm a man!"

"Then you won't mind investigating Victoria's boyfriends and other male figures in her life."

"What will you ladies be doing?"

"Girl stuff, of course."

"You? Do girl stuff? Ha!"

"You want to do it?"

He thought about it. "No, not really."

"Thompson, do you have the interview list?"

"Right here." She handed Angelo the file that Seymour tried to hold on to for dear life. The lieutenant made him give it up after he made a childish scene.

Pulling out a sheet of paper, she handed it to O'Malley. He looked at it, thanking God that it was a short list. "I'll get right on it. Hey, Thompson, can I call you by your first name? What is it again?"

"Susan."

"No you may not, Pat!"

"You're no fun, Angelo. See you around, Susan."

O'Malley walked off.

"So now what?" Thompson asked.

"We are going to check out Victoria's secrets," she said, grinning.

"Pardon?"

"Her residence. I want to see what made her tick. Get inside her head. Find out a bit more about her life and death."

"Oh, all right. Cousin, huh?" Thompson said, grinning.

"Yeah. I'll explain on the way. Let's go."

Chapter Six

    The snow was falling again and visibility was poor. Angelo wondered if this bad weather would ever end. Angelo and Thompson drove a beat up four wheel drive vehicle, procured from the unit, north on I-95 to Victoria Sterling's house in Torresdale. Like a lot of the other homes on the block, Victoria had set up a plethora of Christmas decorations. Most of the houses on the block were dark now, the lights turned off for the night presumably to save electricity. However, Victoria's lights, in full holiday glory, were still on. *Guess she never got the chance to turn them off*, she mused grimly.
    She lived in a pretty, three bedroom row home at the end of the block. Her corner house faced Pennypack Park. For what it was worth, it was a beautiful snow-cover view. Angelo did a quick survey of the outer perimeter. "No sign of forced entry," she said to Thompson, walking back around to the front of the house. Someone, probably the neighbors, had placed flowers on her doorstep as a memorial.
    "No. No broken windows or doors."
    "Tell me what happened?"
    Looking at the report in her hand, Thompson said, "From what they gathered, he forced his way inside through the front door. He must have been waiting for her to come home and attacked from behind."
    "What time?"
    "It's estimated around eleven o'clock."
    "Anyone hear anything?"
    "Neighbor next door," she said, pointing to the adjoining house, "states that he heard a muffled cry, but nothing else."
    "Did he come outside to investigate?"
    "He said he looked out the front bedroom window on the second floor, but didn't see anything. He went back to bed and finished watching the news. The timing was about right."

"Anyone else on the street that night?"

"Not that I am aware of."

"We'll have to go over all the interviews again. All the neighbors."

"Right," Thompson said, writing in her notebook.

"Okay, so about eleven, Victoria comes home from wherever she's been and is attacked from behind, pushed inside the house... then what?"

"I guess she was raped and murdered."

"You have to see the big picture, Sue. A rapist usually uses one of three methods in his attacks. There is the Con. The Blitz. And the Surprise."

"What are they?"

"The Con uses subterfuge. He interacts with his victim."

"How?"

"Let's say he pretends to be a cop and says he's going to arrest you for, oh, I don't know, an open warrant. He handcuffs you, puts you in the back of a car. He drives you to another location and overpowers you. Or he says he injured himself, maybe he has a cast, and needed help putting groceries in a car. Boom, he pushes you in the backseat and rapes you."

Thompson shuddered.

"But our guy doesn't use that method. The next one is called the Blitz. Usually it employs physical force. He punches and renders you incapacitated, gets you in a secured location and attacks. It happens fast."

"You think he blitzed her?"

"No. I think he used the third method. The Surprise."

"Okay, how?"

"The Surprise method usually uses stalking. He'll stalk for a while, making sure you live alone, sneaks in the house and overpowers you with force or threat of force. Maybe even a weapon to make the victim compliant. He does not usually hurt the victim."

"Not hurt them?"

"I said, *does not usually* hurt them. Each case is different."

"The sixteen year old was in her own room at her parents' house. He got in through a window and attacked while she was sleeping in bed. From what she said, he was very nice and apologetic. Told her it was a date and not to make a sound or her parents would catch them. Kind of weird if you ask me."

"Yep."

"You know, you really know your stuff about how the mind of a rapist works."

"I studied behavioral sciences at the FBI academy."

"You were in the FBI?"

"No, I took a course there."

"Why'd you leave Special Victims?"

"I got tired of all the pain and suffering. And the lies."

"The lies?"

"Yes. A few women would cry rape just to get attention or to pay a guy back for some reason or the other. They are the ones who ruin it for the real victims."

"Why would anyone want to do that? Isn't the stigma bad enough?"

"Stigma?"

"You know what I mean."

Angelo shrugged her shoulders.

"Don't you get tired of all the death working homicide? I would have thought that would be worse."

"It is, but I've learned not to take it home. I was younger and less experienced when I worked Sex Crimes. I brought my work home with me. Not anymore. You had better learn from my mistake and not take it home."

"I'll remember that, Bee."

"Yes. If you've got any sense, you won't spend too much time there either. Cops burn out fast in SVU."

"Good to know."

"Why do you do it? You're still young. Why SVU?"

"I have my reasons."

Everyone had personal reasons to want to work sex crimes. Angelo left the issue alone.

"Besides, it's a good place to learn investigations."

"Is that what you want to be? A detective?"

"Yes. SVU is the only place where an officer could work like detectives."

"It's a good start. What you need to do is take the test."

"I'm waiting for the next one coming up in a few months."

"Well, good luck, I'll be rooting for you. If you need any tutoring…"

"Really? Thanks, Bee."

"Yes, well…" Angelo reached in her pocket and pulled out a key to the house. "Let's go inside."

"Don't we need a warrant or something?"

"No. I got permission from her family to do a search."

"Oh."

"Let's take a look into Victoria's world."

They opened the door and walked inside the house. Turning on a light, they surveyed the scene. It was a tidy house, everything for the most part, was in place. Angelo could see the remnants of latent fingerprint dust left by CSU all over the living room.

"Unless you want black fingerprint powder on you, don't touch anything," she said, placing a pair of latex gloves on her hands. Thompson stuck her hands in her pockets.

There were bookshelves and an entertainment system to their right and a sofa and coffee table to their left. Stairs led to the second floor bedrooms. The house was what was called a straight-through. A person entering could walk straight back from the living room to the dining area and into the kitchen. There were also a set of steps leading to a basement.

There were signs of a struggle in the living room. Pillows from the couch were on the floor and the coffee table was on its side, magazines scattered around.

"Tell me what you see, Sue?"

"What do you mean?"

"Get inside her head. Get inside his head too. Tell me what happened in this room after he pushed his way in."

Thompson thought about it for a moment. "She was letting herself in and he came up from behind. Maybe he clamped a hand over her mouth to keep her from screaming."

"Yes, go on."

Thompson could visualize the horrible attack in her head. She walked over to the couch. "He knocks her down onto the sofa and overpowers her. It's not difficult because she's a petite woman. He tells her to be quiet, but she fights and kicks at him, knocking over the coffee table. Maybe he chokes her to make her passive."

Angelo could see that the visualization exercise was making Thompson pale. She would have to get over it if she planned to stay in Sex Crimes. "Okay, concentrate, Sue. Now what happens?"

She looked around and noticed drag marks on the carpet. "He drags her over to the stairs, picks her up and carries her unconscious body upstairs to the front bedroom. Her bedroom."

"Let's go upstairs and take a look."

They ascended the steps and turned left to go into the front room. The Master bedroom. *Funny,* Angelo thought. *They don't call it the master bedroom anymore. Not very PC.* Angelo turned on a light. The bed had been stripped of its sheets, presumably by the Crime Scene Unit to check for semen and hair evidence. Angelo doubted they'd find anything. This guy was clever.

"Okay, Sue, I know it's difficult, but what do you see now?"

"He puts her in bed, removes her clothes and I guess rapes her while she's still unconscious. She wakes up, starts to scream and he strangles her again. Only this time he goes too far. She's not dead, but is gravely injured."

"What do you think he does next?"

"Panics?"

"I don't think so. He takes the time to clean up any evidence."

"What do you mean?"

"Did SVU or Crime Scene find any semen or a condom?"

She looked in the file. "No."

"He didn't mean to hurt her. He didn't think he really hurt her that bad."

"Why?"

"He's what is known as a Power Reassurance rapist. They are usually polite, apologetic, and have a delusional fantasy that the sex was consensual. It was a date in his mind. They can be violent when it suits them. From what I read from the reports, the others did not fight him. They were compliant with his demands."

"Except for Jennifer Tully."

"She fought and he got rough. But he didn't go that far. Not like here. This was an accident. Now he might have gotten a taste for murder. His need might be more than for just rape now. He might want to know what it feels like. She wasn't dead when he left, but the next one might be."

"Why?"

"Just to see what it's like to kill."

"What does it feel like?"

"Powerful. Rape is all about power, but murder is about the ultimate power. The power of life and death. He'll likely kill again even if his victims are compliant."

"Yes. I think so too."

"He thinks himself a Don Juan. A lover. To him all these rapes are consensual. A date. Fighting is rejection. Rejection leads to anger. Anger to murder. He will be the *last* lover his victims ever have. He will hurt them because he knows he can."

"He's sick," Thompson said, feeling queasy.

"Yes." Angelo sat on the bed. "Okay, back to the scene. What does he do next?"

"I guess he leaves."

"Let me see the crime scene photos?" Thompson handed Angelo the photos an over eager cop took before the ambulance took Victoria away. She wasn't sure if she was pissed that the officer took the photo of someone that couldn't consent or pleased that she had *before* shots. "Look at this photo. Tell me what you see."

She was naked with her arms crossed over her chest. Thompson clenched her jaw, teeth grinding. "Looks posed."

"She is. Like he put her in a position of eternal sleep."

"Like a mortician?"

"Yes."

"Shit, you don't think he's a mortician, do you? That just makes it creepier."

"No, I don't."

"Why then?"

"He's feeling guilty about what he did. Another Power Reassurance trait. Who made the call to the cops who found her?"

"I don't know. Came from a phone booth."

"I'll bet you dollars to doughnuts that he called the police after he left."

"I'm confused. Why?"

"He didn't mean to hurt her. He needed to get her some help. He is torn between the need to rape and the emotion to be kind and caring. The lover."

"He's just messed up. I don't care how nice he is, he's still a rapist!"

Raising an eyebrow at the young officer's tone of voice, Angelo said quietly, "Thompson, calm down. I know."

"This guy will get caught and get off like the rest of them! Oh, poor baby's insane."

"The rest of whom?"

She shook her head. "Never mind. Sorry, I'm just having a hard time understanding how this asshole thinks."

"You'll get used to it."

"I'll never get used to it. If I do, I'll become apathetic. I don't want that."

"I doubt that, Sue. You've got too much heart."

She smiled. "Thanks. This guy has some major issues."

"No shit."

"He's arrogant."

"That he is."

"He's self absorbed. Probably good looking. Scores with women, but needs to rape to make him feel more of a man."

Smiling at her protégé, she said, "Now you're getting it."

"Why? That's the question."

"Who knows? Maybe he hates his mother."

"I've read that most rapists were victims themselves."

"That's true. The endless circle of violence continues."

"How are we going to stop him?"

"Did you do that search I told you to do? The one of the convicted sex crime offenders?"

"Yes, but nothing came up yet."

"Keep trying. Maybe we'll get lucky."

"Maybe he never got caught before."

"That could be the only problem with that avenue. He's good. Taking evidence with him. That suggests that he learned from a previous mistake. I think he may have been caught before. Maybe as a teen. Maybe charges were never pressed."

"Juvenile records are sealed."

"There are ways around them. Let me worry about that."

"So, now what?"

"I want to know her habits. Where did she go and frequent? Any of the same places that the other victims hung out?"

"That's an idea."

"Maybe she had a diary or a PDA."

They searched for about an hour until they finally found a PDA hidden in a desk drawer. For some reason Victoria had hidden the PDA. Was there something in it that she didn't want anyone to know about? Looking at it, most of it was in code. She wouldn't worry about that right now. She wanted to read the things she could understand.

"Ah, found it."

"How did you know she'd have one?"

"She just seemed the type who was very organized in life."

"You're very organized. Do you own one?"

"No. I keep everything in my brain," she said, tapping the side of her head. "It's easier to carry around with me. This way I won't forget to bring it along."

Thompson laughed at the little joke. "Wish I could do that."

"It'll come in time, young Jedi," she teased. Angelo perused the PDA for a few minutes.

"Well?" Thompson asked in anticipation.

"Dinner with Mike. Business lunch with Freddie. Date with Bob."

"She was busy."

"Doesn't say where she was having these meetings. The only mention of a business location is a coffee shop."

"Where?"

"Doesn't say exactly, but it says she was having a lunch meeting there with her girlfriends. Day before she was attacked. There is a mention of Happy Hour at a bar."

"What's it say exactly?" she asked looking over Angelo's shoulder.

"It says, meeting the girls at eight. They want to go cruising for guys."

"At the coffee house? Or the bar?"

"I assume the bar since it's later in the evening after work. We need to find these friends of hers and talk to them in the morning."

Angelo looked through the PDA for a few more minutes and came upon a personal note. The look on her face told Thompson that she found something of interest. "What? You look like the cat that swallowed the canary."

Angelo grinned. "Check this out," she said, handing Thompson the PDA.

Thompson read the note aloud. "*God's gift to women hit on me again. What a creep. Thinks he's hot stuff. How many times do I have to tell him to get lost? Jerk doesn't know when enough is enough. I might have been flattered if he didn't hit on every female in a skirt at the café. Maybe I should put him in his place once and for all. Talk to his boss. Better yet, tell his mom what kind of son she raised.*"

"Interesting, no?"

"I wonder who she's talking about."

57

Angelo shrugged her shoulders. "I'm sure we'll find out soon enough." Looking at her watch, Angelo noted that it was four in the morning. "Let's go back to the unit and get that list together. Then we'll head out and talk to the girlfriends at a reasonable hour."

"Right."

"Speaking of reasonable hours, I also want to see Morty."

"Who is Morty?"

"Oh, you haven't met him yet, have you?" she said, thinking of her pal at the Medical Examiner's Office. Morty helped her out on more than one occasion.

"No."

"He's the medical examiner. I want to see if he found anything useful from Victoria's body."

Thompson grimaced. "Oh, okay."

Angelo could see that Thompson wasn't thrilled about going to the ME's office. Who was? Nevertheless, she'd have to get used to it if she wanted to work Homicide. Homicide detectives spent a lot of time at the morgue.

"I'm hoping to get Jenny to open up to me."

"How is she doing?"

"She needs professional help."

"Maybe if I talked to her..." Thompson suggested. "It helps to talk to strangers sometimes."

"We'll see. I'd like to see if Jenny frequented any of the same places as the others."

"That's a thought. Maybe *Don* hangs out there too."

"You're calling him that now?"

"Well, it's better than what I'd like to call him."

Angelo laughed. "My thoughts exactly."

They locked up Victoria's home and went back to the unit. There was much to investigate. Their day hadn't even started. Angelo was right, they were going to work long hours on this case.

***

They got back to the unit in one piece, not that the weather didn't try to take them out on the ice packed roads. Angelo was an excellent driver, but Thompson was still shaking from the four near misses caused by other people who shouldn't have licenses, let alone be driving in that weather.

While Thompson was finding out where the late Victoria Sterling's friends lived, O'Malley wandered over to Angelo and sat on her desk. "How's the rookie working out?" he asked, nodding at Thompson.

"Very well. She's got a good head on her shoulders."

"That's not all she's got." He grinned, leering at Thompson who was leaning over a desk.

"Down, Pat. I'm only going to warn you once to leave her alone."

"Oh, I'm just messing with you. She's young enough to be my daughter."

"Just you remember that."

"How could I forget with you reminding me all the time?"

She smiled wickedly at him. "So, did you call the boyfriends?"

"Yes. Our vic had quite an active social life."

"I kind of gathered that from reading her PDA."

"She was seeing some guy named Bob. Real name, Robert Granger. He's a coworker at the company. He was devastated by the news of her death."

"I bet."

"He agreed to be interviewed in the morning."

"Good. What about the others?"

"They were casual acquaintances. Nothing romantic. Bob was her main squeeze," he said, still staring at Thompson. Angelo elbowed him in the ribs.

"Hey!"

"Sorry. But she is a pleasure to look at."

"Get on with it," she warned through her teeth.

"Anyway, I ran all her male friends. All have clean records. They all agreed to a DNA sample. All had alibis."

"No use doing that since we don't have a sample to compare it to. But we'll keep that in mind."

"Anything else you want me to do?"

"No. Thanks. I'll let you know. I'll take care of Bob."

"You mean I get to go home on time?"

Angelo looked at her watch. Quitting time was an hour away. "Not unless you want to do something else for me?"

"No, not really. I've got a breakfast date."

"Oh?"

"Yeah. You know Selma from Evidence?"

"Yes."

"Me and her, we got a thing going." He arched his eyebrows suggestively at her.

Not wanting to hear about it, Angelo replied groaning, "Gee, Pat, thanks for putting that image in my head."

"My pleasure."

She grimaced. "Do I tell you about me and Sam?"

"No, but I wish you would." He winked at her.

"Pat, I don't want to know. Go away now."

He smiled and walked away, passing Thompson with a wicked smile. She smiled back at him.

I really wish she wouldn't encourage him, Angelo grumbled to herself.

Thompson walked back over to her desk. Angelo motioned for her to have a seat. Sitting down next to her, Thompson said, "The girlfriends all work in the same office. We can probably catch them there."

"Good. We'll grab a bit of breakfast and then do the interviews when the office opens. Her boyfriend works there too."

"Cool. I'm starved."

"What office do they work in?"

"In a building on the Boulevard. Ms. Sterling was an office manager for an accounting firm."

Thompson yawned. Angelo glanced at the clock on the wall. They had two hours to spare. "You sure you want to go with me? You've been working pretty hard tonight. If you're tired…"

"No, no, you warned me it would be a long tour. I want to go the whole nine yards."

"What about Matt?"

"What about Sam?"

"Sam never expects me home on time."

"Well, Matt will have to get used to it too."

"You really need to talk to him."

"Why?"

"I don't want this to stress your relationship."

"It won't stress it any more than it already is, Bee. Don't worry about me." Thompson smiled. Angelo was ill at ease. She knew just how personal relationships could suffer when the job took over.

"I mean it."

"All right, already. I'll talk to him. Maybe we'll fight and then have make up sex."

Angelo's head shot up. "Excuse me?"

"Make up sex. It's always better than regular sex."

"I wouldn't know. I don't fight with my husband."

"Yeah, okay, and pigs fly."

"You're getting awfully bold."

Thompson wasn't sure if she was serious or teasing her. Angelo could see on her face that she was unsure if she overstepped her bounds.

Angelo laughed. "Okay, yeah, you're right. Make up sex is always better than regular sex."

Relaxing, Thompson returned the smile.

"Come on, let's get some breakfast. I'm starved myself."

Chapter Seven

He was just getting out of the shower, feeling good about himself. Wrapping a towel around his slim waist, he stood in front of a full length mirror and admired himself. "Good God, I'm handsome," he said to his reflection, turning and looking around to study his hairless back. "No wonder the girls love me."

Still wet, he walked into his bedroom and flopped back on the king sized bed, staring at the mirror on the ceiling. Looking at himself, his hands wandered over his chest and down his six-pack abdomen. He could feel himself grow excited. He would have to satisfy his need soon. The time between each date was growing shorter. The last one just a few nights ago.

He walked over to a glass curio cabinet and touched the diamond ring he had taken from Victoria's house, its diamond sparkling under the light. It sat next to the other items he procured so far in his quest. He had a collection of over a dozen or more items, each dated and categorized. Different times and different places. Each one an adventure on its own.

God, she was great, but she made me angry. I hate it when they make me angry. I can't be a gentleman. He didn't mean to get so rough and hoped she was all right. He would have liked to visit Victoria again. *She was one hot piece!*

He licked his lips and sat up, reaching for a remote control. He turned on the television. The early morning news was just starting. As the news anchor reported that there was more snow on the way, he got up, dropped his towel, and padded naked into the kitchen to put on a pot of coffee.

He had to go to work and was a little sleepy from all the prowling he did the night before. He didn't have anyone in particular in mind yet. He was still choosing from the many that he encountered. He would be in the coffee house again today, trawling for dates.

But of course, he had to go to work first. *Oh, how I hate actually having to work in that place! They are out to get me. Especially that bitch—my so called* boss. *Do this and do that! She never leaves me alone. Not a moment of peace. No time for myself. Do you think I'm your personal slave? Just as bad as my mother!*

He hated his mother too.

She made him get that godforsaken job in the first place. *Be good for you. Get you out of my house and into the real world.* He did get out of the house, renting a two room apartment far away from the interfering witch. He liked the Northeast part of the city. It was quiet, almost outside the city limits.

Grabbing a cup of hot, fresh coffee, he went back into his bedroom and sat on the bed. The top of the news hour was about to start. He only watched the first ten or fifteen minutes. That was when they reported all the good stuff. Sports and weather, he could live without, although when bad weather struck it was always the top story. *God knows why, with all the tragedies happening in the world.*

He got up and went over to his closet, selecting a white button down shirt from his many white shirts. That's all he ever wore. It was cleaned and pressed with military creases. He liked to look sharp even though no one appreciated him at work. They'd appreciate him someday! Buttoning his shirt, his attention turned toward the television when he heard a familiar name.

"Victoria Sterling, the latest victim of the Don Juan rapist, died late last night after being unhooked from the life support machines that were keeping her body alive. Her family decided to donate her organs as Victoria's last request to help others in need," the anchor stated.

His jaw dropped in surprise. "No! I didn't do that! She was fine when I left her! Someone else did it! I'm not a rapist, I'm a lover. I loved her! The sex was consensual! She wanted it!" he yelled at the television. "She just couldn't live without me. That's what happened. Her family killed her. She could have pulled through. She wasn't hurt that badly. It was just a game! They jumped the gun!"

In his own twisted logic, he believed what he said was the god's honest truth. He had nothing to do with her death.

The news anchor continued with the report. "The case is now being handled by the Homicide Unit. Both Special Victims and Homicide will be working hand in hand to find this vicious murderer and rapist. It is not confirmed yet, but we understand that Detective B. Angelo is handling the case with the help of a Special Victims officer. You may recall a few weeks ago that Detective Angelo, a decorated fifteen year veteran of the Homicide Unit, stopped the *Convict Killer* after the cold blooded murder of her partner, Detective Dwayne Ronalds. The suspect attacked Detective Angelo and her husband in their West Mt. Airy home, but luckily failed in his attempt when a struggle for the knife ensued. He was killed in the altercation. We wish her all the luck in the world catching this individual."

He turned off the television. "It wasn't my fault! She wanted it rough. It was just a game. It's not my fault that she died. Someone else killed her after I left." He paced the floor. He had to talk to someone. "I wonder if Jennifer Tully has returned to her home yet."

He stopped by her house a few times, but found no one home. He didn't hear anything about her reporting the encounter to the police. Not like the others who cried rape. *Yes, she enjoyed it. She wants me to come back.*

"Yes, that's it. I'll pay Jenny another visit. We'll have hot, passionate sex. She'll scream with pleasure. Then we'll have a little pillow talk. She understands me." *When would she be back?* he wondered. He'd have to find that out. *Yes. Jenny.*

He got dressed and walked out the door, locking up his Northeast apartment. He headed out to the job he despised and the boss he hated. At least it paid the bills. Until Jenny returned, he'd have to scope out more prospects at the coffee house.

The thrill of the hunt!

Yes, it was the thrill of the hunt that kept him going. It was an addiction, worse than any drug in the known world.

Chapter Eight

It was still too early to interview Victoria Sterling's friends at work, so Angelo and Thompson decided to have breakfast at an all-night diner on Frankford Avenue. The Diner was famous, or infamous depending on how one looked at it, located in the Northeast. It was not just known for its food, but for its political outspokenness.

Most of the people who frequented the establishment were locals. All dressed in different attire, from the three-piece business suit to jeans and a hard hat, they all ate and talked to each other as if nothing separated their class.

Angelo, a stranger, was noticed right away when they walked in the front door. She got several unwelcome leers from a couple of teenagers. She snarled back at them, making them return their attention to their breakfast. However, Thompson went there often and received a warm and friendly greeting.

"Good morning, Officer Thompson," the waitress said.

"Hey there, Betty," she replied.

"Your usual spot?"

"Please."

The waitress showed them to a corner booth. Cops usually sat in a corner, with their backs to a wall, facing the front door. Just in case something was to happen. A cop never knew what could happen in an unpredictable world. She thanked Betty after she handed them two menus and filled their coffee cups without asking. Angelo asked for a few minutes to look over the selections. The waitress nodded and walked away.

"I take it you come here often," Angelo said, glancing at the menu.

"Yes. I live not too far away. It's an early morning ritual for me. On my way home, I stop here for breakfast. The most important meal of the day, y'know."

"You sound like my husband."

Thompson grinned. "It's true."

"Where exactly do you live?"
"Fox Chase."
"Nice area."
"Yes it's very quiet."
"A lot of cops live up in the Northeast for that reason. Mostly the Brass though. Most of them live in the Far Northeast."
"Cost money to live up there."
"Yes."
"Where do you live?"
"Mt. Airy. West Side." She explained exactly where.
Thompson knew the area; she lived in Germantown for a while. "Oh my, that's just as expensive. Even more than living up this way. How do you afford it? The taxes alone cost a small fortune."
"Long hours," she joked.
"Really?"
"Yes and it doesn't hurt that my husband is rich," Angelo mumbled.
"I can't tell if you're being serious, or not."
"I'm always serious." She grinned, sipping her coffee.
"What does he do? No, let me guess. Lawyer?"
Angelo shook her head no.
"Architect? Doctor? Letter carrier?"
"None of the above."
"Well, what? I give up."
"He's a romance novelist. And a pretty good one at that."
"Now I know you're joking."
"Nope."
"I read a lot of books. Anything I should know?"
"Maybe. Ever read the *Welsh Bride*? That was his first and probably his best."
Searching her memory for the book, it came to her in a flash. "He wrote that!" she exclaimed, nearly spilling her coffee. "Sam Marshall! You're married to Sam Marshall?"
"Shhh!" she hissed, holding her finger up to her lips.
"Sorry, but I love Sam Marshall," she said in a hushed tone.
"Me too. I don't usually tell people who he is, so keep it under your hat. Okay?"
"Oh, okay, but only if you promise to introduce me."
"See, that's why I don't tell people about him."
"But he's so gorgeous," Thompson continued. "A tall, cool glass of water."
"Yes he is. I'm a very jealous woman."
Thompson laughed, and then realized that Angelo was being serious this time. "Oops."

That made Angelo laugh even harder. She liked Thompson's enthusiasm. "We'll see."

"Cool." Thompson stopped to look at the menu although she pretty much had it memorized. Putting it down, she asked, "Bee, why do you work for a living?"

"Pardon?"

"You certainly don't need the money. Sam Marshall is a best selling author. Why do you do the job?"

"It's what I do. I am the job. Without it, I'd just be a bored housewife."

"Is that what it is? Boredom?"

"Of course not. I love the satisfaction I get when I put someone away. I also get satisfaction out of righting wrongs and freeing the innocent."

"That's very noble."

"Noble? No. It's just who I am."

"I hope to be like you some day."

"Work hard and stay out of trouble."

"I'll try. But it's not easy with the *guys* stealing all the good jobs."

What Thompson said was true, but she had to learn to get over it and work twice as hard as the *guys do*. "Why do you do it?" Angelo asked, chewing a coffee stir. She hadn't noticed it before, but recently she had taken up an oral fixation of chewing things. Pens, pencils, and now coffee stirs. *I should buy a pack of gum or something or I'll have to visit the dentist soon.* She took the stir out of her mouth and put it on the table.

"What?" Thompson asked, not understanding the question.

"What do you think I'm talking about? Police work."

"Oh, I guess I want to right wrongs too. I don't want to be a victim."

Puzzled, Angelo wondered what she meant by that. She wasn't about to pry into Thompson's personal life. It wasn't her place. She decided long ago not to get close to anyone on the job. The waitress sauntered over to them, holding a pot of coffee in her hand. She refilled their cups to the brim.

"What can I get you?" she asked.

"Give me the number three," Thompson replied.

The waitress chuckled. "You always get the number three."

"You're just waiting for me to switch up on you."

"Yes, we have a running bet going."

"Yes, I know."

"How about your friend?"

Angelo really didn't have the chance to look at the menu. "Uh, I guess I'll have what she's having."

"Ah, living dangerously. All right, two number threes," she said and walked away.

"So, Bee, you think we'll find out anything from her friends?" Thompson asked when the waitress was out of earshot.

"I don't know. I hope so. I'd like to get to know her pattern. Usually, stalkers follow that pattern. Usually, they return to it."

"You think the others had the same pattern?"

"I'd bet my paycheck on it that they did. They may not have known each other, but there is something that links all six, I mean, seven victims. I think *Don* sees them somewhere and follows them from there."

"You think he lives up here?"

"They usually stay where they feel comfortable. I'd say within a five to ten mile radius. When we go talk to Officer Seymour at SVU I'd like to see how he's doing?"

"You think he'll share?"

"He'll have no choice. I'm not going to play games with SVU. We don't have the time and I certainly don't have the patience."

Thompson grinned. She knew that would burn Seymour's butt royally. She thought that she shouldn't be so petty, but it felt good. Damn, it felt good.

The waitress brought two plates of food over and placed them in front of the pair. "Enjoy."

Angelo looked at her plate. "Holy mackerel! What is all that?"

"Eggs, bacon, sausage links, scrapple, grits and toast," she answered, pointing to each item on the plate.

"It's a wonder you don't have high cholesterol."

"Bee, you've got to live a little."

"If I ate this everyday, I wouldn't stand a chance."

"Sure you would. Dig in."

"How do you stay so thin?"

"Exercise and a lot of wild sex."

"Okay, that was way too much information, Sue."

"Just eat it. You'll thank me later."

Angelo had a lot on her mind so they ate their high cholesterol breakfast in silence. However, she had to admit that it was damn good food.

***

After breakfast, and what seemed to be a bottomless cup of coffee, Angelo and Thompson headed down Rhawn Street toward the Roosevelt Boulevard. The twelve-lane highway, where the speed limit was 45 MPH, was not for the timid. Crossing on foot took several green lights to accomplish safely. Of course, if pedestrians were daring, they could always try to make it across against the light at the risk of their own lives.

Victoria Sterling worked in an office building off the Boulevard on Stanwood Street. From where they stood, Nazareth Hospital could be seen in the distance. The officers walked into the building and up to the security guard at the front desk.

"Detective Angelo and Officer Thompson, Philadelphia Police," she announced, showing the apathetic looking Hispanic man her badge and ID.

"Yes, ma'am?"

"We're looking for the Hoffman and Cohen offices."

"Fourth floor. Suite 407. You'll have to sign in," he told them, pushing the clipboard toward them.

Angelo signed the visitor's log. She didn't like this guard. He reminded her of someone. *Probably locked him up before*, she mused.

Looking her up and down, he said, "The elevator is to your left. Have a nice day." The tone of his voice had a sarcastic edge to it. Angelo chose to ignore him.

"Thanks. Come on, Thompson."

They walked away from the sour security guard and over to the elevator. "What an asshole," Thompson commented.

"Never mind. He's probably getting minimum wage."

"Still, he should at least be polite."

"Maybe he doesn't like cops."

"I have half a mind to put him on my short list. A suspect."

"I'm sure he has a shady past, but he's got nothing to do with this case."

"He works here. Sees our Vic. Could have stalked her from here. He even has shifty eyes. Notice that he didn't meet your eyes?"

"No, he was looking at something else. Further south."

"See. He could be Don."

"It's a very remote possibility, but…"

"But what?"

"He's too short. Can't be more than five six."

"How do you know? He was sitting down."

"His feet didn't reach the floor on the stool. The stool is about three and a half feet off the ground…"

"All right, I get it. Well, it was worth a shot."

"Can't fault you for thinking."

The elevator doors opened and Angelo pressed the button for the fourth floor. All the way up, their ears were assaulted by sugary music pumped into the tiny space through little speakers. Angelo's dislike of elevators revisited her like a bad memory. *God, how I hate these things,* she thought sourly.

When the doors opened, Thompson noticed that Angelo stuck her head out and looked both ways before exiting the elevator. "Why'd you do that?" she asked, trying to keep up with Angelo's long stride.

"What?"

"You looked out of the elevator before getting off."

"Did I?"

"Yes, you did."

"I don't know. Habit, I guess. One time, when I was a patrol officer doing a building search, I got jumped by a burglar."

"Were you hurt?"

"Not as bad as him," she laughed. "But I learned a valuable lesson. Always look before you leap."

"So noted," Thompson said. She was learning something new about Detective Angelo every day. It felt good that someone was taking an interest in her and her career. She didn't know how she could repay her. No one had ever showed her this sort of kindness before. She had always been on her own.

"Suite 407," Angelo said. She knocked on the door before trying the handle. The door was unlocked. Walking up to the receptionist, Angelo pulled out her badge. "Excuse me. Detective Angelo and Officer Thompson. Homicide."

The young black woman behind the reception counter started to tear up, black mascara running down her cheeks. *What now?* Angelo wondered.

"You're here about Victoria, aren't you?"

"Yes. We need to speak with…" Angelo held out her hand to Thompson, who as if reading her mind, gave her a piece of paper. "Tammi Jonas, Princess Dupree, Stephanie Wadsworth and Robert Granger."

"I'm Princess Dupree," the receptionist said, dabbing her eyes with a tissue. "I'm sorry about this." She waved the black mascara coated tissue at Angelo. "It's still such a shock to think that Victoria is dead."

"Murdered," Thompson added. That made Princess cry even harder. Thompson got a stern look from Angelo.

"Yes. Murdered! That bastard took my best friend! I'm sorry."

"That's okay, let it out," Angelo said soothingly.

Calming herself, she said, "What do you want to know? I'll tell you anything and everything I can. He needs to be put down."

"Can we talk somewhere private? Somewhere we can sit and not be disturbed?"

"Conference room. Hold on; let me get someone to watch the front desk. Go back," she said, pointing to a double door down the hall. "I'll be there in a few minutes. I need to wash my face."

"Great. Thanks."

About ten minutes later, Princess entered the conference room. Her eyes were red rimmed and swollen. "Mr. Hoffman said you can take all the time you need in here."

"Appreciate it."

Princess sat down, folding her tissue clutched hands in front of her. "How can I help you?"

"There was a mention in Victoria's PDA that she was meeting her girlfriends. Going cruising for guys was the phrase she used. Did you do that often with her?"

Sniffling, Princess replied, "Yes. She's hooked on Bob. We did the cruising, not her. She was as straight as they come. We kind of made it a girls' night out."

"Did you go to bars?"

"Sometimes. But our favorite hang out was the Koffee Klutch around the corner on Solly Avenue."

Ah, the mysterious coffee house. Finally, a name to go with the place, Angelo mused.

"We'd all hang out there for lunch. You know, because we can't drink during our lunch hour. God, I could use one right about now."

Thompson smirked. So could she.

"We went there every day. Noon to one. Like clockwork, we hung out and drank overpriced coffee and ogled the guys."

"Any of them ogle back?"

"Lots of them."

"Anyone make you nervous? Uncomfortable?"

"No, not really. They are all regulars. One creepy guy always hit on us, but we shot him down every time. Oh, my God! That isn't who killed her, is it?"

"I couldn't say. What does he look like?" Angelo asked, her hopes up.

"Short, fat, ugly white guy. He's got to be at least fifty."

Angelo's hopes were dashed away just as quickly as they came.

"Could it be him? I always thought he was a pervert."

"No, I don't think so. Our suspect is young and muscular. Anyone who fits that description that caught your eye?"

"Not really. Like I said, we just looked. No one touched. Oh, one of the managers at the Koffee Klutch always hit on her, but she turned him down flat every time. He's quite harmless. More into himself than anyone else."

"How do you mean?"

"He's gorgeous on the outside, but very shallow. Surface only. You know the kind of guy I mean."

"Yes. Do you know his name?"

"Sorry, I don't remember, but he shouldn't be too hard to find. He's there every day for the most part."

"Could you give me a list of all the places you and your friends visited with Victoria?"

"Sure." She rattled off over a dozen or so business locations. By the time she was finished, Thompson had a cramp in her hand. Flexing her fingers and cracking several knuckles loudly, Thompson put the pen down. "You mentioned a bar earlier. Now that I think about it, we were at a bar on Frankford Avenue the night she—was attacked. We were all pretty wasted, except for her. She never drank. Well, not when she was the designated driver. She was driving that night. All she had was club soda and coffee. She drove us all home and then went back to her place. I guess that was when she was attacked." She started to tear up again.

Angelo didn't want her distracted. "What time were you at the bar?"

"Between happy hour, um, six to ten. We go there often," she sniffled.

"Any unsavory characters there?"

"All the time."

"What's the place called?"

"Maddie's. It's not too far from her home."

"We appreciate your cooperation, Ms. Dupree. If you think of anything else, please don't hesitate to call the unit." She handed Princess a business card.

"Catch him. Make him pay."

"I will try my best. If you wouldn't mind, could you send in the others one at a time?"

"Certainly." She held out a well-sculptured hand to Angelo. Smiling, Angelo took it. Princess left the room in a torrent of tears.

"Boy, Detective, you sure know how to make them cry."

Angelo didn't answer and Thompson assumed she put her foot in her mouth again. *Stupid, stupid, stupid!* she cursed, mentally banging her fist against her head. Scrunching down in her seat, Thompson picked up her pen and twirled it in her fingers.

"Our Vic is a popular girl. I wonder if she was faithful to Bob."

"We'll have to ask him when it's his turn at bat."

The next girlfriend to walk in the door was Stephanie Wadsworth. She was tall, pretty and definitely a natural blonde. After talking to her for about twenty minutes, Angelo figured that the only thing in between her ears was air. She pretty much gave them the same information as Princess. Angelo sent her on her way with the mission to get the next woman. She hoped she would be able to accomplish that simple task.

Thankfully, she did and Tammi Jonas entered the room. Like Princess, her eyes were red and puffy from crying. She couldn't offer anything new. No one noticed anyone giving them unwanted attention at the coffee house or the bar. After all, they were seeking attention.

Angelo thanked Tammi for her time and asked her to send in Robert Granger. She was saving the best for last.

Robert Granger was a handsome man. About ten years Victoria's senior, he carried himself with dignity and grace. He had sharp eyes, but there was sadness in them. He was heartbroken. Angelo could only imagine what he was feeling.

"Good morning, Detective," he said, extending his masculine hand. After releasing Angelo from his grasp, he sat down in front of her. He looked her dead in the eye. This man knew how to talk to people. Straightforward and up front, Robert Granger appeared to be an honest man.

"Good morning, Mr. Granger."

"You can call me Bob. Everyone calls me Bob."

"Okay, Bob."

"Any idea who did this to my Victoria?" he asked.

"Your Victoria?"

"We were engaged to be married." Tears formed in his eyes. He tried hard not to let them fall, blinking a few times, but his eyes never wavered from Angelo's.

"I'm sorry for your loss, Mr. Granger—Bob."

Sniffling and blinking back tears, he put his head down on the table and wept. Angelo placed her hand on his arm in an attempt to comfort him.

"I'm sorry to have to put you through this, but I'm sure you want him caught as much as I do. See him punished."

Lifting his head, he snapped, his eyes hot with understandable fury, "I want him dead!"

Thompson nearly jumped out of her chair at the outburst. Angelo looked at her, telling her to sit still. "I understand your anger, Bob."

Calming himself, he said softly, "I'm sorry. I'm trying to be strong, but I think the fact that I'll never see her again just hit me. She's dead."

Angelo could say nothing that would comfort him in his time of grief. Nothing could ease his pain. "Bob, could you tell me if Victoria felt threatened in any way."

"Threatened? No. I don't think so. She would have told me or at least one of her closest friends. She tells—told me everything."

"You know that she went out with her friends a lot, to bars and such. This guy could have seen her at one of these places and stalked her. Maybe he caught her in a moment of weakness. Did she drink?"

"No. She was always the designated driver. She was like that. Victoria took care of her friends." It was the same story her girlfriends told. She was the model friend. She never drank and was usually the designated driver. Was she too good to be true?

"All the time? Not once did she get a little drunk? Maybe she encouraged this guy in some way."

"No. She was faithful to me!" he snapped.

"I didn't mean to suggest that she wasn't. In fact, I'm sure she was. You were very lucky to have her. I just need to know if anyone hit on her or made unwanted advances."

"I really don't think so. She would have told me. If they did, I'm sure she'd have blown them off. She was very good at handling herself. That's why it took me so long to woo her. The others would have told me if something was bothering Victoria. They cared about each other like that. They would have told me," he repeated. "We were soul mates. Unless you have one, you have no idea what it's like to lose half of your soul, Detective."

Soul mates. Yes. I understand all too well, she mused.

"I swear to you, Detective. If I find him, God help him! I'll kill him."

Calmly, Angelo said, placing a hand on his forearm, "You will do no such thing. You're upset. Not making rational decisions."

He looked at his hands. "I'm sorry. You're right. I apologize for my outburst."

"No, that's all right. If there is anything I can do for you, don't hesitate to call. Also, call if you get any information that might help us catch him."

"Thanks, Detective…"

"Angelo."

"Angelo." He thought about it for a beat. "*The* Detective Angelo?"

"Um, I'm not sure how many Angelos are in the department."

"Yes. You're the one. The one who caught the Convict Killer last month. It was all over the news."

"Yes, I guess that was me."

He smiled. He could appreciate modest people. "Then I'll put it in your capable hands. I'm positive you will get my Victoria her justice."

"I will, Mr. Granger. I have just one more question to ask you."

"I hope I can answer it for you."

"Was anything missing from Victoria's home that you know of?"

He thought about it for a moment. "Now that you mention it, her engagement ring is missing, I assumed it was lost or stolen when her body was transported to the hospital."

"Did you ask about it?"

"Yes. I asked the police, the fire department and the hospital staff. I even asked the people at the morgue. They all denied seeing it. If it was stolen by one of them, I doubt anyone would own up to taking it. It was worth a small fortune."

"What kind of ring?"

"Two karat teardrop diamond in a platinum setting. It had smaller diamonds around it. It was very, very pretty… just like my Victoria."

Man, that just sucks, Thompson thought.

"I'll look into it for you," Angelo said, writing the description in her notebook.

"Would you? That's very kind of you."

"No problem."

He stood. "Will that be all? I have funeral arrangements to make."

"Yes, sir," she said, standing. "We'll let you know if anything develops."

He nodded and walked out of the room.

"Wow," Thompson commented. "He was intense."

"Yes. Poor man."

"Do you think Don took the ring for a trophy?"

"Perhaps. I wouldn't put it past him." Angelo looked at the clock on the wall. It was twelve thirty. Turning to Thompson, who was putting the yellow legal pad in her briefcase, she said, "How about a cup of coffee?"

"I don't think I could drink another...Oh, the Koffee Klutch!" she replied, getting the hint. "You think he might be there?"

Putting on a dark pair of sunglasses, Angelo said, "Possibly. If he holds true to his pattern. What I really want to do is check out the place, see who's checking out whom, and maybe talk to a few patrons. However, I don't want to give anything away. Wouldn't want to tip him off or anything."

"You got it."

Chapter Nine

The Koffee Klutch on Solly Avenue was packed like sardines with the lunchtime crowd. The two floor building was conveniently located in between office buildings and Angelo guessed that was where the business got most of its patrons. On the outside it looked like a hole in the wall, but the inside was quite roomy.

Angelo opened the door for Thompson and gestured her inside ahead of her. Just as she entered, a young man bumped into Thompson almost knocking her down. He wore a black jacket, white shirt and black tie. He grabbed her arm above the elbow, keeping her from falling.

"Oh, I'm sorry, miss," the man said, helping her keep her balance. He bowed to her in a chivalrous gesture.

"No harm done," she replied, adjusting her clothes.

He smiled and walked away. Thompson didn't even give him a second thought, but Angelo watched as the tall blond man walked down the street and into one of the office buildings a few meters away.

"Coming in?" Thompson asked, breaking into Angelo's thoughts.

"Huh? Oh, yeah," she said, following her partner inside the packed café.

"Didn't know you were the type to check out the younger guys," Thompson teased.

"What? No, I was just making sure he didn't just steal your wallet when he bumped into you."

Automatically, Thompson checked her back pocket for her wallet. To her relief, she still had it on her. "Still there."

Angelo smiled. "I'm just suspicious by nature."

The place was packed with young professionals. Most wore the same as the man who just left. White shirts with a tie, dark slacks, and skirts just above the knee. Angelo didn't spot one casual outfit among the crowd. *Classy place,* she noticed. *Not a dreg in sight.*

They made their way through the tightly press crowd and up to the ordering counter. Behind the counter was a young man in his late teens. He seemed harried. Angelo leaned in close to him, showing her badge in the palm of her hand. She didn't wish to let anyone know she was a cop. The less they knew the better.

"I need to speak with the manager," she said softly, her voice hushed.

"Oh!" he squeaked. "Hold on a sec. I'll go get her." He left his station, much to the chagrin of the other customers who groaned in line behind Angelo, and fetched the manager. She turned to smile at the growing hostile crowd behind her.

A woman in her late forties, with salt and pepper hair piled high on her head, came rushing out of a rear office. She had a worried look on her face. Angelo assumed that the manager thought that when the cops came to your business, there was going to be trouble.

"Can I help you?" she asked.

Again, Angelo showed her badge. "Is there somewhere we can talk in private?"

Seeing that Angelo didn't want to get the customers upset in anyway, the manager said, "Sure. Come back to the office. We can talk there."

Angelo and Thompson followed the woman to the back office. She offered them seats and then sat behind her desk. "Thank you for your time," Angelo said.

"Is there a problem, Detective?"

"Angelo. This is Officer Thompson."

"Hi," Thompson said.

"Your name, Ms..?" Angelo asked, whipping out her trusty notebook.

"Mrs. Kettering. Mrs. Ann Kettering. I'm the owner."

Slowing down only for a second to jot down the name, Angelo explained her visit. "Mrs. Kettering, we're from Homicide. We'd like to ask you a few questions about your customers."

"Homicide? Someone was killed?"

"Yes, ma'am."

"Who?" she asked, but then it dawned on her. "Victoria!"

"Yes, ma'am. We'd like to talk to you about Victoria Sterling."

"Oh, my God! I was hoping it wasn't the same Victoria who came in here every day for lunch with her co-workers. She was such a pleasant young lady."

"Yes, ma'am."

"Why do you want to ask me questions about her? She came in here all the time, but I didn't know her socially."

"I understand that, Mrs. Kettering, but we're following up on a few leads. She was in here a lot, right?"

"Every day. Twelve to one. She only works around the corner."

"Do you know if she was having any problems with harassment? Any of the customers giving her a hard time?"

"Oh, no, never. Everyone here is quite professional. Nothing like that happens here. And if it did, they'd be barred."

"Do you know all the regulars?"

"Yes. Most of them, anyway. I make it my business to know my clientele."

"Good policy. Anyone in here lately that you don't know?"

"A few strangers now and then, but they usually just come in, buy a cup of coffee and leave. They don't hang around like the regulars."

"Anyone fit this description? Tall, white male who is possibly in his twenties or early thirties? Very muscular. Clean shaven. Neat and orderly? Possibly smokes a pipe?"

"Honey, most of the fellas in here fit that description. In addition, this is a smoke-free business. No smoking allowed. Pipe or otherwise."

She was right. Angelo noticed that immediately when she entered the café. Establishments that allowed smokers were few and far between nowadays.

"Any of them a bit odd?"

"Odd? How do you mean?"

"Quiet? Broody? Antisocial? Doesn't like to sit with the others?"

"We have a few of them. But they are just eccentric."

Yeah, I'll bet, she thought.

"You have any names?"

"Well, I don't like to talk about my customers behind their backs…"

"Mrs. Kettering, one of them may be a murderer."

She sighed out of frustration. She was torn between her clientele's privacy and the desire to do the right thing. She wanted to help the police, but at what price? She decided to talk. "One guy named Josh Brady is kind of weird in a spooky way. He comes in every day, gets his coffee, and sits in his favorite corner. Everyone leaves him alone. They know that is his spot and they don't sit there."

"He fit the description?"

"A little bit. But I think he may be in his thirties."

Angelo wrote his name on her note pad. "Do you know where he works?"

"I'm not sure, but it's probably local. Most of the customers are from the area businesses."

"Anyone else come to mind?"

"A young man named Stephen Greystock. He comes in every day between twelve and twelve-thirty. He likes to watch the girls, but never talks to them. My assistant says he's a closet homo 'cause he never approaches them. But then again, Kevin, my assistant manager, doesn't like him."

"Why not?"

"My personal opinion? Kevin doesn't like male competition."

"Excuse me?"

"Stephen is quite handsome."

"I see."

"The girls like him, but he doesn't reciprocate. He doesn't say much, but is very polite."

"Is he in here today?"

"Stephen?" She stood up and looked around the café through the office door for a few seconds. "I don't see him. You must have just missed him. He usually leaves just before twelve-thirty. Guess he only gets a half hour break for lunch."

"What does he do?"

"I think he's a clerk or something menial."

Again, Angelo wrote down a name. "Would you mind if we went out and looked around the café. See if there is anyone else you can point out that fits the description?"

"I guess so, it's a free country, but I don't want to bother the customers."

"I won't talk to anyone. I just want to look."

"All right, follow me."

They went out into the sitting area and Angelo scanned the crowd, looking at every young male in the place. Most of them were conducting business or flirting with co-workers. Every now and then a woman would giggle at a remark one of them made. Most of the men wore suits and jackets. One guy had on an outrageous tie with a fish eating another fish, eating yet another fish. The cycle continued.

"That's Josh over there," she said, nodding in the direction of a lone male in the corner booth.

The man, in his late twenties or early thirties, sat quietly in the corner booth with his hands cupped around his coffee mug. He was leaning forward, his nose only inches from the hot beverage, inhaling the aromas. He seemed to be deep in thought, his eyes focused ahead of him on an invisible spot on the table.

He did fit the general description. Angelo decided to run his name later to see if he had ever been arrested or had any prior trouble with women. He glanced up from his cup and looked Angelo dead in the eye. Just as quickly, he turned away, got up, and walked out of the café, leaving his coffee unfinished.

"That was weird," Thompson said in Angelo's ear. "Should we go after him?"

"No. Let him go. I don't want to spook anyone."

There were a few other men that also fit the description, but they seemed to be with others. They weren't the loner type. Angelo was almost positive he'd be a bit of a loner.

"Mrs. Kettering, do you have a clientele mailing list?"

"Yes, but that's private information."

Angelo could have threatened to get a warrant, but she didn't want to go through the hassle and come off as heavy handed. She'd try a different approach first.

"Mrs. Kettering, I understand that you'd want to keep your client list private, but no one needs to know we have it."

"Still..." she said hesitantly.

"You wouldn't want Victoria's murderer to get away with it, would you?"

"Well, no, but..."

"I'm sure the other women in this establishment wouldn't want to find out that one of the men in here could be a *serial rapist* and *murderer*." Angelo accented her words on purpose. She wanted to play on Mrs. Kettering's sensitivities.

Angelo could see in her face that she struck a nerve. "Oh, all right. I'll get the list off the computer."

"We appreciate that. In the meantime, could you ask, uh, Kevin, to come out to talk to us for a few minutes?"

"Sure. I'll send him out."

Mrs. Kettering left to fetch her assistant. Thompson turned to Angelo and said, "Damn, you're good. That was smooth, Bee. Really smooth."

"Just a little psychology."

"I could have sworn we were going to have to get a warrant."

"That could have been the next step, but I always try to use the honey instead of vinegar approach."

"The what?"

"You get more flies with honey than with vinegar. Hasn't anyone ever said that to you?"

"I guess. Usually in my house it was just vinegar."

"Sorry to hear that."

"Well, your approach seems to work. I'll have to try it some time."

The assistant manager came out of the back office. He did not look happy about talking to a couple of cops. Angelo could tell that the smile on his face was forced. Thompson, on the other hand, didn't notice. She saw a tall, dark and, yes, damn handsome man.

"Whoa!" Thompson mumbled under her breath at the sight of him.

"Roll that tongue of yours back in your head, Officer," Angelo said without even looking at her partner.

"Good afternoon, Detective. I'm Kevin the assistant manager. Mrs. K said you needed to talk to me." He held out his hand. Angelo took it and was surprised by the flimsy handshake.

"Kevin..."

"Oh, sorry. McPherson. Kevin McPherson."

"We'd like to ask you a few questions, if you wouldn't mind."

"Am I in some sort of trouble?"

"Should you be worried?" Angelo asked.

"I don't think so."

"Then no, you're not." Angelo grinned, but he did not return the smile. *There was something odd about the man*, she mused. He wouldn't look her in the eye. In fact, he was actually staring at her chest. She cleared her throat to get his attention.

"Oh, sorry. What do you need to ask me? I'll try to be as helpful as possible."

"Do you know Josh?"

"Crazy Josh?" he spat. "Yeah, I know the lowlife."

Takes one to know one, she thought. "Tell me about him."

"Nothing much to tell. He comes in here, buys his coffee and lunch and stares at people," he told her and then proceeded to examine his well-manicured fingernails.

"Has he ever given you any problems? Or any of the customers?"

"Well, no, not really. There was this one time..."

"Yes?" she prompted.

"His mother came in here one day ranting like a lunatic. She created quite a scene."

"His mother?"

"Yes."

"What happened?"

"She came in here screaming about some girl. When I tried to calm her down, Josh attacked me. He only left with her after I threatened to call the fuzz. Sorry, the police. I didn't see him for a week. I thought we saw the last of him, but unfortunately he returned."

"And his mother?"

"Nope. Didn't see her ever again."

"When was this?"

"A few months back. Folks are scared of him. I don't know why Mrs. K lets him in here. If I had any say in the matter, crazy Josh wouldn't be allowed to step foot in the place."

"What about a customer named Stephen Greystock?"

"Um, don't know much about him. Never gave me any trouble. Comes in stays a half hour and leaves. He's a bit stuck up," he said, glancing at himself in a mirror and checking his teeth.

You would know, Angelo thought. Talk about narcissistic. Just for the hell

Angel of Justice

of it, she asked, "Do you know Victoria Sterling?"

His head shot up from his self-inspection. Angelo thought he could have gotten whiplash from the sudden movement of his head. "Victoria Sterling? Uh, no, the name doesn't ring a bell."

Just by gauging his reaction at the name, Angelo knew he was lying through his pretty, white teeth. "Thank you for your time."

"Anytime." Kevin took the opportunity to look at Angelo's chest one last time before turning and going back into the office.

Mrs. Kettering returned and handed Angelo a floppy disk. "Everything you need is on that disk, Detective. I hope it helps."

"Your cooperation is much appreciated, Mrs. Kettering. I would appreciate it if you didn't discuss this little visit to any of your employees or customers."

"I won't. Just catch the SOB. Get him off the street and make us all safe."

"Here is my card. If you think of anything else, please call me."

"I will. Thanks."

Angelo nodded and Mrs. Kettering walked away.

"What was up with him?" Thompson asked, jerking her chin toward the assistant manager's office.

"You let me worry about that."

"Okay. So, now what? Are we going to go back to the unit and look at the disk?"

"No. *We* are going to go home and climb into bed. I don't know about you, but I'm exhausted."

Thompson hadn't realized how long they had been working. The time just flew by. "Oh."

"Don't worry, Sue, we'll get to it tonight. We'll do it all again tomorrow."

"Right. Looking forward to it."

"I bet you are. Of course, when I was your age, I had the energy too," she laughed. "But I'm an old lady now."

"Bah!"

"Is your car at the unit?" Angelo queried.

"Actually, no, it's in the shop. I got a ride in last night. Hopefully the mechanic is finished with it."

"Okay, I'll give you a ride home. If you need a ride tonight, give me a call."

"Okay. Thanks, Bee. I owe you big time."

"What for? A ride?"

"No, for giving me this chance to make something out of my career."

"Think nothing of it."

"Really, I owe you."

"No, you don't. Quit groveling. Come on, let's go. If I smell any more coffee I'll never get any sleep."

Thompson grinned and followed her mentor out of the crowded café.

***

After Angelo dropped Thompson off at her home in Fox Chase, she drove back to the unit and returned the police vehicle to its rightful spot in the yard. It was about two in the afternoon before she got home. Sam was in the kitchen preparing dinner as usual.

He looked at his watch in an exaggerated manner when she entered the kitchen. She kissed him on the forehead. "Sorry" was all she said.

"For what?"

"Being late again."

"You're always late. I don't really notice anymore."

"I'm sure you do notice, but it's sweet that you don't say anything about it."

"True. I am sweet."

"Where's Jenny?"

"She went home."

Angelo knew she would be going home eventually, but she wished Jenny had stayed longer. Maybe it was for the best. She needed to go on with her life. Going home to the place of the trauma was a start.

"Oh."

"I couldn't stop her," he said.

"I didn't expect you to. Her mind was made up. You know how she can be when she sets her mind to something."

"Yes. Just like you."

"I think I pushed her too hard. I'll have to give her a call later. See how she's doing."

"Maybe you should just give her some space."

"I know. And I'm trying. But damn it, she's hurting. I don't like to see my friends in pain. I don't want him to get away with it."

"You can't save the world, Bee."

"No, but I can try."

He smiled, wrapping his arms around her waist. "I love you."

"I love you too, Sam."

"Go and get some sleep. Dinner won't be ready for hours yet."

"What are you making?" she asked, reaching for the pot's lid.

He gently slapped her hand away from the pot. "No. It's a surprise."

She pulled back her hand. "Oh, God, you know how I love your surprises."

"I know," he said suggestively.

"I'm bushed. Wake me for my surprise dinner."

"Oh, I will. You're going to eat something all right. You're getting too thin."

"I'm not."

"Yes, you are. Don't argue. You need to relax and get your strength back. I'll bet you're running on empty right now."

"Coffee and a high fat breakfast actually."

"I still think it was too soon to go back to work..."

"Sam, I'm not going to argue about it now."

"I'm not arguing. I'm just concerned, that's all."

"I know and I'll always love you for that."

"Go to bed."

She kissed him again, this time on the lips. She could taste fresh peppermint on his mouth. She just adored his mouth and everything else about him. She was more tired than she thought, having trouble climbing the stairs.

She entered the bedroom, drew the curtains closed, and flopped down on the bed, face first. She was asleep in seconds, dreaming. Angelo rarely dreamed, but her exhausted and troubled mind awoke with a vengeance.

She was in a dark place, both figuratively and literally. Confused and alone, she called out for Sam, but only heard her own distressed voice echoing back at her. Holding out her arms and only feeling the darkness that surrounded her, she tried to find some way out. A light. Any light at all would have helped quell the fear in the pit of her stomach. She was not accustomed to fear. She didn't like the helpless feeling it gave her.

Moving slowly forward in the dark as black as pitch, she stumbled into something in the middle of the room, hurting her knees. Feeling around like a blind person, she felt for what was in front of her.

She could feel a cool, satiny cloth on top of what she assumed was a mattress. A bed? Yes, it was a bed. She picked up a small pillow and held it up to her nose. It had an unfamiliar scent. Pipe tobacco. She tossed the pillow down on the bed, like it was hot and burning her hands. She turned away. She had to get away from the bed.

Suddenly an unseen force pushed her back onto the mattress and held her down. Pinned, she couldn't move her arms or legs. Her voice cracked in her throat.

"Who? What?"

A hollow laugh responded to her questions. She tried to scream, but screaming was something she couldn't do. She didn't know how to scream. It was as if her voice had left her. She was a fighter, but there was no way to fight this unseen force that continued to hold her down.

The entity continued to laugh at her. Distressed, she squirmed, under the weight on her chest, calling out for help. She was blind and immobile. What was going on? Sweat broke out on her forehead as something touched her face.

She couldn't see the invisible hand that caressed her face and throat, but

she knew it was an unfamiliar hand of a man. A man that was not her husband.

"Get off me!" she cried out. "Get the hell off!"

The entity laughed as it unbuttoned the top of her blouse and ran its fingers along the scar above her breast. The touch was scorching and she felt it burning her flesh as it traced the scar. The smell of seared flesh assailed her nostrils.

"No!" she screamed. This time it was a scream of terror. "No! Get away! Don't touch me!"

The hands went to her shoulders and shook her.

"Bernadette," a disembodied voice said softly.

"Get off me!" she shouted again, tears running down her face. "Get away from me!"

"Bernadette, wake up." The hands that held her shoulders went to her face and stroked her tear stained cheeks. "Bernadette, honey, wake up. You're dreaming."

Suddenly the pressure was off her body and her eyes snapped open. There was light. Glorious light! Confused and shaken, she turned her head to look at her husband. Concern was etched into his beautiful face. The memory was fading fast.

"Bee, are you all right? I heard you screaming all the way in the kitchen."

"Huh? Heard me?"

"Yes. You were screaming in your sleep."

"I don't scream."

"Christ, if that wasn't screaming, I don't know what is. Bee, you scared the hell out of me."

"I'm sorry, Sam. I must have had a bad dream."

"That must have been one hell of a nightmare."

Sitting up, she wiped the sweat and tears from her face. She was mortified. "It was nothing."

"Want to tell me about it?"

"No," she said frankly.

"It might help you feel better. It'll make me feel better."

"I don't remember any of it." That was only a half truth. She remembered feeling helpless and vulnerable.

"Get off."

"What?"

"That's what you were yelling."

"Sam, I don't remember, okay. Let it be!" she snapped. Swinging her legs over the side of the bed, a wave of dizziness struck her. "Whoa!" She grabbed Sam's arm to steady herself.

"Are you okay?"

"Just got up too fast. It'll pass," she replied, still holding on to his perfect biceps. "What time is it?"

"Seven thirty."

"I slept that long? It only seemed like minutes."

"Yes. You were sleeping so soundly, I didn't have the heart to wake you. I think you need all the sleep you can get. I'm sure you'll be working all day tomorrow too."

"Sorry, Sam, but you know how it goes."

"Yes. I know." He kissed her on the nose. "Come on. Wash your face and come down to dinner."

She smiled. Sam always took care of her, no matter what. "Okay, I'll be down in a few minutes."

"Don't make me come up to get you."

"I won't. What did you cook anyway?"

"My slow cooked pot roast special."

"Yummy. I'll be down shortly."

He left the room.

She sat on the bed a little while longer. Her legs were still feeling wobbly. She looked down and noticed that the top of her shirt was open. She could see the scar above her left breast. Covering herself and still dizzy, she walked into the bathroom and threw up.

Chapter Ten

Sam's pot roast special hit the spot, making her feel a little better. There was nothing like a home cooked meal to settle an anxious stomach. Still unnerved by the dream she couldn't quite remember, Angelo finished washing the dishes as Sam put the leftovers in the refrigerator. He didn't mention her terrifying screams that still echoed in his head. Not yet anyway, but he was worried.

She hadn't suffered from nightmares since his accident and he didn't want to bring up all the traumas of the last month. He was sure they were haunting her subconscious. He knew that she was still troubled by the near death experience, although she never brought it up. He knew he would have to bring it up eventually.

He was certain that she talked to a psychiatrist only because she was ordered to do so, but she would never admit that. He sometimes wished she wasn't so tough. She needed to let down her guard and stop being so hard-headed. She didn't want to talk about it and now with her friend being victimized, he was sure it was taking its toll on her mental health.

"How's it working out with the new girl?" he asked, closing the refrigerator door.

"Fine. Sue has a good head on her shoulders."

"I was afraid you wouldn't want to work with anyone again."

He was talking about Dwayne Ronalds. He could see in her eyes that he hit a nerve.

"I had no choice in the matter. I needed a liaison with Special Victims and she seemed a good choice," she replied, sitting down at the kitchen table. "Besides, I work with O'Malley every day. It's not like I don't play well with others."

"I think it's more than that."

"It's not." She was lying to him and to herself. She didn't like to lie to

Sam. Besides her mother, Sam was the only other person she couldn't deceive. He always knew when she wasn't being straight with him. She hoped he wasn't going to push her. She could see it in his face that he was.

"Want to tell me about that dream?"

"No, not really," she said flatly.

"You know you can always talk to me about anything. I'll understand."

"I know that, sweetheart, and I love you for it. But I don't remember it."

"Tell me what you do remember."

"Sam, it was nothing," she insisted.

"Bernadette, I know something is bothering you. It's not just the dream, is it?"

"You're right. Something is bothering me. You are."

"Don't put that on me," he said mildly.

"Sorry."

"Is it Jenny?"

She paused a second or two, thinking. "Yes. I don't want that man to get away with it."

"That's not all, is it?"

"No. She needs professional help."

"Excuse me for saying this, but that's the pot calling the kettle black."

"I will not excuse you for that, Sam!" she snapped.

He ignored her tone of voice. "Last month was tough on you."

"Yeah, so?"

"I know you're still hurting."

"My hand is fine."

"You know damn well I'm not talking about your hand, Bee."

"Sam, leave it alone, would you please."

"I won't leave it alone and you know it."

She did. Like her, once he wanted to get her to open up to him, he was relentless.

"You were almost killed last month. Not once, but twice. We both could have died."

She looked down at her folded hands in front of her. "Yes, but we survived."

"You need to talk about Dwayne."

"No!"

"You couldn't save him. So now you're trying to save the others."

"So? That's my job."

"You need to save yourself first."

She sighed. "I'm fine. I don't need saving. I can take care of myself."

"Bernadette, just talk to me. Please?"

"Sam, not now. I have to go to work."

"Work! Forget about your blasted job for a minute and think about yourself for a change. Think about me."

"Sam, this conversation is only going to piss me off. I don't want to be angry with you. I hate to go to work angry."

"Too damn bad! We're going to talk about this. You can't wish it all away."

Trying hard to keep her anger in check, she said, "No, but I can certainly try. Look, we'll talk about it later."

He knew he wouldn't get anywhere with her when she was angry. She had a bad temper and when it flared, talking to her was impossible. "Do you promise?"

"Yes, of course. After I get this case sorted out."

"To a professional?"

"Sam," she said warningly. "No head shrinks."

"I mean it. Stop being so damn stubborn. There is no shame in getting professional help."

"Goddamnit, Sam, I don't need anybody getting inside my head. Maybe it's you who needs the help."

"Maybe I do."

She felt bad for yelling at him. "I'm sorry, I shouldn't have yelled. I'm a little on edge at the moment."

"No shit. I think this whole household is on edge."

"Everything will be all right. You'll see."

"Bee, I'm just worried about you. If you're not on top of your game, I'm afraid you're going to get yourself hurt."

"I've never been more careful."

"I'm afraid we're going to drift apart. I couldn't live if that happened."

"You're not going to go all insecure on me again, are you?"

"It's hard not too."

"I won't let that happen. I love you too much."

"Then talk to me."

Exasperated, she said, "You just don't give up, do you?"

"No I don't."

"I have to do it in my own time."

"Why don't you just tell me about the dream? I saw how upset it made you. I saw how it made you ill. That's all I ask."

"It was just a dream. That's all it was. It was just a bad dream. Dreams can't hurt you."

"No, but it's killing me. I'm suffering inside." He clutched his hand to his chest dramatically.

"Fine. I hate it when you do that."

"What?"

"The dramatics."

"You'll tell me then?"
"If it'll get you off my back."
"It's a start."
"I told you I don't remember it, but I got the feeling of vulnerability and helplessness. There? Happy? Now you know. I was powerless in the dream and you know how I hate being a victim."
"Is that what you were? A helpless victim?"
"Yes," she said, worrying her wedding ring.
Sam took her hands in his, stroking her ring finger. "Bee, you are a strong and resourceful woman. No one will hurt you. Or at least you won't give them the opportunity."
"Damn right."
"You know what I think?"
"What's that, Dr. Freud?"
"I think you're uncomfortable with being vulnerable."
"Damn right, I am. No one has ever taken advantage of me physically and I'll be damned if they'd do it to me mentally. This bastard, the one who hurt Jenny and the others, won't make me feel powerless. He won't *mind rape* me!" she stated angrily, pulling her hands free from Sam.
He touched her face affectionately. "Is that what you feel he's doing?"
She paused a moment before speaking. "Yes."
"I see. Don't you feel better now that you've told me?"
She smiled. "I do a bit."
"You don't have to fear looking weak in front of me or anyone else for that matter. Look at me. I'm a cripple and I don't mind."
Her voice softened. "You're not a cripple."
"I have a lot of therapy to go through yet, but it no longer bothers me. I was ashamed to let people see me in this state. I thought people would look at me differently. I was afraid they wouldn't see me as a man, but as a man in a wheelchair. Oh, poor Sam Marshall. Look at him. He can't stand up. He can't even make love to his wife. He can't take care of himself."
"Don't be silly," she said.
"I'm not being silly. You know damn well it's true. You know how I was acting before. But I talked to someone about it and it made me feel a lot better for it."
"I know you're right, but it's hard for me. Give me time."
"You should give the same to Jenny."
"What's that?"
"Time."
"You've got nerve telling me that after the speech you just gave me about talking to people about your problems."
"Ah, but this is a little different. I'm your husband. We have more than just

a casual acquaintance. And our problem doesn't stem from a sexual assault. You ought to know that rape is extremely traumatizing to the mind. Worse than any other assault I think."

"What if it was me who was raped? Would you be saying that? Would you be pushing me like you are now?"

"I couldn't say. Thank God it isn't you. I believe I would give you the time you need to get over it."

"Sam, you never get over it," she told him, shaking her head.

"I'm sure, but hounding Jenny because you want to put this guy away is not the way to go."

"Okay, fine. I have the other witnesses to *hound* for now anyway. I'll let Jenny work it out with or without my help."

"That's my girl," he said and kissed her gently on the lips.

"Speaking of Jenny, I should give her a call."

He gave her a look.

"Just to see how she's doing. I will not say one word about the assault."

Sam smiled. At least something got through that thick skull of hers. "You do that."

Angelo got up from the table and went over to the telephone, dialing Jenny's number. It rang five or six times before being picked up by her answering machine.

"This is Jenny. I'm unavailable at this time. Leave a message at the tone and I'll get back to you as soon as possible."

"Her answering machine," Angelo said to Sam.

Beep!

"Jen, It's Bee. I'm just calling to see how you're doing. I'm about to go to work. Give me a call…"

"Hello?" Jenny answered, picking up the phone. "Sorry, Bee, I was in the shower."

Angelo could just imagine next month's water bill. "Hi, Jen, how are you feeling?"

"Fine. Getting on with life. What else can I do?"

"Good."

"I'm going back to work tomorrow."

"Are you sure?"

"Yes. I think I'm ready."

"Okay, but if you need anything you just call."

"You've done plenty for me. I appreciate it."

"Hey, any time. You have my home number as well as work. Call anytime."

"Thanks. You're a good friend."

"Yeah, that's me. I'll stop by in a few days."

"Okay. Thanks."
"Goodnight, Jen."
"Goodnight."
Angelo hung up the phone. Sam was staring at her. "What?" she asked.
"Nothing. You did well. Your restraint is amazing," he teased.
"You think? I hope so. Anyway, I need to get ready for work. I'll see you..."
"Whenever," he finished. "I'm sure it'll be a very long tour. I feel sorry for Thompson."
"Hey, she knew what she was getting into when she signed on."
"I bet she didn't."
"I'll make it up to you."
"Oh, how?"
"I'm off tomorrow night. We'll do something special. Just the two of us."
"Really?" He grinned at her. "Then I'll look forward to our date." He always referred to the time they spent together as a date.
"Me too," she said, kissing him.

* * *

Angelo didn't have to pick Thompson up for work; she apparently was able to get her car back from the mechanic on time. Sitting at her desk, she picked up the phone message stuck to her IN box. It was from Morty, the medical examiner. He was requesting her presence in the morning.

He had the report she needed on the Victoria Sterling homicide. *Good old Morty,* Angelo reflected. She hoped he had some good news for her, but she seriously doubted it. Victoria Sterling was in the hospital. Any evidence would have been contaminated or washed away. Add the fact that she donated her organs and it wasn't looking promising. Although the hospital did a rape kit, they came up empty.

Still, it would be good to see her spooky pal again. She wanted to thank him for the help he gave her on the last case. She also wanted Thompson to meet him. If Thompson wanted to work homicide, she'd have to get used to visiting the morgue.

Where is Thompson anyway? Angelo wondered, looking at her watch.

She spied O'Malley by the coffee machine, stuffing a doughnut into his mouth. Wandering over to him, she poked him in the spare tire. "O'Malley," she said.

He jumped back. "Jeez, Angelo, don't go sneaking up on a guy like that! You could have given me a heart attack."

"Eating those things will give you that heart attack," she said, pointing to the cream filled dessert.

"At least *that's* a nice way to go."

"Sorry. Look, have you seen Thompson around?"

"No, but I think she called to say she'd be late."

"Who'd she talk to?"

"The Sarge, I guess. What am I, your answering service?"

"Haven't you always been?"

"Apparently."

"Did you finish your interviews?"

"Yup. I put the report on your desk."

"I didn't see it."

"No wonder. How do you find anything with all that clutter?"

"It's my system. Leave it alone."

"I'm not going anywhere near it. You probably keep mousetraps under all that mess."

"Well?"

"The short version is that no one was having a problem with the Vic. None of her former boyfriends, her current boyfriend or any other male associates had any record or history of violence. She didn't associate with any bad boy types."

"No, I didn't think so."

"How's it going on your end?"

"Things are looking up. I'm going to have another list for you soon."

"Oh, goodie," he said sarcastically.

"I think I have a link with the coffee house she frequented. The manager gave me a mailing list. She also pointed out a few men who fit the flash."

"What makes you think he stalked them from this particular place?"

"I don't know. Just a hunch. That's all I've got right now. Might as well go with it until we get something solid."

"Well, your gut's been more than helpful before."

"We'll see, won't we? Anyway, when Thompson gets in, send her right over to me."

"You mean you're going to let me actually talk to your cuz?"

"Don't get your hopes up. Just send her over to me."

He gave her a crooked smile.

Going back to her desk, she found O'Malley's report under a pile of other reports someone left on her desk. Reading it, she found that he was right. It was another dead end. She pulled the floppy disk out of her jacket pocket and slid it into the computer drive. There were two hundred or more names on the list. *Man, that place is popular.*

Hitting the print button, the computer spat out the ten page list of names and addresses. She scanned down the list and found Victoria's name. Highlighting it with an orange pen, Angelo searched for the next name. Josh Brady, the loner. Unfortunately, she didn't find it. Maybe he didn't sign up for the mailing list. She wrote his name down on the bottom of the page.

She did find Stephen Greystock, who listed his occupation as a mail clerk.

Another name on the list caught her eye. Barbara Cotton. She was Don Juan's first victim. Pulling out the SVU file, she searched for the other victims' names on the list. If her hunch was correct, she would find all of them.

Barbara Cotton. Francine Tabor. Paula Clydesdale. Sydney Bayberry and yes, even Jennifer Tully. The only name that wasn't on the list was the sixteen year old, Heather Donnelley.

"Maybe she didn't drink coffee," Angelo said half to herself.

"Who didn't?"

Looking up, Angelo saw Thompson standing in front of her desk. "About time, Thompson. Where were you?"

"Sorry. I had to stop at SVU."

"Why?"

"I needed to pick up the files from Golden Boy."

"And did you?"

"No. He gave me a hard way to go. Said if homicide wanted *his* files, homicide would have to come here and get it themselves. What a jerk off."

"Did he now?"

"Nothing but grief from that guy."

"Don't worry; I'm going to give him a bit of grief myself."

Thompson grinned slyly. "So, did you open the mailing list?"

"Yes. Here," she said, handing her the copy. "Tell me what you see?"

"You mean the highlighted stuff?"

"Yes?"

She read the names and smiled. "All the victims?"

"Bingo."

"This is great."

"The only one not on the list was the sixteen year old. We're going to have to interview her personally. We'll ask if she ever visited the café."

"I hope she's up to it. She was pretty messed up."

"So do I."

"Are we going to run all the males on the list?"

"No. Here comes the grief part. We're going to ask Golden Boy to do it."

"Why?"

"Because we have other avenues to explore and frankly we don't have the time."

"But what if he gets a hit and tries to steal our pinch?"

"What did I say about this not being a competition?"

"That it wasn't a competition."

"Right."

"Sorry."

"Relax, Sue. He'll share if he knows what's good for him."

"I hope you're right."

"I am. Besides, I'm also going to have O'Malley do the same thing."

"You don't trust Seymour any more than I do?"

"It's all checks and balances. O'Malley might find something that Seymour missed. Don't tell him I said this because his head is big enough, but O'Malley is a very good investigator."

Thompson laughed. "Oh, okay."

"We also wouldn't want SVU to think we're not cooperating."

"No, I guess not. So, what have we got on tap tonight?"

"We are going to see the ME in the morning. Dr. Wharton keeps banker's hours."

Angelo could see Thompson's face pale. "Right."

"You'll get used to it, Sue, I promise."

"I doubt that."

"Okay, get your things together. We're going to take a drive to the Special Victims Unit. At least the weather is cooperating tonight."

"Yes, but the news reports say that we're in for more bad weather in a few days."

"Will this winter ever end?" Angelo asked.

"Doesn't seem to be any time soon."

"How many days until spring?"

"Too many," Thompson replied.

"Great. Come on, it's off to SVU we go."

Chapter Eleven

Driving to the Special Victims Unit currently located at the Frankford Arsenal was uneventful. Traffic was practically non-existent and Thompson was very subdued. Angelo wondered what was on her mind.

"Did you get enough sleep?" Angelo asked, glancing at Thompson out of the corner of her eye.

"Yes."

"The long hours a bit of a shock to your system?"

"Uh huh. But I'm used to it. I don't sleep well anyway."

Breaking her own rule not to get involved in other people's personal lives, Angelo asked, "Why not?"

"No reason."

"Something on your mind? You want to talk about it?"

"Something is always on my mind, Bee. Nothing in particular though."

"Oh."

"Last out does something to your internal clock."

"Yes. I've worked it most of my career, so I'm used to it. I spend most of my daylight hours in court."

"I don't get much court. I'm still kind of new at it."

"It'll only get worse."

"I hate court anyway."

"Why? It's fun."

"Fun?"

"Yeah. I enjoy making the defense squirm."

"I always feel bad for the victims. They seem to get victimized all over again in court. It's a wonder anyone even presses charge anymore."

"Oh, well, you've just hit the problem right on the head. But I find that if you do a good job investigating the case, the complainants feel better when they know the doer is going away for a long time."

Thompson noticed that Angelo called them 'complainants' and not 'victims.' She guessed that Angelo saw them differently than she did. To Thompson, they'd always be victims.

Turning at Bridge Street and Tacony, they entered the arsenal. Stopping at the security gate, Angelo said to the guard, "Detective Angelo and Officer Thompson for Special Victims."

The guard looked in the car and at Thompson. "Hey, Sue."

"What's up, Nate?"

"Same old. Weren't you here earlier?"

"Yes, but I'm bringing my heavy this time," she teased, looking at Angelo.

The guard laughed, lifting the gate. "You know the way."

"Could find it in the dark," she replied.

As long as Angelo had been on the job, even working at the unit, she always seemed to get lost there on the winding roads of the arsenal. They drove through the gate and made a few turns until they came across the three story brick building.

Parking under a sign that said 'No Parking', Angelo and Thompson got out and entered the elevator, pressing the code to send them up to the second floor where the Special Victims Unit was located. The creaking crate delivered them to the unit in short order.

Passing the long hallway where the walls were covered with wanted flyers of sexual predators still on the loose, they entered the unit. Corporal Grosse was sitting at the front desk.

"Bee!" she exclaimed, standing up and walking around the desk to greet her.

Angelo unceremoniously hugged her friend. "What's going on?" she asked, looking at all the activity.

"This place hasn't been this busy in years."

"Is that a good thing or bad?"

"Depends on how you look at it." Grosse smiled and looked at Thompson. "So, how is Sue working out?"

"Fine. Good, hard worker."

"In case you didn't know, Sue, that was the greatest compliment you'll ever get on this job from one of the best."

Thompson blushed.

"Where is Officer Seymour? We need to have a little chat."

"He's in the back with the lieutenant."

"Can you tell him that I need to discuss the case with him? I'd also like to talk to the lieutenant as well."

"Sure. I'll go get them."

Corporal Grosse went back to fetch them. A few minutes later, Officer Seymour and Lieutenant Joan Pierce came out of the office. This was the first time Angelo got to see Seymour in person. He was a lot bigger and broader than he appeared on the television.

"Detective Angelo," Pierce said, holding out her hand. She was a thin woman in her mid thirties with sandy brown hair. She seemed the type who didn't take any guff from anyone. Angelo liked her.

"Lieutenant. It's a pleasure to meet you."

"The same here. This is Officer Seymour," she said, pointing at the man by her side. He looked like a faithful puppy standing there. "He's handling the rape cases."

"Yes. I know. Nice to meet you. You know Officer Thompson, my liaison."

Seymour grunted, looking daggers at Thompson. He held out his hand and purposely squeezed too hard. Angelo smiled and returned the pressure right back at him. Seymour's face went white as a sheet. He was not expecting her to have such a grip. He could have sworn he heard bones crunching in his hand.

Letting him go, Angelo asked, "Is there somewhere we can talk? We have information for you about the cases. An interesting link. We can use some help."

"Certainly," Lieutenant Pierce said. "Come back to my office and we'll talk."

They followed her to the back office. She offered Angelo a chair. Thompson and Seymour were left standing. Without a word spoken, Thompson handed Angelo the file. She opened it and pulled out the mailing list from the Koffee Klutch.

"When we interviewed Victoria Sterling's friends we found out that she frequented a coffee house around the corner from where she worked. We asked for a clientele list and the manager was kind enough to give it to us. Upon reading the list we came across the names of four other victims of Don Juan."

"Really?" Seymour said, genuinely surprised.

Angelo failed to mention or highlight Jennifer Tully's name. She wasn't part of the investigation as of yet. Why bring it up?

"The manager also pointed out a few males who fit the flash of Don Juan. One man is on the list, the other is not, but I wrote his name down. I also included male employees."

"What do you need us to do?" Pierce asked. She seemed pleased that Angelo was going to help and not play *I'm better than you* politics. Angelo's reputation of being an honest and steadfast cop was not only true, but also extremely accurate in Lieutenant Pierce's opinion.

"Could you be so kind as to run all the males on the list? Particularly the two men I mentioned. See if anyone comes up with a hit that also fits the flash. Stick with the twenty to thirty age brackets."

"Okay," Seymour said happily. Thompson glared at him.

Yeah, sure you're happy. We did most of the work, Thompson thought nastily.

"Now, we also need the interview records of your victims."

"Why?" Seymour asked. "It's got nothing to do with the homicide."

Oh, going to play hard to get? Okay, Angelo thought. "It has everything to do with leading up to the homicide," she said coolly. "Officer Thompson said that you wouldn't give them to her, but that you'd give up the files if I made the trip up here myself. Well here I am. Can I see it now?"

"Seymour!" the lieutenant admonished. She didn't need any grief from Homicide. Especially from Detective Angelo. Seymour didn't know who he was messing with.

Seymour looked down at his feet. *Ratfink told her rabbi what I said!* he thought hotly. Thompson smiled, pissing him off even more.

"Can I see the files, please?" she asked, holding out her hand. "Please?"

"Seymour, give Detective Angelo the files."

"Yes, ma'am."

"Thanks, Lou."

Seymour stalked out of the room, bumping into Thompson. *Asshole!* she thought, glaring at him. When he returned, he handed over his file to his lieutenant who in turn gave them to Angelo. She looked them over carefully. They were quite thorough.

"Very good interviews, Officer." He smiled and smirked at Thompson. "Very good indeed. Very promising."

"Thank you." He leaned back against the wall.

"However, your interview with Heather Donnelley is incomplete."

He straitened up. "Sorry, I tried, but I couldn't get anything out of her. The moment she saw me, she freaked out and her parents asked me to leave. So I did. What was I to do? Besides, she didn't see him anyway. No use interviewing a basket case."

Boy, you're a compassionate soul, aren't you? Angelo mused.

"The others were more helpful anyway."

"We'll go back and see if she'll talk to us. Sometimes the complainant feels better talking to a woman."

"Suit yourself."

"I will. Well, Lou, thanks for your cooperation. Please feel free to read my report on Victoria Sterling and her co-workers. When you get anything from the males on the list, please call us with the results. We'll do the same if we get anything from Heather Donnelley."

"We will, Detective Angelo. Thank you," Pierce said. "We appreciate all the help you are giving us."

"We're all cops here. We all want the same thing."

"Yes. To catch this man and punish him. He's going away for a long time."

"We can only hope. Oh, Officer Seymour, one other thing."
"Yes?"
"Thompson mentioned to me that Francine Tabor has a Protection from Abuse order in effect against...what was his name, Thompson?"
"Ben Moody."
"Yes. Did you check into Mr. Moody's record?"
"As a matter of fact, I did. The PFA has expired. He hasn't had any contact with her."
"Are you sure?"
"Yes."
"Well, when I looked at the court records I found that he violated that order several times."
"Yes. Last year. But after he was held in contempt, he stopped."
"Doesn't mean he didn't get smarter about violating it."
"He hasn't. I had talked to him already about it."
"And you took his word for it?"
"Sure. Why not?"
"If you wouldn't mind, I'd like to look into it further," she said.
"You're welcome to do what you think is necessary."
"I think I will. Thanks for your time, Officer."

Angelo stood up and extended her hand to Seymour. This time he didn't squeeze so forcefully. His hand was still pounding from the last time. "Detective," he replied out of nothing but courtesy.

Letting go of Seymour's hand, she nodded to the lieutenant. "Lou."

They left the office and headed back to the elevator. "What an asshole," Thompson muttered.

"What?"

"Nothing. He just burns my butt, that's all."

"Don't worry about him. We have more important things to do."

"Yes, ma'am. But I still don't trust him," she grumbled.

Angelo shrugged her shoulders and got on the elevator. They drove back to the Homicide Unit without saying another word about Officer Seymour. He wasn't worth the effort.

***

Angelo and Thompson worked all through the night, going over every last detail of Seymour's reports. Angelo was right when she said he was very thorough. Although the reports were complete and accurate, it told them nothing that they didn't already know.

Each victim reported that they were either coming home or were already home sleeping in their bed when he struck. He was never violent with them, unless you counted the sexual assault. He was very polite and talkative.

He told them that it was a *date* and everything would be fine. Fine as long as they didn't resist. Being that he was twice their size, he easily overpowered them. He only used the threat of violence if they resisted. However, he let things get out of control with Jenny and subsequently Victoria Sterling. A Power Reassurance rapist usually didn't resort to violence. He wanted to keep the rape a fantasy of consent.

Maybe he was going into the next level. The Power Assertive. He wanted to prove his dominance. That was a scary thought. This guy wasn't going to stop. If he felt threatened by the police closing in on him, he might pack up and move. Start somewhere fresh where no one would notice the body count until it was too late.

He probably had roots in the community, but that never stopped them from fleeing the jurisdiction. Since he left no DNA evidence, he could start fresh somewhere else. They had to catch him and catch him soon. Before someone else got raped or murdered.

The only way his victims were going to survive was not to fight him. Angelo hated to think that, but it was better to get raped and live than fight and die. Surely, there would be another attack soon. She didn't know how she would react if it were her in that situation. She'd probably fight to the death. It was not in her nature to give up and surrender.

What were the other factors in the case besides the coffee house? They were all red heads. Angelo noticed a lot of red heads at the café. There was a big Irish community in the Northeast. Angelo wondered if they should put someone in the café to keep an eye on things there.

She'd ask Special Victims if that would be possible for them to do that for her. She was sure they could spare the daytime manpower for that. But they had to be subtle. Could they pull it off without alerting the man? She certainly hoped so.

Everyone was reporting off at eight in the morning, the next shift coming in. Thompson wandered over to Angelo's desk. "So now what?" she asked. She looked tired. Angelo felt sorry for her. She hated overworking her co-workers. Even O'Malley looked tired and beat.

"I only want to do a few things before we log out."

"Okay, what?"

"First I want to talk to Heather," Angelo said, reading Heather's complaint report.

"You think she'll talk to us?" Thompson asked, rubbing her tired eyes.

"I don't know. Maybe. I certainly hope so."

"Seymour doesn't know how to talk to people. Especially young girls or women. I don't know how he ever got into Sex Crimes. Probably has a quarter."

"Probably."

"It probably doesn't help that he kind of fits the flash of the doer himself. Most likely he scared the hell out of the poor thing."

"A possibility."

"Hey, you don't think it could be him?" she asked hopefully. "Wouldn't that be a kick in the pants?"

"No I don't. Don't even joke like that!"

"Sorry."

"But you could be right about one thing."

"What?"

"His presence may have spooked the girl. Perhaps we'll have better luck."

Thompson paused a second before speaking. "Bee, I was just kidding about Seymour being the doer."

"I know, but you shouldn't talk about other cops like that. You can ruin a reputation. I'm sure you wouldn't like it if someone did that to you."

"No, I suppose not."

"We'll take care of Heather first."

"Then where are we going?"

"The morgue," she replied.

"Oh. Would you mind if I skipped that?"

"I *do* mind and you *will* go with me."

"I'm really not up for a trip there."

"Have you ever been there?"

"A few times. I could never take that smell. I'm afraid I'll get sick."

"You'll live."

"Bee, please…"

"You're going. If you don't like it, go back to SVU."

She hated to do that to Thompson, but she had to get over her fear of the dead. If she wanted to work homicide, she'd be seeing a lot worse than a few dead bodies at the morgue.

"Sorry. All right," she mumbled. "But if I get sick, I'm going to chuck all over you."

"Won't be the first time. Let's go."

"Yes, ma'am."

***

Heather Donnelley lived not too far from the other victims. Her home, where she lived with her parents, was a single dwelling off of Rhawn Street. It was a pleasant neighborhood where people took good care of their property. She was a straight 'A' student at a private Catholic school.

From what Angelo gathered, before the incident she was doing well in her studies and was going to have every college after her next year. Angelo wondered how she was doing in school now. Was she too traumatized to go to school? Angelo figured she probably would be and that was the real shame. That psycho ruined not only a lovely young lady, but also probably everyone in her family. No one would ever be the same again.

Thompson followed Angelo in her car so she could drop it off at her house before they headed to the ME's office. Why take two cars? Besides, Angelo didn't want to give her an opportunity to escape. She was going to see Morty if it killed her.

Angelo knocked on the Donnelley's steel security door. She was almost positive that it wasn't there before the incident. A woman in her forties answered the door and stood behind the security gate. She had a haunted look in her eyes and prematurely graying hair.

"Yes? Can I help you?"

Angelo pulled out her badge and showed it to the wary woman. "I'm Detective Angelo. Is Heather home? We need to speak to her for a moment."

"Heather isn't seeing anyone at this time, especially the cops. The last one who came by set her back and she doesn't want to talk to anyone from Special Victims." She spat out the words Special Victims as if it was poison.

Seymour! Damn it! Angelo thought. "Actually, Mrs. Donnelley, we're from Homicide."

"Homicide?"

"Yes, ma'am. It's important that we speak with your daughter. I only want to ask a few questions. That's all and then we'll go."

She looked at Angelo. "I know you. You're the one who caught that Con Killer last month. Your partner was killed."

Angelo sighed. "Yes, ma'am." *Am I always going to be known as the one who caught him and lost her partner in the process?* she wondered.

"Oh. Good work. Now if only you'll catch Heather's attacker. He murdered her inside."

"I'm so sorry."

Mrs. Donnelley opened the security gate and let them inside the house. It was just as nice on the inside as it was on the outside. Everything was neat and orderly. She offered them a seat and a cup of coffee. Angelo and Thompson accepted the offer of the seats, but declined the coffee. They didn't want Mrs. Donnelley to go through any extra trouble.

"So why does Homicide want to talk to Heather about her—assault?"

Even her mother can't say the word, Thompson mused sourly.

"We think the same man killed someone."

"It was on the news," Thompson added.

"We don't watch the news here anymore, Officer…"

"Thompson, ma'am."

"We don't allow Heather to watch anything that might upset her, Officer

Thompson."

"Mrs. Donnelley," Angelo said, "we promise not to upset her in any way. We just need to ask her a few more questions."

"All right. We'll see if she is up to visitors. She might not want to talk to you. She doesn't even talk to me or her father whom she is very close."

"Thank you for letting us try."

Mrs. Donnelley turned and stared Angelo in the face. "But I warn you. If you upset her in any way, I'll throw you out on your ear like I did that last fellow." Her voice was low, but she meant to get her point across. Angelo understood her feelings and didn't take her words as a threat even though they were.

"No, ma'am. That's the last thing I want to do."

Mrs. Donnelley believed the detective was being sincere; otherwise, she would not have let her in the front door. "Follow me."

She showed them up to the second floor and knocked on Heather's closed door. There was no reply from within the room. Mrs. Donnelley slowly opened the door and peered inside. Angelo noted that there were bars on her bedroom window. She was sure they weren't there a month ago. Now she was a prisoner in her own home.

Heather was sitting on her bed, brushing the hair on a doll she held on her lap. She seemed so lost. She was in a world of her own, trying to cope the only way she knew how.

"Heather, dear, someone is here to see you."

Heather didn't look up at her visitors. She kept brushing the doll's hair.

"Sweetheart?" Mrs. Donnelley turned to Angelo. "I'm sorry. When she's like this it's impossible to talk to her."

"May I try?"

Mrs. Donnelley shrugged her shoulders. Angelo walked into the room and sat on the bed next to Heather. She watched her for a few seconds before speaking.

"Heather? That's a lovely doll you have there," Angelo said. "What's her name?"

"Sally," she replied softly without looking up from the doll in her hand.

"Lovely name."

"Picked it myself." Heather didn't seem like a sixteen year old, but a six year old. It broke Angelo's heart.

"Beautiful."

"Thanks."

"How are you feeling?"

"Okay."

"How's school?"

"I'm not in school now. I'm on vacation."

"For the Christmas holiday?"
"Uh huh."
"Can I ask you a question or two?"
"I guess."
"Do you ever go to the Koffee Klutch?"
"I used to work there."
Bingo! There is the link.
"I used to work there," she repeated. "Before...before..."
"Shhh, it's okay. Never mind that. Did you like working there?"
"Oh yes," she said, finally looking up and into Angelo's eyes. "Everyone was so nice."
"Anyone ever give you any problems at work?"
Shaking her head, she replied, "Didn't like Josh. He's creepy."
"Did Josh do anything to bother you?"
"No. He just kept staring at me. I didn't like it when he stared. But Steve took care of that for me."
"Steve?"
"Another customer. Put Josh in his place. Don't like Josh at all. Creepy Josh. Steve's such a nice guy."
"When did this happen?"
"I don't remember. I'm sorry."
"That's okay, honey."
She started to cry. Angelo took Heather's head and placed it on her shoulder, stroking her hair. "I'm sorry. I'm sorry."
"What are you sorry about?"
"Being a bad girl."
"You're not a bad girl. Look at me. You're a sweet and lovely, beautiful girl. You're a young lady. You have absolutely nothing to be ashamed of or sorry for. You hear me?"
"I'm nothing," she mumbled.
"Sure you are. You're a real somebody. You are Heather Donnelley. There is no other like you in this world."
Heather gave a slight nod.
"Do you like school?"
Sniffling, she answered, "Yes."
"What do you like to do? What's your favorite subject?"
"English and literature."
"Do you like to write?"
"Yes," she said, wiping her runny nose.
"You know, my husband is a writer."
She looked Angelo in the eye. "Really? What's he write?"
"Novels. Sam Marshall. Ever hear of him?"

Heather actually smiled. "Yes, but I'm not supposed to read romance novels," she whispered, looking over at her mother.

"Would you like to write novels when you get older?"

"Yes. I think it'd be fun."

"When you're feeling better, Sam can give you some advice on writing."

Another smile crept across her sad face. "You think he will?"

"I know he will."

Heather put the doll down on the bed. Life seemed to return to her eyes. "Thanks. That would be nice."

"Anytime, sweetheart. I appreciate you talking to me."

Heather shrugged and went back to brushing her doll's hair. Angelo got up and walked over to her mother who was crying slightly. She glanced one last time at Heather. The light in her eyes was still there. Closing the bedroom door, Angelo turned to Heather's mother.

"Is she seeing a doctor?"

"We've tried, but nothing seems to help."

"I know someone who is very good with young assault survivors." Again, Angelo didn't say victim. "An expert in the field and won't charge anything."

Angelo wrote the doctor's name on her business card and handed it to Heather's mother. "Thank you, Detective Angelo."

"Call her and tell her that I suggested you take Heather to see her. When Heather is feeling better, please call me so my husband can set her up with some writing lessons. It might help her express her feelings."

"You've been so kind."

"No, thank you for letting me talk to her. She was a great help. If you or Heather have any more information to give me, don't hesitate to call me immediately."

Mrs. Donnelley nodded. "Just catch him."

"I promise, I will."

She let Angelo and Thompson out of the house, locking the security gate behind them. They walked over to the car and Thompson said, "That was impressive."

"What?"

"How you got her to open up and talk to you. Did you see her face when she looked at you?"

"That was nothing. I just know how to talk to people."

"It's a gift."

"No, just experience. You'll learn it eventually."

Thompson sighed. "I certainly hope so."

"Okay, next stop, the ME's office."

Thompson groaned.

Angelo laughed.

Chapter Twelve

After dropping Thompson's car off at her house, Angelo got on the Boulevard and then headed south on I-76. Getting off at the City Line Avenue exit, they entered University City and parked behind the ME's office. Thompson was quiet the entire trip. Angelo could see in her face that she was not looking forward to the visit.

Getting out of the car, Angelo stretched and rolled her aching shoulders. "Almost done for the day," she told Thompson.

"Oh, goodie," Thompson replied sardonically.

"Come on, the quicker we do this the quicker we can get out of here."

Angelo walked ahead of Thompson who was dragging her feet. Take a deep breath, Thompson repeated to herself.

Entering the gloomy building, the stench of death hit them like a bolt of lightning. As long as Thompson lived, she'd never get used to the smell of decay and disinfectant. Angelo knocked on the reception window. The man behind the glass looked up and smiled when he recognized her. "Hello, Detective Angelo," he said.

"Hi, Scotty. What's going on?" she asked the attendant.

"Not a damn thing. It's dead in here." He laughed at his own joke.

Angelo looked around. He was right. There was no one in the waiting area. "Do your jokes get any better, Scotty?"

"Hey, that's one of my best lines."

"Don't quit your day job," she teased.

"Morty is expecting you. He's in cutting room one."

"Thanks, Scotty."

"Hey, don't forget to catch my act at the Improv."

"Wouldn't miss it. Come on, Sue."

They walked back to the autopsy suites and Angelo peered into the window of room number one. Morty was about to examine some unfortunate individual's innards. *Good. Thompson should see this,* she thought. Knocking on the door and pushing it open, she entered the room. Thompson reluctantly followed.

Morty looked up from his work and grinned. "Angie!" he exclaimed. "I'd give you a hug, but..." He held up his blood soaked hands.

"Quite all right, Morty. Next time."

"Good to see you back," he said, sticking his hand inside the man's chest cavity and removing his liver. He tossed it on the scale. The organ made a gruesome sound when it landed in the metal bowl. Thompson winced.

"Yes. Thanks."

"I thought you were on IOD status. I was surprised to see your name attached to the Victoria Sterling case. But hey, you're the best. Why not?"

"I'm a fast healer."

"How are you feeling?" he asked more seriously.

"Fine. I'm just happy to be back to work. I was losing my mind at home."

"Who's your pale friend?" he asked, nodding in Thompson's direction.

Angelo turned to glance at Thompson who was looking very green. Angelo grinned. "This is Officer Thompson. She's assisting me with the case."

"Nice to meet you, Officer Thompson," he said, holding out a blood covered hand. Thompson took a giant step back. "Sorry." He pulled off the gloves and tossed them into a bio-waste trashcan.

"What happened to him?" Thompson asked, pointing at the dead man with his chest wide open.

"He's dead. If he wasn't then, he is now. Ha-ha!"

"You're a sick puppy, Morty," Angelo said.

"Actually, he's just an unattended death. Nothing major."

"Oh."

Out of the corner of her eye, Angelo could see Thompson swaying. "You okay?"

"Fine." Thompson swallowed hard several times.

"Sue, do me a favor. Go out to my car and get my purse." She tossed the keys at her.

"Okay," she replied, catching the keys and bolting for the door.

When she was gone, Morty asked, "New kid?"

"Yeah. I wanted to get her used to this place."

"Hon, you never get used to this place."

"You seem to."

"Ah, but like you said, I'm a sick puppy."

Angelo smiled, leaning over and looking inside the dead man's chest. "You missed his gall bladder."

"Did not. I was getting to it." He thought about something she said as he removed the dead man's gall bladder. "Hey, wait, when did you start carrying a purse?"

"I don't."

"Then why did you send...Oh!"

"I didn't want her to chuck on me. Wanted to give her a little dignity."

"Maybe we should talk in my office. She might feel better." He walked over to the intercom. "Scott."

"Yes, Morty?" Scott's voice said over the speaker.

"When Officer Thompson comes back in, send her to my office, would you?"

"You mean the *green* cop who ran out of here a few seconds ago?"

"Yeah."

"Okay."

He turned off the intercom and faced Angelo, removing his blood stained smock. "Come on, Angie, we'll talk in my office. The files are in there anyway."

They walked down the hall to his office. More like a cubical than an office, Angelo sat down in the ratty chair in front of his desk. Looking at the clutter, she spied a photograph of Natasha. It was proudly displayed next to a golf trophy. Morty loved two things more than life itself: his girlfriend and golf.

"How is Natasha?"

"Great. No, fantastic! We're planning the wedding."

"When?"

"Don't know yet. We're shooting for next September. We hope."

"That's nice. All the best."

"Yeah, thanks. I didn't realize how much work planning a wedding involved. How on earth did you do it?"

"Oh, well, we eloped. Thankfully we knew a priest."

"That's a thought. However, I doubt Natasha would go for it. She has her hopes and heart set on a big wedding. The bigger the better."

"That's every girl's prerogative. You should know that by now, Morty."

"Why didn't you have a big ceremony? You not *girly* enough?"

"I beg your pardon!" she said crossly.

"Just kidding with ya, Angie," he said, patting her on the shoulder. "So why didn't you have a big wedding when you and Sam tied the noose—uh, I mean the knot?"

Angelo grinned. "We couldn't afford it back then."

"You can now."

"Yeah, and we're thinking about having a big ceremony for our twentieth anniversary."

"Twenty! Wow. I'll bet it will be splendid."

"If Sam has anything to say about it, it will be the ceremony of the century. He's the party animal, not me."

"You have got to loosen up, woman. Let your hair down."

"My hair is always down, Morty."
"No it's not. You're a stick in the mud."
"Am not."
"Are too."
"Am not."

The argument would have gone on forever if Thompson hadn't knocked on the office door. "Come in!" Morty shouted. Thompson entered the room. "Are too," he finished.

"Sorry, Bee, I couldn't find your purse anywhere," Thompson said, looking a lot better than before she left.

"Hmm, must have left it at home. Never mind."

"Have a seat, Officer Thompson."

"You can call me Sue, Doctor Wharton."

"Only if you call me Morty. Everyone calls me Morty."

"Okay, Morty." She sat down in the chair next to Angelo.

"Let's get down to business, shall we?" He searched his desk and pulled out an autopsy report. Flicking a crumb off the file, he opened it and said, "The official cause of death was complications due to asphyxiation. She was strangled to the point that not enough oxygen was getting to her brain. Someone at the scene started CPR, maybe the first officer at the scene, but was too late to stop the irreversible brain damage. If she had survived, she would have been a vegetable. Maybe it was for the best that she didn't live. The brain damage was too severe."

"Any other trauma?"

"Besides the sexual assault?"

"Yes."

"No. He didn't beat her. All I found was bruising to her throat and legs. I think he strangled her twice."

"Yes. We believe that the first strangulation was to subdue her. The second time was what caused the most damage."

"Right you are."

"Any DNA? Semen? Hair?"

"Not a trace. In addition, I believe the hospital cleaned her up. They should have known better."

"I'll have to check with Crime Scene and SVU to see if there was anything found at the scene."

"Sorry, but there isn't anything I can tell you that would be helpful to this case."

"I didn't think there would be. But thanks for trying."

"Maybe the next one."

"I pray there isn't a next one."

Changing the subject, Morty turned to Thompson and asked, "So, Sue, where do you hail from?"

"Special Victims."

"You want to work Homicide some day?"

"Yes, but I don't know if I can stomach the sight of so much death."

"Oh, you'll get used to it. You know, the first time I met Angie here, she threw up on my shoes."

"Morty!" Angelo squeaked. "That was never to be mentioned—especially around rookies."

"Oops. Sorry." He gave her a sly grin.

Thompson laughed. "Really?"

"Yes, all right, yes. I chucked on Morty's shoes. *Happy now*? Thanks a lot, Morty."

"You're welcome."

Angelo smiled and stood up. "Okay. Thanks again for your help, Morty."

"Any time, sweetheart."

Angelo and Thompson left the ME's office. Thompson, feeling better after getting some much needed fresh air, got in the passenger seat. "That wasn't so bad now, was it?"

"No." *Who am I kidding?* she asked herself.

"Trust me. In time, it won't bother you so much."

"I'm afraid it'll always bother me, Bee."

"One more stop and then I'll take you home."

"Where?"

"To see Ben Moody."

***

They drove to the auto repair shop where Ben Moody worked. After talking to the owner, he pointed out the gentleman in question. She explained— rather diplomatically — to the boss, that Ben was not in any sort of trouble. She told the owned that they just needed to speak with him for a few minutes.

Satisfied that Ben wasn't going to be hauled off to jail and thus proving that he wasn't going to lose a good mechanic, the owner showed them to the repair bay. Ben Moody was under a car. Angelo could hear him cursing as he banged on God knows what. She made a mental note not to ever bring her car there for repairs.

The owner left them alone to talk. Angelo watched the lower half of Moody for a moment, studying his physical features. He was about the right size and weight to make him a possible suspect. She cleared her throat and announced her presence.

"Ben. Ben!"

"What!" he replied from under the car.

"Can you come out from under there, please?"

He slid out from under the car and looked at Angelo who was bending over to see his face. He was wearing a dust mask over his mouth and nose. She also noted that he was covered in oil and grease from head to toe. He removed the cupped facemask and gave Angelo and Thompson a crooked smile.

"You doing surgery under there?" Angelo commented. "Nice mask. Goes delightfully with the greasy coveralls."

"Who are you? The fashion police?" he asked sarcastically.

"Not quite."

"The gas fumes bother my allergies. What of it?" he growled.

"Nothing. We'd like to talk to you a minute, Ben," she told him.

"You can talk to me as long…" he started, looking Thompson up and down, then saw the badge on her hip next to her gun, "Oh, Jeez, now what?"

"We'd like to ask you a few questions."

"I'm too busy. I got to have this car done in an hour," he said and tried to slide back under the vehicle. Angelo stopped him with a foot on his chest.

"We can do this here or downtown," Angelo said calmly.

He sighed heavily. "What do you want?" he asked, getting up and moving over to a sink to wash his greasy hands. It didn't look like he was having much success removing the dirt. His fingernails were still black with oil. Angelo noted that he was about six foot and built to match. All that heavy lifting he did in the shop gave him a buff appearance. She wondered if he was hairless under those coveralls. She couldn't quite tell just by looking.

"I want to talk to you about your relationship with Francine."

"What relationship? She dumped me a year ago."

"Did that make you angry?"

"Hell yes, it did!"

"Stalked her for a while? Had to have a restraining order put on you?"

"I was upset. I gave her the best five months of my life."

"Wow, *five* whole months," she said.

"I'm over it now. What is this all about? I just got done talking to another detective a few days ago about her. What's she saying about me now?"

"Nothing. Yet."

"Look, I told him and I'm going to tell you. I haven't seen the witch since that judge slapped the contempt charge on me. I almost lost my job because of that."

"I bet that pissed you off."

"You bet. But I saw the errors of my ways and stayed far away from her. I've got a life now. A new wife."

"What's her name?"

"That's none of your damn business."

"It is, if I say it is!" she snapped, making him jump back a pace.

"Her name is Della. Della Portsmouth-Moody."

"Will Della give you an alibi for December 18th, between the hours of nine at night and one in the morning?"

"What? Why?"

"I'll ask the questions. Well?"

"I don't…" He chewed his bottom lip. "No. I was out drinking."

"Anyone see you *drinking*?"

"Sure. I guess the whole bar did."

"You guess? Not! Wrong answer." Turning to Thompson, she said, "You know what, Officer, I believe Mr. Moody here is worth taking a closer look at, don't you think?"

"I think so, Detective," Thompson replied, reaching for her handcuffs.

"I swear I was at a bar called, um, Mason's. Yeah. No, wait. It was called Maddie's. It was something like that. I know it was on, um, Frankford Avenue."

"You don't sound too sure, Benny."

"I was plastered out of my head. I don't remember."

Angelo made a tisk-tisk sound. "Not looking good for you, Benny," she said, shaking her head in disbelief.

"Okay, okay. I was with a girl."

She raised an eyebrow. "A girl? Not your wife?"

He looked down at his feet. "No. It wasn't my wife. Della is pregnant. She won't let me come within ten feet of her. I was feeling, well, you know."

"Ah, I'm starting to see the big picture. Does this girl have a name by any chance?"

"Don't remember."

"Boy, you have a lousy memory, Benny."

"I was drunk."

"Could that girl's name be, oh, I don't know…Victoria?"

"No, no. I'd remember *that* name. That's my mother's name. Oh, God!" He was starting to get nervous, pacing the floor. "Give me time. I'll remember it."

"I'm not believing you here," she said, tapping her foot impatiently.

"I promise. Just let me think."

"Okay, Benny, I'll give you the benefit of the doubt." She handed him her card. "You remember that name in the next day or two and call me. If you don't, I'm coming back here for you. You don't want me to come back." She gave him an evil looking smile.

"Okay, okay. You didn't tell me what this was all about."

"No, I didn't."

He shut his mouth before it got him into any more trouble.

"You have a nice day, Benny," Angelo said, still smiling at him.

"Yeah, yeah," he stammered nervously.

They left the repair bay and a very visibly shaken Ben Moody. Walking back to their car, Thompson said, "There is that bar again."

"Yes." She would have to ask Jenny if she had ever been to that particular bar. It was worth another look.

"What do you think? Can Benny be our man?" Thompson asked hopefully.

"We'll keep him on the short list."

***

After dropping Thompson off at her Fox Chase home and telling her to enjoy her two days off, Angelo decided she needed to make one last trip before going home herself. It was still early in the afternoon and after paging her friend, she drove down town. He told her to meet him at Broad and Arch Street along side of the District Attorney's Office. She'd have to make it a quick visit though because he had to be back in court by three o'clock.

Angelo parked on the northeast corner of Broad Street and flipped her *Police Official Business* placard on the dashboard. The last thing she needed was the parking authority towing her car. They'd do it too.

Getting out of the car, she noticed that the media was around, circling the DA's office like vultures on a carrion. Either they just had a press conference or they were waiting for one to start. Either way, they looked hungry for a news story.

She stood by her car hoping, no praying, that none of the reporters spotted her. She was the media's Golden Girl at the moment and she hated that fact. Angelo turned her head when she heard the side exit door open and a man slip out quietly.

Angelo grinned. "Hey, Tony! Slipping out the back door now?"

"Actually, it's a side door," he replied.

"Semantics."

"Bee, come with me a minute. Away from them," he said, pointing at the reporters.

"Okay."

They walked toward the back of the building and Angelo noted that ADA Vargas looked particularly troubled. "I think it'll be all right to talk here."

"What's going on over there?" Angelo asked.

He sighed heavily. "This Don Juan killer. The media is screaming about the police and the DA's Office not doing enough to stop him. They think we should have caught on sooner. You know how they like to start trouble."

"Hmm, yes. Nevertheless, they are right. We should have caught on sooner."

"You're on that case, right?"

"I am."

"Good. I know you'll make and airtight case against him."

"I'll certainly try, Tony. It's only a matter of time."

"So, what's up? It's not about that case, is it?"

"Not directly, no," she fibbed. Angelo wanted to take another angle on Jennifer's assault. She liked to cover all the possibilities.

"Okay, what then?"

"This is between you and me, right?"

"Of course."

"I remember that you worked with Jennifer Tully on a few cases."

"More than a few, but that was a couple of years ago. I remember that she was a nice woman and a fine attorney."

"Do you remember if any of her cases got—how should I say—ugly?"

"I'm not sure what you mean."

"Did she ever get threatened?"

"Don't we all at some point?" He paused a second before speaking again. "Did something happen to her?"

"I can't discuss it with you, I'm afraid. It's personal."

"Something *did* happen! Don't tell me that this has something to do with Don Juan."

"All I can say is that she wants it kept quiet. Okay?"

"All right. I'll do what I can. What do you need from me?"

"Could you get me her old case files?"

"You've got to be kidding, Bee! There has to be hundreds of cases."

"I know it's a lot to ask, but—"

"Okay, okay. Jenny's a friend and so are you."

"I owe you."

"Can you at least narrow it down for me?"

"Already thought of that." She handed him a piece of paper. He took it, glanced at it briefly and stuffed it in his breast pocket.

"Is Jenny all right?" he asked worried.

"She'll be fine. Really."

"I'll take care of it. Tell her I said hello and I'd like her to come back to the DA's Office."

Angelo smiled. "So would I, Tony. Next to you, she's one of the best."

Vargas held out his hand and Angelo took it warmly. Before letting her go, he said, "Oh, I've been meaning to tell you something."

"About what?"

"Bill Banks."

"Bill? You found him? Is he all right?" Angelo and the entire DA's Office were worried about him since he disappeared last month. She felt bad for suspecting him in the *Con Killer* case.

"He is alive and apparently doing much better. He decided to check himself into one of those New Age wellness centers."

"Bill doing New Age?"

"Yeah. Who would have thought such a thing would happen."

"And?" she prompted.

"He's trying out that *mind over matter* healing."

"And it's working?"

"It seems to be working along with his Chemotherapy. He might be in remission, but they aren't sure just yet. He says that he's not worried about that and at least he is at peace with himself. He is no longer afraid of death and says even if he doesn't beat the cancer, at least he'll be happy. He has found himself. I guess he found God too."

"Wow. That's great news. I'm glad you told me. I was worried. I'll pray that it works out for him."

"We all do. He's a great guy. I'll let him know you're thinking of him. Did you still need to talk to him about a case?"

"Not anymore. It's over with now."

Vargas' beeper went off and he glanced at it. "Oh, heck! I have to go, Bee."

"Sorry to keep you."

"No, don't worry about it. At least the judge isn't DeCello," he laughed.

Angelo smiled.

"I'll call you later when I get the information for you."

"Thanks. You're the best, Tony."

Vargas walked away and up the street toward the Criminal Justice Center on Filbert Street. Angelo was about to walk back to her car when she was descended upon by a reporter from the local rag.

"Detective Angelo!" the fat, little man in a wrinkled overcoat said, stuffing a tape recorder in her face. She slapped it away with her hand.

"Jesus, Bart! Don't jump out at me like that. And get that thing out of my face!"

"What were you and Vargas talking about? Who is Jennifer Tully? Is she one of Don Juan's victims?"

Angelo snapped, her temper getting the better of her. She snatched the tape recorder out of his hand and pushed him up against the wall, pinning him. "You little rat! Were you eavesdropping on a private official conversation?" she demanded as she yanked the tape out of the recorder, destroying it.

"Hey, you can't do that! That's paper property!"

"Shut the hell up! I'll do more than break the tape in a second!"

"Police brutality!" he yelped when he spotted a police sergeant walking by the alley. The sergeant backed up, looked at Angelo and grinned.

"Hi, Detective Angelo," the sergeant said to her.

"She's brutalizing me! Do something!" Bart protested.

The sergeant looked at him. "It doesn't look like that to me. Besides, you probably deserve it," he said and walked away.

Bart turned back to Angelo and spat, "I'm going to file a complaint with Internal Affairs, Detective!"

"You do what you feel you need to do. I don't give a damn. Just you remember that two can play at this game. I caught you eavesdropping on an official investigation. I'll charge you with hindering an investigation."

His face fell. "Are you threatening me? You can't…"

"Just watch me," she said and pulled out her handcuffs.

"Okay, okay, hold on a second, Angelo."

"Let me tell you something else. If I see any of my conversation with ADA Vargas or the mere mention of a certain woman in that rag you work for, I will hunt you down. Then you'll know what brutality really is. Just remember there are shield laws and I enforce them."

"Point taken."

She let him go and smoothed out the extra wrinkles she added to his jacket. "Oh, and one more thing. If you and your paper want to lose every police source in this city and the tri-sate area, go ahead and say something about this little chat."

"You can be a real witch, Angelo."

"With a capital *W*, Bart. Try me and find out just how much of one I really am. I keep my promises."

"Fine. Be that way, Detective. Good day!"

"Good day to you too, Mr. Snodgrass," she replied and smiled.

He walked off in a huff. He was trying to act as if what she said didn't bother him, but it didn't work. She knew he was scared of her. The warning of having him and his paper blackballed by the department was no idle threat. She'd do it and that fact hit home. A reported without a source was useless.

Angelo wasn't worried about him filing a complaint with IAB either. He was a weasel, but messing with a detective with her reputation was career suicide and both of them knew it. She got into her car and went home to her husband. Bart Snodgrass was a fading memory.

***

Just as Sam promised his number one fan, he paid a visit to her book group. Mrs. Carrington asked him to stop by her home and *meet the girls* from the group. They were all looking forward to finally meeting their favorite author. She told him that only a few ladies would be there and it wasn't formal so he was to come as he was.

He wheeled himself up the wheelchair ramp and knocked on the door. A moment later, an older woman Sam guessed was in her seventies, opened the door. He could have sworn he saw her swoon when she saw him. A great, big smile crossed her face.

"Sam Marshall!" she nearly squealed in delight. "Come in, come in, please!" She stepped aside to let him pass. "This way, please, Mr. Marshall."

"Please call me Sam, Miss…"

"Carole. You can call me Carole. Beatrice said you were coming, but we weren't going to believe it until we saw it."

Sam smiled as he followed her into the parlor. His eyes widened. *A few ladies?* There had to be twenty women of all ages in the living room. Mrs. Carrington put the tea set down on the table and walked up to Sam. She bent down and he kissed her on the cheek. She blushed like a schoolgirl.

"Sam, honey, we're so glad you made it. Especially in this weather," she said.

"Oh, I'd brave the Andes for you, Beatrice."

She blushed even more furiously. "Come over here and settle in. The girls are just dying to meet you."

He smiled at the women. "Ah, Beatrice, I thought you said a few ladies."

"Yes, well, that was the plan, but as soon as word got out it was a free-for-all. I couldn't turn them away. This isn't a problem, is it?"

"No, no, of course not. It's not everyday I'm surrounded by beautiful women." The ladies giggled.

"My wife has some stiff competition, Beatrice."

"Sam, you are such a charmer. I'm sure Bernadette can feel quite secure."

One of the women approached Sam. "I'm Mary Mae. When Beatrice told me that you were coming, I dropped everything and flew home from Europe. I had to see it to believe it. And true to her word, here you are. I'm such a fan!"

Sam took her hand and kissed it.

"You're right, Beatrice, he is such a gorgeous gentleman. I'm so jealous." It was Sam's turn to blush.

Beatrice handed over the new manuscript to him. It was in a sorry state, being read dozens of times. "Sorry about the manuscript, Sam. I just loved it."

Looking at the dog-eared, over-read manuscript, he said, "You know what, Beatrice, you keep it. It'll be a collector's item some day."

"Thank you! Thank you so much, but don't you need it?"

"Ah, the power of computers," he chuckled. "I have another copy."

"Thanks again. Okay, girls, give the man some breathing room," she said to the gaggle of women surrounding him. After pouring him tea, she started the meeting. "We, the girls and I, thought up an idea we'd like your input on."

"I'm all ears," Sam said.

"Oh, and quite fetching ears too," one of the women said, reaching out to touch him.

"Fannie!" Beatrice said, slapping her hands away. "Behave yourself!"

"You're no fun, Beatrice!" Fannie said.

Sam had to laugh.

"Sorry, Sam, but some of the ladies are incorrigible."

"Not a problem. So tell me about this idea?"

"We started an amateur sleuth group. You know, a whodunit game. Where we all try to figure it out? No real mysteries, mind you."

"I see. And what do you need from me?"

"We'd all love it if you'd set up the scenarios. It's one of those things where there's a new winner every month. It'll keep us occupied until the new book comes out."

"I can do that for you. It sounds like fun."

"Maybe Bernadette could help."

"I don't know about that. She has enough real life mysteries to solve. But I'll ask her."

"That would be just fantastic. How is she, by the way? We heard what happened last month. Poor Detective Ronalds. I feel bad for misjudging him when he came here. He turned out to be a hero."

"Yes. Bernadette is working out some issues. The loss was a lot for her to handle."

"I can imagine."

Sam smiled again, but Beatrice could see he didn't want to talk about it. "Okay, enough about that. Let's get down to business."

Whipping out a pen, Sam started jotting down notes. "I'm ready when you are."

"Splendid!" Mrs. Carrington shouted. "Sam, you just made a bunch of old crows very happy."

"Beatrice, even crows have beautiful feathers," he said with a wink.

***

Angelo went home. She planned to relax and spend some quality time with Sam. It was their time. Nothing would get in the way of a good time with her husband or so she hoped.

When she got home, she found the house empty. Wondering where Sam could have gotten to, she padded into his office. Knowing that would be the first place she looked, he left a note taped to his computer monitor. Pulling it off, she studied his neat handwriting.

"Gone to a book group meeting at Mrs. Carrington's. Be back at six. Love you. Sam."

"Good for you, Sam."

She pondered how old Mrs. Carrington was doing. She still hadn't gotten the chance to read the new manuscript. Sam had told her that Mrs. Carrington loved the new novel and must have read it fifty times. That made Angelo wish she could read it even more.

She had half a mind to dig into his computer files, but knowing him, he had it locked under some obscure password she wouldn't be able to figure out in a thousand years. She'd have to remember to ask him about it when he returned home.

Bringing her jacket sleeve up to her nose, she could smell the scent of death on her skin. She needed a hot shower big time. A good, hot shower. She would bet dollars to doughnuts that Thompson felt the exact same way. Yuck! Some days she didn't know why the hell she did what she did for a living.

Climbing the stairs to the second floor, she thought about poor Heather Donnelley. It was a pity that such a beautiful and promising young girl had to have her life shattered by that pig. She would make him pay. Justice would not be blind. Justice would be swift. She would put him away for the rest of his life. Better yet, get him the death penalty.

She wished Heather well and promised herself to check up on her progress. She was sure Sam wouldn't mind helping if that was what Heather wanted. Look what he was doing for that lonely Mrs. Carrington. He was such a kind and loving man. *God, how I love him more every day,* she thought. She couldn't wait to have that wedding/anniversary ceremony.

She couldn't wait to see Sam standing at the altar again, looking as handsome as he did the day they got married twenty years ago. The older he got, the more distinguished he became. *Why do men get distinguished and women just get old?*

When they first met, he was a gangly six-year-old. He was literally the boy next door, skinny as a rail and easy picking for the bigger kids. Angelo could remember picking on him herself. Not in a mean way, but they were always very competitive with each other, even at age six. She tormented him to no end.

Eventually, as they grew, he became taller and stronger. Her best friend became her boyfriend when they entered High School and she was allowed to date. Although they never slept together, not until they were properly married, they were inseparable. He was the only man she had ever been intimate with and she knew in her heart that he would be the only man in her life. He was the air she breathed. He brought her to life.

Dropping her clothes where she stood, she jumped into the shower. Letting the hot water slosh over her tired body, she let her mind wander. The heat soothed her aching joints and relaxed her.

After washing her hair several times, making sure she got all the morgue smell out, she climbed out and draped herself with a giant towel. It was Sam's towel, his scent still lingered on it. She desperately wanted to make love to him. She planned on seducing Sam tonight. She was ready for him, warm and moist.

Flopping facedown on the bed, she closed her eyes. A million things ran through her exhausted mind. She would have to check on Jenny tomorrow night. Just to see how she was doing. How she was feeling. She told herself that she wouldn't push Jenny. At least she would try to restrain herself from doing so. It wasn't going to be easy. She wanted Jenny to get the help she needed. Jenny was a dear friend. Angelo didn't have many female friends.

Finally falling asleep, the dream that frightened her revisited her anxious subconscious. She was alone and in the dark with the unseen entity. It laughed at her. Told her that it was no use resisting. She was his prisoner and he was free to do with her as he pleased. There was no one there to help her. She struggled to get free, feeling hot pain in her lower abdomen as it traced its fingers across her skin. She couldn't free herself from its grasp.

"No!" she murmured. She was covered in a light sheen of perspiration. "Why? Why?"

"Because I can," it told her.

"No!"

Her eyes snapped open. Confused, she looked at the clock on the wall. It was a few minutes after six in the evening. The hours passed as if seconds. She sat up, covering her naked body with the bed sheets. She was shivering uncontrollably.

"Damn it," she said to herself.

"Bee?"

Angelo jumped at the sound of another's voice. Seeing Sam in the doorway, she relaxed, her heart calming. "Oh, Sam, you're home."

"Are you okay?" he asked concerned.

"Fine. Why?"

He wasn't about to tell her that he watched her for the last five minutes, fighting in her sleep. "No reason. You just look a little pale."

"I didn't get a chance to eat anything."

"When was the last time you ate?"

"When did you cook last?"

"You know better than to skip meals."

"Yes, Mother," she said jokingly, but Sam was not amused.

"Come downstairs and I'll make you something."

"Don't go through any trouble, Sam. I'm not really up to eating anything heavy."

"How about some soup?"

"Sam."

"I'm in the mood for some soup. It's cold out. There is a storm coming. I can feel it." Ever since the accident, Sam could tell if a bad storm was coming because his bones ached. "Get dressed. It'll be ready in five minutes. No trouble at all."

"What if I don't want to get dressed?" she asked suggestively.

"Oh, then I might have to take you on the kitchen table."

"Hmm, interesting suggestion."

"I'm up to it, if you are."

"Kitchen table? Hmm. I think I'll pass on that one. Besides I have to eat off that thing."

"Oh." He sounded disappointed.

"But if you're up to it, how about right here, right now?"

He raised an eyebrow. "Is that a come on?"

"No, this is." She stood up and walked over to him, pressing her naked breasts to his face. He kissed her, running his hands down her back and buttocks.

"Oh, I love the taste of you." He held her closer, inhaling the strawberry soap she used earlier. He stood up from his chair and pushed her back onto the bed, falling on top of her.

Pulling his shirt over his head, she tossed it on the floor and raked her fingernails down his smooth back. The hairs on his chest tickled her breasts, making them grow taunt. His lips wandered over her face, down her neck and then lingered for a time at the hollow of her throat.

Moaning, she ran the fingers of one hand through his hair and with the other worked on removing the belt from his trousers. She fumbled with the zipper next and when he was finally free of the last barrier between them he climbed on top of her welcoming body. He was ready for her and she for him.

"Wait," she said, pushing slightly away from him.

"What?"

"Remember what the doctor said. You can't strain your back."

"Screw the doctor!" he said.

They made love for nearly an hour, taking each other. The soup was forgotten for the moment. Eating would have to wait until they satisfied another primal need.

Chapter Thirteen

It was cold out again, but he didn't seem to mind. The cold never bothered him. In fact, he reveled in it. Sitting in his heated car across the street from Jennifer Tully's house, he watched her as she paced around her living room. He could see her silhouette through the drawn curtains. She was finally home.

He wondered where she had been and why she was avoiding him. Didn't she enjoy their last date? He certainly did. He had a sly grin on his face as he recalled the encounter. Her skin was so smooth, her hair fiery like her temper. He knew how to cool her temper. All she needed was some serious loving.

He was still feeling a bit upset about how his last date turned out. Pity she couldn't live with herself after he'd left her. Some girls just couldn't deal with him leaving them. Some went to the police out of guilt or died like the last one. He didn't mean for that to happen. He would miss Victoria. Miss her laugh, her smile, the way she sipped her coffee.

Now Jenny was different. She didn't do either. She didn't call the police, but she did disappear for a few days. Maybe she just needed some space. He understood. He wasn't angry. In fact, he was happy. He was very happy indeed. He would pay her another visit soon. He would make her feel like a real woman. A real woman who needed a real man. He told himself repeatedly that she was special and a woman like Jenny deserved a man like him—the perfect lover.

He continued to watch her for a while. She seemed anxious, continuously peering out the front window through the silky curtains at every passing car or pedestrian. Is she waiting for me? Yes, that's what she's doing. *She's waiting for her Don Juan, her lover, to return to her.* She would not have to wait long.

I'm coming back for you soon. Very soon, my sweet. My beautiful Jennifer. I'll take you in my arms and make sweet love to you all night. We'll go slowly this time. Gently and passionately. No need to play games. No fighting.

Just sweet, hot sex.

He licked his lips, tasting the cherry flavored lip balm he generously applied. He liked his lips to be soft, not chapped from being out in the cold for too long. He lit his pipe and let the sweet, smoky aroma waft around his head. *Ah, a pipe. Separates the men from the boys.*

He couldn't stand the smell of cigar or cigarette smoke. It was stale and nasty. He preferred the sweet smell of pipe tobacco. His mother never allowed him to smoke it at home, although she smoked like a chimney. She said it reminded her of his father. That bastard, she'd call him from time to time. *No wonder dad left you, you fat, ugly cow!*

Left her, and him, when he was only five. He had no real male role model in his life. Maybe that was half his problem. He needed a real man to raise him, not some bitch of a mother who drank and smoked too much. Who always had some strange man over. Who never closed her bedroom door when she had company. A different man every week. Sometimes twice a week.

He hated hearing the noises that came from her bedroom. He would hide his head under the dirty pillow in his bedroom. They sounded like sick, depraved animals. That's what they were...animals. Nothing but grunting, slobbering animals.

He was so glad to have finally gotten his own place away from his domineering mother. She was always cross. She was never nice to him. She always beat him for no reason. She was a bitch.

Just like his boss.

She's just like Mother. If I didn't need my job, I'd flatten her pug face even more than it already is. Knock her into the next century. Maybe what she needs was a taste of Don Juan's magic touch.

He shuttered.

God, what a horrible thought! No way would I ever touch that woman. That's disgusting! It would be like touching Mother. Never would I touch anyone like Mother.

Women. They were all the same. They eventually turned on him. Casting aspersions on him. Making him feel less of a man.

But not like Jenny.

She was special.

Even the others he had seduced didn't compare to the beautiful, redheaded Jennifer Tully.

He would have her again.

Soon.

Very soon, Jenny. Very soon.

He smiled, dumped his pipe tobacco out the window, and drove away into the night, giggling. He had to prepare himself. He wanted to look good for his second date with Jenny.

Chapter Fourteen

Getting dressed for work, Angelo stood in front of a full length mirror, buttoning her shirt and adjusting the weapon on her hip. Sam came up behind her. She turned to face him, leaning down and kissing him on the top of his head. He was back in his chair, only able to do short stretches of standing without assistance. But at least he could stand. She was thankful for that.

"I'll miss you," he told her.

"Me too."

"Be careful out there. You know how much I worry about you."

"Aren't I always careful, Sam?"

"Sometimes I wonder."

"No need to worry tonight, I've got a ton of paperwork to get through. I won't be leaving the unit until the morning when I can gets some interviews done at a respectful time."

"That puts my mind at ease. At least for tonight."

"Well, while you're at ease, I'll be getting cranky from a paper headache."

Looking at his watch, Sam said, "You're going in awful early."

"I promised Jenny I'd stop by her house before I went to work tonight."

"You're driving all the way up to the Northeast and then driving all the way back down town? Why don't you just see her in the morning?"

"I won't have time. I have interviews in the morning and she's going back to work. Sam, I promised I'd do it tonight."

"Okay. Just remember that you have to give her some space."

"I know, I know. I am. I'm just making sure she'll be all right to go to work tomorrow. She asked me to come by."

"Fine. Just be her friend, not a cop."

"I am her friend, that's why I'm going to see her. I've pretty much given up getting her to report it. However, I won't give up getting her some professional help."

He pulled her face closer to his and kissed her. He could taste toothpaste and mouthwash. "I better let you go."

"Bye, Sam. I'm taking the Lexus. It's going to snow again."

"Sure." She exited the bedroom, was down the stairs and out the door in less than a minute. It was still early enough to catch Jenny at home before she went to bed. She promised herself that she wouldn't stay long and give Jenny the time and space she needed to recover.

Driving from Mt. Airy to the Northeast was a task in itself, but it didn't help with the weather being as bad as it had been recently. It was cold out. Not bitter, but crisp. Perfect snow conditions. The flurries started to fall half way through her journey up the Roosevelt Boulevard. The windshield wiper blades of the Lexus did their best to keep up with the amount of falling snow.

Flurries my foot, Angelo thought. *There's a blizzard coming.*

Angelo's cell phone beeped. Sitting at a red light, she glanced at the beeping phone. Low battery. It would be dead in minutes. Darn it! She left her car charger in the Toyota. She'd have to charge it at work. Turning it off, she tossed it in the glove box. She didn't need it right then. She rarely used it anyway. It was only for emergencies.

What possible trouble could she get into?

***

He decided tonight was the night he would visit Jenny again. She was alone. He knew that she was always alone. She hadn't had any visitors for the last two days. He knew. He had been watching, getting himself psyched up for their date. It had been way too long. He missed her and would be returning soon. He was her conquering hero—her knight in shining armor—returning from war. That was his fantasy for tonight.

Every light in the house was on. That would not do at all. The first thing he had to do was cut the power. She couldn't see his face. He preferred to remain anonymous. It would ruin everything. It was all part of the fantasy.

Creeping around the back of the house, he found the phone box and the electrical wiring going into the basement. He cut the phone lines first. He didn't want any interruptions. He would have to pull the fuse for the electricity from inside the basement.

Jenny had an outdoor deck in the back. Perfect. Like Romeo, he would climb up to her second floor window and meet his Juliet. He climbed the fence and pulled himself to her second floor deck. The door to the deck was locked, but it was ineffective. He easily opened it and slid inside the back room.

Jenny used the room as an office. She had wall-to-wall shelves lined with law books as well as a desk and a computer in the room. Neat and orderly, just like Jenny. He made his way over to the closed door.

He could hear a shower running. *Ah, she was preparing for his visit. All the better.* He went down the hall, passing the bathroom door on the way down stairs. He went into the basement and found the fuse box by the back door. Opening the gray box, he pulled the main fuse. The house went black.

From the basement, he could hear Jenny turn off the water to her shower. He waited for her in the living room. She would be down shortly. He rubbed his hands in anticipation, smiling and lighting his pipe.

Upstairs, Jenny was in a panic. The sudden darkness frightened her. Wrapping a towel around herself, she went into her bedroom and fumbled for the telephone in the dark room. Picking up the handset, she dialed 911 and listened to the silence. It took her a moment to realize that there was no dial tone.

A wave of nausea hit her. She kept a flashlight in the kitchen. She needed to go down into the basement and check the fuse box. Maybe it was just a power outage from the storm. A pole may have come down on the wires, knocking out the phone and electricity. It happened all the time. It was nothing but her panicking imagination. Nothing at all. Putting on a robe and a pair of slippers, she felt her way down the steps, bumping into furniture along the way.

"It's nothing. It's nothing," she told herself.

She went into the living room and stopped, looking out the window. The lights across the street were still on. It wasn't a power outage after all. It was just her house that was having the power failure. She needed to find a flashlight. Moving toward the kitchen, she halted when she smelled it. Warning bells inside her head were going off at full blast.

Pipe tobacco.

Just my imagination, she thought. *Someone must be smoking next door. It's just seeping though the walls.*

However, the smell was too strong to be coming from the neighbor's house. Besides, they were still on vacation. Someone was smoking in her house. She became alarmed and backed away toward the front door. She didn't care that she was wearing nothing but a robe. She needed to get out of the house. Get out now. Run to the neighbor's house. Call the police. Call Angelo.

Moving silently toward her only way of escape, she ran into something solid. It wasn't a piece of furniture. It was a very large human being. Nearly frozen in fear, Jenny turned to face her monster. She looked at his face. He was wearing a full ski mask this time. She could only make out his eyes. He had cold, soulless eyes. The devil's eyes.

"Hello, Jenny. I'm home," he cooed in her ear.

Jenny stifled a scream that rose in her throat. She remembered that he would become violent if she resisted. She had to remain calm and passive if she wanted to survive this.

"Hello," she responded in a small voice.

"Did you miss me?"

She did not, could not, reply.

"I missed you." He leaned closer and kissed her face. Taking a deep breath, he inhaled her clean scent.

Jenny cringed inside. *Oh, God, no.*

"I asked you if you missed me." His tone had a harsh edge to it. He was getting angry.

"Y—yes," she stammered. *Just let me survive this,* she prayed. She decided to play along as long as she could until the opportunity to escape presented itself.

"I knew you would."

"What...what do you want?"

"Another date."

"I don't even know your name. Tell me your name."

"You can call me Don." He kissed her again. It took every ounce of will power she had not to bolt from him.

"Okay, Don. Would you mind if I got some light on in here? I'm afraid of the dark." She tried to move away from him, to get to the kitchen and a weapon, but he yanked her back by the arm. He pulled her into his body. She could feel his arousal.

"No, I prefer the dark."

Oh, God. Help me!

"Let's go upstairs. We'll be more comfortable," he suggested, pulling her along with him. She did not dare resist.

* * *

Angelo pulled up in front of Jenny's house. *Why are all the lights out?* she wondered. Surely she hadn't gone to bed so early. Jenny knew she was going to be stopping by to see her tonight. She reached for her cell phone, but remembered it was dead.

Getting out of the car, she walked up the front path. She noticed a set of footprints in the snow. The snow had been falling fast, but not fast enough to cover them completely. They were made maybe a half an hour ago.

She followed the fading but large, definitely male footprints. They did not go up to the front door, but around the back. Something was definitely amiss. Tracking them to the rear yard, she spied the phone box, its wires cut.

"Oh, damn!"

The footprints ended at the fence. Angelo looked around to see it they backtracked, but they did not. Looking up, she could see the door ajar on the second floor deck. She had to get up there. Climbing the fence, she pulled herself up and onto the deck. She peered into the darkened room. *If only I had*

127

a lousy flashlight! My kingdom for a flashlight.

Pulling her firearm, she opened the door and crept inside. In the pitch black darkness, she made her way over to the door. She leaned an ear to the door, listening. She could hear voices across the hall. A man's voice and a very frightened woman's.

Slowly opening the door, praying it wouldn't squeak and alert them, she moved down the hall toward the voices. She could smell tobacco. He was here. She knew it—and damn it—so was Jennifer. Fearing that Jenny would be hurt in the crossfire if she used her weapon, she secured it. She was equally dangerous without it.

She moved closer to the door and listened at the master bedroom. She could hear Jenny trying to talk to her assailant. He seemed to be getting impatient with her stalling.

"On the bed, now!" he ordered. Angelo could hear Jenny being tossed down on the bed, its mattress springs creaking.

She tried the door, but found it locked.

Now! Angelo thought as she kicked in the bedroom door.

She crashed inside, taking both Jenny and the man by surprise. He jumped up as Angelo charged him. He was as solid as a rock. It was like running into a brick wall. Angelo was not a small woman by any standard, having more muscle than fat on her lean body, but he swatted her away with a backhand.

Rolling away from the punch, she charged him again. Jenny screamed. The man was quicker than Angelo anticipated and he hurled the bedside lamp at her. She ducked, but it glanced off her shoulder.

He jumped over the bed and out the door. Angelo was about to chase after him, but tripped over Jenny.

"Bee!" she wailed.

Angelo stopped a moment to check on her friend. "Jen, are you all right?" she asked.

"Yes. He didn't...didn't have the chance to do anything to me."

"Good. I'm going after him."

"No!" Jenny shouted, grabbing her hand.

"Jenny, let go!" she shouted, pulling away from Jenny's grasp. He had at least a thirty second head start on her. Angelo ran after him, taking the stairs four at a time. The front door was wide open. She ran out the door and noticed the footprints in the snow heading toward the street. She followed them. He was running toward the park.

Pennypack Woods was part of Fairmount Park, one of the largest park systems in the world.

"Damn it!" She'd never be able to find him in the thick woods if she didn't catch up, but she was going to try. Running into the park's entrance, she followed the bike path for about a hundred yards. The tracks he made vanished into the woods. Angelo's gut told her that he was lurking around somewhere.

Suddenly a huge form rushed at Angelo, slamming into her and making her drop the gun in the deep snow. Like an enraged bull, he charged her again and she lost her balance, slipping on a patch of ice. She tripped headlong into a tree, striking her skull on the nearly petrified wood of a Sycamore.

She was stunned, but not out cold. She could feel blood trickling into her eye. She lay there, deciding to play possum. She hoped he'd come a little closer. He didn't disappoint. He moved in cautiously toward her unmoving body.

Who is this beautiful Angel? he asked himself. *Who are you?* The woods were dark and there wasn't enough light in the park to get a good look at her. He wondered if he had seen her somewhere before. He just had to get closer. He needed to see her face.

Come on. Come in a little closer so I can see your face, you bastard, she thought. She needed to get that ski mask off.

"Not a bad looking creature. Not a redhead, but she might do. I ought to make you pay for interrupting my date with Jennifer. You just had to spoil everything. Maybe it was time I spoiled your fun." He bent over her and reached out his hand, touching her face.

Her skin crawled.

He was taken by surprise when her foot shot up and kicked him in the groin. She missed what she intended, her aim impeded by the bump to the head, but the shot was just as effective. He yelped, cursed her, and jumped back.

"Bitch!" he shouted, doubled over.

Angelo rolled and jumped to her feet, preparing for a fight. He had never seen a woman move so fast and be so aggressive. Her fists went up in an offensive position. She took a step forward, trying to snatch the ski mask off his head. She missed; her balance and depth perception were now affected by the blow to the skull. She wasn't going to let him know that she was seriously injured and she bellowed out a ferocious battle cry.

He immediately saw that she wasn't down for the count like he thought and decided to flee. She was injured and he probably could have taken her in a fight. However, he couldn't risk losing and her seeing his face. Running into the woods, he vanished from her sight.

She was about to take off in pursuit, but a wave of dizziness hit her. The bump on the head was more severe than she first thought. The world was spinning. She steadied herself by holding on to the offending tree. Raising her hand to her head, she wiped the blood out of her eye and looked down at her bloodstained hand. Head wounds were always messy.

"That's gonna leave a mark," she grumbled to herself, wiping the blood off on her jacket.

After finding her gun, she secured it and limped back to Jenny's house.

129

The front door was still open, letting in the snow. She found Jenny sitting on the living room couch, her head in her hands. She was crying. Looking up when she heard Angelo return, she stood and ran over to her.

Clasping Angelo to her chest, she said, "Oh, Bee! Thank God you're all right! Did you catch him?" Seeing the blood on her face and coat, Jenny gasped.

"No, he got away," Angelo grumbled.

"You're bleeding."

"It's nothing. Are you okay?"

"Yes. Yes," she replied, touching Angelo's temple. Angelo winced at the pain.

"We have to call the police."

"No. Please, Bee, not now. I can't do it right now."

"Fine, but you're coming back to my place. When we get there, you're going to talk to someone."

Jenny did not reply.

Angelo made her pack a few personal items and then drove Jenny back to her home in Mt. Airy. She would have to call work and tell them that she was running late. A family emergency. She'd be in later.

Damn him, she thought, touching the side of her head. *Now it's personal!*

* * *

As Sam typed away at his next novel, his thoughts were interrupted by someone entering the house and deactivating the alarm. Only he and his wife had the code. What was she doing home? Something was very wrong. He wheeled himself out of the office and down the hall.

"Bernadette!" he called.

"In the living room," she replied.

He entered the living room and spotted Angelo squatting down next to Jenny who looked visibly shaken. "What's going on?"

Angelo turned around and Sam saw the blood on her face. She could see in his shocked expression that she must have looked worse than she felt.

"What happened?" he asked. "Your face, Bee!"

She put her hand to her head. The blood was dried, but the cut above her left eye was very noticeable. "Nothing," she told him.

"Don't you *dare* tell me that's nothing, Bernadette!"

Jenny jumped at his tone. He saw that he was frightening her and lowered his voice.

"I'm sorry, Sam, it's my fault Bee got hurt," Jennifer said.

"Nonsense!" Angelo scolded.

Sam gave Angelo his patented '*We're going to talk about this later*' look. "I'll go and get the first aid kit," he said, turning and going to the kitchen where he kept the medical supplies.

Angelo moved over to the telephone and called the unit. She informed them that she was running late and inquired if Thompson was there yet. They told her that she was also running late. After she hung up, she called Thompson at home. There was no answer, so she called her cell phone.

"Hello?" Thompson said. Angelo could tell that she was on the road. Angry honkers could be heard in the background.

"Where are you?"

"Just getting on the Boulevard. I'm heading into work. Why?"

"Get over to my house now."

"But..."

"Now, Sue, I have an emergency. Bring your 48 book and interview record paperwork."

"My 48 book? Bee, what's going on?"

"I'll explain later." She gave Thompson her home address. "You got that? It's not hard to find."

"Okay. I'll be there in fifteen to twenty minutes if I can get out of this traffic...Move it, dummy!" she shouted crossly at a crawling motorist.

"Drive carefully. I'll see you in a few. Thanks."

"No problem."

Angelo hung up the phone as Sam entered the room, holding the first aid kit. "Sit down," he ordered.

"But Jenny needs...."

"Bee, let him take care of you. I'm fine," Jenny said. "I'm not the one who's hurt."

"Fine," Angelo growled and sat down. Still feeling a little shaky, she was relieved to get off her feet.

"Want to tell me what the hell happened?" Sam queried.

"I ran into a tree."

He could tell that wasn't all that happened. "And?"

"The tree won." Not so gently, he dabbed the cut with an alcohol swab. "Ouch! That hurt!" she shouted at him, jerking away.

"Sit still and it won't hurt so much," he told her. He finished cleaning the dried blood with a warm washcloth. It looked worse that it really was. She would be needing stitches. "You should go to the hospital, Bernadette."

"No hospitals. I'm fine. Nothing a few aspirins won't take care of."

"Stubborn, pigheaded woman!" he said hotly.

"It's just a little cut, Sam."

"Have you seen it?"

"Yes. I just skimmed the tree, that's all. It's a good thing I have a hard head," she tried to joke. He was not amused.

"Hard headed is right. Did you lose consciousness at any time?"

"I'm still here, aren't I? No, I was awake the whole time."

He got out a butterfly stitch and stuck it to the wound. "You're going to have a black eye."

"It's not the first and it probably won't be the last."

"Here." He handed her an ice pack. "Put that on. It'll help keep the swelling down."

She put the ice pack up to her eye. "Ow!"

"Now are you going to tell me what happened tonight?"

It was no use keeping it from him. He was going to hound her until she told him the whole story. Looking at him with one eye, she said, "I interrupted Don. He broke into Jenny's house."

He turned toward Jenny. "Jesus. Jenny, are you okay? Do you need a doctor?"

"No, I'm fine. Nothing happened. Bee got there in time."

"Well, thank God for small favors. What happened after?"

"I chased him into Pennypack woods. He jumped me from behind. I tripped and hit my noggin on a tree."

"Are you sure you didn't lose consciousness? Even for a second?"

"I'm positive. I played possum. I wanted him to come closer so I could grab the mask and see the bastard's face."

"He didn't touch you, did he?" he asked angrily. The thought of another man touching his wife made him see red. Anger boiled inside of him.

"No, Sam, he didn't."

"You shouldn't have gone after him alone. Where was your backup?"

"My cell was dead. I had to make a decision. I chose to go in."

"You could have been seriously hurt or worse."

"So could Jenny have been if I hadn't gotten to her in time."

"He could have raped you too!"

"He didn't and I didn't get hurt. So stop worrying about what could have been."

Sam couldn't reply. It was just no use arguing with her. She was infuriating. If she had hit her head harder than she actually did, God only knew what the monster could have done to her. "We are going to talk about this later, Bernadette."

"Okay, Sam, okay. Later. I need to talk to Jenny first."

Looking at Jenny, Sam decided it was best if they didn't fight in front of her. She was already upset enough. "I'll go make some tea."

"Thanks, Sam. Do me a favor and unlock the front door. Thompson should be here in a few minutes."

"Why?"

"Because Jenny is going to make an official report to Officer Thompson from Special Victims."

"Bee, I…"

"You are, damn it!" Angelo shouted. No more pussyfooting around with Jenny. She had to get tough. It was for her own good. "I've had it! You *will* report this assault and you *will* report the prior rape! You *will* tell Officer Thompson what happened!"

Jenny lowered her face into her hands and started to cry.

"I'll go make that tea," Sam said.

Chapter Fifteen

Thompson pulled up in front of Angelo's address. She was awed by the immense size of the home. *This can't be the right place. It's not a house, it's a castle,* she thought. She looked at the paper in her hand and read the address again. Spotting the mailbox, she read the name on it. The Marshalls. It was the correct location.

Grabbing her 48 book and interview form, she wondered why Angelo had ordered her to bring them. She got out of the car and walked to the massive front door. She stabbed her finger on the doorbell and Angelo's voice came over the intercom.

"Is that you, Thompson?"

"Yeah."

"Door's open. Come in and make a left in the foyer. We're in the living room."

"Oh, okay."

Thompson turned the brass knob and entered the spacious foyer. Looking at the dozens of landscape painting, she couldn't help but be reminded of a museum. It was like walking into the Philadelphia Museum of Art on the Parkway. Remembering that she was here on official business, she tore herself away from the art and turned left.

She found Angelo in the living room, her back to her, sitting with another woman Thompson assumed was Jennifer Tully. "Detective?"

Angelo stood up and turned around.

"Jesus, Bee! What happened to your face?" Thompson exclaimed.

"Tell you later. Come over here."

Thompson went over to the women. Jenny wouldn't look at her. "Hello," she said to her.

"Jenny, this is Officer Thompson from Special Victims."

"Sue. You can call me Sue."

"She's handling your case."

Jenny looked up and daggers at Angelo. She saw hurt and a little anger in her eyes.

That's right, be angry. Be angry with him.

Thompson, seeing Jenny's distress, sat down next to her so she could look her in the face and not hover over her. She wanted to give Jennifer some personal space. She pulled out her pen and the interview record form. "Ms. Tully, you can trust me."

Jenny turned toward Thompson, but still did not look her in the eye. She was mortified. She felt that Angelo betrayed her trust.

"I know this is difficult. Ms. Tully, it has to be done. It's not just for your sake, but also for every other woman out there. No one is safe until he is permanently put away." Thompson turned her head when she heard someone else enter the room.

"Tea is ready," Sam said.

Looking at the man, Thompson smiled. He was even more handsome than the picture on the dust jackets of his novels. *Well, I'll be. Angelo really is married to Sam Marshall.*

You must be Officer Thompson. Bee's told me all about you," he said, putting the tray on the coffee table. He wheeled himself over to her and offered his hand. Shaking it, Thompson felt weak in the knees. It was a good thing she was sitting down at that very moment.

"Yeah—yes, yes. Hello," she stammered.

Angelo grinned to herself at Thompson's reaction. Sam had that effect on women. Hell, he had that effect on her too.

"I'll leave you ladies alone. Bee, I'll be in my office."

"Thanks, Sam," Angelo said.

Thompson sighed as he vanished from sight. Angelo snapped her fingers at the young officer to get her attention. "Oh!" Turning her attention back to Jenny, she said, "Okay, where were we?"

"Jenny is going to make an official report," Angelo told her.

"Bee, I'm not sure about this. I'm not ready."

"Yes you are. Talk to Thompson. She'll understand."

Looking at the officer, Jenny replied, "How could she?"

"Ms. Tully, I do understand your pain and fear."

"I know you mean well, but I'm sure you don't, Officer."

Angelo wandered over to the fireplace and leaned against it. She could feel its warmth heat her chilled and bruised body. She wanted to give Jenny some space to talk to Officer Thompson. Holding the ice pack to her eye, she listened to Thompson, wanting to observe her technique.

"I do. I understand all too well."

Jenny glared at her, unbelieving. "No offense, Officer Thompson, but you're just a baby. How could you? You don't look as if you've been on the job that long. What are you, about twenty?" If Jenny's intentions were to insult or frustrate Thompson into going away, it did not work.

"Twenty-five, actually," she replied matter-of-factly. "And, no, I haven't been on the job long."

"Well, then..."

"But I do know what it's like to be raped. It happened to me. It was a few years ago, but it is like it happened yesterday."

Angelo's hand slowly came down off her face at the revelation. She figured something was bothering Thompson, but had no idea what troubled her. Surprise was written on her face. "Jesus," Angelo mumbled to herself.

"You?" Jennifer said.

"Yes. It happened when I was a freshman in college. As you said, I was just a baby."

"I'm sorry."

"Why? There is no need to feel sorry for me. I only wish I had done something about it then. Like you, I didn't want anyone to know. I didn't want to have the stigma of being a victim. I regret it everyday. He got away with it and he probably did it to someone else."

Jenny was silent, and so was Angelo.

Thompson needed to tell her story. "I just turned eighteen and was at a frat party. I had no business being there. I shouldn't have been drinking at my age. But you know how college kids are. You just can't tell them anything. I was finally free of my parents. I was on my own for the first time in my life and I wanted to make the most of it. I was—so I thought—an adult, who could make adult decisions. I thought I could take care of myself. Of course, I had to learn the hard way that I wasn't so grown up."

She paused, putting down the incident report she had tightly clutched in her hand on the table. She rubbed her eyes with her hand. Angelo noticed that it was shaking slightly.

"I never told anyone what happened—not my parents, not my teachers and certainly not the police. I didn't even tell Angelo. I was ashamed. I know in my mind that I shouldn't have been, but in my heart, I just felt like dirt. I shouldn't have been ashamed, just like you shouldn't be ashamed."

Quietly Jenny said, "I'm sorry."

"You didn't do anything to me. You didn't do anything to think you caused what happened to you either. It was not your fault. Let me tell you what happened to me. Maybe it'll help you believe that I will understand how you feel."

"Officer Thompson, you don't have to."

"No, I need to tell you. I need to tell someone. I have to get it off my chest, off my soul."

She took Jenny's silence as a go-ahead.

"I was invited to a frat party by a senior who I thought was a nice guy. Nice guy, my ass! He was handsome and charming. I thought he liked me. I certainly liked him, but I found out later that I was just another conquest. A bet. Can you believe that? A lousy bet with his pals. To him, I was just another notch on his bedpost.

"He asked me to the party. Me, like the silly girl I was, was flattered. I said, sure that sounds like fun. He gave me beer after beer and I got wasted. Worse than wasted. I didn't know if I was coming or going. To this day I can't even look at the stuff. I get sick just smelling it."

In a far away voice she said, "Wasted. So wasted. I felt sick. He told me to go upstairs and sleep it off in his room. He told me no one would bother me there. I trusted him and I should have known better. You hear all kinds of stories in college. They're always warning girls never to go in a boy's room if you're drunk, but I did anyway. I remember thinking that was sweet of him to look after me like that. Maybe he really did like me. However, I found out soon enough that he had other intentions. And they weren't noble."

Thompson saw Jenny swallow hard. She stopped long enough to pour her some tea. When she saw that Jenny was ready to hear the rest, she continued with her story.

"I was sick as a dog. He was kind and gentle. He put me to bed and told me to sleep off the alcohol. He told me that he'd check on me from time to time. Oh, yeah, he would check on me all right. Him and a few of his friends."

"Oh, God," Angelo muttered under her breath. "No."

"I don't know how long I was out of it. It could have been minutes, maybe an hour. I can't be sure. All I remember was waking up with a terrible weight on me. I couldn't breathe. I thought I was suffocating. When my vision cleared, I found him on top of me, pushing himself into me. I tried to scream, but my throat was so dry it came out as a whimper. I was in so much pain. He was ripping me apart. I could hear myself crying and he covered my mouth. I could see his face over mine. I could smell his stale beer breath.

"I could hear his friends cheering him on. They were begging for a turn at bat. I'm sure they would have taken turns, but someone yelled something about the cops coming to break up the party. They scattered like the cowards they were. I ran back to my dorm room and shut myself in. I was in shock. I was scared. I couldn't believe what had just happened to me. I was angry, but I couldn't tell anyone.

"My grades suffered because I couldn't concentrate. I suffered panic attacks. I couldn't be alone and I couldn't be with people. I was a prisoner in my own body. I had to leave school because of him. I saw him everywhere I looked. I'd hear him laughing at me. He almost ruined my life. I swore I'd never find myself in that position again. I learned my lesson the hard way.

"I thought for a long time that I'd never be whole again, but I was wrong. It made me stronger. I joined the department hoping to save others because I couldn't save myself. I want to make them pay for what the one who got away did to me. I intend to make the man who attacked you pay. Can you trust me to do that?"

"Yes."

"Tell me what happened to you that night."

They spent the better part of an hour talking. Jenny told Thompson much more than she was willing to tell Angelo. Thompson hung on every word. She did not interrupt or judge Jenny in any way. She was compassionate and loving. She wrote everything down, word for word, on the interview record.

Angelo was impressed with how the young officer was able to put Jenny's fears to rest. Jenny opened up to her. They were kindred spirits. She had a lot more information about Don Juan than she thought she did. She would be a great help to the investigation.

Jenny was drained both physically and emotionally by the time they were finished. However, she admitted she felt a lot better. She was finally free from the burden and no longer feared judgment.

Angelo sent her off to bed, telling her that she could stay as long as she needed. Even if that meant until they caught him. She and Sam and also Officer Thompson would be there if she needed anything. She would be safe there. Jenny thanked Angelo and Thompson for their help and understanding.

Thompson looked wiped out herself. Angelo knew it was hard for her to do what she did, but she was proud of her. It took a lot of guts to survive her ordeal. She did the department proud. Thompson was a trooper. However, she probably wasn't going to like what was going to happen next.

Finishing her tea, Thompson said, "Jen mentioned that she was at Maddie's the night she was attacked."

"Yes, I heard. I remember that night she told me she felt responsible because she had a few too many drinks."

"That had nothing to do with it," she said defensively.

"That's what I said to her. Rape is rape, drunk or sober."

"Maybe there is a connection between the bar and the coffee house."

"Perhaps," she said, rubbing the cut above her eye. "We'll keep that in mind." She paused before speaking. "Sue, I don't know what..."

She knew what Angelo wanted to say, but she didn't want pity. "Forget about it, Bee. It's ancient history."

Angelo knew, in Susan's mind, it was still very much in the present, but she would speak no more about it. "Okay."

"So, now what?"

"We're going to SVU. We have to give Officer Seymour your interview."

"What? Why?"

"Because it's part of his investigation now."

"But…"

"It's procedure."

"It's not fair. I don't see him giving me anything."

"Sue, you've just proved to me that you are a professional. Don't spoil it."

"Fine," she huffed.

"Look, Seymour needs all the information, whether he gets it on his own or you help him out. We need to catch this son of a bitch. It would be wrong to keep this from him. It would be a violation of police procedure. Remember you're a cop first."

"You're right. I'm sorry. He just burns my ass."

"Get used to it."

***

The Special Victims Unit was a madhouse with people running around like chickens without their heads. Angelo and Thompson were nearly knocked down by a rushing officer as they walked in the door. "Oh, sorry," he said and continued down the hall.

"What's going on?" Thompson asked.

"Beats me."

"Speaking of beatings, your eye looks better. I told you a little cover-up would hide most of it."

Touching the butterfly stitch Sam put there earlier, she said, "Yeah, thanks."

They found Officer Seymour barking out orders as if he was a general or something. He didn't see Angelo approach. She tugged on the back of his shirt a few times before she got a response.

"What!" he snapped, turning around. "Oh, Detective Angelo." His sight zeroed onto the cut above her eye. "What happened to you? Get into a fight and walk into someone's fist?" he snickered.

"A tree," she said flatly.

"Did the tree win?" he laughed, but immediately regretted it when the glare he received bored into him. He cleared his throat. "What can I do for you? We're a bit busy at the moment."

"Make time. We have something important to show you."

He looked at Thompson's face. She didn't look happy. "Okay, what?"

"Thompson, give him the 48 and interview record." When Thompson didn't make a move, Angelo exclaimed, *"God, you two are like children!* Give it to him."

Grudgingly, Thompson handed it to him.

"What's this?"

"Complainant number six. The one before Victoria Sterling."

"Excuse me?"

"Just read the report," Angelo huffed. She didn't have time for his bull crap.

He looked at the report Thompson gave him and read it. "Holy shit!" He glared at Thompson. "You knew about this!" he said, pointing a finger at her accusingly.

Angelo spoke up, defending Thompson. "That was my doing. It's a long, complicated story. The victim took some persuading to report this. You should be happy that Thompson got her to open up. This is valuable information," she said, slapping the folder in his hands.

He read the interview. When he got to the part about the second attack, he looked at Angelo, understanding how she received the knot on her head. He suddenly felt bad for the comment he made earlier.

"Where is the victim now?"

"The complainant is...in seclusion. She will not talk to you. She told us that. All the information you need is in Thompson's report."

"Good work, Thompson," he said.

Thompson raised an eyebrow. *What was that? A compliment?*

"You need to get Mobile Crime out to her house and process the scene. I secured it for now. Here is the key." She handed Jenny's house key to him.

"I'll get right on it."

"Tell me what is happening on your end."

"Oh, big news. I was going to call you later with this."

"Sure. Well?"

"We ran those names you gave us from the coffee house. Josh Brady is a creepy little man. A good suspect."

"Really?"

"He has a stalking and assault record."

"Sexual?"

"Well, no, but his profile suggests that it wouldn't be too hard to make that leap. He's clever. He may have learned from his mistakes."

"Maybe."

"We're setting up surveillance on him. The guy actually lives with his mother. How sad is that? He'll be watched twenty-four seven. When he slips up, we'll be there."

"What about the other guy the manager mentioned?"

"Stephen Greystock? No wants and no record. Model employee. From what I'm told, he's also a momma's boy."

"You know, momma's boys could be sexual predators too," Thompson said. "In fact, a lot of serial killers turn out to be momma's boys. It's a statistic, you know."

"Not this one. I spoke to the assistant manager and employees at the café. They all think he's gay or something."

"You shouldn't just assume things about people's sexual orientation."

"I've got a feeling."

"Did you check juvenile records?"

"They are sealed. Look, I'm almost positive that Josh is our boy."

"Okay. Keep me informed. Be careful not to tip him off to us. Are you going to put an officer in the café?"

"No. We didn't want to put an unfamiliar face in there. If he's spotted, Josh might bolt. He'll tail him from a distance."

"All right. Good work, Seymour."

His chest swelled with pride. "Thank you, Detective Angelo. Coming from you, that is a great compliment."

Suck up, Thompson thought wickedly.

"We'll be back at Homicide if you come up with anything."

"Right."

Thompson glared at Seymour one last time before Angelo pulled her out by the arm. "You think Golden Boy has the right man?"

"I don't know. We'll see. Come on, we have work to do and we're already several hours late."

They drove back to Homicide. It was time to check on O'Malley's progress. Angelo was sure her partner would come up with more than Seymour could ever hope to. O'Malley knew how to get into juvenile records. He was a fine detective.

***

"Where's O'Malley?" Angelo asked the sergeant.

One look at Angelo's face and he restrained from commenting on the injury. The sergeant pointed to the coffee station. Angelo looked over and spotted O'Malley stuffing another doughnut into his mouth. *He really needs to cut down on his sugar intake,* she mused.

"Thanks."

Making her way through the crowded room, she stalked up to her partner. He removed the doughnut from his mouth when he saw her approaching. "What the hell happened to you?"

"The next person who asks me that is going to have a matching bandage."

He shrugged his shoulders. "Thompson, you shouldn't go around hitting detectives," he teased.

Thompson opened her mouth to deny the accusation, and then closed it when she realized he was joking.

"Did you run those names?"

"Yes I did. Very interesting group. Mostly professionals and office workers. The gentlemen you singled out were the most interesting."

"Seymour said that only Josh had a hit."

"He did. He's got a violence against women record, but he's been clean for a while. He's in therapy for anger management."

"What about Greystock?"

"No adult record. However..." he said, looking around. "I found some interesting things in his juvenile record."

"I thought those were sealed," Thompson said.

"Shhh, they are," he whispered to the rookie. "Doesn't mean you can't get at them."

"Oh."

"So?" Angelo prompted.

"As a boy, he didn't have much of a home life. Abusive mother. Did poorly in school. Bounced around the state. Got in trouble a few times for fighting, although he was usually on the receiving end. Apparently, he was a ninety-eight pound weakling. Got thumped a lot in school."

"Doesn't make him a killer."

"No. However, he did try to assault some girl. He was only fourteen. He didn't hurt her, but he was sent to a mental hospital for a while. They cured him of his hostility. There has been nothing since. The assault was expunged from the record. I saw his juvie photo. He was a skinny little runt back then. I'll have to pull his BMV records to get an adult photo."

"What about Kevin McPherson?"

"Funny you should mention him."

"Why?"

"Because he has a history."

"Do tell."

"Dug into his criminal background..."

"He has one? What a surprise."

"Are you gonna let me finish or are you gonna keep up the witty sarcasm?"

"Sorry, he just rubs me the wrong way."

"Well, you know what they say about first impressions."

"Okay, all the sarcasm is gone. So what about him?"

"Well, as I was saying before I was so rudely interrupted, he has several private criminal complaints from women for harassment on him and a few *Stay Away* orders in effect."

"Any stalking charges?"

"No."

"Anything else?"

"He also has an aggravated assault charge on record."

"Really? Against a woman?"

"No, actually, a man. Seems our boy was a bouncer in some strip joint on Delaware Avenue. Beat the crap out of some guy. Wasn't really a fair fight. The victim was in his sixties and a little bit of a thing."

"The charge stick?"

"Nah. The victim never showed up for court. Case was dismissed. No victim, no case for the state, no crime."

"Hmm, intriguing."

"Now, you're going to love this part. I had a gut feeling about something. When I checked to see who filed the harassment complaints I was thinking that maybe one of the other victims was the complainant."

Angelo raised an eyebrow. "And were any?"

"No. Then I compared *all* the names from the list the manager from the café gave you. There were three women who frequent the café who did."

"Good job, Pat. Could you talk to these women and find out their stories?"

"Already did. They all pretty much said the same thing. That he's an arrogant son of a bitch who needed to get a life. The harassment stopped after the complaints were filed."

"Did any of them fear him?"

"I didn't get that impression. They seemed more insulted than afraid."

"Why?"

"Because he tried to turn it around on them. Told the judge that they were after him 'because he's so god damn good looking'. His quote, not mine."

Angelo laughed.

"He told them that they weren't worth pursuing anymore."

"It's a wonder he can get through a door with a head that big."

"Do you want him on the short list?"

"You know it. We'll keep that option open for now. Thanks, Pat, you're the best."

He smiled. "I know." He turned to Thompson. "How you doing, Sue? You look just as beat as Angelo. Only you're prettier at the moment. Not all lumped up."

"Shut up, Pat," Angelo said.

Angelo pulled Thompson away from O'Malley and back over to her desk. "So, now what?"

"We'll see how Seymour handles Josh's surveillance."

"Seymour," Thompson said bitterly. An idea struck her like a bolt of lightning. "Hey, Bee, I have an idea."

"What's that?" Angelo asked, shuffling through her paperwork.

"How about I go undercover at the café. I can get a red wig..."

Angelo's head shot up sharply, causing a wave of pain in her eye. "Are you out of your freaking mind!"

"No, Bee. Think about it. If I can get his attention and get him to notice me, maybe he'll come after me instead of some other woman. We'll be able to catch him in the act."

"Let me repeat myself, Sue. Are you totally out of you mind?"

"But..."

"But, nothing! You will not put yourself in harm's way. You will not set yourself up as a target."

"Bee, I am an adult. A police officer, trained and unafraid to face danger. I know how to handle myself. I won't put myself in danger."

"Yeah, like at the frat house," she said, but immediately regretted it. Pain and hurt hit Thompson's face.

"It's not like that," she said quietly.

"I'm sorry. I shouldn't have said that. I'm just being protective."

"I was a kid. I was drunk. It won't happen again."

"How can you be sure?"

"I just am."

"Sue, no. I'm pulling rank. I'm ordering you not to even think about doing that."

"Just a suggestion."

"Well, forget about it. No arguments."

"Fine," Thompson said.

Angelo looked at her and thought, *You'd better get that thought right out of your head, Officer!*

Thompson was thinking something else.

* * *

Leaving Thompson at the unit, O'Malley and Angelo paid a visit to the bar on Frankford Avenue. Named after the owner's mother, Maddie's was a homey, comfortable place to hang out. Angelo could see why Victoria and her gal-pals would frequent the establishment. Although there were a few unsavory looking characters in the bar, most of the customers appeared respectable.

Angelo walked up to the bartender who was wiping down the counter with a wet rag. He was a man in his fifties with a thin build and graying hair. Speckles of gray streaked in his full beard. He didn't look up from his task when Angelo approached.

Clearing her throat, she said, "Excuse me."

"What can I get you?" he asked.

"Information. Were you working here on December eighteenth?"

"I'm here every night. I own the place. Who wants to know?" he replied, looking at her. She held up her badge and ID for his inspection.

"Detective Angelo. This is Detective O'Malley," she announced, pointing at O'Malley who had his hand in the pretzel bowl. He waved casually at the bartender.

"I run a clean operation," he said defensively.

"I see. Very nice place, Mr…"

"Ford. Joe Ford." Her appreciation of his bar seemed to calm his ire. Even to suggest that he didn't run a clean pub was an insult to him. She wrote down his name on her legal pad. "What do you want information about?"

"Have you ever seen this gentleman in here?" she asked, placing a photo of Ben Moody on the counter. She pushed it toward him. "Around the eighteenth?"

He snorted. "Yeah, but I wouldn't call him a gentleman."

"Why not?"

"He was drunk and started to carry on. Had to put him and his girl out."

"What time did you put him out?"

"About midnight."

"Midnight," she repeated. "You sure?"

"Yes. I close at two. He was here a few hours. I stopped serving him when he got too obnoxious. He wasn't happy about that, but when I threatened to call the cops, he left with his girl."

"This girl got a name?"

"Never saw her before."

Angelo wondered if Ben or his girl drove home. She hoped it wasn't Ben if he was as drunk as the owner claimed he was. That in itself could have been a tragedy. Nevertheless, she wasn't there about a DUI investigation.

She showed him a picture of Josh Brady next. "How about him?"

Joe Ford studied the photo. "Nope. Don't think so. He's kind of scary. I think I'd remember him."

"You know a guy named Stephen Greystock?" she asked.

"Hmm, I don't know. Got a picture?"

"Unfortunately, no."

"Sorry, the name doesn't ring a bell," he said, shaking his head.

"How about a guy Kevin McPherson? Sorry, no photos of him either."

"Now, that name sounds familiar, but I'd have to see a photo to be sure."

Angelo stuffed the photographs back into her briefcase and came up with a few more. This time female. "You see any of these ladies here?"

Again, he studied the women's faces. "I know her," he said, tapping Victoria's picture.

"Victoria Sterling?"

"Yeah, that's her name. Lovely woman. She comes in here with her girlfriends. In fact, I believe she was in here on the eighteenth. She doesn't drink, or at least not that night. I believe it was her turn to be the designated driver. Her girlfriends, however, got pretty plastered."

"You let people get plastered?"

"Hey, I'm a responsible bar owner! I knew they had a designated driver, so I let them get as hammered as they wanted."

That was kind of you, Angelo thought sourly. "Okay, any of the others ring a bell?"

"Her," he said, pointing at a photo of Jennifer Tully. "She was in here with a few friends about a week or so ago. Boy, can she knock 'em back. I believe she lives down the block."

"And being the responsible bar owner that you are, you let her?"

"Angelo," O'Malley said mildly. He saw something in her eyes and in the tone of her voice.

"She wasn't driving. She only lives down the street," he said petulantly. "Did something happen to her?"

Yeah, you big oaf, she got raped!

"No," Angelo lied.

One of the patrons yelled at the bartender, holding up an empty beer mug. "Yo, Joey! How 'bout another?"

"In a second, Jake! Hold your horses!" he shouted back. He turned to Angelo. "Will that be all? I've got customers waiting."

"Yes. Thanks for your time, Mr. Ford." She handed him a business card. He looked at the card and saw the word *Homicide* on it.

"Homicide?" It looked like a light bulb went on in his head. "Oh, my God! The girl on the news. That Victoria?" His face paled.

"You keep running this responsible bar, Mr. Ford," Angelo said, stepping away from the counter.

Angelo had a problem with bar owners who would let someone get so drunk that they were in danger of killing someone or getting themselves killed. Drunk drivers were the worst kind of murderers. Moreover, bar owners should be held accountable. Even after an extensive personal investigation, Angelo never found out which bar the intoxicated man, who almost made her a widow, was drinking that cold, rainy night in November.

O'Malley could tell that something was troubling his partner, but he didn't bring up the subject. He knew why her husband was in a wheelchair. He knew how she was and how she would react if he stuck his nose in her business. If she wanted to talk to him, she would. They went back to the unit, leaving the bar and its *responsible* patrons.

Chapter Sixteen

Thompson was subdued the rest of the night. Angelo had her doing paperwork, typing up the handwritten interview records of Victoria Sterling's coworkers and boyfriend. Thompson was quite the little typist, rivaled only by Sam in Angelo's opinion.

She knew Thompson was unhappy that her suggestion to go undercover to catch this man was shot down. She thought Angelo didn't trust her to handle herself in a tight situation. She wanted to prove her wrong in the worst way. She wasn't a rookie. She wasn't stupid, but she was young and impulsive.

Angelo was fairly certain that Thompson would follow orders and not try anything on her own. However, she'd be keeping an eye on her anyway. She hoped that Thompson didn't think she thought differently about her because of her past. Far from it. What doesn't kill you will make you stronger.

Thompson walked over to Angelo's desk and plopped the typewritten reports on it. "All done," she said.

Angelo looked up; removing the pen she nearly chewed to pieces out of her mouth. "Thanks, Sue. I appreciate the help. I'm not the fastest typist. Now, Sam, he can type."

Thinking about Sam Marshall, Thompson grinned. "I bet he's got some great hands."

"Hey, you keep your oversexed mind off my husband!"

"Oh, you're no fun. It's hard not to. He's such a hunk." She sat down in a chair by the desk. She didn't know if she should broach the subject of Sam. Angelo seemed to keep her personal life private. "Um, Bee, why was he using a wheelchair?"

"Sam had an accident last year."

"He's okay, right?"

"He's getting better, but it wasn't looking very good at first. With therapy, he'll be fine."

"I'm sorry, I didn't know."

"That information wasn't made public. Sam didn't want people to know he was paralyzed."

"Paralyzed? Like in, can't move?"

"Yes. From the waist down."

"Bummer."

"I don't like to talk about it," she said flatly.

"Oh. I understand. You don't really know me and you don't want to talk about your personal life."

"It's not that. It's just hard to bring up the past."

"Tell me about it," she murmured. Thompson knew just how hard it was to talk about bad experiences.

Angelo took a deep breath. To Thompson's surprise, she told her anyway.

"A little over a year ago a drunk driver hit Sam's car head on while he and his agent were driving on West River Drive. His agent was killed and so was the drunk in the other car. I heard the call come over radio. I panicked when I saw the wreckage and the bloodstained sheets that covered the bodies. I thought Sam was dead too. I ended up collapsing and being rushed to the hospital. I found out later that he wasn't dead after all, thank God, but in a coma. However, he would be paralyzed. The doctor's didn't give him much hope of recovery. They didn't think he'd ever walk again."

"And now?"

"Thankfully he's proving them wrong. He can stand for very short periods of time, but he's got a lot of work and therapy before he'll ever be fully recovered. If he ever fully recovers."

"Is that hard on your marriage?"

"It was for a time, but I love Sam with all my heart. I'd never abandon him."

"Is that what love's all about?"

"Yes."

"If the doctors didn't have much hope, how did he get better?"

"Another freak accident. I'd rather call it a miracle."

"What happened?"

"When I was attacked in my home last month, Sam came to my defense."

Thompson remembered hearing the story, but not all the details were made public. It was even hushed around the department. No one wanted to talk about the incident last month. Maybe they kept it quiet for Angelo's sake.

"I was disabled by a Taser and Sam was knocked down the main stairs in the house."

"Those huge stairs in your foyer?" She recalled how grand the staircase in her home was.

"Yes, those stairs."

"Jeez."

"By some miracle, the fall freed up the nerves pressing on his spine. Sam was able to crawl up the stairs and get to me. I was almost certain I was going to die. I wasn't worry about myself because I was prepared, but when I saw Sam in the doorway of our bedroom, I feared for him. I thought for sure that Sam would be killed. A thousand thoughts raced through my brain. It's moments like that that remind us how much we really love someone. I knew I couldn't live if anything happened to him. They fought, wrestling on the floor. Sam is a strong man, but the other man had psychosis on his side. I was powerless to help. I was bound to the chair. So I do know how it feels to be defenseless. It's not a nice feeling. I never want to go through that again."

"No, it's not a nice feeling."

"Anyway, we were lucky that night, Sam got the upper hand. But I'll never take life for granted ever again and neither should you."

"I don't. I live my life without looking back."

"That's a good way to look at life, Sue. I'm only trying to protect you by nixing your undercover idea. I don't want you to get hurt. It has nothing to do with your past."

"I know that, but you have to realize that I'm not a little girl."

"I understand that, but I swore that I wouldn't let another partner get hurt."

"You're talking about Detective Ronalds, aren't you?"

"Damn it, yes."

"I'm not him."

"That doesn't stop me from worrying about you."

"Don't."

"You have a long career ahead of you. There will be plenty of opportunities to work undercover once you make detective. Just not now, okay?"

"Okay, Bee. I got that. You've made it perfectly clear."

Angelo hoped she got the message and removed all thoughts of doing something rash out of her head. "Is it?"

"Yes."

"Okay, then. There will be no more talk about it."

"Bee, I appreciate the fact that you trust me enough to talk about uncomfortable subjects."

"I'm glad you feel you can tell me yours too."

"I do."

"While you were keeping busy, doing all my typing, I checked out Maddie's. I also got a hold of Ben's mystery side-piece."

"She alibi him?"

"Yes."

"You believe her?"

"Well, yes."

"Why?"

"She was pissed when she found out he was married, but she still gave him an alibi anyway. I know I wouldn't have if it were me who found out I was just a roll in the hay while his wife was unavailable." She laughed.

"Guess not."

"The bar owner remembers Ben being there at the bar the night Victoria was attacked, but says he was there until midnight and he was with his girl."

"Victoria was attacked about eleven."

"Right."

"So Ben's off the short list?" she asked disappointed.

"For now. I also showed him a photo of Josh and, just for the hell of it, asked about Stephen and Kevin."

"And?"

"He doesn't remember seeing Josh and doesn't recall anyone named Stephen. Kevin was a maybe."

"The bar is a dead end?"

"Just because the owner didn't see or know them, doesn't mean they weren't there. Even he says he might not have noticed them if they didn't cause a problem. For argument's sake, we'll keep it in mind, but I honestly think the coffee house is the link."

"Okay." Thompson yawned, but quickly covered her mouth with her hand. "Oh, sorry. I'm tired."

Angelo looked at her watch. "Go home. The shift is over anyway. We don't have anything else to do today."

"Really? Okay, I'll see you tonight."

"Yes. Get some well earned rest."

"See ya," she said, packing her gear and leaving the unit in a hurry.

Angelo sat at her desk for a while, thinking. Rubbing her temples, she closed her eyes and made a silent prayer that everything would work out. She had a headache. The knot on her skull was pounding like a bongo drum.

Getting up, she said her goodnights to her supervisors and O'Malley, who was at the doughnut box again, and went home. She needed a couple of strong painkillers and a few hours of uninterrupted sleep. She was running on empty, not just physically, but mentally. She needed her husband. She needed Sam. He knew how to make it all better.

***

Officer Thompson did not go home right away like she told Angelo she would. Instead, she made a pit stop at a wig shop in Center City. She didn't want anyone who knew her questioning her motives. Especially other cops.

Angel of Justice

She walked into the shop, the doorbell chimed as she entered. A young girl dressed in a Gothic outfit with raven black hair and a pale complexion, looked up from her reading. She was reading a vampire novel and dreary music was emanating from the earphones she had on her head. Thompson could never understand Goth music. *No wonder those kids were depressed. Well, to each her own,* Thompson mused.

Taking the earphones off, the Goth girl smiled at her, the diamond stud through her eyebrow sparkling in the light. Thompson wondered just how many piercings the girl had. She couldn't have been any more than eighteen.

"Hey," the teen said.

"Hello," Thompson responded.

"You want something?"

"I'm looking for a wig."

"Duh, I kinda figured that out. Why else would you be in here?"

"You don't work on commission, do you?" Thompson asked slightly sarcastic. *With an attitude like that, it was a wonder.*

The girl missed the sarcasm completely. "As a matter of fact, I do. Why?"

"Never mind. I need a wig."

"Well, then you've come to the right place." She stood up and walked around the counter. She was a tiny thing, but she wore what looked like six inch heels on the leather boots that reached all the way up to her knees.

"How do you walk in those things?"

The girl smiled, showing perfect white teeth behind the black lipstick. "Practice," she said.

Thompson shook her head in amazement.

"What color?"

"Red."

"Oh, you want to be a redhead, huh?"

"Yeah."

"You've got nice hair. Why don't you just dye it?"

Thompson had to think up something fast. "Uh, my boyfriend wants to know what it's like to date a redhead. He's got a thing for red hair. Instead of worrying about him straying, I thought I'd try a wig. I'd rather not dye it."

"You know a bit of leather and handcuffs might help."

"Ah, I don't think so. That might scare him."

"That's the point."

Thompson laughed. "Say no more."

"What length?"

"A medium if you got it."

"We've got all kinds of lengths." The Goth girl pointed with short black painted fingernails, showing her a selection of red wigs. So many to choose.

"What do you recommend?"

"Depends on how real you want it to look."

"Very real."

"Then you'll want to go for the human hair, not that synthetic crap. It's more expensive though."

"Not a problem."

The sales girl smiled. Here was her chance to get a real commission. "This one is real human hair. Have no idea where they get it, but it's pretty. It would be a little longer than shoulder length. You can pin it up. Braid it. Or you can let it hang straight. I don't recommend getting it permed. If you want curly, you can get the wavy version. Whatever your boyfriend likes."

"It's nice," she said, stroking the soft locks.

"Here, try it on." The girl helped Thompson put on a stocking cap to tuck her own hair under. When she tried on the wig, she was surprised that she looked so different.

"Wow."

"Yeah. Can't even tell it's fake. I still think you look better as a blonde, but hey, that's your thing."

"I'll take it."

"You sure? It's expensive and not returnable."

"Positive. He's going to love it."

"Okay. I'll wrap it up for you. Will that be cash or charge?"

Since Thompson didn't carry that kind of cash on her, she pulled out her credit card. This was going to set her back a bit, but it would be worth it if she could catch this creep. Maybe she'd use it as a tax write off.

"Credit card."

She handed the girl her credit card and waited a few minutes while the purchase was approved. She signed the receipt and walked out the door with a new look. It was time to go home and try it out. She had the whole thing worked out in her head. She just hoped it worked out when she put it into practice. Her tour of duty was just extended. Too bad she wasn't going to get paid for it.

***

Angelo on the other hand went straight home. She was glad the weather had cleared up slightly. The plow trucks made short work of the snow on the expressway. Taking the Lincoln Drive exit, she got on the serpentine like street. It was like driving on a ski slope. She drove it slowly, her headache keeping her under the posted 25 MPH speed limit. She got a few dirty looks from the other motorists who took the winding street entirely too fast.

One man in a gray business suit flipped the finger at her and honked impatiently as he passed on the right. There was going to be a nasty accident if people didn't slow down. Why did people drive in bad weather as if it was a clear and sunny day? Even on a nice day, Lincoln Drive was a treacherous stretch of road.

As Angelo passed the 92nd District at Gypsy Lane, she saw that the driver who passed her on the road was pulled over by a patrol car. *That's right, give him a ticket,* she thought evilly. She waved at the officer and smiled at the ticked off, red-faced motorist, who was steaming even more when he saw her give the officer the thumbs up sign.

She got off Lincoln Drive at Wissahickon Avenue, and then turned left. Only a few more blocks and she could take a hot shower and a couple of painkillers. Her head was pounding even worse than before. She was starting to wonder if she might have hit her head harder than she thought. She didn't want to see a doctor, but if the pain persisted, she might not have a choice in the matter.

Pulling up her driveway, she turned off the engine and got out of the car. She was starting to really like Sam's Lexus. Maybe it was time she traded in her old Toyota for a newer model. Maybe an all wheel drive. After patting the hood of the car like a cherished pet, she went inside the house and shrugged off her coat.

Sam was in the kitchen as usual. He was making breakfast. "Hi, sweetheart," she said to him.

"Hey there, lumpy," he said, winking at her.

"Smells good. I'm starved."

"Really?" He was glad to see she had an appetite. "It'll be ready in about five minutes. I'll bring it to you in the dining room."

"Thanks." She kissed him then went over to a cabinet. She looked through the medication bottles until she came up with the one she wanted. She grabbed the aspirin and threw down a couple of tablets with some orange juice.

"Head hurt?"

"A little." *Hell, a lot.*

"Not surprised. How's the eye."

"I can still see out of it."

"You look beat."

She glared at him.

"I mean as in tired. I want you to go to sleep right after breakfast."

"Yes, Mom," she said, bowing to him and backing out into the dining room.

She sat down at the table and waited for Sam. He did not disappoint, placing the plate in front of her. The tempting aromas wafted up to her nose. He had made his own plate as well, but he gave her the loin's share.

"Trying to fatten me up?"

"Yes, as a matter of fact."

"Didn't think you were into chubby women," she teased.
"Even if you were Rubenesque, I'd still love you."
"I'm not big bones enough to be a Ruben girl."
"Still…" He pointed to her plate, encouraging her to eat.

She ate her breakfast as if she had been starved for a week. Pushing her empty plate away, she said, "That was fantastic as usual."

"Why, thank you. Now, off to bed."
"In a minute."
"Got something on your mind?"
"I have a lot on my mind, Sam."
"Want to talk about it?"
"Maybe later." A thought struck her. "Where is Jenny?"
"Ah, she went to work."
"And you let her go?"
"What was I going to do to stop her? Did you want me to cuff her to the radiator?"
"I guess not."
"She said that she was taking control of her life. She was no longer going to hide and she was ready to face her fears."

Angelo sighed. "I guess she's got to do what she's got to do."
"I think talking to you and Officer Thompson last night helped. She got it off her chest and finally feels free."
"Maybe."
"You should try it."
"What?"
"Talking about what's bothering you. Get it off your chest. I know I'd like to get a few things off mine."
"I know what I'd like to get off your chest."
"What's that?"
"Your shirt," she said walking around behind his back and hugging him. She started to work on the buttons of his shirt.
"Bernadette, that's not going to work," he said, grabbing her hand and stopping her.
"What?"
"Seducing me into changing the subject."
"I'm not doing that to change the subject."
"Then what are you doing?"
"Can't I fondle my husband without being accused of having an ulterior motive?"
"No."
She straightened up, taking a step back. "Fine, be that way. I'm going to bed. *Alone.*"

"Bernadette," he said softly.

She did not reply, walking out of the room. She went up to their bedroom and sat on the edge of the bed. *He was not going to let it go*, she thought sourly. The pain in her head was still there. She lay back on the bed and closed her eyes. She needed to rest. As exhausted as she was, she didn't find sleep easily.

She was restless because she was overcome by worry—worried about Jennifer, worried about her and Sam and most of all, for some unknown reason, she was worried about Susan Thompson.

***

The Koffee Klutch at twelve noon was busy and packed as usual. Thompson walked in the door dressed in her best business suit and red wig. She was impressed how different it made her look. A few people noticed the stranger walk in, but only paid her a brief glance before going back to their own conversations. Kevin, the assistant manager, appeared to be too preoccupied with himself to notice her. If he did see her, she didn't think he recognized her.

Thompson ordered a coffee and a bagel with cream cheese. After she got her lunch, she sat down at one of the few empty tables available. She wanted to sit as close to Josh Brady as possible. However, soon after, when the café became even more packed, a few people asked her if they could share her table.

She told them that she would be happy to have the company because she was new in town. She explained to them that she came from Ohio looking for work. She wanted a cover story that couldn't be easily discounted. She didn't want people to catch her in a lie if she said she worked in one of the local businesses. She told them she was putting out résumés and looking for interviews. The men and women at the table offered her their business cards.

Out of the corner of her eye, she could see Josh Brady watching her. He kept peeking over his coffee cup. A few other men tried to pick her up, but she politely turned them down. They were not the intended target. She was sure that Don Juan wasn't going to just walk up to her and introduce himself.

She waited until one, watching every young man enter and exit the establishment, before she said it was time to go back to her job hunting. She thanked everyone at her table for their kindness in welcoming the new kid on the block. She said she'd be back for lunch the next day.

She looked at Josh one more time before leaving the coffee house. She was tired after the long day. She hoped that her plan would work and she'd get the attention of Don Juan.

***

She got his attention, all right. He watched her as she entered and automatically made friends. A pleasure to talk to and certainly a pleasure to look at. He loved the way her red hair sat straight on her shoulders. So nice and silky looking. He wished he could run his fingers through it. She was almost too good to be true.

He licked his lips. She could be the one he was looking for. Jenny had been such a disappointment. She called the police after all. After his little altercation with the tall brunette in the park, he went back to Jenny's place. He watched as the brunette, who kicked him good in the family jewels, bundled Jenny into her car and drove away.

A few hours later he saw a crime scene van pull up in front of the house and go inside. They spent the good part of two hours inside the house. So she did call the police after all. Too bad. She was just as bad as the rest of them.

It was time to move on to another young woman. The new girl who was looking for work seemed a possible choice. He would have to see if she returned the next day. He noticed a lot of the other guys trying to get her attention, but she turned them down flat. Could that be a sign that she was his perfect date?

He hoped so. He couldn't wait until tomorrow's lunch break. Something in the back of his mind told him that he had seen her somewhere before, but for the life of him couldn't remember when or where. He'd remember sooner or later. He just hoped it was sooner.

But now he had to get back to work. His boss was barking orders at him again. He gritted his teeth and swore under his breath, at the same time smiling at her. *She'll get hers some day,* he thought bitterly.

Chapter Seventeen

Right after dinner, Angelo called Jenny at home. She did not return to Angelo's house, so she assumed she decided to go back to her place. She was correct in her assumption. She couldn't blame her. She realized that she was really being a nag and Jenny had every right to want to be on her own for a while.

"Are you sure you don't want to stay here with us?" Angelo asked.

"No. Honestly, I've been trouble enough."

"Don't be silly. It's no trouble at all."

"You're just saying that to be nice."

"A lot of people would disagree with you. I don't say anything just to be nice." That wasn't strictly true.

"Don't worry about me. I had an alarm installed and I also got a little extra protection for the house."

"You didn't go out and buy a gun, did you? You need to be trained in their use."

"No. Not a gun. You know me, I hate those things."

"Then what? Stun gun? Pepper spray? Mortar? Ball and chain?"

Jenny laughed at Angelo's suggestions. "No. I got a dog. A rather large one. His name is Caesar. He's a brute and is police trained."

"Well, that's better than a gun, I guess. It's a lot of responsibility though; you have to walk a dog."

"It'll give me something to do."

"Did you go back to work?"

"Yes."

"How'd that work out?"

"Fine. No one asked any questions. I guess I look rather pathetic. They all thought I had the flu. I had a lot of work to catch up on. It kept my mind busy."

"I'm happy for you."
"I couldn't do it anymore."
"Do what?"
"Be a prisoner. I had to take charge of my life. I'm sure you can understand that, Bee."
"Of course I understand. You're a take charge kind of woman."
"That I am. He won't make me any less of a woman."
"That's the spirit, Jen. You know you can always call if you need me. It won't mean you're weak or anything."
"I know. Tell Sue I said thanks. She really helped."
"I will."
"You were right. I needed to talk to someone who understands how I'm feeling. I'm also going to see a counselor."
"You are?"
"Yes. I guess it took a little persuasion to get it through my thick skull."
"I hope you didn't think I was badgering you."
"You were badgering me, but it wasn't you who finally made me see reason."
"It wasn't?"
"No. It was Sam. He sure knows how to get his point across."
"Yes he does," she mumbled.
"Well, I better let you go now. I'm sure you have to get ready for work. And I need to walk the dog."
"Uh, yeah in a bit. Can I ask you a quick question?"
"Sure. What?"
"Do you regularly visit a place called the Koffee Klutch?"
"Yes, I do. Why?"
"Do you know a Josh Brady?"
"Josh? Um, yeah. He's a quiet, spooky man who hides in the corner of the café. Why?"
"No reason."
"There has to be a reason why you're asking me about him. You don't suspect him, do you?"
"He's one of a few on the short list."
"It's not him," Jennifer said suddenly.
"It's not?"
"Can't be."
"Why do you say that?"
"He's quiet and a little broody, but he's harmless. I don't think it was him who attacked me."
"Are you sure?"
"Pretty sure."

"You can't just be pretty sure. You have to be positive."
"My gut says it wasn't him."
"He's got the build."
"Yes, but Josh doesn't talk."
"Doesn't talk?"
"You sound like a parrot."
"What is he, a mute?"
"No, he can speak, but he doesn't say much. Doesn't really talk to people at all. He's a loner. I think I'd know it if it was Josh who attacked me."
"How? How can you be so sure, exactly?"
"My attacker spoke to me. Josh rarely speaks to anyone, except maybe to order his lunch at the café. Josh has a deep voice, kind of gravelly. My attacker had a young, higher pitched voice."
"Are you sure?"
"Stop asking me that. Of course, I'm sure. I'll never forget that voice as long as I live."
"I'm sorry. I didn't mean for it to come out like that."
"Oh, and Josh has hair. He's pretty furry in the chest department."
"How do you know that?"
"Hell, you can see it sticking out of his shirt."
Angelo thought she had better mention this to Seymour. "Listen to me; don't go back to the Koffee Klutch for a while, okay?"
"Oh, my God, you think Don is stalking women from there, don't you?"
"You didn't hear this from me, but yes we do."
"Oh, hell."
"Yes. Just stay out of there."
"Sure. Anything you say."
Angelo knew she could trust Jenny not to say anything about the suspicions. Jenny was an ex-prosecutor. She knew how detectives worked. She certainly wasn't going to do something to ruin an investigation.
"We have the place under surveillance."
"Okay, thanks for the warning. I hope you catch him, but I'm telling you, it wasn't Josh."
"I'll call you later."
"Goodnight, Bee."
Angelo hung up the phone. She had to talk to Officer Seymour and tell him that Josh might not be the man they were looking for after all. She found his pager number and called him. She left a message for him to call her back right away. He didn't return her page. She called Thompson next. There was no answer at her house either. She'd have to try again later.
Where is everyone? she wondered.

***

Angelo sat down at her desk and called the Special Victims Unit. A Sergeant Carter answered the telephone. He sounded annoyed. "Special Victims, Sergeant Carter. Can I help you?"

"Sarge, this is Detective Angelo from Homicide. Is Officer Seymour there? It's important that I speak with him now."

"He's busy at the moment, Detective. Can I have him call you back?"

She thought it might be a while before he called back. It had been hours since she tried to page him. "I'll hold."

"It's your dime. Hold on." He put her on hold for a good fifteen minutes before Seymour finally graced her with his voice. It was a good thing Angelo was a patient person.

"Officer Seymour," he said. He sounded just as annoyed as the sergeant did.

Does everyone in that place have a bug up their butt tonight? she wondered. "Seymour. Detective Angelo."

"Oh, Detective, I was just going to return your page."

This century?

"What's going on over there?"

"It's crazy."

That didn't answer her question, but she gave up asking. "I can tell."

"What can I do for you?" he asked.

"I've got a bit of information for you."

"And what's that?"

"I think you're looking at the wrong guy."

"Really?"

"Yes, really," she snapped.

"And how do you know?"

"I spoke to Jennifer Tully tonight."

"Victim number six?"

"The complainant, yes."

"And?"

"She is sure it wasn't Josh Brady who attacked her."

"Did she see his face? In the report, it states she didn't see him." Then he added, "You didn't even get a good look at him."

If that was meant to sting, it worked. "Well, no, but—"

"Then how can she be sure it wasn't him?"

"His voice."

"Look, Detective Angelo, I know you mean well, but based on surveillance of the nut job, I'd bet my paycheck that we've got the right guy."

You'd lose, you arrogant jerk, she thought angrily.

"I think you should keep your options open," she said much calmer than she thought she could. Her temper was at the boiling point.

"I've got a warrant for his arrest."

"Based on what? What judge in his right mind would give you one on suspicion only?"

"It's just not suspicion."

"What then?"

"Based on his connection to the victims, his past stalking and assault record and other information."

"What other information?"

"One of the victims ID'd him."

"How?"

"I showed a photo array and she picked him out."

"Had it ever occurred to you that maybe she picked him out because she sees him in the café all the time? In fact, a lot of people know that he frequents the place and most think he's a bit odd. She probably assumed it was him."

"I don't think so."

Can't talk to this young pup!

"What's your plan?"

"We plan to pick him up for questioning tomorrow. You're welcome to attend the interrogation."

Gee thanks.

"I'll be there."

"Fine, I'll call you."

You'd better call me.

"Probably be some time late afternoon. We want to snatch him up after he leaves his place of employment."

"I'll meet you at SVU then."

"I'll look forward to seeing you. Oh, and you can bring Thompson along. Maybe she can learn a thing or two."

What a jerk!

"Sure. Goodbye." She hung up the telephone. "Asshole," she said out loud.

"Who?" Thompson asked.

"Seymour."

"Are you just figuring that out?"

Angelo didn't reply.

"What's he done now?"

"He's going to arrest the wrong man."

"He is? Who?"

"Josh Brady."

"How do you know it's not Josh?"

"Jenny says it wasn't him."

"Is she sure?"

"Very."

"Doesn't mean he didn't attack any of the other women."

"That's true."

"So, what's Golden Boy have planned?"

"They are getting an arrest warrant based on some really circumstantial evidence at best. They are going to pick him up tomorrow afternoon. He'll be interviewed at the Special Victims Unit."

"Not here?"

"Not yet. Seymour has invited us to attend, God bless his heart," Angelo said sarcastically.

"When?"

"He said he'll call."

"Yeah, when it's all over."

"Oh, I made sure he'd let me know right away."

"Okay, I'll be there."

"Where were you this afternoon?"

"Excuse me?"

"I called your house after I talked to Jenny."

"Uh, I was out." That was all she stated, but Angelo got the feeling she was holding back.

"Doing what?"

"I do have a life. I went shopping," she snapped, but caught herself. She hoped Angelo didn't notice her tone. She did. Nothing slipped by her.

"Okay. Sorry. Didn't mean to pry. That's your business."

"No, I'm sorry; I'm just tired and a little tense."

"Why?"

"I don't know. I just am."

"You want to go home and take the night off?"

"No. I'm fine. I'm sure that sludge you guys call coffee will wake me up."

"That'll probably kill you," she joked about the coffee.

"Probably."

"Well, if you want to work I have a stack of paperwork that needs typing."

"You're so kind, Bee," she teased.

"Aren't I though?"

Angelo kept Thompson busy the rest of the night while she caught up on some old jobs. Thompson had other thoughts going through her mind. If it wasn't Josh, then who could it be? One of the other men? She didn't notice anyone else paying her any covert attention. She seriously doubted it was any of the men who hit on her at the café. Surely he wouldn't be so bold. Or would he?

***

The night went by at a snail's pace. There was nothing going on in the city, let alone the case. After Thompson typed up all the reports Angelo could find for her, she was sent home. Thompson decided to use the spare time to catch up on some sleep before she returned to the Koffee Klutch. She wanted to be fresh and totally aware.

She found another suit and headed out to the café. She hoped she would be able to get the guy to surface before she ran out of suits. She only owned a few business suits. Most of the time she wore semi-casual attire, even at the unit.

She was running late. It was nearly twelve-thirty when she opened the door to the Koffee Klutch. She ran straight into a man exiting the establishment. He knocked her off balance. It was the same man who bumped into her before. He didn't seem to recognize her.

"Oh, sorry," he said, helping her.

Automatically she reached for her wallet, but realized that she wasn't carrying it in her back pocket. She forgot she was wearing a skirt suit. "That's all right. My fault. I'm clumsy."

"No, you're not," he said, smiling. He reached out his hand toward her hair. She stepped back out of his reach. Seeing that she was jumpy, he smiled again. "You have something in your hair."

"What?"

He picked a small leaf out of her hair and handed it to her. "Here."

Taking the leaf from his well manicured hands, she said, "Oh, thanks."

"No problem. I'm running late returning to work. My boss is going to have a fit. Goodbye."

"Yeah, see you."

"I hope so." He walked away and down the street. She turned back and went into the café.

"Sue!" someone shouted.

Who knows me? she wondered, and then realized that it was the people she met the day before. They were holding a seat for her. That was nice of them.

"Oh, hi." She ordered coffee and a bagel and sat with her new friends.

"Any luck on the job hunt?"

"Not yet. But it's looking hopeful."

She turned her head and noticed Josh staring at her. The instant he saw that she was looking at him, he turned his attention back to his coffee. She continued to observe every male in the café, taking mental notes. She didn't notice anyone else paying her any unwanted attention. Maybe Jenny was wrong and Josh was their man after all.

Thompson looked forward to seeing how Seymour handled the man. Josh didn't seem the type who'd break easily under interrogation. *We'll see,* Thompson thought as she nibbled on her bagel.

***

About quarter to seven in the evening, Angelo's pager went off. It was Seymour calling her from the Special Victims Unit. "I guess they arrested him," Angelo said to Sam as she went over to the telephone to return the page.

"You don't sound so confident. I thought you'd be happy," he said.

"If it was the right guy, yes. Personally, I think Seymour's making a big mistake. But what does a detective with years of experience know."

"You doubt it's him?"

"Yes I do. I've got a gut feeling and it's telling me that Josh Brady isn't our rapist."

She called the unit and Seymour answered the phone. "Seymour."

"Angelo."

"We're going to start the interrogation in about a half an hour."

"You expect me to get to SVU in a half an hour?"

"Sorry, but we want to start right away before any lawyers show up."

"You mean he hasn't asked for a lawyer yet?"

"Not yet. I'm hoping he'll be cocky enough not to want one."

"Okay, I'll call Thompson and be there within the hour."

"Right. See you then."

Angelo hung up the phone. "The bonehead isn't going to wait for me. He's going to screw it up, I just know it."

"Better get up there quickly."

"I am. Catch you later." She kissed him, called Thompson, headed out the door and up to SVU. She hoped that Seymour would be smart enough not to push Josh too hard and force him into calling a lawyer before she got the chance to talk to him.

She made it in record time. However, Seymour had already started his interrogation. Angelo walked into the outer room and watched from behind the glass mirror as Seymour bore down on him. Josh looked angry. Seymour looked even angrier.

"Come on, Josh, we know you did it. We got witnesses. You were picked out."

"I had nothing to do with it," Josh Brady replied, the veins in his head looked as if they were ready to explode.

"We have evidence that says otherwise."

"What evidence? I didn't leave any evidence."

"Ah, so you admit that you cleaned the scenes."

"What are you talking about? I didn't do anything. I wasn't there, so I couldn't have left any evidence."

"I know you're lying. You stalked those women at the Koffee Klutch."

"No, I did not," he said emphatically.

Seymour's hands came down hard on the table in front of Josh. "I say you did."

Josh didn't even flinch. Calmly he said, "I want a lawyer."

That's done it, Angelo thought crossly. Once a suspect requests a lawyer, all questioning must cease or it would be inadmissible in court.

"Are you sure? Got something to hide?"

"No I don't."

"Then you don't need a lawyer."

"I know my rights."

"Yes, I bet. You've been arrested before, haven't you?"

"A long time ago. I'm in therapy now. I'm under control."

"For what?"

"None of your damn business!"

"I can make it my business."

"Go right ahead. Knock yourself out. I've got nothing else to say to you. I want a lawyer now." He leaned back in the chair and folded his arms across his chest in defiance.

Seymour growled and stalked out of the room. He ran into Angelo standing by the door. "He's lawyered up," he told her.

"Yes. I see that," she replied dryly.

"I don't want him to get away with this on a technicality. He'll get his damn lawyer."

"Mind if I talk to him a minute?"

"Anything he says will be inadmissible."

"No, really?" she said sarcastically.

He raised an eyebrow at her tone. She had to put her temper under control.

"I know. I just want to ask him something. See his reaction."

He shrugged his shoulders. "Be my guest."

Angelo went into the other room and sat across the table from Josh. "Hi," she said, smiling.

"Who are you? Good cop?"

"Who me? No. No, I'm better at the bad cop routine."

"I'm not saying another word until my lawyer gets here. I told the boy detective that already."

"I heard."

"Then why are you wasting my time?"

"I don't think I'm wasting my time, Josh. I want to make sure we get the

right guy."
"I told you that I had nothing to do with it."
"I believe you, Josh. I don't think you did it."
That caught him by surprise. "You don't?"
Leaning in closer, she said, "No, I don't."
"Then why the hell am I here?"
"Not my call. However, I don't think you killed anyone. In fact, I think you can help me."
"I didn't kill or even rape anyone. I have an anger problem, yes, but it's under control."
"You knew those women at the Koffee Klutch."
"Yeah, sure. They were in there every day. So was I."
"I know."
He suddenly recognized her. "I saw you in there with that younger woman. You looked at me. I remember thinking to myself that you had *cop eyes*. That's when I left the café."
"Yes. That was me. You did leave in quite a hurry that day."
"I had somewhere to be. I was late for an appointment," he explained.
"I see."
"She's been in there the last two days."
"Who?"
"The young woman who was with you that day."
His statement took her totally by surprise. Angelo did a double take and said, "What?"
"Your partner, I assume. She's been staking out the place. She's wearing a red wig."
I'll murder her myself! Angelo thought angrily. "Are you sure?"
"Of course. I never forget a face."
"Never mind her. So you're saying that you never stalked any of those women."
"No. I swear I only looked."
"What about Heather?"
"She's just a teen and probably half my age. What on earth would I want with a baby? I looked at her once and that asshole, Steve, got in my face."
"Steve?"
"I don't know his last name. He's a regular at the place."
"He got in your face about Heather?"
That was the second time Steve came up in conversation. Maybe he needed a closer look. She'd ask O'Malley to dig a little deeper. Like a Jack Russell dog, O'Malley was a pro at digging. By the time he was finished he'd know the size of the person's underwear.
"Yes. So I stopped looking at her. That's what I do. I like to watch people

166

interact with each other. It's called people watching. You know, like bird watching. It is part of my therapy. It calms me."

"Can I ask you one more question? Off the record?"

"What?"

"Do you have a nipple ring?"

"A what? No. I don't wear any rings. Nipple or otherwise." Angelo noted that he wore no jewelry at all.

Angelo looked at his chest. His tie and the top button of his shirt were undone. She could see thick, dark hair sticking out of the top of his shirt. Jenny was right. He was furry in the chest department.

"Josh, tell me about your mother." Angelo had a gut feeling that the man she was looking for had a deep-seated dislike, even hatred and loathing, of his mother. She wanted to gauge Josh's reaction to the mention of his mother.

"What the hell does my mom have to do with this?"

"I heard there was an altercation at the café a while back."

Josh snarled, "Kevin! Christ! That happened almost a year ago. That has nothing to do with this situation."

"Tell me about it."

"Why? I demand to know why?"

"Please. Just humor me."

He sighed. "My mom can be a little overbearing and overprotective of me. She always has been. Some girl found my wallet and, trying to be a Good Samaritan, dropped it off at my house. My mom flipped. She thought the girl was after something."

"Why would she think that?"

"Because—well, I just ended a bad marriage. My ex-wife, Hanna, ran off with my best friend and business partner after taking me for everything I had. My house, my car, and even my business left with her. I've been staying with my mother since then. Mom isn't a bad sort, just overprotective of me. She knew where I go for lunch and came by the café. The argument was partly my fault. I was angry that she would accuse me of being stupid. That I couldn't judge a woman. Mom knew that I was being taken for a ride way before I did. She tried to warn me about Hanna, but I wouldn't listen. She was my wife. I loved her. When Mother came by the café, I let my anger get the better of me. But you know what? If you think my temper is bad, you haven't seen bad until you've seen my mother's."

"Go on."

"She created a bit of a scene and that jerk, Kevin, got involved. He thinks he's a bouncer or something. He put his hands on my mother. *No one* touches my mother! I went crazy. I mean, he has no respect! He called her all sorts of foul names. I could have killed him, but my mom had me calm down. I guess she saw that I was over the edge. I almost killed the last man who touched my mother. And he was my father."

Angelo placed her hand on his arm.

"Anyway, I calmed down and took her out of there. That was the end of that."

"Josh, how do you feel about your mother?"

"I—I love her to death. She can be a pain in the ass, but I would do anything for her and she would do the same for me."

"I see."

"I don't. I still don't know what that has to do with what I'm being accused of."

"Trust me, knowing helps me. And you."

Josh shook his head. "If anything, you should take a long, hard look at Kevin. He's got some real issues about himself and women."

"What do you mean?"

"Come on. You can't tell me you hadn't noticed how he is. He thinks he's God's gift to women. He just doesn't take no for an answer."

"I'll personally look into it. Okay, Josh? You wait for that lawyer," she said, patting him on the forearm.

He grabbed her hand, squeezing hard. She did not pull away and looked him dead in the eye. "You really don't think I had anything to do with it, do you?" He stared at her with his face full of concern. His eyes never left hers.

"No, Josh, I don't."

He let go of her hand. "Well, tell him that," he said, pointing at the two-way mirror.

"I told you, it's not my call. You just wait for that lawyer. I advise you to remain silent."

Angelo got up and went back into the other room. Seymour was red-faced, going into the stroke zone. "What the hell was that!" he yelled.

This time Angelo raised her eyebrows at his tone, but held her comments to herself for the moment. "It's not him."

"The hell it's not! I can't believe you just told him to remain silent! Now we'll never get anything out of him."

"It's his right. I'm telling you that Josh is not your man."

"How the hell do you know that for certain?"

"I just do. Call it experience."

"Not good enough. You screwed this up, Angelo!"

She sighed. "Have you noticed that he's got a chest full of hair?"

"So?"

"All the complainants state that he was hairless."

"So, he let it grow back. My old man can grow a beard in two days."

"That amount of hair just doesn't grow back like that after a waxing. It takes weeks, maybe even months, to grow back. In addition, he said he doesn't have a nipple ring. Something else the complainants stated the doer had."

"Oh, well, why don't we just take his word for it then?"

"And he loves his mother," she added.

"What? What the hell does that have to do with this?"

She wasn't in the mood to argue with him any further. "Look, he's lawyered up. Any half decent attorney is going to have him out in less than a day. You've got not one shred of evidence."

"I've got witnesses."

"Tenuous at best. No one saw his face. Have you noticed the tone of his voice? He's a bass or at least a baritone. The complainants state his voice was younger, higher pitched."

"I'm telling you, he's got something to do with this, Angelo."

"Well, while you're wasting your time with him, the killer is still out there. Scott free. And another thing, *Officer Seymour*," she said, finally losing her temper and growling through her teeth, "don't you *ever* take that tone with me again. My title is *Detective* Angelo."

The door opened and Thompson walked in the room. "I miss it?" she asked.

"You!" Angelo shouted, pointing a finger at her protégé. Thompson jumped back, shocked, and frightened. She actually thought Angelo looked furious enough to hit her.

"Sorry I'm late. I got stuck in traffic."

"I want a word with you!"

"Me?"

"Yes, you! Outside *now!*"

"Oh, okay." Thompson left the room.

"It's not him," she told Seymour one last time and followed Thompson out of the room. She grabbed Thompson by the elbow and pulled her, not so gently toward the elevator, stabbing the call button with an angry finger.

"What's going on? Bee?"

She rounded on Thompson, her eyes full of molten fury. "That's *Detective Angelo* to you, Officer!"

Taking another step back, Thompson said, "Sorry. Detective. What did I do?"

"What the hell were you thinking?" Angelo seemed to be in an angry rage, but she was more worried and concerned than she was mad.

"I don't understand," she said, confused.

"Don't give me that. Did you think I wouldn't find out?"

Thompson gave her a blank stare.

"Red wig? Coffee house? You tell me."

Oh, damn. "Uh. I can explain that."

"Oh, you will explain all right! Then you will cease and desist! I ought to have you busted back down to patrol for this stunt you pulled!"

Thompson looked down at her feet, tears forming in her eyes. "I'm sorry. I thought I was doing the right thing. I thought I was taking the initiative."

"Initiative? I ordered you not to do it. You disregarded a direct order from a superior officer."

"I know, but—"

"No buts, Susan!"

"Yes, ma'am."

"Sue," she said a little calmer. "You could have gotten hurt, or worse. Never do anything without backup. You broke a cardinal rule."

"I know. I'm sorry."

"Then why did you put yourself in jeopardy?"

"I want him."

"So do I."

"I thought I got Josh's attention."

"It's not Josh."

"What? But he was looking at me."

"First of all, he's a people watcher. Second of all, how do you think I found out about this? He recognized you."

"Oh, shit."

"You got that right."

"How do you know it's not him for sure?"

"Remember how the complainants said that the doer was hairless. Not even any short and curlies?"

"Yeah."

"Well, Josh is far from hairless. The man could make a sweater from his chest hair alone."

"Oh. I never thought of that."

"Look, Sue, I'm sure your intentions were noble and all, but that was a stupid risk you took. I know you want to catch this guy as bad as I do, but please don't put yourself in harm's way again. I'm only going to say this once. Do not go back there for any reason. Got that?"

"Yes," she murmured.

"What was that?" she asked, holding her hand up to her ear.

"Yes, Detective." Thompson replied, still looking at her feet.

"Hey, look at me!"

Thompson raised her head and tried very hard to look Angelo in the eye. It was a difficult task, but she managed it.

"I mean it. If I find out you went back there, I would have you busted back to patrol so fast your head will spin and your children will be born dizzy. You'll never make detective. You'll be pushing a patrol car around for the next twenty years, if you last that long."

170

"I won't. On a stack of Bibles, I swear." She held up her right hand.

"You'd better not," Angelo said, poking her in the chest.

Like Josh, Thompson continued to remain silent the rest of the night. She didn't dare talk to Angelo about her unauthorized surveillance. She realized that what she did was incredibly stupid and risky. She should have listened to Angelo. Now she feared that her mentor had lost all respect for her and didn't trust her anymore. She'd have to do a lot of kissing up to get back into her good graces.

***

Assistant District Attorney Tony Vargas was true to his word. When Angelo got back to the Homicide Unit, she found two large boxes of files on her desk. Vargas narrowed the field down by only including men who fit the general description Angelo gave him. However, he still came up with a little over one hundred case files. There was a note stuck on the top on the box.

"You owe me big," it said.

"Boy, do I," she said to herself and sat down at her desk. She started by stacking the list of men in categories. Men who were still in prison and those who were released. Most of the men were still incarcerated, but that left her about 25 who were free on probation or parole. She knew it was going to be a long night and definitely was going to need help shifting through all the names.

Looking around for her partner, she saw him seated at his desk reading a newspaper. He saw her watching him and grinned. She wasn't sure if he was smiling at her, or at what he was reading. She'd soon find out. He got up and walked over to her desk.

"Hey, Angelo, you made the local rag."

"Excuse me?" she asked, snatching the paper out of his hand.

"Don't be so rude, Angelo. I see that Snodgrass has a bug up his rear end for you."

"They all do," she said, looking at the article.

"I see they put it next to the *Rover ate my alien baby* article," he snickered.

Reading the article, she was thankful that Snodgrass had taken her threats seriously and did not mention the conversation he overheard with Vargas. Most of the article was bashing Angelo about being secretive and saying, No comment. Basically it was a lot of nothing.

"Did you really say, No comment, Angelo? Somehow I can't see you even talking to the bum."

"I didn't talk to him. I threatened to beat the living crap out of him."

"Now *that* sounds more like you."

She shoved the paper back to him. "Get that rag out of my sight."

"Sure thing, Detective *No Comment* Angelo."

"Since you're not doing anything constructive at the moment, how about helping me out with this?"

"What's this?" he asked, looking at the piles of folders. "They look like court files."

"They are."

"What are you doing with those?"

"Look, it has something to do with Don Juan. But I need you to keep this quiet."

"Why?"

"Why do you always ask so many questions?"

"I'm a detective. I'd be a lousy one if I didn't ask questions."

"True."

He looked at the files. "Hmm," he said to himself. "I'm seeing a common factor here."

"I'm sure you do. That's why I don't want anyone else hearing about it. Got that? Only a few people know about the situation, okay?"

"All right, I'll help you and ADA Tully."

"Thanks. I knew I can count on you," she said, patting his arm. "I really appreciate it."

"Yeah, well, don't get all mushy on me," he replied, looking at her hand.

"Who's mushy?"

"You are."

"No comment."

Chapter Eighteen

Angelo decided that she wanted to pay a visit to the Koffee Klutch and have a word alone with Kevin McPherson. She knew he was lying to her and was going to call him on it. The case was getting frustrating and if she didn't start adding or eliminating suspects she'd go mad.

The Koffee Klutch opened early and, even at eight in the morning, it was packed with customers getting their coffee and breakfast. As she entered the café, she scanned the room looking for her target. She found him almost immediately.

Kevin was standing behind the counter, but he wasn't helping anyone. He just stood there with his arms across his broad chest as if he were a slave overlord. Occasionally, he'd take a break from his hovering to examine his fingernails or look at himself in a mirror.

Walking over to the crowd of people standing in line, she bucked the queue to the front. She got a few under-the-breath comments that were no doubt uncharitable, but one look from Angelo silenced them.

"Kevin. I'd like a word with you." Her statement wasn't a request; it was a demand.

Kevin huffed irritably and walked around the counter. He tried to smile, but she could see the annoyance in his expression. "What can I do for you, Detective, uh…"

"Angelo," she told him. *He knows damn well who I am*, she thought. Again, she noticed that instead of looking at her face, he was ogling her chest. "Hey! I'm up here, Kevin!"

"I'm a very busy man, Detective. What do you want?"

"Yes, I can see that." *Must be terribly hard to watch other people work*, she mused. *You don't get enough 'me' time.*

"Well?"

"I'll get to the point. You *lied* to me."

"I did? About what?"

On a hunch that he was the '*God's gift to women*' Victoria mentioned in her PDA, she said, "You told me that you didn't know Victoria Sterling. I found out that you did in fact know her. Very well."

His face fell because he knew that he was caught in the lie. "Okay, so I knew her."

"This is a good start, Kevin. Now that you're being honest how about you tell me why you lied to me."

"I don't like to be called a liar," he snapped.

"All right. Why did you omit the facts?" she asked sarcastically.

"No reason."

"Oh, come off it. Do I *look* like I just fell off the turnip truck?"

"Fine. I thought she might have filed a complaint on me?"

"Why would she have done that?"

"They all do. No good women. Just because a guy hits on a woman doesn't make him a criminal."

"True. But harassment is a crime."

"Who says it was harassment."

"Uh, a judge, perhaps?"

"Please. Look at me. I can have any woman I want. I don't need to harass anyone. Vicki liked to play the game. She flirted worse then her friends."

"She was engaged."

"So? Doesn't mean squat. They all play games. I'll bet even you play them."

You'd lose, buddy, she thought.

"Eventually I would have won."

"Really? How?"

"I always win."

"You didn't seem to win with the three women you, uh, hit on."

"Losers. All of them."

"You know what I think?"

"What's that?"

"I think you have a huge ego and that ego makes you think you're hot shit. But you know what, Kevin, that makes you the loser."

"Your opinion of me don't mean dick."

"I'm sure it doesn't."

"Yeah, so I got a big ego. It comes with the rest of my anatomy," he said, crudely thrusting his pelvis at her. "No man likes to be rejected, especially me. I'm the type of guy who just moves on to the next one. Plenty of fish in the sea, so they say. And I like to fish." He licked his lips suggestively.

"I see."

"Will that be all, *Detective*? I have a business to manage." This time he didn't try to hide behind pleasantries. He was being down right rude.

"You do that. And, Kevin," she said with a serious look, "I'll be watching you."

He ginned, spreading his arms wide. "Watch away, darling. I've got plenty of eye candy for you to look at. When you want a piece, you just call me. I'll bet I could make your day."

She shook her head at him as he walked away, swishing his butt at her. *Did he just hit on me? Asshole!* she thought as she left the café.

***

Before Angelo went home, she stopped by the newly built Forensic Science Unit at Eighth and Poplar Streets. The multi-million dollar building had the distinction of being one of the most advanced forensic units in the country. It was so much nicer than the cramped quarters in the basement of Police Headquarters.

The unit had DNA and drug testing labs that could rival the FBI. In addition, the Firearms Identification and Crime Scene units moved into the building, giving them more room to do their investigations. The building even smelled new.

Angelo walked in the front door and the officer behind the glass barrier greeted her. "Hey, Bee," the officer said as she watched Angelo sign in. "What are you here for? Shouldn't you be home resting."

"Rest? What's that?" she replied. "I'm just here checking on the progress of one of my cases."

"Have you ever been here before?"

"No, this is the first time I've had the chance to come to the new building. I'm not sure I know where I'm supposed to go."

"Go back to the Crime Scene Unit. They'll help you out," the officer said, pointing over her shoulder.

"Thanks, you're a dear."

"Shhh, don't let that get out," the officer joked.

"Your secret is safe with me."

The officer buzzed her into the main entrance and Angelo walked back to the Crime Scene Unit. She knocked on the door and a tall, nice looking officer answered it. "Detective Angelo!" he said.

"Hi, Tag."

"What can I do for you?"

Everyone is always so nice at this unit, she thought. "I'm checking on one of my cases." She read off the file number to him.

"Hold on, let me look it up."

They walked over to his cubical and punched in the case number. Angelo looked around the room. Everyone had a desk and a file cabinet. The desks were adorned with family pictures and other pleasant items. It made the place seem lived in and a nice place to work.

Tag broke her out of her straying thoughts. "Jennifer Tully?" he asked, bringing up the file on the computer.

"Yeah."

"It says it's an SVU job. What's Homicide doing with it?"

"It's connected to a homicide case."

Tag shrugged his shoulders. "We're not finished with processing the scene's evidence, but so far we got nada. Your doer knows how not to leave evidence."

"Yes, that's the problem with this case."

"I think the lab is processing the bed sheets. I'll take you to the lab. We'll see if they got anything yet."

"Thanks, Tag."

They took the elevator to the next level and entered the lab. Men and women in white lab coats sat at their stations. The room reminded Angelo of her high school chemistry lab. Everything was so nice and orderly. It certainly was a change from the usual mess.

"Hey, Mary, can you spare a minute?"

A woman in her late forties looked up from her microscope and smiled at Tag. "Anything for you, sweetie."

He smiled back at her. "Detective Angelo needs to see if anything came back from the Tully scene?"

"Uh, Tully? I'm afraid not. We did an alternate light source test and didn't find anything from the doer. Found a few hairs from the victim and possibly some from another female on scene, but nothing male."

Ugh, even I left evidence at the scene, Angelo thought to herself, *but not this jerk!*

"No seminal fluid, saliva or blood found."

"The attack was interrupted. He was wearing a ski mask. Any fibers from that?"

"Not that I found. I can go over it again if you'd like."

"That would be nice. I appreciate your help."

"No problem at all."

"Come on, Bee, I'll give you a tour before you go home."

"Tell you what, Tag, so far I'm very impressed."

He smiled as if she was talking about his child. "We try."

Angelo could have spent hours in the Forensic Unit, but she didn't have the luxury of time. She was tired and annoyed by the slow progress of the case. Thompson's little outing was also on her mind. What if something had happened to her? *Rookies! When will they learn!*

After stopping by the Inspector's office and chatting with her for a few minutes, Angelo left the unit. She hoped with all the new technology, they'd find something to help her case.

***

The second day that he saw the pretty, new girl at the coffee shop was the day he decided to follow her home. Faking illness, he left his job right after lunch and watched as she got in her car and drove away. She lived a little outside his prowling grounds in Fox Chase, but he was sure she'd be worth the effort.

She lived in a single dwelling. There would be no connecting walls to neighbors to worry about. There would be no one to interfere or hear the wild night of excitement he had envisioned. He could visualize the magical night that he had planned in his mind's eye. He couldn't wait to taste her sweet body.

She must have another job, he reasoned. He assumed it was the kind of job that took her away at night. Maybe that was why she was looking for day work. Some people just weren't creatures of the night. Not everyone could be like him.

Later that afternoon, he made his way back to her Fox Chase home. He sat across the street and watched her house with interest. He would wait there patiently for her to come out of the house. He knew she was home, but she hadn't left the house yet. Maybe she was sleeping. He wondered if now would be a good time to pay her a visit. He looked up at the sun, which would be setting in less than an hour.

No, not now, he thought. Not yet. He wanted to be sure that she was the one. He had to uncover her pattern, see who visited her and where she went during the day. He wanted to catch her in the wee hours of the morning. However, if she had an overnight job, that could pose a problem. He'd have to wait to catch her on a night off.

In the meantime, he'd just wait and watch. After all, the watching was as much fun as the actual date. He anticipated the victory. He'd bide his time.

A spiffy red Chevy Corvette pulled up to the front of the house and a man in his late twenties got out. He was wearing what looked like a flight jacket. *Don* couldn't read the emblem on it from where he was sitting. He watched with interest as the man walked up to her front door.

Who is this? Boyfriend?

He observed that the friend was of average height, maybe a few inches shorter than he was. He had a thick build. He wasn't muscular, but looked as if he had been losing weight and trying to bulk up with exercise.

He's not a bad looking man, but of course, not as handsome as I am. No one can be this good looking.

The man knocked on the front door. She opened it and had a surprised look on her face. Obviously she wasn't expecting company. She appeared to be preparing to go out, her head covered with the hood of her jacket.

Don pulled out a sound amplifier and pointed it in their direction. He listened intently to their conversation.

"Matt, what are you doing here?" she asked.

"Can't I come over and see my girlfriend?"

"Matt, I'm going out at the moment. I have things to do."

"You always have things to do that don't include me. If it's not work, it's something else."

"You're not being fair. You know how important my job is to me."

"Am I not important to you?"

"Of course you are."

"I'm starting to wonder. Are you seeing someone else?" he blurted out.

She took a step back as if slapped. "How could you say that? How could you even think that?"

"It's hard not to think something is wrong with our relationship."

"What?"

"You don't leave me any alternative. What am I to think?"

"Honestly," she huffed. "Stop being so insecure. It's not a good feature on you."

"How can I not be? We haven't seen or been with each other for weeks."

"That's not my fault. Our shifts conflict. You knew that when we first hooked up."

"It's never been this bad. You used to make time for me."

"And what about you? Why is it always me who has to make the time?"

"Sue, I don't want to fight out here like this. Let's go inside."

"No."

"Then why don't we go out and do something now?"

"I told you, I have things to get done before I go back to work tonight."

"I'll tag along."

"No. I have to do something personal."

"You are seeing someone else!" he accused.

"No I'm not, damn you!"

He remained silent.

"I don't need this right now. I'm under a lot of stress with my job."

"I don't need this either."

"Then I guess there is nothing left to say. Good-bye, Matt. Don't bother coming over or calling. It's over!"

"Over? I don't think it ever got started."

She locked the front door and walked away toward her car. "Goodbye," she repeated.

"Sue!" he shouted.

She ignored him, refusing to continue the heated argument. She really didn't need the stress. She started the car and revved the engine. Peeling away from the curb like a madwoman, she left Matt standing on her front step. He looked completely stunned, as if he just got his heart ripped out of his chest.

Don grinned. *I guess I don't have to worry about him anymore*, he thought. No boyfriend meant there wouldn't be any interruptions when it was time for their date. He continued to watch as the man called Matt got in his 'Vette and left the area. Well, that solved one problem. The only one left was catching Sue home alone on her day off.

A few days, my sweet, he mused. *Just a few more days.*

***

Reports that the Don Juan Rapist had been captured were all over the news. No doubt someone at SVU leaked that bit of information to the media. There was no talking to Seymour. He insisted that they got their man. Only time would get a confession out of Josh Brady. Angelo still had her doubts. At least they didn't release his name to the general public.

"They are setting themselves up for a big, embarrassing fall," Angelo told Sam as they watched the news over dinner.

"There has to be some reason why they arrested him. They have to have evidence."

"Circumstantial at best. I still think they got the wrong guy. I'm starting to feel sorry for poor *people watching* Josh."

"How can you be so sure?"

"I just am, okay. I think Special Victims is being put in a corner because of the media hype and the politicians breathing down their necks."

"Wouldn't be the first time they arrested the wrong man because of politics."

"And it won't be the last time either," Angelo said bitterly. "In the meantime, the real killer is still out there and no one is looking for him. I fear he might bolt now that he knows we're on to him."

"Is that such a bad thing? If he leaves the city, then the women of the Northeast can feel safe again."

"They'll never be safe. He'll only be some other jurisdiction's problem. More women will be hurt, raped, and maybe even murdered. I'm surprised you even suggested that it would be a good thing, Sam."

"You know I didn't mean it the way it sounded."

"The one thing about him that makes me think he'll stick around the city is that he's arrogant and comfortable here. He won't stop until someone stops him. By then it might be too late."

"What about the man in custody?"

"Josh? I'll bet you that once Don attacks another woman, they'll have to realize that Josh's the wrong man and let him loose."

"Or they could just say it was a copy cat."

"That's a possibility. He'll make bail. Either way, they can't hold him for long."

"It's a shame another woman has to be assaulted before that can happen."

"That's why it is imperative that we catch him soon. I don't want another woman to be added to his list of conquests."

"Do you think Jenny will be safe?"

"Now that she has reported it, yes."

"Why?"

"She was the only one not to report the assault and was attacked a second time. I believe this guy thinks because she didn't report the rape it was okay to pay her a second visit."

"Interesting theory. How do you figure?"

"Calling the police was an insult to him. A let down. Maybe he thinks that because the others reported it, they weren't worth a repeat. None of the others were attacked a second time. Only Jenny."

"I hope you're right."

"So do I. You know, I've checked everywhere for a possible suspect. I even tried a different angle and looked into Jenny's old case files from her time at the DA's office."

"And?"

"Nothing. I had poor O'Malley checking dozens of possible suspects and we came up with absolutely nothing. All had alibis, were back in jail or out of the state. Even Jenny said none of those men threatened her. She said she'd know if it was one of her old defendants. A complete dead end and waste of time."

"I wouldn't say that. Nothing you do to investigate is a waste of time. That's what I love about you. You're so thorough." He grabbed her hand and squeezed it gently. She brought his hand up to her lips and kissed him. He could tell something else was bothering her. "What's wrong?"

She let out a big sigh. "I'm worried about Susan."

"Why?"

"She went and did something stupid."

"What was that?"

"She bought a red wig and went to the coffee house to attract Don's attention."

"And you let her do that?"

"No, I did not! She did it on her own and against my orders not to."

"I hope you stopped her."

"Damn right I stopped her foolish behavior. Gave her a royal ass chewing as well."

"Are you sure she listened this time."

"She knows better now. I threatened to bust her back to patrol." Angelo wondered if Thompson really would listen. She didn't want to be back on patrol, but Thompson reminded Angelo a lot of herself. She would risk that demotion and the real possibility of physical harm to get the bad guy.

"And you would bust her back down to patrol too, wouldn't you?"

"Hell yes. It would be for her own good. As much as I like her, she still disobeyed a direct order. She could have gotten hurt."

"She's young and impulsive. Sounds like someone we both know."

"Who would that be?" she asked, faking ignorance.

"You know damn well, who."

She smiled. "I just hope she didn't get his attention. With him on the loose, she can be in danger."

"Do you think she'll need protection?"

"I hope not. I'm going to tell her to keep vigilant. If she feels threatened in any way, I want to know about it immediately."

"She's going to have to trust her instincts."

"Yes."

"She may be a rookie, but she is also a woman. Women have that intuition we men lack. It tells them that they are in danger. I'm sure she'll be on guard."

"I hope so. If anything happens to her…" She paused. "I don't know what I'd do. I don't think I could take the guilt."

"She's not Dwayne."

"I know she's not, but I don't want a repeat of what happened to him."

"Neither do I. Have you had a chance to talk to someone about Dwayne?"

"Yeah, the head shrink at EAP."

"Bee, the guy you talked to over there isn't enough. You talked to him, what? A full five minutes?"

"More like ten."

"What you need is a few hours maybe weeks with a real professional."

"Are you going to start that again?"

"I'm going to start every chance I get until you listen to me."

"Sam," she said warningly.

"I'll go with you. I'd like to get a few things off my chest."

"Then you go."
"I think you need it more than me."
"I don't."
"Have you always been this stubborn?"
"Yes."
"You say you love me."
"Of course I do."
"If you loved me as much as you claim, you wouldn't make me suffer so much," he said.
"Don't start with the dramatics. Listen, if it'll make you feel better and get you off my back, I'll talk to someone...later. After this case is over and done with and Jenny's rapist is behind bars for a very long time."
"Do you swear?"
"You have my word, Sam."
"And I know your word is your bond. I'm going to hold you to it."
"I just know you are." She kissed him. "I really do love you, Sam. Dramatics and all."
"So do I. More than you know."

∗∗∗

Thompson got the feeling that someone was watching her. She wasn't even sure if she was just being paranoid or if there was some truth to her nagging intuition. She was wondering if she should mention this to Angelo or not.

They said they caught the guy, but Angelo insisted that Josh was the wrong man. If it wasn't Josh, then whoever this man was he was still out there. Could she have made a really bad decision and actually gained Don's attention? If she had, then she could be in mortal peril.

She entered the unit and looked around for her mentor. Finding O'Malley instead, she went over to him and asked if he had seen her.

"She's running a little late," he told her, holding out a doughnut and offering it to her. "Want one?"

She shook her head no, and thanked him anyway.

"Something bothering you, kid?" he asked genuinely concerned for her wellbeing.

"No," she lied.

"I was going to tell Angelo this when she came in, but since you're here, I'll share it with you first."

"Really?" She was stunned that she was so readily accepted by the detectives in the unit.

"Sure."

"Okay, what's the scoop?"

"Remember how Angelo wanted the information on Stephen Greystock?"

"Yes."

"I pulled his driver's license photo."

"And?"

He handed it to her. "Did you see him at the café when you went there?"

He knew about that! She was silent for a moment.

He was confused by her silence. "When you went with Angelo?" he prodded.

Oh.

"Well?" She looked at the BMV photo. Thompson couldn't help but think that all driver's license photos looked like mug shots. Especially her own license.

"Well, I'll be." The same guy in the photo bumped into her at the café. Not once but twice.

"I'll take that as a yes," he said.

"Yes. I saw him."

"He's got a juvie record for assault, but he's clean now. Or so everyone thinks."

"You don't think it's Josh Brady either?"

"Those bozos at SVU wouldn't know a rapist if they got raped themselves by one. Oops, sorry, Sue. I wasn't talking about you. You're the exception."

"No problem."

"I'm with Angelo on that. Josh is not our guy. I'd take a closer look at Stevie here. If I were a betting man, I'd say he's a possibility. I want to dig a little deeper."

Thompson kept quiet and O'Malley glanced over her shoulder.

"Here comes your cuz now."

"What's going on here?" Angelo queried.

"Nothing. Just sharing some information with Sue."

"What information would that be?"

"Stephen Greystock." He handed Angelo the photograph.

Looking at Thompson, she said, "Isn't that…"

"Yeah. The guy who bumped into me at the café. You thought he might have stolen my wallet."

"I knew there was something about him that wasn't right."

"Um," she ventured, "I know you're still pissed at me about going out there on my own…"

"That little stunt you pulled? Yes, I'm still pissed."

"Um, well, he actually bumped into me twice."

"Did he touch you?"

"No. Just apologized again and walked away like he did before, but…"

"But what? Spill it."

"He kind of looked at me funny."

"Is that all?"

"It was the way he looked at me. I automatically went for my wallet."

"I wonder if this is the same Steve who got in Josh's face about Heather."

"Nice guy Steve?"

"Yeah, him."

"Could be. I don't remember seeing too many Steves on the mailing list. Um, Angelo, I don't want to sound paranoid or anything, but I think someone's following me."

"What!"

"You know how that little voice inside your head tells you when things aren't right?"

"Your intuition?"

"Yeah. Well, mine is sending up flares. Maybe I'm just being paranoid like I said. Maybe I'm too close to the situation."

"Don't ever discount that little voice. Saved my life a hundred times."

"I was worried I was just making this stuff up in my head."

"Have you noticed anything indicating that you're being watched?"

"I don't know."

"Anything at all?"

"Well, I'm not sure. I found some footprints around my house. But that could have been the mailman or some city worker, checking the meters."

"What else?"

"The other day Matt came over and we had a little argument in front of the house."

"So?"

"It wasn't anything major, but I didn't think of it until later. I saw this guy in a car across the street watching us. At first I thought it was just a Good Samaritan who was concerned because we were arguing, but then I started thinking about it. It stuck me a strange."

"Did you get a look at the driver?"

"White male. That's all I recall."

"How about the car? What color?"

"Burgundy. Older model foreign car. I'm not good with cars. I couldn't tell just by looking. Some cop I am, huh?"

"Don't say that."

"It's true. I didn't take any notice of it."

"Hmm," Angelo said thoughtfully, sticking a pen in her mouth.

"I'm just being paranoid, aren't I? It's all in my head."

"Maybe, but I've always believed that you should trust your first instincts. It will inevitably save your life."

"What do I do now? Move?"

"I don't think that will be necessary."

O'Malley piped up. "What about Kevin? I thought he was at the top of your short list."

"He's still on my short list, but on the bottom."

"What made you change your mind?"

"I had a chat with him. He's arrogant, a prick and a pervert, but if that was against the law, I'd have to lock up half the police department," she joked. "He lied about not knowing Victoria because he said he thought she filed a complaint on him. But I think it was because his ego was hurt."

"Not because he had something to hide?" he asked.

"I'm sure he has plenty to hide, but not about this. He's an asshole, but not a rapist. He'd probably *deflate* the second someone rejected him."

"That's a vision you had to put in my head," O'Malley said.

"He is too assertive to be a *power reassurance* rapist. His ego is so big he certainly doesn't need the reassurance. He actually had the balls to hit on me."

"Oh, man, that really takes some balls," O'Malley teased. "I hope you turned him down." O'Malley was one of the worse culprits when it came to hitting on her, but he only did it in fun. Angelo never took him seriously.

"Ha, ha, Pat."

"So, now what?" Thompson asked.

"I really hate to do this, but I think you should go back to the café."

"Excuse me?" That wasn't the response Thompson expected.

"It might be too late. He may have already set his sights on you."

Angelo could see Thompson swallow hard. Why was she being so nervous now? Wasn't that what she wanted? "I don't know, Bee…"

"We should try one more time and see if this Steve guy gives you a second glance."

"Really? You're gonna trust me not to foul it up?"

"We really don't have a choice, do we? We might as well strike first."

"Um, yeah," Thompson said worried.

"You're a professional, so you keep telling me. I trust you can handle yourself. However, this time you'll have backup."

"Thanks for believing in me."

"Don't thank me yet. What you will be doing is very dangerous. You can get seriously hurt."

"I risk that every time I go to work."

"O'Malley," Angelo said.

"What?" he asked, chewing a doughnut.

"Time for a little stakeout. We're not going to let Sue out of our sight."

"You think the captain is going to approve the overtime?"

"Hell no. That's why we're going to do this on our own time."

"We are?"

"Yes."

"You know, you're lucky that I like your cousin," he grumbled.

Angelo smiled. She knew O'Malley would never let anything happen to another officer. "Sure."

"When do we start?" Thompson asked.

"Tomorrow at lunch. From now on, you will always have one of us watching your back. Think of us as your permanent shadow until he is caught."

"Thanks, Detective Angelo. Thanks, Detective O'Malley."

"Like I said, don't thank us just yet."

Chapter Nineteen

Sitting in the back seat of the unmarked police car with Angelo and O'Malley, Thompson checked the red wig on her head. After making sure no stray blonde hairs were visible, she turned to Angelo.

"How does it look?" she asked.

"I like you as a redhead," O'Malley commented.

"You'd like any color as long as it belonged to a female," Angelo teased.

"You know me so well, partner."

"Are you all right?"

Thompson swallowed hard. "I'm just a little nervous. I don't know why because I've done this before."

"Just relax. You'll be fine. We've got your back."

"Aren't you coming in?" she asked Angelo.

"I can't. He quite possibly could have seen my face." She pointed to the now healing cut over her eye. "It was dark, but I don't want to take any chances. O'Malley will be in there with you."

"Oh, okay." She smiled at O'Malley.

"Let me give you a bit of advice before you go into the lion's den."

"Don't call it that. I'm allergic to cats," she joked halfhearted.

"Just go in there and have your lunch. Try not to look so nervous. Talk to the people you've already met."

"Right. What if they ask how the job hunt is going? What do I tell them?"

"Just tell them that you'll be hearing from them soon."

"What if they ask where?"

"Tell them you don't want to say because you're superstitious or something."

"Oh. Good idea,"

"If you get his attention, do not return it. If he talks to you, be polite, but under no circumstances are you to encourage him. Do not be forward in any way."

"Why not? I thought we wanted to draw him out."

"That might push him away. He's probably not going to like forwardness in a woman. He wants to be the dominant one. If you come on to him, he will reject you. Be shy and demure."

"What's demure?"

"Kids," Angelo said, glancing at O'Malley who had a large grin on his face. "Just think Melanie from Gone with the Wind."

"I can do that, Scarlet."

"When you're talking about work, say that you're glad to be finally going back on day work. Do not use the phrase *Last Out*. That is a police term. If he is watching, he'll probably know your work schedule. He'll know you are not home at night, so don't lie about that. Mention that you are off this weekend and look forward to a nice quiet evening at home. This way we'll try and get him to make his move in the next two days."

Thompson was feeling a little queasy. "Okay."

Sensing that Thompson was uneasy, Angelo asked, "You sure you want to do this thing? It's not too late to pull out."

"I have no choice now. I screwed it up, making myself a target on my own. I'll have to fix it."

Angelo looked at her watch. "It is now ten minutes to twelve. O'Malley is going in ahead of you to get settled in. You will follow shortly after. He will keep an eye on you and I'll keep in touch by cell phone. You will not have any contact with him. He is a fly on the wall."

"Buzzz!" O'Malley said. "Unobtrusive is my middle name."

"You surprise me, O'Malley."

He raised a bushy eyebrow at Angelo. "Why's that?"

"I didn't think you knew what unobtrusive meant," she teased.

"Har. Har," he snorted, playfully punching Angelo in the arm.

Angelo snickered at her partner, and then turned back to Thompson. "Ready?"

"I'm ready as I'll ever be," Thompson answered.

"You?" Angelo asked O'Malley.

"Angelo, you know I was born ready," he said, grinning.

O'Malley got out of the car and strolled into the coffee house, leaving Angelo alone with Thompson. She turned to the young officer and smile. "It'll be all right, Sue. You're perfectly safe. Nothing will happen to you in there."

"I know."

"What's on your mind then?"

"I'm just worried about what is to come. Later when I'm home alone and he strikes. I just know he's going to come for me. I just know it and it's not my paranoia talking."

"No, it's your sixth sense."

"I'm scared, Bee. I don't want *it* to happen again."

"*It* won't. I'll make sure of that."

"I trust you, Bee. Okay. I'm ready. Let's do this."

Angelo patted her on the shoulder. Thompson exited the car and adjusted her clothing one last time before heading toward the café. Upon entering, she went over to the counter and ordered her usual coffee and bagel, then sat at an unoccupied table in the center of the room. Her stomach was so full of knots that she wasn't sure she could eat anything without wanting to throw up.

Scanning the room, she noticed that the lunchtime crowd had not yet arrived, but people were starting to trickle in. She saw O'Malley sitting on a stool at the bar designed for single customers. He was sipping what appeared to be a large latte. He did not pay her any attention, but watched her out of the corner of his eye. He really could be unobtrusive when he wanted to be.

She also noticed that Josh's table was unoccupied. Even though he was not in the café, no one dare sit there. They must be scared of him. Well, he was a spooky guy. *Just like Box Five,* she mused, thinking of the Phantom of the Opera. Her intended target, Stephen Greystock, was not there yet either. From what she recalled, he only had a half hour lunch break and was in and out by twelve thirty.

Shouldn't be too long now, she thought.

She didn't have to wait long. Within minutes, the crowd gathered and her new friends joined her at the table. Of course, they inquired about her job hunt. She was about to answer them, when she saw Stephen Greystock walk in the door. He was groomed and perfectly tanned. The perfect Adonis. Just what she thought Don Juan would look like. He was arrogant and self assured. With a body like that, it was a wonder the women weren't all over him.

She quickly turned her attention back to her friends and said loudly enough for him to hear, "Yes, I may get that job I've been fighting for."

"Oh, where?" a woman at the table asked.

Remembering what Angelo told her, she replied, "I don't have it just yet and I don't want to jinx it. I'm superstitious that way."

"We understand. We're all like that in some way, aren't we Brett?" the woman said to her male companion.

"We sure are."

"Good luck, Sue."

"Thanks. I'll be glad to be finally able to quit my night job. Third shift does a number to your social life. Wait. What social life?" she joked. "Actually, I just broke up with my boyfriend."

"Oh, he'll come around," Brett said, flirting with her. "If not, I'm here for you."

"Maybe he will and maybe he won't. I never know with him. Once I get a day job, I'll be able to spend a quiet evening at home for a change. I don't remember the last time I actually spent a weekend night at home. I just want to relax and soak in a hot tub filled with expensive, exotic oils."

"That's a fascinating picture you paint, Sue," Brett said.

"We're rooting for you, Susan."

Out of the corner of her eye, she could see Stephen watching her with interest. He licked his lips thoughtfully. That's right. *Got your attention now, don't I, you bastard*, she thought.

"If it all works out, I'll be starting on Monday. I'll have the whole weekend to relax and unwind. I plan on getting myself a nice bottle of wine and just zoning out. Maybe even a little drunk." Just thinking about getting drunk had Thompson sweating. She hadn't had a drink since that night at the frat house.

"Sounds like a plan," Brett said. "You sure you don't want to spend the weekend at my place in the Poconos?"

"That's sweet of you, Brett, but I don't think your wife would appreciate it," Thompson told him.

"How?"

The woman sitting next to him started laughing so hard she was crying. "Got you there, Brett."

"How did you know?" he asked again.

"You have a wedding ring tan line."

"Damn," he said, covering up his ring finger.

"I think you better put it back on before you get yourself into trouble."

He reached in his pocket and retrieved his wedding band, slipping it on his finger. "Guess nothing gets by you, Sue. You ought to be a cop."

"A cop? Hell, no. I'm a big chicken."

They all laughed as lunch continued.

Outside, Angelo watched as people entered and exited the café. She saw Stephen enter the coffee house and gave O'Malley a heads-up by cell phone. Looking at her watch, she noted that it was almost time for him to go back to work.

Then she saw a familiar looking man walking up the block toward the café. Craning her neck to get a better look, she recognized him and said out loud to herself, "Oh, shit!" Quickly, she dialed O'Malley's cell phone.

"Talk to me," he said, sounding like a businessman.

"Trouble coming your way."

"Who?" he asked, then saw the man enter the café. "Damn!"

"Get her out of there before he sees her."

"How the hell do you expect me to do that? Damn it, too late. He's already spotted her."

The man saw Thompson sitting there with the others. Anger was in is eyes. He stalked over to her and grabbed her arm. "What are you doing here!" he demanded under his breath. She looked like a deer caught in a pair of headlights. Everyone at the table was stunned. They never heard him talk, let alone become physical with a stranger.

Standing up, but still being held by the arm by the man, she whispered, "Not now." The man who held her by the elbow was Josh Brady.

Suddenly someone grabbed Josh by the arm and spun him around. "Don't touch the lady!" It was Stephen.

"Back off, Steve!" Josh growled, getting in his face, nose to nose. They looked like they were about to come to blows.

Thompson could see O'Malley getting off his stool to intervene, but stopped when he saw her eyes telling him that she had the situation under control. He did not interfere and backed off, sitting down at the bar. He was still prepared to launch himself at the pair to defend her.

"Gentlemen, please," Thompson said calmly, sounding like a southern bell. She pulled away from Josh's grip.

"We don't want you here," Stephen told Josh. "Your kind is not welcome."

"I have every right to be here, Steve," he spat.

Thompson said gently, "Let's not cause a scene. Everyone back in their corners. No harm done."

Josh glared at her one last time, but thankfully didn't blow her cover. He walked away and sat at his table, mumbling to himself. Everyone thought he lost his mind.

"Are you okay, miss?"

"Fine."

"You know that crazy jerk?" he asked, looking daggers at Josh.

"No. Never met him before. Maybe he has me mistaken for someone else. It happens all the time. I guess I have one of those faces."

"You have a lovely face," he said, stroking her cheek.

Thompson could feel the acid in her stomach rise. She suddenly had an idea. "Oh," she cried, collapsing into his chest.

"Are you all right?" he asked, steadying her.

"I'm sorry; I suddenly got a little faint. I'm all right now. I have to go. Thanks for the chivalry," she said, walking away and out of the café. Stephen watched as she exited and followed a few minutes later, having to return to work.

Getting in the back seat of the car and ducking down, Angelo could see she was sweating. "You did good, kid."

"How'd Josh get out?"

"I told you that they wouldn't be able to hold him for long. He probably posted bail."

"That was close. He almost blew my cover."

"But he didn't."

"I wonder why."

Angelo shrugged her shoulders. "He probably wants this guy caught as much as we do."

"Maybe."

O'Malley returned to the car and got in the front seat. "That was great," he said.

"Great? My heart still hasn't settled."

Patting Thompson on the shoulder and nearly knocking the breath out of her, he said, "That's your adrenaline. What a rush! You handled yourself well. I'm really impressed, and it takes a lot to impress me."

"Really?"

"Damn, fine work, kiddo."

Thompson smiled at O'Malley.

"Yes," Angelo agreed.

"I'm a little confused by that little fainting spell you did in there. Are you feeling okay?" O'Malley asked.

"Yes. I feel fine."

"You fainted?" Angelo said surprised.

"No. I was just satisfying my curiosity. And guess what?"

"What?"

"I was right. He has a nipple ring."

"He does?"

"Yes. On the same side that Ms. Tully said there was. Left side."

"That's very interesting."

"You think we got his attention?"

"Oh, yes," O'Malley said. "If you didn't before, you sure as hell have now. You didn't see him because you had already left, but if a man looked at my daughter the way he was leering after you, I'd have to kill him."

"Let's hope that won't be necessary," Angelo said. "Come on, let's go back to your place and set everything up. Tonight might be the night he strikes."

"I'm honestly not looking forward to it. Chasing criminals is one thing, but being the bait is a whole different matter entirely."

"I know. Trust me, I know."

"Think of it this way, kid," O'Malley said. "Tonight, we might just pinch Don Juan."

***

The set up was simple. Thompson would stay at home and try, as hard as it might seem, to relax. She would go about her usual routine. Meanwhile,

Angelo and O'Malley would tail Stephen Greystock in separate cars so he wouldn't become suspicious that the same car was following him all night. If he spotted her or O'Malley, he'd know it was a set up right away.

Although Angelo and O'Malley would be on the street, Thompson would not be left alone. Thompson protested because Angelo would have to enlist the help of Officer Seymour. He would be her back up, staying with her and watching her house during the night.

Of course, they'd have to ask him first.

"You think he'll do it without bitching?" Thompson asked, offering the detectives soft drinks as they sat in her living room. They needed the sugar rush.

"He'll probably complain and whine about it, but he'll do it if he knows what's good for him and his career," Angelo said.

O'Malley remained silent. From what he heard about the officer, his opinion of him was not very high.

"He'll do it because he wants the pinch and he's welcome to it."

"Why can't you stay with me and let Seymour do the tail?" Thompson asked, sipping her diet soft drink.

O'Malley answered her. "He doesn't have the experience. Angelo and me. We're a team. We read each other. It takes years of working with a partner to know how they operate."

"A compliment, O'Malley? I'm touched," Angelo joked.

"Don't get that big head of yours too inflated, Angelo. Besides, I'd rather have a man watching Sue."

"I beg your pardon!" Angelo protested.

"That's not what I mean and you know it. Hell, I'd rather have one of you watching my back than twenty men."

"Gee, thanks. I think I'm gonna get all misty eyed."

"Don won't expect a man to be at Sue's house. It'll give him an edge if there has to be a takedown."

"Maybe you're right," Thompson said. "Take him by surprise and push him off balance."

"Right. He's all about control," Angelo said. "Well, I guess I should call Seymour." She picked up the telephone and called him at home. It was still early in the afternoon.

It rang twice before being picked up. "Hello?" he said sleepily.

"Seymour?"

"Yes? What?"

"Angelo. We need to talk."

"About what? If you're waking me up to talk about Josh—"

"Forget Josh. If you want to catch Don, you'll meet us at Thompson's house."

"What the hell are you talking about? We caught him. It's only a matter of time until we get more evidence and a confession."

"It's not Josh and we'll prove it."

"How?"

"Get here now or I'll call in someone from Homicide to take your spot in the arrest."

"Hold it; I didn't say I wasn't coming. Won't you at least tell me what the hell is going on?"

"When you get here all your questions will be answered in short order." She gave him Thompson's Fox Chase address.

"All right. This better be worth it."

"Believe me, it is."

"I'll be there in thirty minutes or less."

"Just like my pizza guy," Angelo joked.

"Excuse me?"

"Never mind. Just get here." She hung up the phone. "He's on his way."

"One question, Bee, shouldn't we tell a supervisor what we're doing?"

"Already done. Trust me. I play by the rules. He is not going to get off on a technicality. The captain gave us his blessing. The Brass wants this joker even worse than the politicians."

Thompson nodded.

"His exact words were, 'Whatever it takes.' And he meant it."

"Oh, good. I was worried we've gone rogue cop or something."

Angelo laughed. I've learned a long time ago never to play cowboy. It could get you fired or worse—killed. Something you should have learned by now."

"Oh, I've learned that already. Trust me."

"Good girl. Now all we have to do is wait for Seymour and then the game begins."

***

Seymour stabbed his finger on Thompson's doorbell and held it there for a few seconds. While waiting for a reply, he stomped his feet impatiently in the snow. She opened the door and glared at him in a not-so-friendly way. He returned the hostile stare. They looked like two boxers ready to go at it in the ring, growling at each other. He appeared tired and unshaven. Even more, he looked very annoyed.

"This better be good, Thompson," he nearly snarled at her.

"Hello to you too," she replied, standing aside to let him in. He brushed past her and she closed the door behind him.

"Where is Angelo?"

"*Detective Angelo!*" she shouted from the living room. "In here, Officer."

Thompson suppressed a smirk. *Damn, Angelo has some sharp hearing.* "This way," she told Seymour, showing him the way.

As they entered the living room, Seymour stared at the man with Angelo. He did not know him, but he had seen him before. "This is my partner Detective Patrick O'Malley," Angelo explained.

"You will call me *Detective O'Malley*," he said.

Seymour could see that the detective had a low opinion of him. *Probably Angelo's doing*, he thought bitterly. *Who cares?* "Is someone going to tell me what the hell is going on? Why was I dragged out of bed?"

"All in good time. Have a seat."

"You want a soda or something?" Thompson asked, trying to play the gracious hostess.

"I don't have time for this game you are playing!" Seymour snapped.

"You better watch it, boy," O'Malley growled at him. Immediately Seymour took a step back.

"Listen up, Officer," Angelo said.

He tore his gaze away from O'Malley and looked at Angelo. "I'm all ears."

"We have reason to believe that Stephen Greystock, not Josh Brady, is Don Juan."

"How?"

"We pulled his juvenile records and even though it was expunged, I found that he has a record of assault against a girl. He's been clean ever since."

"So? If he's been clean what makes you think he's our guy?"

"Just because he hasn't got an adult record doesn't mean he's been clean all this time. Don Juan is a clever bastard. He knows how to keep his identity a secret. Don't you think he could have learned from his one mistake?"

Seymour shrugged his shoulders.

"Susan has been undercover and believes she is being stalked." Angelo did not mention that her little undercover operation was unauthorized. Why make an issue out of it?

"Are you positive?"

"Reasonably."

"Not one hundred percent?"

"Nothing is one hundred percent. If we were that certain we would have gotten a warrant. But we need more proof."

"So tell me what makes you think Susie is being stalked and not just being paranoid?"

"I'm not paranoid, you jerk!" Thompson snapped. Susan took that as a major insult, especially on the professional level.

Angelo continued, ignoring their little comments to one another. "Earlier today we went back to the café and subtly announced that Sue will be home alone this weekend. We noticed Stephen paying particular attention to her. We think he took the bait. If we can catch him in the act of stalking, we'll have enough to get that warrant to search his apartment. He's a trophy taker. He's bound to have the stuff there. All we need is probable cause for the warrant. We have a two day window for him to strike."

"If he strikes."

"No, I believe he will. He's arrogant. He will try. I feel it."

"Okay, fine. What's the plan?" It was easy to tell he was a little skeptical of the entire thing, but he played along. He didn't want to end up with egg on his face if Angelo and Thompson ended up being right.

"O'Malley and I will tail him after he gets off work. If we have to follow him around all day, we will. However, I'm certain he'll strike between eleven in the evening and six in the morning. That's his pattern. They don't usually stray."

"Yes. To strike while the victim is home alone in bed or about to enter the house late at night."

"Right."

"Okay, go on."

"We will follow him in two cars and keep everyone advised by mobile phone." She pointed to the coffee table where three mobile-to-mobile phones sat charging in their bases.

"What will I be doing during all this?"

"You will have the most important part."

"And that is?"

"You're going to be watching Thompson's back."

He glared at Thompson. "In her house?"

"Yes. You got a problem with that?"

"No."

"For now, you can stay inside, but once it gets late, you will be outside in your car to watch the street. If you see him or his burgundy car, you will watch him. He drives an older model Mazda. If he makes one move toward the house, you will call in the Calvary. We shouldn't be too far away ourselves. We will attempt an apprehension before he can get to Susan."

"Right."

"You will take great care and back Thompson at all costs, got that?"

"Of course. She may be a pain in the ass…" he started.

"Hey!" Thompson shouted at Seymour.

He ignored her. "But she is an officer. I've got her back."

"You're so kind," she said sarcastically.

"When do we start?"

Angelo looked at her watch. "In about two hours. Stephen gets off at five. We'll be there when he does. It's going to be a long day. O'Malley and I will probably need relief. Do you think you guys can handle it here?"

"I think I can stand to be in Thompson's company for a few hours."
"Bone head," she mumbled.
"I'm sure you've cleared this little venture with the captain."
"Of course. Yours and mine. Don't worry you'll get paid."
"I'm not worried about that."
"No?"
"No. I just wanted to make sure this little stunt was authorized."
"I know how to do my job, Officer," Angelo snapped.
"I'm sure you do. I'm still not convinced it's Stephen Greystock. Stephen the momma's boy. It's a stretch."
"All I know right now is that it is not Josh."
"We'll see who is right about this," he said smugly.
"Oh, you can bet your boots, we'll see."
Seymour grinned at Thompson. "I guess I'll have that soda after all."
"Get it yourself!" Thompson snapped, pointing toward the kitchen. "I'm your partner tonight, not your slave."
Angelo laughed. It was going to be an interesting evening. Hopefully the two young officers wouldn't end up killing each other.

***

At exactly five minutes past five, Stephen Greystock sauntered out of the office building, put on a pair of dark sunglasses, and got into his burgundy Mazda. O'Malley was half a block away in his beat up Ford, watching with a pair of binoculars. He keyed his mobile phone.
"Elvis has left the building. He's on the move," he informed Angelo.
"Okay. Let me know which way he's headed so I can pick up the tail."
"Ten-four, good buddy."
O'Malley watched as he drove off, heading south on the Boulevard and turning onto Rhawn Street. He continued north on Rhawn until he hit Torresdale Avenue and then turned left. He pulled in front of a small red-bricked apartment complex and got out of the car, checking his reflection in the side view mirror.
"Boy this guy is self centered," O'Malley commented over the cell phone.
"Probably very narcissistic."
"Damn right. This boy's got some major issues to iron out. And I thought Kevin was bad, but man, this boy takes the cake."
"Tell me about it. Okay, what's he doing now?"
"Looks like pretty boy is going into his apartment building."
Angelo checked the BMV records. She read off the address on his driver's license. "Is that the address?" she asked.
"Yup. He's home."
"I'm a few blocks away. Is there any other way in or out of the complex?"

"It's not a big building. Maybe twenty apartments. I see fire escapes on the east side, but the entrance seems to be the only way in front."

"What about the west side?"

"It's connected to another building."

"I'm going around back to see if there are any back doors."

"Okay."

He waited a few minutes until Angelo contacted him again. "O'Malley, there is a rear exit, but entry can't be gained."

"One way exit only?"

"Yes. Well, his car is out front. I don't think he's going anywhere just yet."

"Probably preening himself," O'Malley said in disgust.

"Is there somewhere we can meet and still keep the building and car in sight?"

O'Malley looked around. "Shopping center across the street on the east side."

"Meet me there."

"Okay."

They met in the shopping center's parking lot across the street. O'Malley parked his car at an angle where he could see the front and rear of the building as well as the fire escapes.

"We're in luck," Angelo told him as she got into his car.

"Yes. We can see everything from this vantage point."

"So, I guess all we can do now is wait."

He yawned. "Do you think we should call in that manpower?"

"I think so. It's been a long day and we need to be on our toes tonight. Let me make a few phone calls. We'll get someone to take our post and watch him until about eleven. This way we can get a few hours sleep before we take over again."

"I'd like to take a shower. I'd like to be fresh as a daisy when we catch this sonofabitch."

"I'd prefer it too," she teased, waving a hand in front of her nose.

"For a minute I thought you were gonna make us stay here all night."

"I'm not that cruel. Besides, I'm tired. I can't think when I'm tired."

"You are cruel. You might be able to get by on a two hour nap, but I need my beauty sleep."

"Tell you what. Instead of you going all the way back to southwest, you can bunk at my place for the afternoon and sack out. Sam might even feed you."

"Oh, my God! Are you asking me to sleep at your crib?"

"Sleep. That's all you'll be doing there, Patrick. Remember, Sam will be there to protect my virtue."

O'Malley laughed. "Oh, okay then. Are you sure you've got enough room?

I can take the couch."

"Not the *Chippendale*."

"Huh? You have strippers there?"

"No, what...? No, you great lummox, the *sofa's* a Chippendale. Never mind. I've got plenty of room."

"Deal. I've always wanted to see your place."

"Here is your chance. Your last chance if you don't behave."

"What about the kids?"

"Who?"

"Thompson and Seymour."

"They can get all the rest they want at Thompson's place."

A sly grin crossed O'Malley's pudgy face. "Lucky dog."

"I wouldn't say that. We'll be lucky if they don't try to kill each other."

"That's a thought. Seymour's got a bug up his ass about Sue."

"She's got one up hers about him too. Aren't you glad we don't fight?"

"Since when?"

She didn't answer. "Let me make those calls and get us some relief."

Angelo called the Homicide Unit and requested two detectives from Two Squad to help with the surveillance. They were happy to help. Afterwards she called Thompson and told her that they would be at her house in Mt. Airy getting some rest. She advised her and Seymour to do the same and said that she'd call about eleven. Thompson agreed.

When the two detectives from Homicide showed up it was a quarter to six in the evening. After giving the relief a photo and pointing out the car, they were instructed to keep a low profile and follow him wherever he went. They were to keep a log of all the places he visited.

They were told not to make a move on him unless he did something criminal and a life was in danger. She didn't expect him to, but there was always a chance. If he made a move on Thompson, she was to be called immediately. They were to protect Thompson and Seymour at all costs.

After everything was set up and Angelo thanked them for the help, she headed home with O'Malley following in his car. By now, she really needed some sleep.

***

Seymour was making himself at home—in her home! Feet propped up on her coffee table as if he lived there; he stretched out on the couch. Thompson glared at him.

"Hey!" she shouted. "Do you mind? This is not your house. It's mine. Get your stinking feet off my coffee table!"

He slid his feet down to the floor. "Sorry," he said.

"If you want to sack out, there is a spare bedroom upstairs."

"I'll be okay here. You can go up and rest if you want."

"Gee, thanks."

"You don't like me, do you?"

"How did you guess?" she asked caustically.

"Why not? I'm not so bad."

"Since when do you care about what people think of you?"

"I've got feelings, y'know."

"Really? I find that hard to believe."

"Why?"

"Because you're a pain in the ass."

"So are you," he said, grinning.

"Am not."

"Well, neither am I. So there." He stuck his tongue out at her, doing his best impression of a three year old.

"Baby!"

"So, why don't you like me?"

"You want to know why?"

"Yes I do."

"You stole my investigation."

"Yours? How was it yours? The lieutenant gave it to me."

"Yes, mine!" she said, holding her hands on her hips.

"How?"

"I uncovered the link between the cases. I gave it to the supervisor. And what does the lieutenant do? I'll tell you what she does. She gave it to you. Her Golden Boy!"

"Granted, but I have more experience in the unit. I have more time on the job too."

"Yes, you may have the time and the experience, but I did all the work on my own. Put it all together, piece by piece. That should have counted for something."

"You went to Angelo."

"So?"

"Everyone knows Angelo's reputation. You got lucky, getting her to listen to you." At that point, he was almost harassing her, but he was mostly trying to intimidate her. He wanted her to think that she didn't deserve the case. Thompson wasn't that weak.

"Angelo got involved because of her friend. I don't see anything wrong with going to her. You did that with the supervisor."

She had him there. "Yeah, but even my supervisor is afraid of Angelo. She's a somebody in the department. How do you think she got on the Victoria Sterling case? She was on IOD status. Wasn't just sheer luck and good timing. She asked for the case. No. I bet she *demanded* it."

"Angelo is a great investigator and I'm not just saying that. She's not conceited or above everyone else. She's just a regular cop. She's just good at what she does. She started helping me because of her friend, not because I asked her. She would have done the same for you if you had only asked."

"Perhaps."

"She would. I'm telling you."

He thought about it for a moment. "Her friend was victim number six, right?"

"She has a name, Seymour."

"Sorry. Jennifer Tully. How'd you get that job?"

"The corporal gave it to me because she was doing Angelo a favor. It was a dead job. Her friend didn't want to report it, but Angelo did. Something about the case bothered me so I took the initiative and found out about similar cases. Angelo had nothing to do with that. I did it on my own. I only brought it to her attention after the lieutenant gave the jobs to you. I didn't go looking to make trouble for you, although I was pissed. I didn't go looking for a rabbi."

"But she is yours now. Why didn't you tell me about Jennifer Tully if you knew it was connected?"

"I told you. She didn't want it reported."

"Are you sure that's the only reason?"

"Well, to be honest, I didn't want you to steal that from me too."

"I'm not a thief," he huffed.

"Call it rookie paranoia. Look, I'm sure once this is all over with, I'll go my way, and she'll go hers. I'm just doing this for the experience. I'll take all the instruction I can from Angelo."

"How about we call a truce?"

"I'm not at war with you."

"Seems that way."

"Well, I'm not. We're going to be here a while, so we might as well try to get along. I can do it if you can."

"I can. I promise not to murder you in your sleep."

She laughed. "I'll try to do the same. Not murder you, I mean."

"Sue, I really do have your back on this. I won't let anyone harm you."

"Nice to know. And I got yours too."

"Go and get some sleep. You're going to need it. If you're right about this stalking thing, you can be in some serious danger." He paused, lowering the volume of his voice. "I wouldn't want anything to happen to you," he mumbled.

"What did you say?"

"Nothing. Go to sleep."

"Okay. You can either stay here on the couch or utilize the spare room."

"I'll be fine here."

"Just keep your grubby feet off my coffee table!"

He smirked at her. Thompson turned and headed up the stairs. She went into her bedroom, closing the door behind her. Out of nothing but sheer habit, she locked her bedroom door.

What's wrong with me? Seymour is not a threat.

Old habits die hard.

Will I ever get over it? she wondered, settling down for a nap.

Chapter Twenty

O'Malley followed behind Angelo in his car. When they pulled up the driveway, he had the same reaction that Thompson had earlier. He couldn't believe his eyes at the size of the house. *This can't be her house. Not on a cop's salary, even with the overtime.* He knew she lived in a ritzy area of Mt. Airy, but he didn't expect this. It wasn't a house, it was a mansion. He'd be able to fit three of his houses in hers.

"Jesus Christ on stilts, Angelo!" he exclaimed, getting out of his car. "You can't be serious."

"What?"

"This is a rental. You rent an apartment, right? One of the rooms?"

"What are you talking about? No, it's all ours. Mine and Sam's."

He shook his head in wonder. "If I didn't know you better, I'd think you were pulling my chain. But you don't joke like that, do you?"

"Nope," she said grinning. "Sam makes a pretty good living out of writing girly romance novels."

"No wonder you don't invite your coworkers to your crib."

"I invited you, didn't I?"

"Yeah, after what? Five years of working with me? God, I can't wait to see the inside," he said, rubbing his hands together in anticipation.

"Just keep your grubby paws off the antiques."

"You collect antiques? Would have never guessed that."

"I don't, Sam does. And you know how he likes to protect what's his."

He smirked. "Yeah."

"Stop gawking and come on inside. It's cold out here."

"I smell a fireplace."

"Sam probably has one going."

"I love fireplaces," he remarked, walking with her to the front door.

"Me too."

She opened the door and they walked into the grand foyer. O'Malley's mouth dropped open even more. He looked like a codfish. "Holy…"

Angelo ignored him and walked into the living room. Sam was sitting by the fireplace, reading a book. "Hi, Sam."

"Hello, sweetheart," Sam replied and looked behind her. "Good afternoon, Detective O'Malley."

"Pat. Call me Pat."

"Call you stunned more like it," Angelo teased.

"Good to see you again, Sam," O'Malley said, reaching out his hand to him.

They shook hands as if they were long time friends even though they met for the first time only four weeks before. After Sam killed the man who attacked his wife, it was O'Malley's job to interview him at the unit that day. Sam liked O'Malley instantly. As much as Angelo bitched about him, he knew that she really loved him like a brother. O'Malley had on one occasion saved her life. Sam would be forever grateful.

"Um, O'Malley's gonna get some sleep here this afternoon. We have a stakeout tonight."

"That's great. You're welcome any time, Pat."

"Really? Thanks!" he said, sounding like a thrilled child.

Angelo rolled her eyes. "Now we'll never get rid of him."

Sam laughed out loud. "Can I get you something to eat?"

O'Malley opened his mouth to answer, but looked at Angelo first. He didn't want Sam to go through any trouble. "No, better not. I can't nap on a full stomach."

"Since when is your stomach ever empty?"

"You know, Sam, you're wife is incredibly mean to me."

Sam shrugged his shoulders. "She's like that with everyone."

"I beg your pardon!"

"Tell you what. I'll pack you two a lunch for your stakeout."

"Wow, Angelo, if I didn't know better I'd think your hubby is setting us up on a date."

"In your dreams," Angelo said.

He would have said something lewd, but refrained. He wouldn't dare, not with Sam in the room. He had too much respect for him. Besides, Angelo would probably punch him in the head for it.

"Pat, go out the way we came in and go up the stairs. Go down the hall and pick a room."

"Any room?"

"Yeah. Just stay out of mine. I don't want you pawing through my things.

It's bad enough that you do it at the unit."

"Oh, okay. Hope I don't get lost."

"If you do we'll send out the St. Bernard."

"With the whiskey?"

"Not while on duty. I need you sober."

"Spoil sport. Are you gonna trust me not to steal anything?"

"I'll be sure to check the inventory later. I need to talk to Sam. I'll catch up to you in a few minutes."

"Right. Nice seeing you again, Sam."

"Same here, Pat."

When O'Malley left the room, Sam asked, "What's up? Something on your mind?"

"Nothing really. I just wanted to keep you informed with all that's going on."

"Has to be serious if you're letting O'Malley stay here."

"We have to stick together tonight."

"So what's going on?"

"We set up a trap for Don Juan."

"You know who he is?"

"We have a strong suspicion, but no proof. We need to catch him in the act."

"And just who is the bait?"

"Thompson."

"I thought you nixed her idea?"

"I did, but it might have been too late. We can't undo what's been done, so we might as well use it to our advantage."

"You'll be careful?"

"Of course. Plenty of backup."

"What about Susan?"

"I have an officer with her at all times. At the moment, two detectives are keeping an eye on our suspect. We will take over the surveillance about eleven."

"We?"

"Me and O'Malley. That's why I want him here with me. Wouldn't want him to get lost. You know how he is."

"Yeah, sure."

"I'm going to check on him and make sure he gets some sleep. Can you wake us around ten?"

"Sure. No problem. And I'll pack you guys that dinner."

"Thanks Sam. You're a love."

"I know."

"I love you," she said, kissing him.

"Ditto, Bee. More than you can ever imagine. Be careful."

"I will. Not to worry."

She kissed him again and left the living room to go upstairs. She knocked on the guest bedroom door before entering. God forbid she'd walk in on him naked or something. She found O'Malley playing with the entertainment center.

The sight of O'Malley watching TV was enough to annoy Angelo. Not only was he making himself at home in her house, she knew what the job they were going to would require. "Pat, you're here to get some sleep. Not watch the television." She reached for the remote control.

"Oh, come on. I've never seen a TV this big before."

"Off!" she said, turning off the television.

"No fair, Mom!"

"You can play later. After we arrest the suspect."

"Oh! You promise? You mean you're going to invite me back?"

"If you behave. Now, you have a private shower and plenty of smelly soaps in there. You'll smell just like that fresh daisy."

"Cool."

"Sam is going to wake us at ten. That should give us enough time to get back on post."

He looked at his watch. Three hours sleep was better than nothing at all. "Okay."

"See you later. Enjoy your shower," she said, leaving the room.

She could hear him turn the television back on. She rolled her eyes and went into her own room. She flopped onto the bed, her legs hanging over the side. She inhaled deeply, smelling Sam there. Within minutes, she was fast asleep.

Thankfully, this time she did not dream.

***

Just as Sam promised, he packed them an overnight picnic basket full of the largest sandwiches and best tasting, overpriced coffee O'Malley had ever had in his life. They were back on post by eleven that evening, relieving the detectives already there from the afternoon.

Parked across the street where the suspect's apartment building could be seen front and rear, Angelo walked over to the unmarked detective's car and leaned in the window.

"Any movement?" she asked.

"He went out about eight. Drove to a restaurant on Rising Sun Avenue and had dinner. We followed him inside, but he didn't notice us. He was too preoccupied with himself to notice anyone. Kept looking at himself in the stainless steel napkin holder and fixing his hair. And I thought women were vain."

"Then what?"

"He had a rather large meal, ate it, and then came back home. That's all he did since we've been here."

"Filling up on carbs, no doubt."

"Angelo, you really think it's this guy?"

"It's a very strong possibility."

"Well, I hope so. We need to end this."

"I totally agree with you, Carl. That's exactly what I intend to do."

"Good luck and be safe."

"We will. Not to worry. Thanks for your help."

"Anytime, Bee. You know that."

She winked at him and patted the roof of the car as they drove off. Going back to O'Malley, she got into the passenger's side of the vehicle. O'Malley was already digging into his corn beef sandwich. "Mmm," he was saying to himself.

"Enjoying?"

"You bet. You know, Angelo, if Sam wasn't your husband, I'd be after him myself."

Angelo laughed at her partner. "Gee, Pat, I'm glad you're secure with your sexuality."

"Shut up," he mumbled with his mouth full.

Angelo opened the Thermos that held the hot coffee and poured him a cup, handing it to him. "Here. This is a hundred times better than that crap you drink at the unit." He took the steaming cup from her and took a sip. He practically sighed when he tasted it.

"Oh, God, it's better than sex," he commented. "You've ruined all other coffee for me."

She shook her head and took a sip herself. "Yes," she replied.

"So, what did Carl and Phil have to report?"

"Greystock only left to go out to dinner. We'll have to be ready for him when he makes his move."

"You think he will make his move tonight?"

"I hope so. He needs to be stopped."

"Stopped or punished?" he asked. He knew this was personal for Angelo.

"Both," she admitted, rubbing the cut above her eye. "He hurt a good friend of mine. He got the better of me in a fight and you know how I hate to lose a fight."

"Don't I ever."

Changing the subject, she asked, "How's the sandwich?"

"Fan-freaking-tastic! Corn beef. Just what an Irishman like myself lives for."

"Glad you like it. Sam has this need to feed people."

"Not a damn thing wrong with that. You know food is an aphrodisiac."
"Is your mind always on sex?"
"Ninety nine percent of the time, yes. Like most men."
"I don't know how you guys get through the day."
"Not easy. You can't tell me that women don't think about it."
She grinned wily. "Well, not all the time, but it does come up on occasion."
"How'd you get so lucky?"
"Huh?"
"To snag a great guy like Sam?"
"Fate."
"What do you mean? Fate?"
"Destiny. You know. Meant to be. That sort of thing. I've known Sam most all my life. We grew up together. We were both six when he moved next door to me. We've been together ever since. I'll always love him. There will never be anyone else."
"You mean there wasn't anyone else besides him? Ever?"
"Never."
"I wish I had that," he sighed.
"I believe there is someone for everyone. You just have to find them."
"I thought that someone was my ex-wife, but she just couldn't handle the long hours and constant attention I had to give the job. That's why she divorced me. That was about fifteen years ago now."
"Ever try to work it out?"
"Yeah, but I don't think we were really meant for each other. Not like you and Sam. I mean, sure I loved her—I still do—but the job always got in the way."
"The job can do that. That's why I don't let it."
"How do you do it?"
"What?"
"You spend more time at work than you do with your husband. How do you keep it strong and fresh?"
"Like I said, we're soul mates. We make the time for each other."
"I'm happy for you guys. I wish you the greatest happiness."
"Thanks, Pat. That means a lot to me." She took another sip of her coffee, inhaling the aroma. "You have kids, right?"
"Yeah. A son and a daughter. They are grown now. Peter is in college, studying to be a medical doctor and Patricia, my eldest, is getting her Ph.D. in criminology. I've very proud of them."
"So you should. Your daughter taking after her old man?"
"Yes. I've always been close to my daughter. Even after the divorce. That's why I want this guy caught so badly. If anything like that ever happened to my

daughter, I'd kill him with my bare hands. Slowly and painfully."

"You can't take the law in your own hands."

"Screw the law! My daughter means everything to me. I wouldn't care if I spent the rest of my life in prison as long as she was avenged and justice was served."

"I understand."

"Why don't you have any kids? Sam would make a great father."

Angelo looked down at her hands, watching the steam rise from her cup of coffee. "I have a problem conceiving." She couldn't believe she just told him that.

"Gee, that bites. Anything the doctors can do?"

"I guess. However, I'm not sure I want children right now. I know for sure that Sam wants them desperately but..."

"But what?"

"I'm afraid," she mumbled.

"You? Afraid? That's the funniest thing I've ever heard you say."

"No. Seriously. What kind of world would I be bringing a child into?"

"You can't think like that, Bee. Children are the greatest gift God gives us."

"I know, but still...."

"Ever think of getting some medical help? You know the things doctors can do with infertility these days is amazing."

"Pat, you're starting to sound like Sam."

"I mean it."

"I know. I think it's more of a mental thing with me, than an actual physical problem. I can conceive. It's just..."

"Just what?"

She wasn't sure she wanted to be discussing her personal feelings, let alone her problems, with her partner. She didn't even tell Sam. *Oh, what the hell. It might make me feel better.* "I got pregnant a little over a year ago."

"Really? I didn't know. What happened?"

"I lost the baby when Sam had the accident. It was my fault. I rushed to the scene and was so traumatized that I miscarried. I didn't even know I was pregnant until the doctor told me at the hospital."

"How did Sam take it?"

"I never told him. He doesn't know and you had better not say a word to him! I swear, I'll kill you myself if you do!" she snapped. She started to wonder if revealing that little secret to O'Malley was a wise choice.

"I won't say a word. I promise. You have my word as your partner."

"Sorry. It's still a touchy subject with me."

"Why haven't you told him?"

"He had enough problems with his paralysis and the loss of his agent,

Kathy. I didn't want to add the fact that I just lost our first born because of the accident too."

"Oh."

"He's been bringing up the baby subject again. I don't know what to do. I do want to have his children, but I'm afraid to lose another one."

"Who says you're going to lose the next one?"

She shrugged her shoulders.

"Bee, listen to me. You're the strongest, most intelligent woman I have ever known. And I know a lot of women."

She grinned.

"You need to talk to Sam. Stop making up excuses about why you don't want to have a baby. You're not getting any younger."

"Hey!"

"I'm serious. A child would bring you something that is missing in your lives."

"Who says anything is missing?"

"I do. It will make you stronger. But you'll never know until you talk to Sam."

"Maybe."

"I'm right about this. Look, you're my partner. I may pick on you, tease you, and even hit on you, but I love you like a sister. Maybe even like a daughter."

"Really?" O'Malley never talked to her like he was doing now. She was grateful to have him as a friend and a partner.

"Yes. You and Sam have something special. You have nothing to fear. Any future children you two have would be lucky to have you as parents."

"Do you really believe that?"

"Hell, even I want to be adopted by you and Sam."

She laughed. "Sam made you corn beef. I think he has already adopted you."

"Seriously. Talk to him. He'll understand why you are hesitant. He might be upset that you didn't tell him about the miscarriage, but once it's out in the open you'll feel better. I promise."

"You're right. And that doesn't happen often."

"I know I'm right. Take it from a father who would do anything for his children. I wouldn't steer you wrong."

"Okay, Pat. Point taken."

When there was nothing else to say, they continued watching the suspect's apartment in silence. It was going to be a long night. Full of thinking and lots of hot coffee.

***

About quarter to midnight, Stephen Greystock made his move. He left his apartment and got into his car. O'Malley elbowed Angelo in her side, getting her attention. "Hey, he's on the prowl," he told her.

She looked across the street. "Right. Follow him. I'll follow behind you," she said exiting his car and getting into her own. O'Malley drove off first, following discreetly behind the suspect's car. Angelo trailed a few blocks behind, keeping in touch by mobile phone.

"He's getting on the Boulevard," O'Malley informed her.

"Which way?"

"South toward Cottman."

He was moving away from Thompson's residence. Where was he going?

"I'll pick up the trail at Cottman," she told him.

Angelo bucked ahead of them and waited at the Cottman Avenue exit on the boulevard. She spotted the suspect's vehicle and was surprised when he got off the Boulevard there. He turned right on Cottman and drove into the mall parking lot.

"What's he doing?" O'Malley asked. "Do you see him?"

"Yes. He just went into the mall."

"This time of night? The mall is closed."

"I'll follow and let you know."

She did not cut through the mall's parking lot behind him. There weren't any other cars in the lot and she didn't want him to spot her following, so she went around the block. There were only a few exits that he could take to get out of the mall. She could see all of them from the street.

"He's turning right on Bustleton. Getting on Bliegh. Wait, he's parking."

"Where?"

"Movie theater."

"He's going to see a movie?"

"How should I know?"

She parked and watched as he got out of the car and sauntered over to the box office. O'Malley parked his car next to Angelo.

"A movie? He's going to see a freakin' movie?"

Angelo shrugged her shoulders. "Midnight showing."

"You think I should go in and keep an eye on him?"

She thought about it. "Well, he's not going anywhere without his car. Just go up to the box office and see what's playing."

"Okay." O'Malley walked over to the theater and checked out the playing times. He returned a few minutes later, getting back into his car and turning up the heat. "God, I hate the winter."

"Well?"

"Only one midnight movie and it's three hours long."

"Maybe he was bored at home and needed something to do before he

made a move on Sue."
"Revving himself up?"
"Yeah. He usually strikes in the early morning hours."
"Well, the movie's over at three. I guess we'll just have to wait."
"That's all we can do for now. Let me give Seymour and Thompson a call."
Angelo keyed her mobile phone to contact Seymour. He picked up the phone.
"Seymour here," he responded.
"He's out."
"On his way?"
"Not quite. He's gone to the movies."
"Excuse me?"
"He's at the mall catching a midnight movie."
"Why?"
"Who knows. Maybe he wants something to do for the next couple of hours."
"Or you can be wrong and we're wasting time."
"Don't start with me, Officer."
"Sorry."
"Remember that he usually strikes in the early morning hours when his victims are already home."
"Right."
"In a little while, I want you outside in your car. Make sure the house is secure front and rear. Stay out of sight, but don't let the house out of your field of vision. When he makes his move, we'll let you know. Remember; don't try to apprehend him by yourself. He could be dangerous. We shouldn't be too far off ourselves."
"Don't worry about us."
"Have Thompson stay in her bedroom."
"Will do."
"Be careful."
"I will, stop worrying. I won't let anything happen to Sue."
"I know you won't."
After Angelo hung up, Seymour went over to Thompson who was having a cup of tea in the living room. "What did Angelo have to say? Is Greystock on the way here?"
"Not quite. He's gone to see a movie."
"Weird."
"I just hope we're not wasting our time following this guy around all night."
"It's him. Stop being such a Doubting Thomas."
"The boss wants me outside. Doesn't she know it's cold out?"
"She's out there too, y'know."
"Yeah. I don't know why I just can't stay here."

"Perhaps it's because you wouldn't see him coming until it was too late. You have to grab him before he gets inside."

"I guess you're right."

"I made you some coffee," she said, handing him a large thermos.

"Thanks."

"No, thank you."

"For what?"

"For watching my back."

He shrugged his shoulders. "I'd watch any cop's back."

"And I thought you finally liked me. I guess I was wrong."

He could see that he had hurt her feelings. "Sue, I do like you," he said, then added, "a little."

"You do?"

"Yes, of course." He smiled, holding up the coffee thermos in a salute. "Thanks again for the coffee. Make sure the house is secure."

"I will, don't worry."

After checking all the doors and windows, Seymour left and got into his car parked across the street. He turned on the engine and the heat, but not the headlights. He could observe her home without being spotted by anyone. All he needed was a neighbor calling the cops on him. He slouched down out of sight in the front seat of the car and watched the house and street.

Thompson lived on a corner property and he could easily see the front and the rear, but he could not see the east side of the house. He wasn't too concerned with that. There was only one lower floor window on that side of the house and it was very secure. He honestly didn't think that entry could be gained from that window. The most likely point of entry would be through the back. She had one of those useless sliding glass patio doors. Seymour hated those types. They weren't very secure. However, he would check on the east side of the property from time to time.

Inside, Thompson got into a pair of sweat pants and a t-shirt and climbed under the covers of her bed. She was wide awake, her gun stashed under her pillow. She wasn't taking any chances. Turning out the light, she waited.

***

Two hours into the movie, Stephen Greystock slipped out the back door of the theater. However, instead of going to his car, he caught a bus. He never took his personal car to one of his date scenes. He didn't want anyone to see it and get the license plate number. That was how they caught the Son of Sam. He was caught because of a lousy parking ticket. He learned by seeing other people's mistakes. He would never make such a blunder. He was too perfect.

He waited about a half a hour for the bus and took it to the Fox Chase section of the city. He was looking forward to his date with the redheaded enchantress named Sue. He wondered what her last name was. He'd have to remember to ask.

His plan was that he would sit and watch her house for a while, making sure she was home alone and unaware. He would also make sure no one else was on the street to see him. With all the media hype about Don Juan, people would be more vigilant. They'd be calling the cops for every suspicious person they see in the neighborhood. *Oh, well, that made the game even more exciting.*

He was always prepared, staking out the house earlier and bringing the items he'd need to help him gain entry quickly and quietly. He knew that the east side of the house would be the safest way in. He would not be seen from the street and the tall bushes on the next door neighbor's side of the fence obscured the view.

Didn't anyone ever tell them that tall bushes were dangerous? he mused, giggling to himself. *Burglars just love tall bushes and shrubs in front of windows.*

He crept through the neighbor's back yard and past their sleeping dog. He ducked back behind a bush when the dog raised its head and sniffed the air. The dog was old and probably deaf as a post because it didn't even notice him creeping around the house. Some guard dog! The dog soon placed its head back down and went back to sleep.

It hadn't snowed in the past few days so he wasn't concerned with leaving any footprints behind. Moving from behind the bushes, he made his way over to the only window on the lower floor of the east side of the house. It was an older wood framed window, not the newer kind that was made out of plastic. Her windows were made from real glass. Real, breakable glass panes.

Perfect.

Reaching into his pockets, he pulled out a pair of thin, black leather gloves and a roll of masking tape. Placing the tape on the pane above the lock, he covered it completely and then quietly knocked out the glass. It shattered noiselessly, all the glass shards sticking to the tape.

Quickly and silently, he removed the broken glass, reached inside, careful not to cut himself, and unlocked the latch. He was in. He knew from his reconnaissance of the home that she didn't have any pets or an alarm system. Even better for what he had planned.

He slid the window open and climbed inside the dark living room area. Letting his eyes adjust to the darkness, he sniffed the air. He could smell coffee. She must have made some earlier that evening, probably not too long ago before going to bed. He made his way into the kitchen and felt the coffee pot with the back of his hand. It was still warm.

He helped himself to a cup of the left over brew and sat down on the living room couch, making himself comfortable. He needed to prepare mentally for his date. He also wanted to make sure she was alone and asleep. He would finish his luke warm coffee and then go upstairs to make sweet, beautiful love to his redheaded goddess.

Looking at his watch, he observed that it was quarter to three. Yes, three. His lucky number. That would be the perfect time to have his date.

Perfect, he mused, licking his lips and tasting the coffee.

Perfect. Just like his date.

***

The movie let out about five of three in the morning. Angelo and O'Malley watched as the dozen or so moviegoers left the theater and got into their vehicles or walked home. After a few minutes, Angelo started to get a bad feeling in the pit of her stomach. The only car left in the lot was Stephen Greystock's and he was nowhere to be found.

"Oh, shit, O'Malley," she said.

"Where is he?" He was starting to worry as well.

"I don't know. I didn't see him leave."

"I'm going into the theater," O'Malley said, getting out of the car. "Maybe he fell asleep or something." He rushed over to the locked theater and banged on the glass with his badge. The manager came out and told him that there was no one in the theater except for a few employees cleaning up. After checking for himself, he returned to Angelo. His face had an increasingly worried look.

"Well?"

"He's not in there. Slippery little bastard!" O'Malley said angrily.

"Son of a..." Angelo looked around the mall parking lot. "Maybe he slipped out a little early to get something to eat or drink. There are a few bars around here."

"Yeah, but the bars close by three."

"Then he should be back soon."

"I don't like this," O'Malley commented, wiping the perspiration from his brow. As cold as it was outside, nerves were making O'Malley sweat like a pig.

"Me either."

"What do we do now?"

"Look, stay here and watch the car. He's bound to come back for it. I'm going to Thompson's place."

Putting a hand on her arm, he said, "Be careful."

"Contact me immediately if he returns."

"I will."

Angelo sped off in her car out of the parking lot and down the street. She hoped she wasn't too late. *How the hell did he slip by me!* she wondered.

"Damn it! Damn it!" she cursed, dialing Thompson's home phone number. She had to be warned that they lost Greystock. The line rang a dozen times. She tried again, worrying even more when the phone just kept ringing and ringing without being answered.

Her heart pounding in her chest, she prayed she wasn't too late.

* * *

Thompson's telephone was ringing off the hook. Something went wrong, she could feel it. Her intuition was warning her, but warning her about what? Reaching for the phone, she froze when she sensed a presence in the room with her. A noise. A smell. The scent of pipe tobacco. She just about had her hand on the telephone when someone clamped a gloved hand over her mouth.

He stifled her scream and breathed in her ear, "No interruptions tonight, Susan."

Oh, crap! she thought. *It wasn't supposed to happen this way. The plan was that he would never get this close to me. Where is Seymour? He was supposed to be watching my back! Where is Angelo!*

Slowly, she removed her hand from the still ringing telephone. Maybe it was better that she didn't answer the call. If it was Angelo phoning, she would definitely think something was a miss at the house. Surely, she'd call in the Calvary. Thompson thought that was her only hope at surviving the *date*.

"If I remove my hand from your mouth, will you be silent?" he asked in a smooth voice.

She shook her head in the affirmative. He removed his hand and stroked her hair. She wasn't wearing the wig, but he couldn't see its color in the darkness. That was a good thing, but she couldn't see his face either. However, she knew who he was. She knew his voice.

It was Stephen Greystock. He was Don Juan after all. Angelo was right.

They had their probable cause now, but would she survive that night to see it put to good use? Would they be too late to save her? Would he rape and kill her like he had Victoria? She knew that if she resisted he was likely to harm her, but damn it, she wouldn't let him rape her either.

Maybe she could talk to him. Delay him until help arrived. They were bound to know she was in danger by now. Delay him. Talk to him. Just long enough.

"Who are you?" she asked.

"You can call me Don if you'd like," he replied, sitting next to her on the bed. She dared not move.

"Okay, Don, what do you want?"

"I want a date with you. I want you."

"Isn't this the wrong way of going about it?"
"What's wrong with it? Don't you find it exciting?"
"It's scary, Don. I'm scared."
"No need to be, my little lamb. I won't hurt you if you play nice." He touched her face, causing a wave of panic to course through her mind and body.

Think, damn it! Think!

"Okay, Don, what do you want me to do?"

He was confused. None of the others ever asked him that question. Usually they screamed and fought him. What was she playing at? He would put her to the test. "I want you to touch me."

"Where?" she asked, sitting up in bed.

He unbuttoned his shirt. "Touch my chest."

With a shaky hand, she moved toward him, touching his hairless chest with tentative fingers. His eyes rolled in the back of his head as he moaned with pleasure. She needed to stall him just a little longer. Getting the feel of his muscular chest, she continued to caress him. She could feel the nipple ring he wore and played with it.

Suddenly he placed his hand over hers. "Stop."

"What's wrong?"

"I want to touch you now."

'Oh, God!

Pulling at her t-shirt, he said, "Take off this...thing."

"Please, Don, it's cold."

"I'll keep you warm," he replied, reaching under the shirt.

Where the hell is Angelo! Where the hell is my backup!

Chapter Twenty One

Angelo called Seymour on the mobile phone, sounding out of breath. "Seymour, we lost him!"

"What!"

"He slipped by us. He ditched his car at the mall. I called Sue, but she didn't answer her phone. Go check on her."

"Hold on. I'll check on it now." Seymour got out of the car and rushed over to the house. He checked the doors and windows, then went over to the east side of the property. That was when he noticed the broken window. "Damn it!"

"What's wrong?"

"The window is breached. I'm going in."

"No, wait. I'm only two minutes away. I'm calling in backup."

"It might be too late. I'm going in now!"

"Seymour!"

He wasn't listening and wasn't going to wait. He was responsible for Thompson's safety and he blew it. Pulling his gun, he unlocked the front door and went inside. He could hear voices on the second floor. He took the stairs two at a time, rushing to her aid. He had to get there before it was too late. He feared that he might already be too late.

Thompson lay back on the bed as he kissed her bare neck and shoulders. Her mind was running a mile a minute. What could she do? Then she remembered the hidden gun. Slipping her hand under the pillow, she reached for it. She could just about reach the butt of the gun, feeling its plastic grip with the tips of her fingers.

Her hand clamped over the gun, she was about to pull it from beneath the pillow when someone came crashing through the bedroom door, shouting her name.

"Susan!"

Both she and her attacker jumped up, just as Seymour charged them. Stephen caught Seymour in his arms as they both went tumbling over the side of the bed and onto the floor. Thompson screamed, dropping her gun. The two men fought viciously on the floor. Seymour was about the same size and build, but Stephen had a slight advantage, his eyes were more accustom to the darkness.

Thompson scurried over to them and tried to intervene, pulling off the bandanna that covered her attackers face. Swatted away by Stephen, she was knocked to the floor, stunned. When her vision cleared, she could just about see her gun under the bed. She reached for it just as Stephen bashed Seymour over the head with a table lamp.

With Seymour down, Stephen made a break for it. He jumped up and bolted for the door. He stopped when he heard sirens in the distance. He turned and looked one last time at Susan. She could see his face in the light. She would never forget it.

"I'll be back for you!" he snarled at her.

"No you won't!" she said pointing her gun at him. "Freeze! Stop where you are!"

He looked at the firearm, wondering where she got it. He smiled at her. "You won't shoot me."

"Don't bet on it!"

He turned to leave, ignoring her orders.

"I said, freeze! I'm not going to tell you again!"

He turned his head and looked at her, still smiling, then bolted from the room just as she squeezed off a shot. She wasn't sure if she hit him or not. He was gone. Hearing Seymour moaning as he regained consciousness, she turned her attention to him.

"Are you all right?"

"Ow, my head," he said, touching the goose egg on the back of his skull.

She jumped over the bed and turned on the light, not realizing that the only thing she had on was a lacy black bra. She went back over to him and examined the knot on his head. It looked worse than it probably was, the blood matting his dark blond hair.

"You'll be okay," she told him.

He looked at her, seeing that she was half naked. "Please tell me I wasn't too late. Please, Sue, I'm sorry."

"What? Why?" She looked down, realizing that she was in a state of undress. She grabbed the t-shirt off the bed, throwing it over her head.

"I screwed up, Susan! I'm sorry."

"Calm down, Seymour. Don't worry, I'm fine. You were just in time. He didn't do anything to me. I was able to stall until you arrived."

"Really?"

"Yes, of course. I wouldn't lie to you." She hugged him to her chest. Seconds later, Angelo and five uniformed officers burst into the room, guns drawn.

"Jesus Christ! Are you two all right?" Angelo could see blood on Seymour's head and Thompson's hands. Turning to an officer, she shouted, "Get a rescue unit here now!"

"Yes, ma'am!"

Going over to the officers, Angelo bent down. "Sue, are you hurt?"

"No. Seymour jumped him. He didn't have time."

"Where is he?"

"He ran out. I took a shot at him, but I'm not sure I hit him."

Angelo turned and looked at the door. There was a small amount of blood on the doorpost. "You may have winged him, or that's just a blood transfer from Seymour. It doesn't look like enough to be a serious wound. Either way, we'll test it for DNA."

"It was Stephen," Thompson said.

"Are you positive?"

"Absolutely. I pulled off the bandanna," she said, holding it up in the air and showing Angelo.

Angelo called O'Malley. "Pat."

"Go 'head, Bee."

"He was here."

"Is Sue and Seymour all right?"

"Yes. Get that arrest warrant for Stephen Greystock and secure his vehicle."

"I'll get the warrant," Seymour said, standing up.

"No, you need medical attention."

"I don't need it. I'm fine," he said and bolted out the door.

"Wait! Seymour!" He wasn't listening. "O'Malley. Just secured the car. Call for a patrol car. If you see him, lock him up."

"Will do."

"Have several patrol cars go to his apartment and secure that too."

"Right."

She turned back to Thompson. "Are you sure you're okay? He didn't touch you, did he?"

"No, he didn't have the chance."

"Thank God. I don't know what I would do if..."

"He didn't. Don't worry about me."

To the officer in the room, she said, "Secure the house as a crime scene. Call for a supervisor. Police discharge. Have the supervisor call for the detectives, Mobile Crimes and IAB."

"Yes, ma'am," he said, getting on his radio.

"What about Seymour?" Thompson asked.

"I'll get him."

"I'm going with you."

"No. You'll stay here. You discharged your weapon. You have to talk to the IAB shooting team."

"But—"

"But nothing, Susan. We will follow the directives."

"What about Seymour? Don't let him do anything stupid."

"He won't be doing anything stupid. Just wait for the supervisor. I'll call you later."

"Okay."

"You did a great job. Just try to calm down and relax."

"I'll try, but I don't think it'll be that easy."

"I know." Angelo keyed her mobile phone. "Seymour, where are you?"

"On my way to SVU to get that warrant."

"Wait for me there."

"Okay."

"I mean it. I've got cops on his car and his house. He's not going to get away. I'll meet you at SVU in half an hour."

"Fine. I should have the warrant by then. Angelo…"

"What?"

"I'm sorry I was such a dickhead. You were right all along."

"Forget it. I'll see you in half an hour." She cut him off before he could say anything more.

"I'm worried about him," Thompson said. "He's taking this personally."

"Who isn't?"

"I'm serious. You better get to him before he does something stupid like going after him by himself."

"I'll see to it that he doesn't. When the supervisor gets here, tell him what happened. Call your supervisor and let them know also. I'll talk to you later."

"Okay."

Angelo smiled. "You did well. I'm proud of you," she said and left, heading for Special Victims. There was no time to waste.

***

Wounded! Scarred! Bitch shot at me! he cursed silently as he checked out the blood soaked shirtsleeve. It was only a graze wound, but it stung like hell. *Ruined my perfect body. Saw my face. Ruined everything! How could she? More to the point, where'd she get the gun? And who the hell was that*

man who interrupted our date?
There was something wrong with this picture.
He made his way back to his car in the mall parking lot, but stopped when he saw a half a dozen police cars, their red and blue lights bouncing off the movie theater walls. They surrounded his car.
What the hell!
They couldn't know who I am. Not unless—I was set up! Damn it. That's it. I was set up. She set me up. I need to go home and regroup. But wait, if they know my car, they'll know where I live. They'll be waiting for me there.
Where to go? Where to hide?
Mother's?
That may be my only option. I really hate to go there. I hate mother. What else can I do? Where can I go? Damn, damn, damn!
He chewed his fingernails and worried as he watched the police activity around his car. "Oh, that traitor! Susan! She'll get hers. She'll pay for her betrayal."

***

Just as Seymour promised, by the time Angelo reached the Special Victims Unit he had an arrest warrant for Stephen Greystock and search warrants for his apartment and vehicle, signed by a judge and ready to be served. He was now a wanted man. They would serve the search warrant on his home as soon as possible. When Angelo walked into the unit, she noticed that everyone was frenzied. Not only because they finally identified Don Juan, but also because he attacked one of their own.
The second Seymour saw Angelo he handed her the warrants. "My God, that was fast," she said.
"The judge who signed the warrants is a friend of mind."
"Speed dial?"
"As a matter of fact, yes. He wants this guy just as much as the rest of the city."
"Is everything in order?"
"Of course."
"All right. I have O'Malley on the car and the apartment is secured by the Eight District personnel."
"Any sign of him?"
"Not yet. But he can't get far."
"We hope."
"Let's hope he left some evidence at his apartment for us."
"What kind do you expect?"
"He's a trophy collector. Hopefully he keeps it at the apartment."

"Or he could have buried it somewhere."

"That's a possibility. He's arrogant. I'll bet he has it at his apartment so he can look at them and admire his handiwork."

"Right."

"Ready?"

"Oh, yes."

"We'll take my car."

"You're in charge." They left the unit to the cheers of the other officers. Don Juan's rein of terror was over or so everyone hoped.

Driving to Stephen Greystock's apartment, Seymour was quiet. Angelo turned to look at him while sitting at a red light. "Something on your mind, Seymour?"

"No."

"Oh, okay." Turning her head, she stared straight ahead.

"I blew it," he blurted out suddenly.

"No you didn't," she responded quietly.

"I knew the east side of the property was unsecured. I should have checked on it more often."

"I'm as much to blame. I should have had someone else with you."

"No. I insisted that I could take care of Susan by myself. I was arrogant. I was certain you had made a mistake. I thought it would be a wasted night. I let my guard down. I did the one thing a cop should never do. I got complacent. Complacency could get someone hurt or killed. It almost got Sue hurt. Hell, it got me a goose egg on the back of my head," he said, rubbing the back of his skull.

"Look, don't blame yourself."

"I can't help it. What if he had hurt her? What if I didn't get there in time? He could have raped or killed her. I was supposed to be her backup and I blew it."

"Hindsight is 20/20, Seymour. If I had to do it all again, I would have sent O'Malley into the theater after him. I would have had you stay inside the house with Sue. I wouldn't have let Susan get into the situation in the first damn place. We all screwed up in one way or the other. All we can do is learn from our mistakes. We know what not to do now."

"I guess."

"He'll not escape. In an hour, his face will be plastered all over the tri-state area. On the news and in the papers. Where is he going to run? You'll be a hero. The man who caught Don Juan."

"I didn't do a damn thing. I had my sights on Josh. I was stupid not to listen to you. You did all the work. You and Sue."

"I don't want the credit. The pinch is yours and Sue's. After all, you had him."

"Yeah, until I got my brains knocked out."

Angelo laughed. "If it's all the same to you, so did I," she said, pointing to the cut above her eye. "And I'm a hell of a lot tougher than you are, junior."

He smiled. "Okay, live and learn."

"That's the spirit."

They pulled up in front of the apartment building and parked behind Eight-Andy car. Getting out, they made their way toward the sergeant. There were five patrol cars there altogether. Two to help serve the warrant and three more to fend off the media that gathered around.

"How the hell did those vultures get wind of this?"

The sergeant shrugged her shoulders. "Beats me, Angelo. Loose lips."

"Great to see you again, Sergeant Gannon," Angelo said, shaking the sergeant's hand.

"Same here."

"Any sign of our boy?"

"No. I guess he knows you're on to him."

"Maybe," Angelo said, scowling at the media.

She could hear the media shouting questions at them. "Is this Don Juan's apartment?"

"Who is he?"

"Was he arrested?"

"We heard that he attacked another woman. Is that true?"

"Jeez!" Angelo growled, rolling her eyes toward heaven. She walked over to the news reporters, something she rarely did, and spoke to them. "Look, can I have your attention?"

The media fell silent.

"You'll have all your questions answered in a few hours. If you go to the Public Affairs Officer, you'll get all the information you'll need for the early morning broadcast."

"Detective Angelo, you know the PA officer won't tell us anything."

"Bart," she said to the reporter. "I'm telling you that he will. I told him to give you the information as soon as possible."

"Why can't you just tell us now?"

"I can't. Look, I have work to do. You guys can all waste your time standing around here for nothing or go to the PAO and get a picture for the air. You know I wouldn't lie to you."

A few reporters mumbled and packed up their gear. "No, but why are you being so helpful, Angelo? You're never helpful to the media."

"I beg your pardon, Bart, but you're absolutely right. I hate you guys, but I want his face on the air. I don't have a picture for you here, but if you get your scrawny butts down to the Police Headquarters, you'll get one so you can air it. You have my word."

"And your word is good?" Bart asked.

"How can you ask me that? Remember what I said to you the last time we had a little conversation? I keep my promises." Her tone was harsh.

"Damn it, Bart!" another reporter shouted. "Don't piss her off!"

"Now, if you'll excuse me, I have a warrant to serve."

Angelo stalked off and entered the apartment building. Two patrol officers at the door and the superintendent met her with a key. He handed her the key and stepped aside. With guns drawn, they unlocked the door.

"Search warrant!" Angelo announced even though she didn't think anyone was in the apartment. They entered and the officers cleared the rooms.

"All clear in this area."

"Same here."

"Okay. Search for anything that could tell us where he is likely to go. Look for any evidence that proves he's Don Juan. We need proof positive to seal this case up tight. Touch nothing! Leave that for CSU."

"Angelo," Seymour said from the adjoining room. "Come and look at this."

She went into the other room and met Seymour standing by a curio cabinet. "Well what do we have here?" She took out a pair of latex gloves and slipped them on her hands. Pulling open the glass door, she picked up the visor cap from the Koffee Klutch.

"He's got everything labeled. You were right. He is arrogant," Seymour stated.

"Yes. The hat belongs to Heather Donnelley."

"He's a freaking trophy collector."

"And here is the missing engagement ring from Victoria Sterling's house."

"Stick a fork in him. He's done."

"Call for Mobile Crimes. Have them photograph everything. Bag and tag. We're not letting him get away with any of these attacks. We'll follow procedure down to the letter."

"Hey, Angelo, he's got almost twenty items here. Dated back almost ten years. What's he about? Twenty seven?"

"Yeah."

"Some of these places on the labels aren't even in this city."

"We'll have to check the dates with the cold case files and also with the counties."

"Ten years, Angelo. Ten years he's been doing this."

"Probably longer than that."

"Jesus."

"Well it's over now."

"Thanks to you."

"No. Everyone had a hand in the investigation."

"How can you be so humble?"

"I'm not. I call it like I see it. Enough about that. Call Mobile Crimes and get them out here now. I want this scene processed immediately. I've got the vultures off our backs for now, but they are going to want blood in a few hours. And we're going to give it to them."

"What about Thompson?"

"She's going to be tied up with the IAB shooting team for a few hours. They'll want to talk to you also."

"Why?"

"You were there."

"I was knocked out."

"They'll still want to talk to you. The sooner you guys finish with them, the sooner we can get on with apprehending this asshole."

"You got it," he said, calling the Crime Scene Unit on his cell phone.

"You are history, Stephen," Angelo said more to herself than anyone else.

Chapter Twenty Two

By six o'clock in the morning, Stephen Greystock's name and photograph was all over the news. Every police department in the tri-state area was on the alert and hunting for him. He attacked a police officer. He would not escape. Angelo secured an updated photo of the suspect and issued it to the press as promised.

They figured that he probably knew they were on to him by now and he would not return to his home or work. He was arrogant, not stupid. He certainly would not return to the Koffee Klutch, not unless he wanted to be lynched by the regulars. He would most likely flee the city and quite possibly the state.

Angelo talked to his neighbors, who were totally shocked by the revelation that they had a serial rapist/murderer in their building. She was told that he didn't have any close friends that they knew of. He was a loner, more preoccupied with himself than anyone else. He had no girlfriend who visited, nor did he have friends over. Angelo was sure that if he had a girlfriend, she would have ratted him out by now. If not for the reward money, then on principle.

Where would he run? Who would help him knowing what he was? What rock could he hide under until he could slip out of the state? Those questions had to be answered before they could find him.

Seymour was sipping on a cup of coffee watching Angelo type up the crime scene report. A thought struck him and he said, "You mentioned that he lived with his mother for a time before he got that apartment."

She reached for the file. "Yes. She lives in Wissinoming."

"You think he'd go there?"

She thought about it for a moment. "Maybe."

"Would she harbor him?"

"I don't know. A mother's a funny creature. They could hate you or love you no matter what you do."

"He is a momma's boy."

"That's what everyone assumes. Stop calling him that. Gives the good momma's boys a bad name. Remember that most serial rapists don't have good or remotely healthy relationships with their mothers or any other female who holds control over them. His juvenile record indicated that they bounced around a while."

"Well, I think it's worth a shot."

"Yes it is." She put the file away and took a moment to finish her typing. Turning off her computer, she said, "Get your gear together. We'll head up that way."

"What about Thompson?"

"Hopefully she'll be done with IAB. Did you talk to them already?"

"Yes. I could only add so much to their investigation. I was knocked out for a few seconds."

"At least you got it over with. She'll probably be put on limited duty for a few days. I'll call her on her cell and see if she's finished with them."

Seymour looked over Angelo's shoulder and nodded. "Never mind, Detective, here she comes now."

Thompson walked into the unit and over to Angelo. She looked no worse for the experience, but she did look very tired. "Hi," she said.

"I was just about to call you," Angelo said.

"How are you feeling?" It was Seymour who asked her.

"Okay, I guess. Tired."

"That's understandable."

"Does everyone who discharges their weapon have to go through that inquisition? I thought they were going to bring out the Rack."

Angelo laughed. "Afraid so. Be thankful you didn't kill anyone. You'd still be there."

"You've been in how many shootings?"

"Two. Three if you count the one with O'Malley. That time I didn't discharge my weapon. So technically I've fired my weapon twice."

"Did you feel…upset?"

"Yes, of course. That's natural. That's why the department gives you time, counseling and a refresher at the range. Did you get restricted duty?"

She sighed. "Yes. I guess I'll miss out on the apprehension."

"Don't worry, Sue, you'll share in the pinch," Seymour said.

"Thanks, Seymour."

"You deserve it."

She actually blushed, hating herself for doing it. "I mean, thanks for everything."

"Don't mention it. I'm just glad you weren't hurt."

She didn't reply.

Angelo said, "Go home, Sue. Get some rest."

"I have no choice now. You will keep me advised?"

"Of course. You'll be the first to hear."

"I'll be glad when this is all over and done with."

"You and me both."

She smiled and walked away. She received several pats on the back from her co-workers on the way out. She was blushing even more. Angelo noticed that she seemed a little disappointed that she was put on restricted duty, but it was police policy in a shooting.

Angelo turned to Seymour, who watched Thompson as she was leaving the unit, and cleared her throat. "Seymour."

"Yes, Detective Angelo?"

"Are you ready?"

He glanced one last time at the exit door. "Yes. Let's get this son of a bitch."

***

Greystock's mother lived in the Wissinoming section of the northeast on a clean, albeit busy, street with perfectly manicured lawns and the usual holiday decorations. Although the property was neat, the home was not decorated or cheery in any way.

"Guess she's not one for the holiday spirit," Seymour commented to Angelo as they pulled up in front of the house.

There was a media van parked half way up the block. The van's broadcast antenna stretched high into the sky. It looked like they were about to do a live remote. That particular channel was not the type to be discreet and Angelo wondered why they were keeping their distance. She would soon find out why.

Walking up the path to the front door, Angelo pulled her badge out and let it hang over her outer garment. She knocked on the door and waited a few minutes before knocking again. She was about to knock a third time when the door flew open. Seymour took a step back, but Angelo held her ground. They were faced with a behemoth of a woman holding a broom. She looked as if she was about to use it, and not to sweep the floor.

"I told you sonsofbitches that I have no comment!" she screamed.

Angelo blinked. "Who, ma'am?" she asked calmly.

"You news bastards."

"We're the police. Not the news." She held up her badge. The woman in the all too tight orange running outfit examined at her badge.

"He ain't here."

"So you know why we're here?"

"The whole freaking block knows why the police are looking for Steve. That little bastard! If he dare show his face here, I'd knock his teeth out and shove this broom up his ass!"

"We have a search warrant to search the property," Angelo informed her, handing over the signed warrant.

"Search away. He's not here. He won't be coming here if he knows what's good for him."

She stepped aside and let the detectives inside. Like the outside, the house was clean and perfect, although it reeked of stale tobacco smoke. Angelo glanced at the coffee table and observed two dozen or more cigarette butts in the ashtray. Again, she noticed that there were no holiday decorations inside the house either.

Maybe she's Jewish, Angelo mused.

They checked the entire house from top to bottom, looking in every space that a man could possibly secrete himself. The only thing they found was more cigarette butts. Man, this woman is a human smokestack. It was a wonder she didn't have a heart attack with her weight added to the smoking.

When she was satisfied that he was not hiding in the house, Angelo went downstairs. Mrs. Greystock was lighting another cigarette. She wasn't surprised that Stephen wouldn't come here and she couldn't blame him. His mother was as warm as a polar ice cap.

"I told you he wasn't here, Detective," she said, blowing smoke in Seymour's direction. He waved his hand in front of his face to clear the smoke. To Angelo's surprise, he didn't say anything to her.

"We had to check, you understand." She handed her a copy of the warrant.

She took the warrant and tossed it on the couch next to her. "Will that be all? I have to finish cleaning."

"Mrs. Greystock, your son is in a lot of trouble. It would be wise if he turned himself in."

"Well, obviously the boy is stupid."

"He could get hurt if he doesn't surrender."

"I don't care if you shoot the little bastard on sight."

Wow! Seymour thought. *What a bitch.*

Angelo was thinking the same thing, but she didn't let it register on her face. "Have you any idea where he might go? Does he have any friends?"

"How the hell should I know?"

"When did he move out of here?"

"About two years ago. Wasn't soon enough. He's been a thorn in my side since the day he was born. Nothing but grief from that boy."

"If he comes by or calls, please call us or tell him to turn himself in. We don't want to hurt him."

"If he dares to show his face here, he won't have to worry about the police hurting him. They'll be taking him out of here in an ambulance or a body bag."

Angelo sighed. Obviously, the woman had no heart. "Thank you for your cooperation."

She grunted and opened the front door. Seymour couldn't wait to get out of the house and into the fresh air. He would need to take his allergy medication soon. Walking back to the car, Seymour said, "No wonder he has some serious women issues."

"She's controlling and domineering, I'll grant you that. She probably never showed him any love or affection. And if she did, it was the wrong kind, no doubt."

"I'm seeing an insanity defense in the making."

"Yes."

"I still don't feel sorry for him. He could have walked away when he was old enough to do so. But instead he stayed with that horrid woman."

"It's not so easy to walk away. Mental abuse is just as bad as physical."

"Maybe it is and maybe it isn't," Seymour snorted. "Where to next?"

"There is no where else for us to look now. We'll have to rely on someone spotting him."

Looking over at the idle news van, Seymour suggested, "Maybe we can use the media to get the word out for him to give himself up."

"That's an idea. Let's catch that van before they leave."

"You want to talk to them?"

"No. If he hears it coming from a woman, especially a woman in authority, he'll not respond. The media is all yours."

He smiled. "Gee, thanks. Nice to know I'm good for something."

They gave the thrilled news crew an impromptu press conference before they retired for the day. Angelo reminded Seymour to contact the other media outlets and give them the same statement. She also reminded him to be careful and watch his back. Stephen might be angry enough for revenge.

She was tired; it had been a long tour of duty. All she wanted to do was get some rest. She was sure Seymour and Thompson felt the same way.

***

Finally able to go home, Angelo walked into her house. Wondering where Sam was hiding, she wandered down the hall to his office. The door was closed, but not locked and she could hear him typing away like a madman on his computer. Not wanting to disturb him, she turned around and went upstairs to bed.

Stripping to her underwear, she flopped face down on the bed. She was tired, but had no idea just how exhausted her body felt until she was finally able to relax. The previous night's activities continued to run through her mind. It was only a matter of time before he was captured.

Then why was she so disturbed? Why couldn't she turn off her brain? It was running almost as fast as Sam's fingers on the computer keyboard. All she wanted was sleep. Eight hours of uninterrupted, dreamless sleep.

She would get the sleep, but it wouldn't be dreamless. Nor would she feel rested. Her subconscious opened to the dream world and all the things she tried to bury made their way to the surface. And they intended to make their presence known.

In the dark room again, she felt herself pinned by the unknown, unseen and merciless entity. Unable to move, panic seized her in genuine female distress. A woman always in control of herself and the situation around her, she was now helpless and unable to fight. She didn't like the feeling. Not one bit.

The stranger's harsh laughter grabbed her attention and she looked to her left. It seemed the only thing she could move was her head. In the pitch darkness, she could see what appeared to be a steel table. A morgue table, like the kind Morty used to dissect bodies.

Like a macabre theater play, a spotlight illuminated the table and she found herself staring in horror at Dwayne Ronalds' body, a knife sticking out of his chest. He was pale and had the look of death in his cloudy eyes. His eyes were wide open and staring at her.

"Oh, God! No!" she cried.

The corpse grinned and glared at her with cold, dead eyes. "It's entirely your fault, Bernadette!" it accused. "I thought you had my back!"

"I did! I did! I couldn't get a clean shot."

"It's your fault that I'm here on this table!"

"I'm so sorry, Dwayne!" she whimpered. "Please forgive me!"

He closed his eyes and turned away. That was worse than anything he could have said to her. "You failed me."

The spotlight went out and he was gone. The room was filled with that hateful, maniacal laughter again. Hate was not usually in Angelo's heart, but she was starting to hate this unseen force that had her captive.

"Stop! Stop! Why are you doing this to me?"

"Because I can," it told her once again.

"I won't let you! Damn it! I won't! It wasn't my fault that Dwayne died. I did everything I could to save him."

"It wasn't enough, was it, Bernadette?"

"I'm only human, damn you!"

"How are you going to save her?"

"Who?"

"Her!"

The spotlight came on again and the table reappeared. This time it wasn't Dwayne on the table. It was Sue Thompson. She was naked and bleeding. She looked just as dead as Dwayne.

Angelo screamed, "No!"

The laugh echoed in her head, piercing her mind like a thousand shards of glass, as she continued to scream.

"No! No! No!"

Angelo awoke, tumbling out of bed in a tangle of satin sheets. She fought to get free, falling to the hardwood floor with a loud thud. Sweat broke out all over her body and she shivered from the cold.

"Oh, God. It was just a dream. Just a bad dream," she told herself.

Covering herself with the sheets, she glanced around the room. She was alone. Thank goodness Sam wasn't there to see her in that sorry state. She would have never heard the end of it.

Maybe Sam was right and she felt responsible for Dwayne's death. Maybe she really needed counseling. Someone to talk to about her feelings of guilt and remorse. She needed to get over it before she could move on. She needed to swallow her pride. That was something that would be harder for her to do than anything else.

Getting off the floor, she made her way into the bathroom, and for the second time that week, threw up her lunch.

***

After a hot shower to calm her nerves, Angelo went down stairs for dinner. She could smell whatever it was that Sam cooked for that night. Although hungry, Angelo didn't think her stomach could handle food. Even food prepared by Sam. He would definitely know something was wrong.

Nerves! Nerves! I never have nerves, she thought sourly. Even after the thorough teeth brushing, she could still taste the bile in her throat.

Entering the dining room, she noted that Sam had already set the table for two. He was lighting the candles when she entered. He looked at her, but did not smile as he usually did. Instead, he had the look of worry on his face.

"Bee, don't take this the wrong way, but you look like hell warmed over."

"Thanks, Sam. Always nice to hear that from my husband." She tried to make it sound biting, but it fell flat. She knew she looked like crap, and after everything, she didn't really care.

"I'm serious. Are you sick?"

"Just tired, Sam."

"Did you sleep?"

"A few hours."

"Want to talk about last night?"

Instead of an answer, she just shrugged her shoulders. She did want to talk about it, but didn't want to burden him. He had his own problems.

"I'll take that as a yes. But first I want you to eat something."

"I'm not really hungry." Her stomach growled, betraying her.

"Right," he said, grinning. Without another word, he went into the kitchen and returned with her plate. He placed it in front of her, the steam rising from the dish.

Looking at him, she said, "Aren't you going to have something?"

"After you have something."

He's just too protective. Picking up her fork, she stabbed a carrot on the plate. She hoped she'd be able to hold it down. Running from the table to throw up again wouldn't look very good. Thankfully after a few bites the nausea subsided. *All I needed was some food to settle my nerves,* she thought.

"How is it?"

"Why do you always ask me that?"

"My ego needs stroking."

"As usual, it's fantastic," she told him. "Oh, and Pat says to tell you thanks for the lunch you packed last night. He loves you now."

"You know that the way to a man's heart is through his stomach."

She laughed. "Are you hitting on my partner now?"

"Maybe. I owe him."

So do I. "Well, if that's the case, it's a wonder we stayed married for so long. Since I can't cook."

"I can always teach you."

She thought about it for a couple of seconds. "No, I'd rather leave that in your wonderful hands. Be thankful for small mercies."

He sat and watched her for a few more minutes to make sure she was eating. Satisfied she would continue, he got his own plate and joined her.

"Are you working tonight?"

"Actually, no. My SDO."

"I take it that everything is under control in your investigation." He knew that she even worked through her days off when a major case was in progress.

"It's only a matter of time."

"I saw the news reports."

"Of course you did."

"I was surprised that you used the media this time."

"They might be vultures, but like vultures, they have their uses."

"Yes, when it suits you."

"Sure, why not?"

"You know if you start letting them have information, you'll never get rid of them."

"Oh, that's why I let Seymour handle them. I played the brooding detective part to them."

"A method to your madness?"

"Certainly."

"How's Susan?"

She raised an eyebrow at him.

"They mentioned that a female officer was attacked during the apprehension. They said she was from SVU and that she shot at him. Now, since you promised to call me if you ever got into another shooting, I assumed it wasn't you."

"You think you're so clever."

"Aren't I?" he said and grinned.

"Sue is fine. She wasn't hurt, but..."

"But?"

"She could have been. My shortsightedness could have gotten her hurt or worse."

"You can't say you blame yourself? Things go wrong, you know that."

"Lately, things seem to go wrong for me all the time."

"Not all the time."

"Could have fooled me."

"Is that why you're having trouble sleeping? Dreams?"

She was about to deny it, but she knew that he'd never believe it. Then of course, he'd be angry with her for lying to him. "Perhaps."

"Tell me about the one you had this afternoon."

"How?"

"I know everything."

"It was just weird."

"Weird? I'd say scary from the way you reacted."

"Were you spying on me while I slept?"

"No, but I've got ears. You made enough noise to wake the dead."

"I beg your pardon. I don't make noise," she huffed.

A wry grin crossed his lips. "I wouldn't say that. Sometimes, you're quite vocal."

"Shut up."

"No seriously."

"Okay. If I tell you, will you lay off?"

"Maybe."

"Maybe isn't good enough."

"I can't promise you anything. I love you too much."

"Jeez, you're a pest."

"You bet. Talk to me."

235

She pushed her food away; the sight of it was making her queasy again. Sitting in silence for a while, Sam kept quiet and didn't push her. She would tell him in her own time, at her own pace. Nevertheless, she would eventually tell him.

Finally she spoke. "I think I told you about the dreams before."

"You mentioned very little. Only that you felt vulnerable."

"Helpless, for lack of a better word."

"Okay. Go on."

Angelo swallowed hard, her mouth suddenly dry. Lifting up her wine glass, she took a sip. She drank the wine, not only to soothe her parched throat, but also to calm her nerves. "I'm in a dark room. No, it wasn't just dark. It's black as pitch. I'm on this bed. It's not familiar to me. I can't move. I'm not restrained by ropes or anything, but by some kind of force. It's evil. I just know it. This—thing—laughs at me. Tells me terrible things. Torments me."

She paused, not knowing how else to explain it. Sam sat quietly and said nothing. He did not prompt her.

"In this last dream, a light comes on. At first, there is just a steel table in front of me, but then...Dwayne is laying dead on it. Only he's not quite dead. The knife used to murder him is sticking out of his chest. There is blood. So much blood. He looks at me. He tells me that I failed to back him. I was the reason why he was dead on the table."

Sam had to speak. "No, Bee, it wasn't your fault."

She shook her head. "I know that in my head, but in my heart..." She stood up and started to clean off the place in front of her. She didn't know what to do with her hands.

"Leave it, Bee," Sam told her, placing his hand over hers. "Sit back down. Please."

She didn't want to tell him the next part. It frightened her more than the restraint or even Dwayne. "Sam, I can't talk about it any more."

"You've told me most of it. Just continue with the rest."

She sighed and sat back down. Looking into his big, blue eyes, she felt safe with him there. "The light went out and Dwayne was gone. I was relieved. I didn't want to look at him. I was ashamed I let him down. Then the voice returned. It asked me how I was going to save her."

"Her, who?"

"That's what I asked. The light came back on and there was another body on the table."

"Was it you?"

"No. I wish it were. I could understand that."

"Who then?"

"Susan. She was just as dead as Dwayne was. The voice told me that I would fail again. She would die too."

"I see."

"You see what? I don't even understand it. How could you?"

"Your mind is playing with you."

"How do you figure?"

"You refuse to talk about Dwayne. It's eating you from inside. You say your so-called shortsightedness almost got Susan hurt. You feel that you need to protect her. Bernadette, you did nothing to risk injuring your officers. Sue is not Dwayne. She also seems to know how to handle herself from what I've seen and heard. You can't go blaming yourself every time an officer gets injured on your watch. You can't blame yourself every time something goes wrong."

"Wrong? I got my partner killed. I almost got my liaison killed!"

"Bernadette, listen to me. You did not."

She chewed on her bottom lip. "Okay, okay, fine," she said, holding up her hands in surrender.

"You need to talk to someone about how you feel about your loss. Not only the loss of Dwayne, but also your loss of control. If you don't it will continue to feed on your mind, body, and soul, for that matter, until there is nothing left."

"I'm talking to you, aren't I?"

"God, you're stubborn! I'm talking about a professional."

She remained silent. "Maybe I do," she mumbled finally.

"I'm glad you see it my way."

"What choice do I have? Go insane or be hounded by you every minute of the day."

"Ha, ha. You're so funny."

"Okay. I see your point about Dwayne, but what was Sue doing in that dream?"

"Do you think she could still be in danger?"

"I don't know. Stephen Greystock never returned to the victim once the police were involved."

"Yes, but this time he knows he was set up. He might be crazy enough to try something. He's cornered. He's got nothing to lose now."

"You're not helping ease my concerns."

"Maybe that's what your overworked brain is telling you, but you're too tired to understand the significance."

"God, maybe you're right. I need to get her some protection." Angelo stood up and stalked over to the phone. She spoke to someone for a few minutes, but from her tone and angry expression, Sam guessed she wasn't getting anywhere with them. She slammed the phone down on its cradle. "Stupid idiots!" she shouted to no one in particular.

"Calm down. What?"

"Special Victims doesn't think it's necessary to put someone on her. They don't think she's in any danger. He's on the run, hiding from the police and not a threat. There is no way he's going to go after a cop. Bull crap! Who knows what goes on in the mind of a psychopath? What a bunch of assholes!"

"Why don't you just give Sue a call and ask her to stay here for a few days."

"I don't want to scare her."

"Just tell her that it would make you feel better. Or maybe that you need help with paperwork or something."

"She's on limited duty. She'll think I'm just trying to give her something to do."

"So let her. What's wrong with that?"

"Nothing." She leaned over and kissed him. "Thanks, Sam. You're a peach."

"Speaking of peaches, I made your favorite. Peach cobbler."

"I knew there was a reason why I married you."

"Great sex?"

"Yeah. And your cobbler."

Chapter Twenty Three

Angelo called Thompson at home. It rang several times, worrying her when there was no answer. She was about to hang up on the twentieth ring when Thompson finally answered. Angelo was relieved just to hear her voice.

"Hello?" Thompson said breathlessly.

"Sue? It's Bee."

"Oh, hello, Detective Angelo. What's up?"

"Why are you out of breath?" she asked more out of curiosity than worry.

"Just got in from my evening run. Got to keep fit, y'know. I heard the phone ringing and did my final sprint into the house."

"Oh."

"Do you need something? Are you okay? You sound a bit off."

"I'm fine. How are you?"

"Getting curious. Why?"

"Um, I'm just wondering. How long are you on limited duty?"

"Three days. Got to see the head shrink at EAP tomorrow and then I have to report to the academy."

"Yes, the range. How would you like to hang out at my house for a few days?"

"Sounds like fun, but why?"

"I could use some help with the paperwork."

Thompson paused a second. "Bee, why do you really want me there?"

Can't get anything by her, Angelo mused. "Okay, you caught me. I'm worried about you being alone with Greystock still out there."

"I'm fine here. There is no reason to believe he'll come back for me. Not when he's on the run."

That's what those bozos at SVU said, she thought sourly. "Look, I don't want to scare you, but I just have a bad feeling. Remember what I told you about intuition? That inner voice?"

"Yeah."

"I always listen to mine and it's telling me that he might not be done with you yet. I called your boss, but he doesn't think he'll retaliate either."

"But obviously, you do? Why?"

"I can't say exactly."

"I'm fine here."

"It would make me feel more comfortable. I'm not sleeping very well. Knowing you're safe will put my mind at ease. Ask Sam. He's not getting any sleep because of me. Besides, he says he wants the chance to meet you under better conditions."

"Just sweeten the pot, why don't you?"

"You'll come over then?"

"Sure, but my car has gone mechanical again. Damn mechanics don't know what's wrong with it this time."

"I'll pick you up," Angelo said automatically.

"I can catch a cab."

"Nonsense. I insist. I'll be there in an hour."

"It's late, Bee. Don't go through any trouble. How about tomorrow?"

Angelo looked at her watch. She hadn't realized it had gotten so late. It was almost nine o'clock. "It's not that late, Sue. Humor me. An hour."

"All right."

She hung up before Thompson had a chance to change her mind. Sam was sitting on the couch behind her in the living room. She didn't see him until she turned around.

Holding her heart, she said, "Oh!"

"Sorry," Sam said.

"You're not sorry."

"So, is Sue coming over?"

"Yes. I'm going to go and get her. Her car is not working."

"Good. Hopefully, you'll be able to relax now."

"I'm relaxed."

"No you're not. You're wound up like a watch. But you'll be able to once you know she's safe."

"I don't like to worry and I've been doing too much of that lately."

"I know. I look forward to talking with her. I didn't get a chance to formally meet her."

"That's what I told her. She's a big fan."

"I know what I'll do. I'll show her the new book."

"Hey, how come everyone gets to see it except me? I'm your wife for God's sake!"

He smiled.

"Okay, I'm leaving." She kissed him. "Be back in an hour and a half or so."

"Take your cell phone with you."

"Of course. Like I'd forget that," she said, holding it up. "Love you."

***

Thompson packed a few items in an overnight bag, still wondering what had gotten into Angelo. In the few days of working with the detective and knowing her reputation of being cool and calm under pressure, she was confused by Angelo's sudden paranoia. Surely, Stephen Greystock wouldn't dare show his face around her.

She was a cop. He knew she was a cop. But then again, the man who had attacked Angelo in her own home not four weeks before knew she was a cop and still tried to murder her. He was mad of course. Stephen could be just as insane. Especially now that he was cornered and had nowhere to run. Maybe Angelo was projecting her fear of losing another partner onto her.

Picking up the pace a bit, she halted when she heard a knocking noise down stairs. She looked at her watch. That couldn't be Angelo banging, not unless she had wings. It would take at the very least a half an hour to get from Mt. Airy to Fox Chase.

Thinking it was better to err on the side of caution, she slid her off duty weapon out of its hiding place. "Damn it," she cursed, going down the stairs to investigate the noise. "Now I'm getting paranoid."

She flicked on the light in the living room. All was quiet, the front door still closed and locked.

"Hmm," she said to herself, "I better check the back door."

She turned to go to the rear of the house when suddenly a large body slammed into her. Tripping over a chair, she dropped her firearm as the form leapt onto her exposed back. She screamed like she never screamed before as her hand searched desperately for the gun that slid under the sofa.

The man grabbed her by the shoulders and yanked her to her feet. He spun her around to face him. She stared into the face of madness. He no longer looked quaffed and orderly, but disheveled and filthy dirty.

"Get your hands off me!" she shouted, pulling away, but he backhanded her. She tumbled over the overturned chair and hit the floor hard. In pain but not stunned, she could see the gun under the sofa.

Reaching for it, he stomped down hard on her hand and yanked her to her feet again. He shoved her into the wall, this time stunning her. He continued to slam her into the wall, playing with her as a cat tormented a mouse.

When he believed she was no longer a threat, he pulled her up again and tossed her onto the sofa. She didn't dare move a muscle. She needed to regain her strength.

"You think you can do this to me and get away with it?" he asked viciously.

She didn't know how to respond. She was afraid to set him off again. Unless she could get to that gun, she was helpless. She needed to make one last attempt to get it. Leaping off the couch, she reached under the sofa, frantically searching for the gun. She almost had it when he grabbed her and swatted her back onto the sofa. He bent down and scooped up the gun.

He studied it for a moment, gently touching it like one would caress a lover. "Looking for this?" he asked, pointing the gun at her. "Well, you can't have it."

"Stephen, what do you want from me?" she asked when she finally got her wind back.

"As if you have to ask. I want to finish our date. Then I want to finish you. Victoria was an accident. I didn't mean to kill her. However, for you I'll make an exception. This time there will be no interruptions."

"You'll have to kill me before I let you touch me!"

"Oh, but that won't be any fun. Do you think you could over power me? I think not. Not without your equalizer," he said, holding up the gun.

She knew that he was probably right, but she had to try. He was going to kill her and she definitely wasn't going to die without a fight. She tried to stand up, but he punched the gun into her stomach. She doubled over, coughing. "Son of a bitch!" she spat.

"Ah, I see you've heard about my mother. Lovely woman, isn't she?" Still fingering the gun in his hand, he said to Thompson, "You know, I hear a gut wound is very painful and isn't always instantly fatal. You could linger for minutes, maybe even hours."

She continued to cough as he grabbed her hair and leveled her face to look into her eyes. He saw hate and fear in her teary blue eyes.

"You're not even a real redhead. Blonde! How could I let a blonde fool me?"

"It was easy," she spat.

He ignored her mocking remark. "I've never shot anyone before. I've always wanted to know how it felt. I always wanted to try it out on my mother. I would be doing the world a favor. Maybe after I'm done here, I will pay Mother a visit. First, I want to deal with you. It's payback time for your shooting me. You scarred my perfect arm. Just look what you did!" He rolled up his sleeve and showed her the bandage. It was still seeping blood.

"I should have put one in the back of your head!" she snarled.

"Oh, getting out your fangs. Is that any way to talk to your date? The best date you'll ever have. And the last?"

"Bastard!"

He laughed. "Yeah, I'm that too."

***

Angelo made it to Thompson's house in no time flat. She was lucky enough to hit every green light on the Boulevard. The roads were plowed and salted; the Streets Department finally able to get a handle on the snow covered roads. It hadn't snowed in a few days, giving them a chance to catch up.

Walking up the shoveled path leading to Thompson's front door, Angelo was feeling a little better that Thompson was going to stay with her. At least for a few days until Stephen Greystock was captured.

Angelo knocked loudly on the door and waited. After a minute, she tried again. This time much louder, but still with no success. Angelo was starting to worry again.

"Oh, please," she mumbled to herself, leaning an ear to the door and listening for any sounds within. She didn't hear anything inside. No voices, television, or movement of any kind. Pulling out her cell phone, she was about to call for backup when a voice called out.

"Look out, Angelo! He's got my *off duty* piece!"

Angelo jumped back and to the left side, just as a bullet ripped through the front door. Without thought for her own safety, Angelo kicked in the front door and dived to the left as another bullet whizzed past her ear. She dived behind an EZ chair, pulling out her own weapon. Luckily, she was able to recall the layout of Thompson's living room.

A third bullet ripped into the recliner. She couldn't tell where the shots were coming from and did not dare expose her head to look. If she recalled correctly, Thompson owned a five shot Smith and Wesson off duty gun. That was why Thompson shouted out that it was her off duty piece. She was warning Angelo how many shots he had.

Angelo dived behind another chair for better cover and concealment. Another shot rang out, but it didn't come her way. She glanced around the corner of the chair and saw Thompson struggling for the gun. The fourth shot went into the ceiling when she punched Greystock in his wounded arm. He cursed and tried to push her away from him.

He succeeded in pushing Thompson away and pointed the gun at her. Angelo shouted to distract him from shooting Thompson and took the opportunity to charge at him. She ran headlong into his midsection, knocking the breath out of him. The fifth and final shot discharged and went harmlessly into the couch.

She could hear the click of the gun as its firing pin struck the used bullet casings. He soon realized that the gun was empty and tossed it at her. It glanced off her shoulder. Suddenly he had two women attacking him, punching and scratching. He soon found out that women fight differently than men. Women fight dirty. They had to.

He knocked Thompson down and out of his way. He outweighed her by at least a hundred pounds and was a foot taller. Angelo was a different story. She was almost equal to his height and all lean muscle, but not as heavy. He couldn't shake her as easily.

Seeing that his arm injury was re-opened, Angelo punched his biceps, hoping she hit the brachial nerve that ran up his arm. She hit her mark with pinpoint accuracy and he screamed in pain. Instead of the result she was hoping for—that his arm would go numb—he seemed to get stronger. He lifted her up off the ground and tossed her into Thompson who was still trying to get up. Both women went down in a tangle of arms and legs.

He didn't press his advantage. He did what was familiar to him. He ran. He bolted out the door and around the side of the house to the back yard. It didn't take long for Angelo to get up and pursue him. Thompson struggled to get up, and after grabbing her gun, followed them.

For his size, he was very fast on his feet. He bolted out of the yard and onto the train tracks that ran behind Thompson's house. Chasing him up the train trestle, Angelo shouted at Thompson to call for backup. Call for an assist. Thompson darted back into the house to retrieve her cell phone and call for help.

She had to watch her step on the tracks. The ground was uneven and icy. Not only that, the high-speed Regional Rail train could come through there at any moment. Getting hit by a train was a fast way to go, but it certainly wasn't pleasant—and it was messy.

Although only several steps behind him, she could feel her legs starting to protest and quiver with fatigue. She was sure he was feeling the same thing. If it wasn't for the surge of adrenaline, she was sure both of them would have collapsed by now.

"Give it up, Stephen! I don't want to hurt you!" she shouted at him.

"All you women want to hurt me!" he shouted back at her, not losing any steam.

"Stop or I'll shoot you!" she warned.

"You won't shoot me in the back."

"Just watch me. The law says I can shoot a fleeing felon in the back if that's what I have to do to stop you from escaping." What she told him was true. However, Angelo didn't think she could shoot him in the back even though the law would be on her side if she did.

He seemed to slow down at the bridge, giving Angelo the opportunity to catch up to him. Then he did the unexpected. He climbed over the railing. It was a fifty-foot drop down to the street. "I'll jump!" he told her.

Angelo slowed down her pace and stayed about thirty feet from him on the other side of the tracks. She wanted him taken alive. All police officers, if they could help it, would rather take a suspect in alive.

"I mean it!" he hissed at her.

"Look, Stephen," she said, putting her gun in its holster and holding her empty hands out to him. "You need help. I know you didn't mean to hurt those women. You didn't mean to kill Victoria."

He started to cry. "I didn't. They were my dates."

"I'm sure you believe that. You can tell that to a judge."

"No! No! They won't believe me!" he lamented.

"Stephen. There is no where for you to run." She paused, listening.

He seemed to listen as well. They could hear sirens in the distance.

"You hear that? Soon there will be a dozen or more cops out here. You've got nowhere to run. Come peacefully with me and I'll make sure you're safe. You have my word."

"No! They'll hurt me!"

"No, Stephen. They won't touch you. I will make sure of that."

"You're a woman. I can't trust you."

"Stephen, listen to me. A train can come through here at any minute. I don't want you to get hurt," she said, inching herself a little closer.

"You lie. You want me dead!"

"No, I swear. I'll protect you."

Out of the corner of her eye, she could see Thompson puffing up the hill behind her. She had her off duty weapon out and pointed at Stephen. Obviously reloaded, she aimed it at him. She had anger in her eyes.

"Maybe you don't, but she does," he said, nodding his head in Thompson's direction.

Angelo looked quickly over her shoulder at Thompson. "Put it down, Sue," Angelo ordered.

"But—"

"Down! Now!"

Grudgingly, Thompson lowered her weapon, but did not holster it. She was prepared to use it at the slightest provocation. How she wished right then and there that he would provoke her.

"See, Stephen, I can help you. I'm not angry that you shot at me back there. Neither is Susan."

"I'm not?"

"Sue! You're not helping."

"No, Stephen, I'm not," Thompson said grudgingly.

"Come on, just let me help you."

Finally what she was saying to him started to sink slowly into his confused brain. He looked as if he was coming to his senses. Angelo could see a childlike fear in his eyes. He started to climb back over the rail when suddenly the loud, high pitched horn of a train blasted into the night air.

The train, traveling in excess of 60 miles per hour, blasted its horn again and then there was a screeching of brakes. It would not be able to stop in time to avoid them. Angelo grabbed Thompson, pushing her out of the way of the train, and then dived down after her just as it barreled through. When Angelo looked up, the train was past them and Stephen was gone.

"Oh, shit!" Angelo said, jumping up and darting across the tracks. She looked over the side of the rail and saw Stephen sprawled at the bottom of the ravine. He wasn't moving. "Oh, shit," she repeated. "Call for Rescue. Now, Sue, now!"

Angelo did an end-run around the bridge and slid down the steep embankment, rushing over to his unmoving form. She could see a large amount of blood all around his head. Thompson followed her down. "Rescue's on the way."

Feeling for a pulse, Angelo said, "He's still alive. Just." She placed a hand on his back. "It didn't have to end this way, Stephen," Angelo said to him sadly.

"Maybe it did, Bee," Susan whispered.

They stayed with him until the ambulance arrived to transport him to the hospital. Don Juan's reign of terror was finally over. The residents of Philadelphia could feel safe again.

At least for a little while....

Epilogue

Angelo and Thompson stood by Stephen Greystock's bedside at Nazareth Hospital. The beeping monitors and breathing apparatus kept a steady, but hopeless pace. His head was bandaged and his face was pale. He looked like a dead man, tubes coming out of his nose and throat. His chest rose and fell in time with the ventilator.

A brown crucifix hung over his bed. Looking at it, Angelo could not help but feel a little sorry for him. Possibly if he grew up under better circumstances, he would have been a different man.

The doctor walked in, looked at the chart, and gave Angelo a dispassionate stare. Then he shook his head and walked out. It seemed that the doctor had no hope in his recovery. At this point, neither did Angelo. He was probably better off.

"Do you think they'll pull the plug?" Thompson asked.

"I don't know. He doesn't have a living will."

"What about his mother?"

Angelo gave her a look.

Remembering what Angelo told her about Stephen's unloving mother, she said, "Oh, never mind."

"He'll probably stay on the life support until his body gives out. Or the courts unhook him from the ventilator and feeding tube." Angelo studied him for a moment. "He might even regain consciousness. Only God knows, but miracles do happen. I know that for a fact."

"That doesn't seem likely, does it?"

"No, it doesn't. Shame," Angelo said, touching his arm gently.

Looking at Angelo's hand on his arm, Susan said, "Don't tell me you feel sorry for him!"

"In a way," she admitted quietly.

"You're joking. After all that he did? After what he did to your friend Jenny?"

Poor Heather? The five other women? Me for that matter?"

"The courts would have taken care of that. Justice would have been served. I truly believe that. I have to believe that."

"Perhaps. And maybe he would have gotten off on an insanity plea."

"Everyone has a right to a fair trial. Seeing him like this makes me feel…"

"Unsatisfied?"

Angelo looked Thompson in the eye. "Sad. Just sad."

"You're a strange woman, Bee," Thompson said, shaking her head.

Angelo took one last look at Stephen Greystock before walking out of the room. "No, I'm not strange, just fair. Come on, let's go home."

As the hospital room door closed quietly behind them, neither Angelo nor Thompson noticed his fingers twitching….

THE END

Additional Books from Just My Best, Inc.

Scarlett, First Knight of Vandora - By Megan Blue Terry
The road had been tough on Scarlett, mainly because she had grown soft with the leisure of not having to wage war. They had ridden hard, stopped only to catch a nap or a snack, and finally after almost three days of harried travel they entered the realm of Ofenhaus. PB $18.98 + S&H

Possibilities - By Janet Sue Terry
She had definitely wanted to avoid the scene he threatened. But there had been more to it than that. A war was being waged within her. On one hand she hated Blake Baxter, and on the other, he fascinated her. And in this case, her weaker side won. PB $16.98 + S&H

Resolutions - By Janet Sue Terry
"There are many resolutions, the trick is finding the right one." Could their marriage be saved? Or was it too late? Would Blake's hasty move to kidnap Nora, and hold her captive in his ramshackle cabin in the woods backfire in his face? Or could he possibly reclaim her heart? PB $16.98 + S&H

Angel of Death - By Rosanna Filippello
She had three murders and not one witness or suspect. She didn't like dead ends. What did these three guys have in common? They had all gotten away with crimes. They were all on probation or parole. She would have to check with the Parole Office in Spring Garden. PB $16.98 + S&H

Vacant Spaces - By Mark Andrew Ware
To discover the truth behind her friends mysterious disappearance, Ashley Malone must uncover the evil secrets of the residents in the sinister old brownstone and unveil the truth of her own forgotton, diabolical past! PB $16.98 + S&H

Logon to http://www.jmbpub.com
Email jst@justmybest.com

Or send check or money order to:
Just My Best, Inc., 1746 Dailey Road, Wilmington, Ohio 45177

Note: Also available at most online book stores.

Printed in the United States
23253LVS00001B/61-72